To Curt

Henrietta Allen West

When Times Get Rough

Henrietta Alten West

This book is a work of fiction. Many of the names, places, characters, and incidents are products of the author's imagination or are used fictitiously. Any resemblance to actual events or locales or person living or dead is entirely coincidental.

Llourettia Gates Books, LLC
P.O. Box #411
Fruitland, Maryland 21826

Hardcover ISBN: 978-1-953082-06-0
Paperback ISBN: 978-1-953082-07-7
eBook ISBN: 978-1-953082-08-4
Library of Congress Control Number: 2021909952

Photography by Andrea Lõpez Burns
Cover and interior design by Jamie Tipton, Open Heart Designs

This book is dedicated to the tireless health-care workers who saved our lives when COVID-19 struck and to the scientific researchers who worked day and night to develop a vaccine.

Contents

CAST OF CHARACTERS

Elizabeth and Richard Carpenter

Elizabeth and Richard live in a small town on the Eastern Shore of Maryland. Richard is a retired pathologist who did some work for the Philadelphia Medical Examiner's office many years ago. Elizabeth is a former college professor and CIA analyst.

Gretchen and Bailey MacDermott

Gretchen and Bailey live in Dallas, Texas. Bailey is a former IBM salesman, oil company executive, and Department of Defense intelligence agent. He currently is making another fortune selling commercial real estate. Gretchen works in the corporate world as the head of an HR department. Because she is so competent at everything she does, she actually runs the company she works for.

Tyler Merriman and Lilleth DuBois

Tyler and Lilleth live in southern Colorado. Everyone suspects that Tyler flew the SR-71 Blackbird for the U.S. Air Force during his younger years. After he retired from the military, he made millions in commercial real estate. He flew his own plane around the country. Lilleth is a psychologist who works on a reservation counseling Native Americans. She is a superb athlete and a beautiful younger woman.

Sidney and Cameron Richardson

Sidney and Cameron have several homes and their own private plane. Cameron is a former IBM wunderkind who went out on his own to start several globally-known computer companies. Sidney is a retired profiling consultant who owned an innovative, successful, and fast-growing business before she married Cameron.

Isabelle and Matthew Ritter

Isabelle and Matthew live in Palm Springs, California. Matthew is a retired urologist, an avid quail hunter, and a movie buff. Isabelle has transitioned from her career as a clinical psychologist and now owns a popular high-end interior furnishings store and design business.

Olivia and J.D. Steele

Olivia and J.D. live in Saint Louis. J.D. is a lawyer who gave up his job as a prosecuting attorney to found his own extremely profitable trucking company. He is a logistics expert. He knows a great deal about watercraft and owns several boats. Olivia is a former homecoming queen, a brilliant woman who worked as a mathematician and cypher specialist for the NSA.

Rosemary and Harrison Davis

Rosemary and Harrison used to live in Seattle. Harrison is a geneticist who has been studying the Covid-19 virus. Rosemary teaches advanced chemistry at a magnet school. Someone wants to silence Harrison because of what his research has uncovered. His laboratory has been destroyed, and his life is in danger. Rosemary and Harrison are on the run.

Alexandra and Owen Bruce/Dana and Brian Ridenour

Someone is trying to murder the Bruces, and they have no idea why. They are hiding out at the Albergo Riposante in Paso Robles under false identities, pretending to be the Ridenours. Owen is an aggressive billionaire businessman, and many competitors would like to steal his brilliant ideas. But maybe the person who wants them dead is someone much closer to home?

PROLOGUE

Cancelled?! Say it isn't so! Most of the members of the Camp Shoemaker reunion group had seen it coming, but a few had held out hope that somehow they would be able to make their yearly trip together. It was not to be, and the final blow came when their venue, the resort they'd chosen for their annual get together, decided to cancel all upcoming reservations for the foreseeable future. It was 2020, and COVID-19 quarantine rules had shut down pretty much everything in the country that was any fun at all. The group who were mostly septuagenarians knew it was for the best, the wise thing to do. It was still a crushing disappointment.

Elizabeth Carpenter was especially depressed about the cancellation. She loved the Camp Shoemaker crowd and looked forward to seeing them every year. Because she was disabled, the annual trip with her husband's childhood camp buddies was one of the few times during the year she chose to travel. She was very down for days after the trip for 2020 was scrapped. When she received an email from the Albergo Riposante in Paso Robles, California, she grabbed onto this glimmer of hope that a reunion might be salvaged.

The Albergo was a wonderful inn where Elizabeth and Richard had spent several delightful vacations. The inn was offering a "Quandanche Quarantena." Roughly translated, this meant "even though it's a quarantine" or "in spite of the quarantine." The resort had designed a week-long package for frequent guests who were known to the staff at the Albergo. Only a few would be invited, and fewer still would be allowed to attend.

There were strict rules, and everyone had to agree to abide by them. You could bring a group of friends—provided they also all agreed to follow the Albergo's rules. Daily COVID-19 tests would be administered. Temperature checks would be required throughout the day and before guests were permitted to attend certain activities. Social distancing would be enforced. Masks were mandatory, except when eating in the dining room and drinking cocktails on the piazza. Rooms would be assigned in dedicated wings of the hotel for groups of ten or more. Menus and activities were described. There would be exclusive winery tours. Special meals at wineries and local restaurants could be arranged and would be private and safe. A limousine or town car would be provided as transportation for each group. Golf would be available at several of the local courses, and even swimming would be allowed.

Each group or couple would have one waiter or waitress assigned to them for their entire visit. Likewise with housekeeping. One team would clean the same rooms each day. Wait staff and cleaning staff would be tested daily. The breakfast room with its usual fabulous breakfast buffet was closed. Breakfast would be ordered the night before and delivered to guests' rooms each morning. All of this was not offered at a bargain rate. There was a significant "pandemic surcharge" to cover the costs of keeping guests safe.

Elizabeth was excited and hoped her friends would be willing to take a chance and pay the extra fees to enjoy this unique opportunity. She forwarded the email, complete with photos of the Italianate Albergo Riposante, its graceful courtyards, flower-filled patios, and arched colonnades. Included were pictures of the hotel's beautifully presented cuisine produced by Rialto, the hotel's three-star kitchen, along with detailed explanations about the safety measures that would be taken to insure everyone's good health. Elizabeth's husband, Richard, was completely on board and thought it would be the perfect way to safely spend time with their friends. Elizabeth had checked with the Albergo, and the week in September that the Camp Shoemaker group had originally scheduled for their reunion would be available to them. She put a temporary hold on six rooms for that week, including a handicap accessible room for herself and Richard. The Camp Shoemaker group would have their own wing of the hotel.

She heard back immediately from two couples. They were enthusiastic and excited about the Albergo and the other events that were planned. They had never been to Paso Robles but had heard good things. Isabelle and Matthew Ritter could easily make the five-hour drive from Palm Springs. Olivia and J.D. Steele were planning to spend three weeks at The Circle Bar Q Dude Ranch and Stables in Ojai, California just before the proposed week in Paso Robles, so they would already be in the neighborhood.

Nobody wanted to fly. The Carpenters would be driving from their winter home in Tucson. One sticking point for some of the couples was that everyone had to quarantine themselves for two weeks before they arrived at the Albergo. Cameron Richardson was so busy, he wasn't sure he could do the two weeks of required pre-trip quarantining. Sidney was all in and said she would come alone, even if Cameron didn't. Gretchen

MacDermott still had a job, although she was now working from home. She and Bailey were up in the air about whether or not they could make it. They had decided months ago they would not get on an airplane until after there was a vaccine available. Lilleth and Tyler initially said they couldn't make it. Elizabeth decided she would hang on to the six rooms as long as she could. Maybe things would work out and plans could be rearranged.

The group of dear friends had been celebrating their lives with a yearly reunion trip for the past eleven years. They had visited well-known and unknown places, and at this stage and at this age, they wanted the accommodations to be comfortable, even luxurious. They were well past the era when they sought out rugged camping trips and pitched tents in the wilds for fun.

The men were in their late seventies, but they were an energetic group. A few continued to insist that they wanted to prove themselves with rigorous physical activities. The golf courses in the area and trips to the local wineries would provide sufficient exercise for most in the crowd. For those who were so inclined, there was the Reservoir Canyon Trail and countless other hiking opportunities in the hills along the nearby Pacific Coast. The younger wives and girlfriends as well as the older women were excited about the full-service spa at the Albergo. A vigorous therapeutic massage sounded like the perfect kind of exercise to most of them.

Great food was a mandatory requirement for these reunions. Paso Robles had more than three hundred wineries in the immediate area, and there were so many outstanding restaurants, the group would never be able to include them all in their dining itinerary. Some difficult choices would have to be made, but what happy choices these would be. They were in an excellent area for outstanding cuisine. And of course, with all those wineries, the wine would be spectacular.

The men in the group had been friends since they were little boys. When they were eight years old, they'd all been assigned to Cabin #1 at Camp Shoemaker, a church camp in the Ozark Mountains. As kids, they had spent their summers together and created countless memories. When they became adults and no longer went to camp, they drifted apart, as work and family responsibilities made inevitable demands on their time.

More than a decade ago, Matthew Ritter had decided he missed his old friends and had organized a reunion for the group of former campers. The boys from Camp Shoemaker, then in their sixties and with their current wives and girlfriends, had spent a long weekend in Palm Springs. It was as if they had never been apart. The women of the group had formed their own special bond, and this congenial group had enjoyed the time of their lives. Every year since, they'd been meeting for their reunion in places that had interesting things to do.

They treasured their friendships, and everyone looked forward to the fun. What they wanted most of all was to spend time together, talking about the past and hoping for the future. They cherished the memories from their younger years, and they were having an extraordinarily good time making new memories as older people.

The past few reunions had provided more than reminiscing about old times and indulging in superb food and wine. There had been adventures, mysteries, and way too much excitement for most in the crowd ... or so they claimed. They all said they wanted a relaxing vacation this year, a reunion without drama, murders, and mysterious goings-on. The question on everybody's mind was, hadn't they kind of enjoyed the escapades, the exploits, the unexpected undertakings of the past few years? Would these still-sharp travelers be content to have a reunion devoid of action? These seniors were not shuffleboard or knitting types by any means.

This was the year of the pandemic, so everything in everyone's world was different. Given quarantines and strict social distancing rules, there would probably not be any opportunities for action-packed intrigue. A ruckus might ensue if someone failed to wear their mask as required, but this did not rise to the level of nefarious activity this group was used to being involved in. Maybe this really was the year to kick back and rest. No one was getting any younger.

CHAPTER 1

C*ameron decided he didn't want to be left out, so* Sidney had a fairly easy time convincing him to quarantine ahead of the trip to Paso Robles. They would spend the fourteen days in isolation at their ranch in New Mexico. Cameron stepped up to the plate and offered to fly Bailey and Gretchen to California. Because of the pandemic, he didn't want to risk flying to Dallas as too much could go wrong at that over-crowded and busy airport. He agreed to pick up his friends at the smaller Midland-Odessa Airport. Gretchen and Bailey would make the five-hour drive from Dallas to west Texas.

At the last minute, Tyler and Lilleth decided they, too, wanted to join their friends in California. They cancelled everything on their schedule but were wary of taking a commercial airline flight. They would drive to the Richardsons' New Mexico ranch, and Cameron would fly them to Paso Robles. The Paso Robles Municipal Airport was small but it was located just four miles from downtown. A week before the reunion, everyone's plans were set. Elizabeth was happy she had hung on to her reservations for six rooms.

Darryl Harcomb, one of their camp friends, had briefly given some thought to making the trip to California. His second wife, Elena Petrovich, had died two years earlier from poisoning at the Camp Shoemaker reunion in Bar Harbor, Maine. Darryl had never known Elena was a Russian spy. She had been murdered right in front of his eyes at a restaurant in the resort town. Darryl's shock at losing Elena combined with his chronic high blood pressure had resulted in his having a stroke. He had been in a rehabilitation facility, regaining his physical strength and skills. He was now almost completely recovered. He had fallen in love with Mallory, his younger physical therapist, and it looked like she was on her way to becoming Mrs. Darryl Harcomb #3. Because of the pandemic, Mallory wasn't able to schedule the vacation time to go to California. Darryl didn't want to make the trip without her. Maybe next year?

One of their group had died a few years earlier after a long battle with Parkinson's disease. His widow kept saying she might attend a reunion, but she hadn't been able to do it yet. Another former camper was in an assisted living facility in Little Rock, and he no longer did any traveling. It made everyone sad that some of their own were no longer able to participate in these trips, but they had some wonderful memories from the years when they were traveling with a full force of camp friends.

There would be six couples quarantining for the trip this year. Because they were in a vulnerable age group, most of them had not been anywhere for many months except the grocery store parking lot and their own backyards. They had been looking forward to their week at a fancy resort in West Virginia, but were delighted that this year's reunion had been salvaged with the substitute trip to Paso Robles. They trusted Elizabeth completely and knew the Albergo Riposante would be a first rate experience—even with COVID-19 lurking.

And so these longtime friends made their way from New Mexico, Arizona, Texas, Missouri, Colorado, and Palm Springs to be together on California's Central Coast. They had all been strict about their weeks of quarantine and knew it would be safe to enjoy the company of their close friends when they arrived to celebrate "Quandanche Quarantena." They needed some fun and more than a little bit of socializing. This might be the most eagerly anticipated reunion yet for the Camp Shoemaker boys and their partners.

Elizabeth made sure all the couples knew what the Albergo's rules were for the week. She had consulted everyone multiple times via email and had arrived at a schedule for socially distanced and safe events at restaurants and wineries in the area. All businesses were anxious to have customers and had laid out sensible programs for patrons to follow. It would take some extra effort, but everyone was determined that this year's reunion was going to be another winner.

Their rooms were all in one wing of the Albergo, and the couples were delighted with their accommodations. The rooms were spacious and newly renovated, and all had views. The first night they were to meet for cocktails on the Albergo's patio, followed by dinner at Rialto, the Albergo's signature restaurant. A favorite destination for wedding receptions and large parties, the piazza (the Albergo's name for its very large outdoor patio) was the perfect venue for a socially-distanced event. Out of deference to staff and other guests, masks were required while walking through the public rooms of the resort, but once they arrived at their own table on the piazza, they could take off their masks. It was difficult to drink a glass of wine or a margarita through a bandana or an N95 face mask.

The piazza was a magnificent creation, and they could have been in the courtyard of a palacio in Umbria or anywhere in

Italy. The centerpiece was a grand double staircase descending from a bell tower. Arched colonnades lined all four sides of the open, flower-filled expanse. There were fountains everywhere, and the sound of water gently trickling down worked its magic on these quarantine-weary souls.

Designed as a site for weddings and large galas, only four groups were seated in the enormous piazza on this magnificent September evening. It was cool, but not too cool. The sun was about to set, but there was just the right amount of magical light still surrounding them. It was a Goldilocks night. Everything was just right. They were so happy to see each other, they almost forgot they'd agreed not to engage in any hugs. Elbow bumps and air kisses tossed from well-sanitized fingertips were the only exchanges of affection these friends would allow themselves this year.

They had already ordered their first round of drinks via the television screens in their rooms. They had also ordered their meals from the televised electronic dinner menu. The chef had appeared on screen, live from the kitchen, complete with his toque and checkered pants. He had described in detail each offering for every course. When was the last time a chef had personally told anyone in the Camp Shoemaker crowd or anybody else about what they could order for dinner? All couples had successfully entered their preferences for cocktails, food, and wine. A few in the crowd were true electronics geniuses, but everyone had passed this challenge for dining in an era overwhelmed by a pandemic. They were understandably proud of their abilities.

They had so much to share with each other. Each had a story to tell about interacting with children and grandchildren via Zoom and Facetime. When they arrived in the piazza, they found an enormous round table reserved for their group. Twelve people could easily sit around the tile and stone tavola.

Other groups of guests were also having cocktails in the piazza. A group of four was seated in the corner opposite the Camp Shoemaker crowd. A solitary couple sat in each of the other two corners. They were too far away from each other to be able to see any faces, and this suited them all just fine.

A kind of salon had developed over the years, in which members of the group shared their hobbies and interests with their friends. Matthew Ritter had become a movie fanatic when he retired. He would show his movie montages at most of the pre-dinner cocktail get-togethers. Matthew had arranged for a room to be set up that provided the equipment he needed to show this year's selection of thought-provoking and humorous movie clips. Because they were dining al fresco on this first night, Matthew had not planned to show any movie montages.

For tonight, Elizabeth had arranged a short game for her friends. She'd attempted to convince each of them to divulge at least one secret about the way they had found to cope with the COVID-19 crisis. Some had shared with her what they'd longed for during the days when they'd been confined to their homes. She had talked some of them into revealing the intended and unintended lapses in their vigilant quarantines.

Elizabeth would read one of the confessions, and the rest of the group would try to guess which one of their friends they thought had submitted the story about a particular longing, lapse, or guilty pleasure. The guessing game was for fun, but it was also a way for the group to disclose what they might otherwise have kept to themselves. They needed to laugh and share how difficult it had been to be cooped up inside for so many months. No one was allowed to judge, or even wanted to. It was funny but also good therapy.

A masked waiter pushed a multi-tiered trolley through the piazza and left it close to their table. Olivia, always the perfect hostess, moved to the trolley to deliver each person's drinks. The Albergo had included a plate of warm, deep-fried squash blossoms, the specialty of the house, accompanied by a fragrant thyme and mustard sauce. These delicacies were a delightful and unusual appetizer. They were devoured in an instant. Sidney said she wanted an entire plateful as her dinner entrée, and the heck with the Dungeness crab Mornay she had already ordered. The mushroom sandwiches were another unique appetizer, and they were addictive. Tyler and Isabelle disagreed over the contents of these toasted triangles stuffed with a creamy minced mushroom concoction. Fresh tomato, olive, and pancetta bruschetta rounded out the delicious trio of appetizer offerings from the Rialto kitchen.

A few in the group had ordered glasses of the local wines, and Bailey and Lilleth were raving about a particular Zinfandel that was from a winery several of them had passed on their way from the airport. Why had they never heard of this Zinfandel before? Elizabeth relaxed, knowing that her choice of hostelry was a success. Her friends loved the food and the wine. They always managed to make their own fun. Elizabeth decided it was time to get her game underway.

The first confession was that someone had worn her or his nightgown all day long, almost every day since March 6th. She had put on underwear, street clothes, socks, and shoes only three times in more than six months. Cameron joked out loud that he was sure the person who had confessed to that particular foible was Bailey. Bailey was famous and infamous for his disguises and wigs. He had appeared at a restaurant in Bar Harbor two years earlier, dressed as a woman and wearing a curly blonde wig. Gretchen had been furious and humiliated. Bailey had promised not to bring his disguises and wigs on the reunion trips anymore, but of course he had not been able to help himself. He had donned disguises several times the previous year in Colorado Springs, but he always tried to keep it a secret from Gretchen. J.D. and Cameron were joking when they pointed their fingers at Bailey as the person who had not been able to get out of his nightgown. Bailey swore that this was not his own particular peccadillo. He said his COVID transgressions were much worse.

Another confession was from a person in the group who had arranged to have Amazon deliver a standing order of two pounds of cheese straws every week, regularly and without fail. The snack had soothed the isolation anxieties and attacks of the munchies. Someone guessed that they thought Cameron had been the person who had ordered the weekly deliveries.

Cameron was outraged. "Hell, no. I make my own cheese straws. Why would I order them delivered from Amazon?" Everybody laughed when Cameron turned to his wife Sidney and quietly asked, "What's a cheese straw?"

Confessions were made about how the couples had remained friends in such close quarters and without the welcome relief of interacting with people outside their nuclear families. One person hinted that they might have reorganized their closets more than a few times . . . a day. Everybody knew who had contributed that story. One household had refused to allow their cleaning lady to clean for them during the pandemic because they were afraid she would bring the virus to their home. They didn't realize for four months that their vacuum cleaner was missing. One person, to remain unnamed, had gained thirty pounds so far during the pandemic. Everyone knew who this was, but nobody said a word. One secret sharer revealed that he had hired an Uber to pick up an order from Taco Bell. The food had taken forever to arrive, and the total charge had amounted to $44.00. The three supreme tacos had cost $4.00, and the Uber had cost $40.00. There had been a long line at the drive-through, and the driver had kept the meter running as he waited.

One member of the group admitted to using a nail file to keep her toenails under control during the quarantine. She wondered if anyone realized how incredibly difficult it was to file down toenails with a nail file.

One reunion goer had become obsessed with the Mars landing. All agreed that this seemed like a healthy and constructive way to have endured isolation. Another member of the group had written that she'd read everything there was to read on the internet about UFOs As a result of her research, she had become convinced that alien beings were visiting the plant earth on a regular basis. Reactions to this confession ranged from total agreement with the conclusion to castigating whoever it was for being over the top "woo woo."

CHAPTER 2

R*ichard Carpenter received a text on his cell phone* that their group could go to dinner. They put their masks back on and proceeded from the piazza along the east colonnade to the large ballroom. Elizabeth estimated that the room could easily handle a seated dinner for 250 people. Tonight there would be only twenty.

Again they had a very sizeable round table for twelve, covered by a white tablecloth. Those who knew about tablecloths wondered where in the world the Albergo had ever found such a large round one. Another tiered trolley appeared from the kitchen, and they took turns serving the courses to each other. Soups and salads were fresh and interesting. The favorite salad was a fruit and nut salad with a raspberry vinaigrette dressing. Entrees ran the gamut but were mostly Italian cuisine. The porterhouse Fiorentina for two was gigantic and would have been enough for six. It came with a light chimichurri sauce that enhanced the flavor of the beef. Several people had ordered pasta, and how delightful was it that all of the pastas were handmade? The pasta was so delicious, noodles with butter alone would have been a filling and yummy meal.

Just when they thought they could never eat another bite, a new trolley appeared with all the accoutrements necessary for coffee and tea service. A tray of finger-sized desserts of all kinds accompanied the after-dinner beverages. There were fruit tarts, miniature cannolis, small cups of panna cotta and chocolate mousse, and delicate lace cookies. Richard ordered a glass of port over his phone. A masked waiter pushed it to their table on its own small trolley.

The Camp Shoemaker friends were curious about the other people who were dining in the ballroom. They were able to see the couples at the tables on either side of them, but the table for four on the diagonal all the way in the other corner remained too far away to see what anybody looked like.

At one of the nearby tables, a distinguished, well-dressed couple was laughing together. They were older and probably married, but they seemed to still have a lot to say to each other and to laugh about. The very attractive woman wore a beautifully flowing colorful silk dress. She had a silk mask/scarf around her neck made out of the same multi-colored silk as her dress. She also wore a long string of large, perfectly matched pearls. Her husband was very good looking. He had a white moustache that made him look like British royalty from a bygone era. This pair was well-known to the staff at the Albergo. They had clearly spent more than a little bit of time at the resort over the years. They were obviously wealthy, but without the arrogance and demanding attitude of entitlement that the very wealthy sometimes exhibit. Everyone at the Camp Shoemaker table was curious about this interesting couple. Cameron thought the man looked familiar, like somebody he ought to know.

The two people seated together on the other side of their table for twelve were more serious. This couple was also married, or so everyone speculated. They were both in their late sixties, and she was quite beautiful. Her thick blonde hair did not have a single gray streak. How could that possibly be? She wore black pants and a soft pink tunic top that complemented her delightful curves. Not everyone looks good in pink, but it was definitely this woman's best color.

But she seemed tired and worried. Her forehead was creased, and she was holding on to her husband's arm as she spoke to him. It almost seemed as if she was pleading with him. Her husband would have been as handsome as she was beautiful if he had not looked so exhausted and so stressed. There was something about him that screamed brilliance. But his coloring was pale and gray. He did not look ill, really. He looked worried, almost frightened. He looked sick at heart.

Elizabeth was curious about these two, and she could see both psychologists in their group stealing glances at the worn-out couple. What could possibly be troubling them while they were at such a relaxing inn? It was puzzling. Under other circumstances, Elizabeth would not have hesitated to go over to the table and introduce herself. Olivia would have also been that bold. But with COVID, people didn't do that anymore. Everyone kept their distance these days. They stayed away.

Elizabeth wondered if she might be imagining it, but she thought she saw the woman in pink begin to cry. Tears trickled down her cheeks, just as the buffet of desserts arrived at her table. How could anyone cry when presented with sweets that looked as inviting as those the Albergo had created. Elizabeth was now beside herself with curiosity. She glanced at Olivia. Olivia's eyes were wide. Olivia had also seen the tears. Olivia didn't miss anything.

This was going to be a real vacation. QQ was already a success. Breakfast would be served in their rooms the following morning. The El Paso de Robles Historical Society exhibits located in the former Carnegie Library Building on the town square were on the schedule for the next day. The library was not usually open on Tuesdays, but their group had paid to have a private talk with a knowledgeable member of the society. The Albergo was providing a picnic lunch for twelve. A limousine would drive them to the library and then to a special scenic spot overlooking the Pacific Ocean for their picnic. In the afternoon, the limo would take them to visit three wineries. The group would return to the hotel for happy hour, and dinner would be at Tio Theo, a popular Mexican restaurant.

The tour of the building where the El Paso de Robles Area Historical Society had its headquarters was a success. The current exhibit was "Seeking Gold. Finding Grapes." and presented a collection of rare bottles and tools that were in use during the days of the California Gold Rush. The history of the California Central Coast was new to many in their group, and the history buffs had questions for their guide. Even more popular than the exhibits was the building itself. Built as a library with a grant from Andrew Carnegie, the Classical Greek Revival architecture of stone and brick had been a familiar and well-proportioned fixture in Paso Robles since 1908. It stood like a decorative piece of art, enhancing the charm of the downtown square.

Running behind schedule, the limo driver was anxious to depart for the Pacific Coast and their lunch picnic. Highway 46 was the scenic route, and it deserved its reputation. The scenery between Paso Robles and the Pacific Coast was a feast for the eyes. The green rolling hills along this short drive to the ocean were unlike anything one could find elsewhere in California. This landscape might be unique west of the

Mississippi River. They oohed and aahed about the beauty that surrounded them on both sides of the two-lane road. The lush green countryside begged to be explored and was vastly different from other wine-growing areas farther north in California. They wondered if it was the ocean air. Did this area have more rain that other places in California? Didn't grapes in wine-growing regions usually beg for an arid climate? Several in the limo who had traveled to Scotland pointed out the similarities of the vistas. The green hills of the Scottish highlands evoked the same feeling as the scenic environs on the route between Paso Robles and the Pacific coast.

Their picnic destination was a private spot close to the Cayucos State Beach. Elizabeth was concerned that her wheelchair would not be able to make it to the picnic area from the parking lot on the rustic pathways, and she was prepared to eat her lunch in the car. As it turned out, parts of the pathway to the picnic area were paved. She would not dine alone.

Several in the group wanted to hike before lunch, and they went off to do their thing. Elizabeth and Olivia found a spot in the warm September sunshine and looked out over the majestic Pacific Ocean. They inevitably began to talk about the COVID-19 crisis and where it all had come from. What Elizabeth had not realized was that when Olivia had worked at the NSA, one of her areas of expertise had been Communist China. Olivia had retired more than a decade earlier, and she never spoke about the work she had done at the No Such Agency. Once in a while she made a knowledgeable and insightful remark about foreign affairs, and her friends were reminded of her former position in the intelligence community.

As they talked, Elizabeth was fascinated with the depth of knowledge Olivia had about China. She urged Olivia to give a short talk to their group that evening about the very difficult and complicated country that China had always been.

"I don't know. Matthew has his movie montages all lined up to show, and most people are much more interested in those than they would be in anything I might have to say about China." Olivia never tooted her own horn.

"I disagree. I think we all would like to know more about China. It's a country that's been shrouded in mystery for its entire existence. Even though it's now open to Western tourists, and the government seems eager to have us come and spend our hard currency there, I suspect there are many secrets that are being kept from the eyes of casual visitors. I would love to hear the inside scoop. China is such a big country area-wise and has an enormous population. But I feel as if I know very little about it." Elizabeth wanted to convince her friend.

Olivia laughed. "The Chinese Communist government doesn't want anybody to know much of anything about what they are doing over there. They encourage tourists to see a few picturesque places, but access to the rest of the country is very tightly controlled. China's rulers want most of the country to continue to be obscure. They get away with terrible things by keeping the rest of the world in the dark. The Wuhan Laboratory and the wet markets are only the tip of the iceberg."

"This is the kind of thing I know our group would be fascinated to hear about."

"You realize there are many things I can't disclose," Olivia warned.

"Of course. I understand. I wouldn't want you to breach any of your confidentiality agreements with the government, and we don't need to know any of that secret stuff. I would just like to understand the country better. I will bet most of the others in the group also feel as if they know hardly anything about China. The Mao Zedong era got a great deal of hype because of his flamboyant, narcissistic personality and his Little Red Book, but there is much more to the place than the terrible legacy of Chairman Mao. Venezuela has collapsed. If you don't count poor pathetic Cuba, China is the last remaining Communist state in the world."

"If you really think the group would like to learn more about The People's Republic, I'll talk to Matthew about giving me a few minutes to talk about China this evening." Olivia reluctantly agreed.

"We are having cocktails by the pool tonight. Matthew's movie equipment is all set up in a special room inside. He's not planning to show any movies tonight anyway."

The hikers straggled back to the picnic area. The hotel had packed a white cardboard box with a gourmet lunch for each guest. Everyone was hungry, and the Albergo's track record so far on food was better than first class. The sightseers knew they were in for another gastronomic treat. The hotel had sent a dozen large glass bottles of Evian and six bottles of assorted local white wines in a cooler. A second cooler held more ice, and a dozen real wine glasses had been carefully and safely arranged wrapped in white linen napkins and were laid on a wooden tray. Chilled wine glasses ... wow! An old-fashioned picnic hamper held plates, silverware, cloth napkins, and everything else one could possibly want for an elegant picnic.

Each cardboard box held half a roasted chicken that had been glazed with a lemon and garlic sauce. Even those who didn't usually eat the skin of the chicken could not resist this delicious and crispy concoction from Rialto. There were a variety of elegant finger sandwiches, sliced tomatoes, and individual containers of French potato salad in each large white box. Olives and celery stuffed with cream cheese had been included. Miniature cupcakes with a variety of fillings and icings completed the delicious lunch. They finished off the wine and drank all the bottled water. A few who had been particularly enthusiastic about the white wine were wishing they could return to the Albergo for a nap rather than continue on the afternoon's winery tour.

Before lunch, J.D. had been looking out to sea through his very powerful Leica binoculars. In the distance, he'd noticed what he thought might be a submarine lurking just below the surface of the water. The wraith-like shape had been so far away, he wasn't certain he'd seen anything at all. Maybe it had just been a mirage or an optical illusion. He knew there was a navy installation in the area, the U.S. Naval Amphibious Training Base at Morro Bay. Maybe what he'd seen was an exotic new vessel that the U.S. Navy was trying out.

J.D. had been a Colonel in the U.S. Air Force Reserves. After his active duty years, he had served in the reserves, and he'd had several other civilian careers since. He continued to read about and study all kinds of military equipment and transport vehicles, including amphibious craft. What had looked to him like a submarine, as he'd viewed it miles out in the ocean, had not looked like a U.S. submarine. It was the wrong shape to be one of ours or even one of NATO's. J.D. was keen on details and paid attention. The submarine he imagined he had seen had looked like a foreign submarine of some kind. If it was from a rogue nation, he couldn't help but wonder what it was doing so close to the Pacific Coast of the USA. Weren't U.S. Navy P-3C Orions still supposed to be tracking and keeping tabs on all the submarines in the world? When he looked again for the submarine, it was gone. Maybe it had never been there in the first place. J.D. put away his binoculars and opened his box lunch.

The winery tour was also a tour of the beautiful vistas around Paso Robles. Their limousine driver knew where he was going and carefully wended his way through the twisting and looping narrow tree-lined roads outside of town. Guiding a limo as long as theirs in this terrain was no small feat, and all were thankful they'd not tried to drive themselves. Tasting wine and driving was never a good combination.

Their first stop was Calcareous. Calcareous had a large wine-tasting building with magnificent views and both outside and inside tables. Situated at the top of a very steep hill, it could only be reached by negotiating a winding and dangerous road. Nothing in Sonoma or Napa was as lovely as the Calcareous setting and the views from their terrace. The group tasted a particularly popular red Zinfandel. They tried another wine blend that had "violets" in the name and had them exclaiming and asking for more. And Calcareous was good at marketing. Several couples signed up for their wine club before the tasting was finished.

One of the other wineries on the tour was quite small, but it had a pair of adorable llamas in residence, one of which was named "Dolly." The other was named Andy, short for Andean. Everyone was taken with the cute and friendly pair and their clever names.

CHAPTER 3

J.D. Steele had been an athlete and a scholar in high school before he matriculated at the University of Oklahoma. He was handsome and outgoing as well as smart. He joined a fraternity and dated many women, but he also managed to make good grades, at least good enough for him to be admitted to the University of Oklahoma College of Law after he finished his four undergraduate years. After law school, J.D. fulfilled his obligation to Uncle Sam and was stationed in El Paso, Texas with the JAG Corps. J.D. had always wanted to be a prosecutor. He had a strong sense of right and wrong and wanted to help make sure the bad guys were found guilty and put in jail. He would devote twenty-five years of his life to this cause, and he became a legend in Tulsa legal circles. His specialty was trying the most complex and difficult criminal cases, including murder, rape, and drug cases. He was a relentless defender of justice and a dispenser of appropriate punishment. He was always prepared and performed brilliantly in front of the jury. J.D. seemed to thrive on convicting the worst of the worst, and he could count the cases he'd ever lost on one hand!

J.D. and his first wife were married just after they'd finished college. They were both too young, and neither of them was ready for marriage. The two had almost nothing in common, and after less than a year, they realized their union had been a mistake. They had no children and few assets, so their divorce was relatively amicable. They remained friends.

After his divorce, J.D. became one of Tulsa's most eligible bachelors and was quite the man-about-town for a few years until he met Signa Karlsson. It was a love match, and they married and had twins—a boy and a girl. Signa had her pilot's license and loved to fly. Both of their children had graduated from college when Signa was killed in a plane crash. She was a passenger in a friend's private plane. J.D. was devastated and terribly angry. He was convinced that if Signa had been flying the plane, there would not have been an accident. He didn't handle his enormous grief well and vowed never to marry again. He resigned abruptly from his job as an assistant district attorney, abandoned his beautiful Art Deco mansion without even cleaning out the refrigerator, told no one except his grown children goodbye, and left the country for French Polynesia.

This was where J.D.'s life and marital history became murky. Some say he married again on the rebound... two times! But no one is really sure whether he ever married again at all, or if he did, whether it was once, twice, three or even four times. Rumors flew, and J.D. wasn't talking about it. It didn't matter. J.D. never went back to Tulsa, and his house was sold. He eventually returned to the United States, and with the money he had saved, combined with an inheritance from his now-deceased, well-to-do parents, he bought a trucking company. The company's headquarters were in Missouri, and J.D. bought a condo in St. Louis.

He'd never thought he would enjoy anything as much as he'd enjoyed being a prosecuting attorney, but he found he loved running his own transportation empire. He was good at logistics and good with people, and RRD Trucking made him ten times more money than he'd ever dreamed he would make in his lifetime. He bought a cattle ranch. J.D. liked to travel to Washington, D.C. to lobby his legislators in person about transportation issues. It was on one of these trips to the nation's capital that he met Olivia Barrow Simmons.

Olivia Barrow had been a cheerleader and her high school's homecoming queen. She was beautiful and outgoing. She was the prettiest and the most popular girl in her school, and she was also smart. After graduating from the University of North Carolina with a degree in mathematics, Olivia moved to Washington, D.C. where she shared an apartment with three other young women. Olivia had landed a job as a cypher specialist at the National Security Agency, so she wasn't able to talk to anybody about what she did at work.

Because Olivia was so attractive and had such a winsome personality, the NSA quickly identified her as a person who could represent the agency at Congressional hearings and other official public events. She always had all the answers, and although she would rather have been spending her time working on the complicated puzzles, mathematical constructs, and computer coding she loved, she was happy to be the pretty face of the No Such Agency. It was during one of her appearances before the Senate Select Committee on Intelligence that she was introduced to Bradford Simmons, the youngest man ever to be elected to the United States Senate. He was from Colorado, and he had a reputation as a womanizer.

Once he'd laid eyes on Olivia, he had to have her. She was young and vulnerable and flattered that a United States Senator wanted to date her. The women with whom she shared her apartment were envious and urged her to continue going out with Bradford. Olivia was eventually persuaded by the young senator's attentions, and within eighteen months, they were married. Olivia was devoted to her work and insisted on keeping her job at the NSA. Olivia and Bradford had three children, and Olivia chose to stay married to the senator until all three had graduated from college. Then she divorced him and took him for everything she could get. Simmons had continued his womanizing behavior all during their miserable marriage, and Olivia had finally had all she could stand of the ridiculously handsome and adulterous cad.

Olivia vowed she would never marry again, and she focused her life on her children, her grandchildren, and the career she loved. Olivia had an exceptionally high security clearance and was a valuable employee at the NSA. Nobody could ever know exactly what she did, but whatever it was, she was extraordinarily good at it. She knew lots of secrets about everything and everybody, but she was a person of the highest integrity. No one ever worried that she would suffer from "loose lips."

Many eligible bachelors in the nation's capital wanted to date her, but she was done with men ... or so she said. Even in her late fifties, she was a beauty. She was a fascinating conversationalist, and everyone, men and women, wanted to sit next to her at dinner. It was at one such dinner party, hosted by her best friend, that Olivia was seated next to J.D. Steele. The two hit it off immediately and were roaring with laughter before the main course was served. The hostess, who had known Olivia for decades, had thought J.D. and Olivia would appreciate each other's company, but she'd greatly underestimated the enormous amount of fun they would have together. For Olivia and for J.D., there was nobody else at the party.

They were inseparable from that night on. J.D. bought a townhouse in Georgetown and courted the woman who had swept him off his feet. He had never expected to fall in love like this so late in life, but he adored Olivia and didn't want to be away from her. Olivia was just as shocked to find herself head over heels in love with J.D. She liked men, but after her disastrous marriage, she wanted nothing more to do with romance. But these two were a match that was destined to be. They had such a good time in one another's company. Each of them had a wonderful sense of humor, and they could always make the other one laugh. Even their skeptical grown children had to admit it was a beautiful thing to behold.

It was Olivia's idea to move closer to where J.D.'s business had its headquarters. The couple bought a house in St. Louis. She hated to leave her job at the NSA, but it was time to retire. Because Olivia insisted on spending one week out of every month near her children and grandchildren, who all lived in the D.C. metropolitan area, they kept the townhouse in the District. This was fine with J.D., and he usually came East with her. They traveled and enjoyed their lives. In spite of love and compatibility, Olivia was skeptical about marriage for many years. She didn't see why it was necessary. J.D. finally convinced Olivia that being married would not be the kiss of death, and they ended up tying the knot when they were both in their late 60s.

CHAPTER 4

The group was having cocktails by the Albergo swimming pool that evening before the limousine arrived to drive them to Tio Theo for dinner. Matthew couldn't show his montages outside, so he was happy to defer to Olivia. Matthew's movies would be the main attraction the following evening. Elizabeth told some anecdotes about herself to soften up the crowd for the hard core facts about China.

"The People's Republic of China burst onto my radar screen in the middle of the 1980s. Mao's Cultural Revolution was finished, ending with his death in 1976. China had an abundance of labor and had decided to reengage with the world economy. They were making things, cheap things, and lots of them, and I was shocked to realize how many of these things they were selling to me!"

"You and everybody else on the planet." Tyler had an MBA and knew about foreign trade.

Elizabeth continued. "I had been shopping. I'd been to a big department store and a few other stores at my local mall. That was back in the day when department stores still existed. I had three small children and very little time to do anything.

Shopping had to be accomplished while the kids were with a babysitter, and I literally threw things hand over fist into my shopping cart as I raced through the store aisles. Checking labels to find out where the girls' clothes had been manufactured was the last thing on my mind. When I got home, I dragged my purchases into the kitchen and began to sort them out. I always washed every new item before I put it away. This meant I had to cut the tags off each piece of clothing before it went into the washing machine. I'd bought a dozen cereal bowls on sale that day and had to remove the price stickers from the bottom of each one before I put it in the dishwasher. As I struggled to remove these stickers, I noticed that all twelve bowls I'd purchased had been 'Made in China.' Everything used to say it was 'Made in Japan.' I wondered to myself if anything was 'Made in the USA' anymore."

Elizabeth worried she might be boring her audience, but at least the women, the primary purchasing agents in everybody's family, were with her. "As I checked the tags on my kids' clothes, I realized that every single item of children's clothing I'd purchased had also been manufactured in China. I felt sick to my stomach. Why was I supporting a Communist country with my dollars? And I hadn't even known I was doing it. It had snuck up on me. Everything I'd bought that day had come from the so-called Peoples Republic. Ugh! The clothes were bought; the bowls were bought. The tags and the stickers had been removed. I washed the clothes and the cereal bowls. My kids wore the clothes, and we ate out of the bowls. But, I vowed that day that I was not going to purchase one more thing made in the Peoples Republic of China. None of my U.S. dollars were going over there anymore."

A couple of the women chuckled, as if they'd also been down that road. "What I realized after making this absurd vow to myself was that, if I wasn't going to buy anything that was made in China, I really couldn't *buy anything at all.* Everything was being made in China. How had this travesty come to pass? I was furious with myself and with the world. That's the story from my first economic encounter with the Chinese." Elizabeth paused and turned to her friend. "My anecdotes are just those of a clueless consumer. I am now going to turn my soapbox over to Olivia who is the real expert on what makes China ... Tik Tok." Everyone who had kids and grandkids got it.

Olivia began, "I don't really have any kind of speech to make. Elizabeth knew China was one of my areas of expertise when I was working for the federal government, and she thought a little history might be interesting in light of what we've all experienced in the past few months. So, from the wonderful folks who brought you Tiananmen Square, they now bring you the coronavirus, COVID-19. Goodbye Mao. Hello Wuhan." Nobody was laughing.

Olivia pulled no punches. "To be fair, China is and always has been a completely ungovernable country. It is vast and incredibly diverse in every possible way. It has too many people and covers too much territory. It has too many languages. But the Communist regime that has ruled the Chinese mainland since 1949 is driven by imperialism and authoritarianism and is engaged in an ongoing and constant crusade to accumulate and subjugate more people and more territory. They cannot govern what they have, but they are historically tyrannical and acquisitive and are constantly grasping for more of whatever it is."

Olivia continued. "I'm not telling you anything you don't already know. The recent protests in Hong Kong made it all too clear, as if anyone needed a reminder, that the Communist Chinese government has no clue how to handle dissent. They only know how to try to crush it. The Chinese people don't want to be browbeaten by the Communist thugs who rule their country. The people of China are the tragic victims here. They have no say whatsoever about who governs them and makes decisions about their lives. The protests in Hong Kong let the totalitarian leaders in Beijing know and let the world know how the Chinese people really feel about their government's despotic policies. Hong Kong does not want to be a part of China. No part of China wants to be under the suffocating shroud of Communism."

Olivia had made her opening statement and was now going to launch into a little bit of recent Chinese history. Since Mao's clique had taken over China after World War II, nothing they'd done had ever made their Communist rulers look good. "In 1950, China decided that Tibet belonged to China. The Chinese military invaded Tibet and attempted to subjugate the Tibetan people, who were primarily Buddhists, to their own atheistic Communist culture through slaughter and persecution. Tibet's eighty-year long adversarial relationship with the Chinese government receives a lot of attention because of the Dalai Lama. He has been forced to live in exile, expelled from his homeland of Occupied Tibet. The Dalai Lama brings attention to the Chinese oppressors.

"But China's imperialistic ambitions, and its efforts to destroy those who refuse to knuckle under, have much deeper roots and more wide-ranging consequences than the well-publicized campaign to silence the Dalai Lana and destroy the Tibetan people. The Chinese government has had an ongoing program of 'cultural genocide' in Tibet since 1950." It was clear Olivia knew a great deal about Chinese history, culture, and politics.

She continued. "Let me go back in history a little bit, before 1950. The Republic of China elected its first president, Sun Yat-sen, in January of 1912. This was China's first foray into democracy after thousands of years of being ruled by authoritarian emperors. When Sun Yat-sen died in 1925, Chiang Kai-shek became China's political and military leader. His goal was to unify China and build a modern democratic society. Unifying and ruling China was never going to be an easy task, and Communist forces were constantly challenging and trying to destroy the young democracy. Chiang Kai-shek led The Republic of China throughout the days of World War II, until 1949. After a prolonged civil war that took place after the end of World War II, Mao Zedong's Communist Party finally prevailed and drove Chiang Kai-shek and his non-Communist followers out of mainland China, into exile on the island of Taiwan. Many countries continued to recognize the Chinese Nationalists, based in Taiwan, as China's legitimate government. You may not know this, but the Republic of China under Sun Yat-sen was one of the founding members of the League of Nations. Under Chiang Kai-shek, The Republic of China was a founding member of the United Nations. But, in 1971, the United Nations voted to take China's U.N. seat away from Taiwan and give it to Mao and Communist China. Thank you, Richard Nixon. When Communist China took over Taiwan's position in that organization, the Communists also acquired China's powerful role as one of the five ruling members of the United Nations Security Council.

"It is difficult to understand why the Communist Chinese want more people and more territory to govern. Their myopic central planners have done a terrible job of handling the people and the land they already have. But Communist China has never been able to keep its imperialistic drives in check, and so they continue to dig themselves into more and more trouble.

"What I think is most pertinent about China today is its human rights atrocities. This is also well-known world-wide, but the United Nations has pretty much chosen to turn a blind eye to these travesties. China continues to have an enormous and on-going problem with its ethnic minorities. The Communist government has never found a way to keep a lid on these difficulties, let alone resolve them. They have tried every repressive and dictatorial measure to control their people, but without success. They want to make their citizens into automatons who are as alike as possible and will, above all things, obey orders. This is, of course, an absurd goal, but it is by definition a basic one of all Communist regimes. Individuality and diversity are disapproved of and looked down upon in the Communist Chinese ideology. China's government wants what they think of as 'real Chinese people,' well-behaved robots, interchangeable citizens who willingly kowtow to their leaders' rules. Kim Jong-un can't achieve this kind of uniformity and compliance, even in his tiny, culturally homogeneous and punitive police state of North Korea. How ridiculous that the ham-handed Communist central planners in Beijing think they can achieve it. But they never stop trying."

"The Chinese have been struggling with their ethnic minorities for a very long time. In the name of Sinicization, which is in reality cultural imperialism, the Communist Chinese government periodically forces relocations of large portions of its population into areas where ethnic minorities, which the Communist rulers consider to be non-Chinese people, are causing trouble and will not toe the authoritarian line. The government wants to crush these minority groups into obedience.

"The Han Chinese are considered to be the 'real Chinese people' who have the right values. The government wants to spread the Han Chinese culture with its language, societal norms, and ethnic identity throughout the country, to dominate the entire population of China. To give you some idea of how all-pervasive this campaign is, the government constantly intervenes to try to influence everything about the people it rules. The areas they are attempting to control are diet, writing, industry, education, language, law, lifestyle, politics, philosophy, religion, science, technology, culture, value systems, even architectural style. That just about covers everything, don't you think?" Olivia paused, clearly upset to have to think about the many areas in which the Chinese Communist government was attempting to brainwash its people. "The people of China are being bombarded with authoritarian propaganda in every possible aspect of their lives."

She sighed deeply and continued. "In 2008, the Communist government forced 20,000 Han Chinese to leave their homes in China's eastern heartland and move to the Xinjiang Province. These Han Chinese were compelled to relocate and could not opt out of what was an unbelievably harsh and unjust program. Their lives were destroyed. They had no option but to abandon their homes and friends and neighborhoods and move to an entirely unknown place. They had absolutely no choice in the matter. They were forced into exile, forced to move to an outpost of the Xinjiang Production and Construction Corporation, an arid border territory that is home to a large Turkic Muslim population. The totalitarian manipulators in Beijing decided in 2008 to send these Han Chinese far away from their homes to try to influence the pesky, native people of Xinjiang. The goal again was Sinicization, sometimes referred to as Chinalization. None of the people involved wanted this to happen. The Han Chinese did not want to leave their homes. The Uyghurs of Xinjiang did not want the Han Chinese moving into their territory. The Communist government is determined to make all its ethnic minorities into Chinese yes-men and yes-women. They will even move enormous numbers of their 'real Chinese' people around the country to try to dilute and destroy ethnic diversity. The Communists abhor ethnic diversity and cultural differences. They want everyone to be alike, and they want everyone to obey."

Once again, Olivia sighed, took a deep breath, and seized on a small diversion. "The whole point of Mao's 'Cultural Revolution' was to try to make every person who lived in China into a follower, a person who obeyed the rules in the Little Red Book. This was not successful under Mao. Recent Chinese leaders have also failed to destroy the diverse cultures within their country. The consequences of these government-imposed machinations for actual human beings forced into China's relocation drives, are all too real and all too horrible. China is a despicable Communist dictatorship. There is no freedom in that country. Everybody in the world already knows this. I am not telling you anything that is not widespread knowledge. But China persists in pursuing its imperialistic goals.

"And so it continues. The Chinese government's battle against its own people never ceases. These tyrants have not yet figured out that freedom lives in the hearts of all people, no matter where they are. The Chinese people are the ones who suffer. They are just like people everywhere—they want to live in freedom. They do not want a government dictating to them every facet of their lives. The more the Communist bullies seek to impose their edicts on a non-compliant people, the more unrest and subversion they will have to deal with."

Olivia continued. "At some level the Communist government realizes they have too many people for the resources available to them. Whenever I think about China and its population to viable land ratio, I am unfortunately reminded of the word 'Lebensraum.' Everyone in the world who has been paying attention is all too familiar with the Chinese government's draconian fertility edicts, forced abortions, and other punishments. Their latest bizarre project has been to attempt to literally manufacture more land in the South China Sea. The Chinese government is building islands on top of coral reefs by filling the sea with dirt, sand, and rock. Their destruction of the coral reefs is inexcusable. Why China feels entitled to build these islands in the South China Sea is complicated. Their aggression has to do with explorations of these waters the Chinese made hundreds of years ago, as well as a fantasy territorial designation of their own invention called the '9 dash line.' The Chinese are desperate for oil, natural gas, and other resources located in and around the South China Sea. They have built naval bases on their seven man-made islands, to intimidate, threaten, and dominate their neighbors. They want to control shipping channels through these waters as well as the airspace above the South China Sea. Names to make note of in this contest for resources are the Spratly Islands and China's Cabbage Strategy. The Chinese are stealing from the other countries in Southeast Asia. They have to do this in order to support their exploding population. And the United States and the rest of the world has been allowing them to get away with all of this for decades.

"And they continue to get away with it. The South China Sea misadventure demonstrates not only how lacking these people are in common sense, but also how desperate they are to fabricate more territory and garner more resources and power. They have destroyed the coral reefs and put landfill in the ocean. It seems like a bizarre undertaking. But because the world remains passive, the strategy is working for them.

"China has had hundreds of different languages and dialects for centuries. As you might imagine, this has presented a long-standing problem with communication. Throughout the centuries and throughout the country, there have been and continue to be, on-going ethnic, religious, and cultural conflicts. It is an untenable situation. The Soviet Union fell apart in the last century. Communist China and Communist Cuba are the last two remaining hopes for Lenin's pipedream."

Olivia felt she had spoken for too long. She was going to have to wind things up. "Because of its size and diversity, China really should not be one country. Of all the large countries in the world, China is one that should be divided up into several countries. Its various regions might have a chance of surviving and even thriving if the country were allowed to break apart. China pretends that it is centrally planned, like all 'good' Communist countries have claimed to be. In fact most of their commerce is not now and never has been centrally planned. If central planning was ever really successful anywhere, Communist China is certainly one place where it has never worked and will not work going forward." Olivia paused. "I promised myself this would not be a lecture in economics. I will try to leave those discussions to Elizabeth.

"I could regale you for days with countless tales of the horrible things China has done to its citizens as it has attempted to control the size and behaviors of its population. Mao's Little Red Book and his repressive regime, if it had not resulted in so many deaths, might, in retrospect, be viewed by the world almost as a joke. Big fat Chairman. Little Red Book. Mao's Cultural Revolution was ridiculous theatre from whatever perspective you want to look at it. But it was also a massive tragedy of unbelievable proportions. Mao's policies resulted in many millions of people starving to death.

"In summary, since the Communists took over after World War II, China's brutal leaders have constantly been in the process of attempting to crush their minority ethnic populations. In the name of 'national unity' or Chinalization, they have stopped at nothing and will stop at nothing, to try to make their people conform to their suffocating vision of totalitarianism. It has never worked, and it never will work. No matter how many vicious relocation programs, forced abortions, reeducation strategies, concentration camps, ethnic cleansing regimens, genocides, and on and on that they impose, they will never be able to beat freedom to death. "

Olivia decided she had said enough. "If I can leave you with one fact about Communist China, it is that the clique which rules China today, and has been in power since the end of World War II, is a brutal regime that is dedicated, even obsessed, with crushing China's ethnic minorities. My prediction is that they will ultimately destroy themselves as a nation as they try to scrub diversity from their territories."

"Well, that is all very interesting, but what does that have to do with their latest gift to the world, COVID-19? Baby clothes and cereal dishes made in China are annoying, but this latest thing they've screwed up is killing us." Tyler wanted to have information that was relevant to the current crisis.

"They tried to poison our pets with their crap dogfood. Remember that? Then they added melamine to their infant formula—to the formula they were exporting *and* to the formula they were feeding to their own Chinese infants. Next they contaminated the drugs they were making and selling all over the world. They have been trying to kill us and our four-legged best friends one way or another for many years. This latest scheme of death didn't just start up in 2019." Richard was reminding the group of things they already knew but might have forgotten. "The Chinese are always up to something nefarious. And we know they are incompetent. It's the line between malicious intent and just plain stupid bumbling that is difficult to determine."

"When the Soviet Union screwed up in Chernobyl, they pooped in the punch bowl. With the COVID-19 disaster, China has pooped in every punch bowl in every country in the world. I contend that the Chernobyl disaster and all the lying and cover-ups the Russians did after it happened were some of the reasons the Soviet Union fell apart. Is there any hope that the Communist Chinese government will fall as a result of the lies and the cover-ups that have surrounded this latest debacle? Or are they 'too big to fail?' Or 'too big to fall?' Tyler had invoked the infamous phrase that became part of the world's lexicon after the financial catastrophe of 2008.

Cameron had been fidgeting in his chair, clearly wanting to get in on the discussion. Finally he could not stand it any longer and took the stage. "I'm a businessman. I don't know much about virology or pharmaceuticals. But I do know about making a profit. And it is all about making as much profit as possible that has led to our dependence on China. We've allowed them to make too many of our things, especially the things that are vital to our existence and national security. American companies and companies around the world found that they could build factories in China, factories to manufacture anything and everything. These factories in China, along with an inexhaustible supply of Chinese workers, could make it, whatever it was, for less, much less. That of course has meant more profits. This has got to be obvious, even to the poor soul who got a D in college economics. Over the past several decades, we have allowed the profit motive to drive relocation of huge chunks of the world's manufacturing to China. It's not just baby clothes and cereal bowls any more. And it's not just iPods, iPads, iPhones, and every other electronic gadget you have in your house. It is critical pharmaceuticals. It is critical PPE. It is N95 face masks and acetaminophen. It is life-saving drugs and ventilators. And it has to stop.

"One thing about the Chinese Communists is that they will steal whatever they can from you. They have been notorious for decades about not respecting the contracts they sign. You might as well not even bother to sign a contract with them. They will always take whatever they want. Nothing is proprietary. They will steal your technology in a microsecond. The

Chinese are not very creative or innovative, but they are great at stealing other people's ideas. They have stolen my ideas. Don't kid yourself. We are in a war with China. It is not a war with guns and bombs, but it is a war just the same."

Cameron wasn't finished. "Some of my companies have been guilty of chasing profits by delegating manufacturing to the Chinese. But that is not going to happen anymore. We are already investing huge amounts of capital to build factories in the United States. The products my companies produce are not critical to our national defense per se, but we have made the long-run decision to close all of our Chinese factories. We will no longer feed the beast. Our products will be more expensive, but I am betting the American people will be willing to pay more going forward for something they know is made in the USA." Several in Cameron's audience were nodding their heads.

"I am also a member of a group of CEOs who get together on a regular basis to talk about these issues. I predict that other large companies—companies that make everything, will be pulling out of China in future months and years. The Chinese never respected the contracts they signed with anybody, but now our most vulnerable flanks have been exposed. The Chinese are welcome to continue to make our cereal bowls. 'China from China' has kind of a nice ring to it. But things that are vital to this country's health and safety, critical industries, and anything important to our national defense must in the future be made in this country." Cameron spoke with a passion he rarely exhibited. He obviously felt strongly about this subject.

Lilleth began to clap. She was delighted to hear such a strong statement from Cameron. "I wish it had not taken a world-wide pandemic for us to learn the error of our ways. Hopefully, the globalists will be going out of fashion and fading into the woodwork. We've had too many of them in positions of power for too long."

Tyler still wanted to talk about how the Chinese had screwed up the entire world economy with their bats and pangolins and Level 4 Wuhan Laboratory. "I guess we will never really know what happened over there, will we? We know these people are not great on quality control, given all the intentional or unintentional bad stuff they've sent our way in the past. With their desire to avoid responsibility and maintain secrecy at all costs, no worthwhile investigation will ever get to the bottom of where all this COVID mess came from. It's so frustrating. Somebody needs to pay for this."

Isabelle spoke up for the first time. "Human nature is such that we want to know the truth. We want to know what really happened. We want to know why. We want to know who is responsible. The Communist Chinese government won't ever admit to anything, but there are plenty of individuals in China who know things. No one person may know it all, but eventually their secrets will be exposed. Don't you think that more than a few journalists have smuggled scientists out of Wuhan by now and are in the process of writing tell-all books about what really happened? I guarantee there's more than one effort going on in that regard. The story may come by way of Australia, or it may come from the British. It may come from someone who defects from China. But eventually we will have answers. The world is too small these days. There are too many leaks and too much hacking to keep anything confidential forever. Like it or not, there are no more secrets."

"I hope you're right. No one may ever be held accountable for this mess, but let's hope all countries will make big changes in their domestic economies. In the future, let's hope the United States will no longer allow itself to be held hostage to the lies and treachery of the PRC. Thank goodness for that!" Tyler was definitely an advocate for "Made in the USA."

CHAPTER 5

They met in New Orleans when he was a fourth-year medical student at Tulane and she was a freshman at Newcomb College. They both had roots in Tennessee, albeit at different ends of that very long state. Their first few dates had long-term relationship written all over them. Isabelle Blackstone was considerably younger than Matthew Ritter, but he was committed to being eternally young and worked out every day to stay that way. They made a handsome couple. Isabelle was blonde and beautiful, and Matthew knew she was the one. He was in love, but he wasn't ready to settle down. He had places to go and people to see. He had an internship and a residency to do, and he had signed up to fulfill his obligations to his country by spending two years working for the United States Public Health Service. She had just finished her freshman year in college. Matthew was moving on to California for his internship, the next chapter in the long quest to become a urologist. Would Isabelle go with him or would she stay in New Orleans?

In the end, she decided he was worth it. She would transfer to UCLA and complete her undergraduate studies there. Her parents were not happy when their nineteen-year-old daughter told them she wanted to leave Newcomb College and move to California to complete her degree. But they trusted her and agreed to pay her tuition in California. She was an excellent student and worked hard to graduate with a dual degree in psychology and sociology. Isabelle and Matthew married after Isabelle finished her undergraduate studies, and they moved to the Phoenix area where Matthew served his two years in the U.S. Public Health Service, working on what was then called an Indian Reservation. While they lived near Phoenix, Isabelle earned a master's degree in clinical psychology at Arizona State University, and she later opened her own counseling practice in Palm Springs, the same year Matthew joined a thriving urology group in that California city.

The professional corporation Matthew Ritter joined was the leading group of urologists in Southern California. Movie actors and other famous people from Los Angeles drove to Palm Springs for medical care, especially when they had an embarrassing problem they didn't want anyone in L.A. to know about. Matthew was bound by the Hippocratic Oath and the covenant of professional confidentiality not to talk about his patients. And he never did. He kept many confidences about highly-placed people in all walks of life. In addition to the Hollywood crowd, he treated wealthy businessmen and politicians, including two governors of Western states, several United States Senators, and assorted Congressmen and judges. His group was known for its medical expertise as well as for its discretion. Matthew knew scandalous things—secrets quite a few famous people hoped he would carry to his grave. He would, but did they all trust that he would always abide by his commitment to confidentiality?

Isabelle likewise knew her clients' secrets. She was an effective therapist and a warm and caring human being. Her patients loved her. She had a successful practice within a year of hanging out her shingle and had to begin hiring additional counselors to join her. There was a lot of money in Palm Springs. There were also some large egos in residence, a not unexpected circumstance, as the financially successful wanted to live, vacation, and retire in this golf course mecca that was reputed to have more sunny days than any other place in the United States. There was a great deal of infidelity, and many people came to her with problems that were associated with their addictions to drugs and alcohol. There was domestic abuse. Women who did not want to be seen in public with a black eye or a broken arm, left Beverly Hills to hide out and seek counseling in Palm Springs. Isabelle listened and dispensed advice to the rich and famous.

Isabelle was sometimes called to testify in court, something she hated to do. She didn't like to break a confidence, but sometimes, she was legally bound to respond to a subpoena to appear in court and to testify honestly when questioned under oath. She had almost been called to testify in the extraordinarily high-profile murder trial that involved a famous football player and his second wife. Everyone knew the athlete had been beating up his wife on a regular basis. He'd finally killed her and was on trial for murder. Isabelle thankfully hadn't had to testify in that case. But there were other cases where her testimony had resulted in an unstable parent being denied custody of their child or children in a divorce. She had received direct and personal threats as a result of some of these court cases.

She had struggled to work, at least part-time, while she raised the couple's two children. Isabelle had household and babysitting help, and she spent as much time in her office as she could. She knew she needed the stimulation of doing her own thing while dealing with diaper changes, wiping down counters, making endless peanut butter and jelly sandwiches, and driving her children to their after-school activities and numerous sports events. When her children graduated from high school, Isabelle realized she was burned out being a clinical psychologist, and she began to look for a new and less stressful career.

She found her next identity as an interior designer and owner of an elegant high-end shop that sold European antiques, lamps, and other delightful and expensive accessories for the home. Isabelle's store, *Blackstone White*, immediately became everybody's favorite place to find the perfect piece to make a room both interesting and classy.

What Isabelle had not expected was the extent to which being an interior designer and a store owner would call on her skills as a therapist. People came into the store to talk and sometimes to cry. Her clients had a great deal of money, but they did not always have much happiness or contentment. Isabelle was a good listener. She was patient and kind. People she barely knew poured out their hearts to her. If a husband was laundering money, his wife might express her disgust or her fear about his activities to Isabelle. If a boyfriend was involved in the drug trade, the girlfriend would confide in Isabelle. There were plenty of Mafiosi living in Palm Springs.

Isabelle sometimes helped a client disappear. It started with a woman who was a prolific shopper and regular customer of Isabelle's. The woman came into the store one day, terrified that her husband had sent his henchmen to kill her. She begged Isabelle to allow her to hide in the storage room at the back of *Blackstone White*. Isabelle trusted her gut and helped the woman lie down, well-concealed behind a pallet of oriental rugs. Sure enough, two greasy looking tough guys with tattoos all over their arms, arrived at the store, and without asking, searched high and low for the gangster's wife.

Isabelle was frightened, but she was also angry. The mobsters were unable to find Isabelle's client, and as soon as they'd left, Isabelle called the police and reported the two for bursting into her store, turning everything topsy-turvy, and searching her property without her permission. She knew nothing would come of the police report she'd filed, but felt she had done the right thing.

Isabelle hid the frightened woman in her own home for several days and then drove her to Mexico. The woman had a secret bank account in L.A. and hoped to start a new life south of the border. The incident had been terrifying, but Isabelle had found a new calling. She was now an interior designer, store owner, and rescuer of the abused. It was a lot to take on, and Isabelle often asked herself if she had merely traded one stressful job for another even more stressful job.

The interior design part of her business was booming. Isabelle had excellent taste. Everybody wanted her to design the addition to their house; consult with them about the space planning in their new kitchen; and do the paint, curtains, and new furniture in the family room renovation. She had more business than she could handle. She spent a lot of time in clients' homes and often drew on her counseling skills to settle disputes within their families. The husband, who was paying the bill for the redecorating project, didn't like white walls. The wife, who would be spending most of her waking hours in the room, wanted only white walls. He dug in his heels. She refused to talk about it. The interior designer/marriage counselor came to the rescue and brought a compromise and reconciliation. Isabelle often wondered how interior designers without experience in clinical counseling were ever able to accomplish anything.

Isabelle saw and heard many things she never wanted to see or hear. She kept her secrets, but she sometimes wondered if an angry father, who had been denied access to his children because of his mental illness, would remember her court testimony and come after her. She worried that the women she'd helped disappear would be found. Would the assistance Isabelle had given to rescue and hide these victims be exposed? Would an angry abuser come after her?

CHAPTER 6

The limousine arrived on time, and everyone wore their masks as they walked through the Albergo to the front entrance. They could take their masks off in the limo but had to put them back on again when they arrived at the restaurant. Once seated—always at a significant distance from any other tables—they could remove their masks to drink and eat. The restaurant staff and waiters never removed their masks. The COVID crisis had gone on long enough that everybody knew what they were supposed to do.

Tio Theo was a popular Mexican restaurant in Paso Robles and had several dining rooms. All were colorfully decorated with piñatas and sombreros and other south-of-the-border artifacts. The reunion table for twelve was set up in the largest room, and three other carefully-placed tables for two were set up in the same room.

Several of the women in the reunion group noticed that one of the couples who shared the dining room with them at Tio Theo that night were also guests at Albergo Riposante. The women noticed the couple because the woman seated at one of the tables for two wore an eye-catching colorful turquoise serape. The light-weight wool fabric was embellished with exquisitely hand-embroidered crewel work designs in all the colors of the rainbow. Gretchen remarked, “It’s a work of art, really, and should be hung on the wall rather than worn to a restaurant. Who would risk spilling salsa or margaritas on that beautiful creation?” The well-dressed couple was definitely staying at the Albergo.

The reunion group’s drinks and their meals had been ordered ahead. Menus in restaurants were now either paper to be discarded after one use or electronic orders placed and paid for before patrons ever reached the restaurant. Their margaritas and Mexican beer arrived on a tiered trolley, and the “Mexican tapas” appetizers were served family style.

The group discussed the views from Calcareous, who had joined the wine club, and the adorable llamas they’d met at the smaller vineyard. A discussion ensued about where llamas originally came from. Somebody Googled it to settle the argument. The answer was North America, but they’d migrated to South America three million years ago. The llama story was complicated. Understandably, nobody wanted to talk about China or the depressing and disheartening information Olivia and Cameron had shared with them about The Red Dragon. Anything remotely connected to the PRC was not on the menu tonight.

The food at Tio Theo was, as advertised, some of the best Tex-Mex you could find in California. The group of friends nearly forgot that COVID-19 had tried to destroy their world. Only when a trolley of fresh drinks arrived at the table were they reminded about masks and social distancing and the importance of staying safe. Flan, individual tres leches cakes, fried ice cream, brownies iced with dark chocolate frosting, and sopapillas with honey arrived to round out the meal.

Sopapillas with honey are so delicious, but they are very messy. Those who had indulged in these clouds of warm pastry wanted to visit the restroom to get the honey off their fingers. The limo was already waiting in front of the restaurant, but there was a line for the bathrooms. Only one person was allowed in at a time, and after each use, an attendant entered and sprayed sanitizer around the room. This was the annoying but necessary bottleneck in the evening's festivities. A few decided to use disposable hand wipes and live with the honey on their faces. The group of twelve was trying to get itself masked and ready to depart when they heard a loud crash at one of the tables nearby.

The man who'd accompanied the woman in the turquoise serape had collapsed on the floor beside his table. He appeared to have had a spell or a seizure of some kind. He'd stood up from his chair and reached his arms out across the table toward his wife. His arms had fallen back down to his sides, and he'd grabbed hold of the tablecloth as he collapsed onto the floor. He had dragged everything on the table down with him and lay on the wooden floor covered with Mexican desserts and whatever had remained in the margarita glasses that had been on the table. He was unconscious in a pile of broken glass and salsa and fried ice cream – laid out with his arms sprawling. Amazingly, not a drop of the table's remains had splashed onto his wife's beautiful clothes.

Matthew and Richard, both physicians, did not hesitate. They made sure their masks were in place and dug into their pockets for the vinyl gloves they'd been carrying everywhere with them for the past several months. They rushed to the man who lay on the floor and tried to find a pulse.

The others in the reunion group were paralyzed, remembering a similar situation they'd experienced in Maine two years earlier. The wife of one of the Camp Shoemaker boys had fallen face first, dead, into her cake, a victim of poisoning. Darryl Harcomb had never known that his wife Elena Petrovich was a Russian sleeper spy. Someone had murdered her in the Cuba Libre restaurant. Seeing a man collapse in a restaurant for no apparent reason was all too reminiscent of the scene they'd witnessed at the Cuban restaurant in Bar Harbor. None of them had ever imagined they would see a murder of any kind. None of them had ever imagined they would see someone they knew die in front of their eyes from having been poisoned. This could not be happening again.

But sure enough, Mr. Turquoise Serape was down. The question was, could he be saved? Was he still alive? What had caused him to collapse? Neither the retired urologist Dr. Ritter nor the retired pathologist Dr. Carpenter knew what had brought the man down, but they determined he had a pulse and was still breathing. Gretchen was watching from a distance, masked and ready to leave the restaurant. She reached into her bag to find her phone. She was ready to call 911. When Mrs. Turquoise Serape saw Gretchen's phone come out, she shouted, "No! Don't!" Gretchen looked up to see who was shouting. The woman begged her. "Please don't call 911. He can't go to a hospital."

Gretchen, who was the most sensible person one could ever meet, countered the plea not to dial 911. "Why not? Don't you want to save his life? He needs an ambulance and a hospital." Gretchen looked at Matthew for the okay to call for help.

Matthew answered Gretchen's questioning look. "It's possible he's had a heart attack and ought to go to the ER, but I really think he has just fainted. He seems to be coming around. His pulse is strong and his color is good. I really don't think he's having a heart attack or a stroke. If his wife says not to call, let's wait a minute or two. Ordinarily I would not hesitate for even a few seconds to call 911, but I don't think, in this particular case, that he needs the EMTs." Gretchen kept her finger poised above the send button on her phone, but she didn't push it. In the world of COVID-19, nobody wanted to go to an ER or to a hospital, and nobody wanted their loved ones to go to those places.

Richard spoke up. "I think you all should go back to the Albergo and leave us here with our patient." Most of their group had congregated near the restaurant door, ready to leave to go to the limousine. Sidney had been bold enough to take a seat at the table across from the distraught woman everyone assumed was the fallen man's wife. Admittedly, Sidney was the youngest wife in the Camp Shoemaker group and the least likely to succumb to COVID-19, and she was masked. But she was still taking a risk, sitting down at a table with the well-dressed woman whose face was ashen. Sidney tried to engage her in conversation, hoping to determine if the pale and shaken woman was in danger of passing out. Nobody wanted another person to faint or fall and end up in the mess on the floor.

Matthew seconded the plan for the others in their group to leave. "We will find an Uber or ride back with our fellow guests here. Please go on. It's best for everyone. We may be retired, but we have this covered. The rest of you need to go back to the hotel."

Matthew knew that, under different circumstances and in a different year, he would never have hesitated to call 911. But with the COVID-19 crisis, everything had changed. He assumed that Paso Robles had a decent hospital, but he had no idea how far away it was. He asked himself what he would do if it had been Isabelle who had collapsed and was lying on the floor. This was the test that all responsible physicians use to determine if they are making good decisions. Matthew was satisfied that, all other things being equal, if it were his own wife who was down, he would not call the EMTs in this particular situation. An unnecessary trip to the emergency room in these pandemic times might lead to something worse. If at all possible, it was best to avoid the hospital.

Sure enough, the man lying under the tablecloth opened his eyes and began to speak. "What happened? Where am I?" He tried to stand up, and Richard gently restrained him and pushed him back down on the floor.

"You just had dinner at Tio Theo in Paso Robles, California. You collapsed and fell. Your wife is right here. I am going to ask you a few questions to check out your mental state."

The man was angry and belligerent. "My mental state is fine. What in the world are you talking about? Who made all this mess?"

"You stood up and reached out to your wife. Then you fainted and collapsed and pulled the tablecloth off the table as you fell to the floor. That's why this food is all over the place. You are the one who made all this mess." Richard was giving the man the truthful answer to his question.

The downed man seemed to grasp the situation. "Sorry, I was disoriented there for a minute until I figured out what had happened. I don't remember standing up or fainting or falling or any of it."

"Hardly anyone ever remembers fainting. Just lie there a little bit longer, and we will get you up into a chair." Richard had done his share of ER duty during his years of training and when he was in the military. The United States Army had required even its pathologists to do rotations in the emergency room. Richard Carpenter had attended to many live patients as well as to many deceased ones.

Dana Ridenour was frightened. "Owen, please do as the doctors are telling you. Lie still for a while. You went down with a tremendous crash, and I'm worried that you might have hurt yourself in the fall."

"I'm fine. And don't call me Owen. My name is Brian, and you are Dana. We are the Ridenours." Owen or Brian or whatever he said his name was, scowled at his wife and then promptly vomited on the floor. The two physicians were used to people being sick, but Dana Ridenour looked as if she might fall out of her chair at any moment. Tossing his cookies seemed to help Owen or Brian get his attitude under control. "Sorry, I don't know what's wrong with me. I'm not myself."

"This is why we don't want you to get up too quickly. I know it's uncomfortable to be lying in a puddle of glass and salsa, but we don't want you trying to stand up and keel over again. You could hit your head or worse." Matthew was more used to dealing with non-compliant patients than Richard was.

"You've said you don't remember fainting. What is the last thing you do remember?" Matthew was trying to figure out what had caused the man to collapse.

"I remember the dessert trolley arriving at the table. I took two brownies and one of those little cakes. The brownies were covered with powdered sugar. I am not a fan of powdered sugar, but I love chocolate. So, I took the two brownies, in spite of the powdered sugar. Both the cake and the brownies were delicious, but as soon as I'd eaten them, I began feeling queasy. Then my legs began to feel numb. I was short of breath. I knew something bad was happening to me, but I didn't understand why I felt so weird. That's all I remember until I woke up lying on the floor in this mess, looking at the two of you. Are you real doctors?"

"No, I just play one on TV." Matthew wasn't really offended and knew he shouldn't make smart aleck remarks. He reminded himself that this man had just experienced some kind of near-catastrophic health event. He should cut the guy some slack and forgive his rude question. "Of course we are real doctors. We both graduated from Tulane University Medical School, class of 1969."

"That's a really long time ago." Brian Ridenour tried to focus his eyes and get a good look at the doctors. "I guess I should be thankful you guys were here to come to my rescue. If you hadn't been here, the restaurant would have called 911. I'd be in the hospital, and then my goose really would be cooked." Brian began to unbutton the cuffs of his shirt. He rolled up his sleeves and began to scratch his arms. "Look at that. What in the world ...?" Huge hives covered both of his arms. Matthew rolled up the cuffs of Brian's pants, and sure enough, the man also had hives all over his legs. Opening his shirt, what both doctors suspected was confirmed —the hives had spread to his torso.

"You've had a massive allergic reaction to something. It is a good thing you vomited whatever it was that you're allergic to." Matthew signaled to a waiter and asked him if someone in the restaurant could find some Benadryl. It wasn't the best treatment, but it was better than nothing. An Epi Pen or a shot of epinephrine would have been a more powerful antidote for the allergic reaction, but who had a shot of epinephrine handy? If Tio Theo had been full, the chances would have been greater that someone had an Epi Pen.

By now, everyone except the two doctors, the Ridenours, and the staff had left the restaurant. Someone found an old bottle of liquid Benadryl. It had expired years earlier, and in fact it was the pediatric cherry-flavored variety. Richard poured it all into a clean drinking glass he grabbed from a nearby table and told Brian to drink it. It wasn't much, and it probably wouldn't help. At least it wouldn't hurt.

Matthew looked at Richard, and Richard looked at Matthew. They didn't say anything out loud, but both were very relieved that Brian Ridenour's episode had been an allergic reaction and not an attempted poisoning. They'd been down that road two years earlier when their friend Darryl Harcomb's wife, Elena Petrovich, had been poisoned in a restaurant and died.

"Can somebody go to an all-night pharmacy and buy me some OTC epinephrine?" Mathew had cash ready for whichever masked waiter stepped forward to volunteer for the errand. There probably wasn't any OTC version of the Epi Pen, but who knew these days. It turned out that one of the restaurant staff had an Epi Pen and was willing to give it up. She was allergic to bee stings, and the injectable epinephrine had languished unused in her purse for several years. She told the doctors it probably wouldn't work anymore, but they could have it for their patient. She went to her locker to retrieve her purse.

Matthew stabbed Brian in the thigh with the outdated Epi Pen, and after a few minutes, the hives began to fade. Richard insisted on paying the waitress for relinquishing her medication. She said she needed to get a new prescription from her doctor anyway. Richard tucked two fifty-dollar bills into the young woman's purse.

The Lincoln Town Car that had driven the Ridenours to Tio Theo was waiting at the curb. Richard had summoned an Uber. Brian Ridenour and Matthew Ritter would return to the Albergo in the town car, and Dana Ridenour and Richard Carpenter would take the Uber. The doctors had decided Brian should have room to lie down on the back seat of the town car for the ride back to the Albergo. The mess inside the restaurant was left for the staff to clean up. Brian Ridenour mumbled something about contacting them the next day to pay for the damages his allergic attack and subsequent fall had caused. The last four patrons of the evening finally left through Tio Theo's front door, heading for the vehicles that would return them to their hotel and hopefully a good night's sleep.

As they'd expected, Brian was unsteady on his feet. Matthew was supporting one of his arms, and Richard was holding him up by the other. He was woozy and swayed dangerously as they helped him to the car. The driver from the sedan service opened the door to the back seat. Just as they were guiding Brian inside, shots rang out. Richard thought they were gun shots, but the noise had sounded exactly like firecrackers. Everybody fell to the ground, including the driver of the town car. Only a few seconds passed before they had confirmation that the sounds they'd heard had been gunshots, not firecrackers. Brian Ridenour was bleeding from the side of his head, and Dr. Richard Carpenter had been hit in the shoulder. They did not know from what direction the shots had come or why they'd been targeted.

Dana Ridenour's face was white as a sheet again, and she grabbed for her husband. Blood was gushing from the side of his face. Matthew Ritter had, at some point, stuffed a clean cloth napkin into his pocket, and he'd forgotten to put it back on one of the tables when he'd walked out of Tio Theo. He pulled it out and began to apply pressure to the side of Brian's face. Ridenour was one lucky man. The bullet had only glanced off the top of his ear. The wound had produced copious amounts of blood, like injuries to the head and neck always do. Brian Ridenour's clothes were already a mess, so the blood that was streaming down the side of his face and onto his shirt was not going to make things much worse.

Richard Carpenter realized he had also been hit, but it wasn't serious. He'd felt the bullet hit his shoulder and knew he'd also been extraordinarily lucky. If the shot had gone a few inches either way, he could have had a bullet through his carotid artery or through his heart. Richard knew he was going to have to go to the hospital to get his gunshot wound taken care of. He struggled to take off his windbreaker and used it to apply pressure to the wound. Brian Ridenour was already screaming that he had hit his ear on something when he'd fallen into the car. He was not going to the hospital.

Richard left Matthew to sort out what to do about the Ridenours and climbed into the Uber. He would have to go to the hospital alone. He told the driver to take him to the closest emergency room that could treat a gunshot wound. The Uber driver had seen and heard it all, and he'd almost driven away when the shots were fired. He looked terrified, but he stepped on the gas and drove his wounded fare to Central Counties Medical Center.

CHAPTER 7

C*ameron Richardson had always loved to build* things. From the time he was a child, he'd been taking things apart and putting them back together again. He loved to tinker. He loved to invent. He liked to change something, even just a little bit, to make it work better. That was the way his mind worked. There were stories of the rockets he and a friend had constructed and tried to launch when they were only kids in junior high school at the time. There were stories of gunpowder explosions in the woods and the resulting craters in the ground. Of course he would study science when he entered Sewanee. He transferred to a university with an engineering program for his last two years, and upon graduation, he was immediately recruited by IBM.

Mastering the technology of computers opened up a whole new world to Cameron, and it wasn't long before he was out on his own, inventing and tinkering and making things better. He built an innovative and tremendously successful computer empire. Then he built a second revolutionary electronics enterprise. The man lived to challenge the status quo, and his head was always in the future.

Cameron's businesses dealt with enormous amounts of data, and thanks to computers, this data could be accessed relatively easily. It made him millions. It was inevitable that the U.S. federal government would, from time to time, come asking for help with something. Cameron was a straight shooter, a good guy. He was an entrepreneur of the first order, but he was also honest, through and through his character and soul. He would not knowingly do something that was illegal or wrong. Sometimes he helped out the feds, and sometimes he didn't. He knew how to say no, even to Uncle Sam. When he said yes, it was never for his own gain but because he felt a patriotic duty to lend his expertise. He helped get into their cell phones that led to the arrests of terrorists. He helped out whenever he felt it was the right thing to do. He didn't want his part in any of these operations to become public, but there were some people who knew he had been instrumental in tracking down and gathering evidence on the bad guys. The question was, did any of the bad guys know that Cameron Richardson had helped to finger them and put them away?

There was no question about it. Cameron had information on everybody and everything. He didn't use it for illegitimate purposes, but he did have it. Anybody who knew what his companies were all about knew he had the goods. Anyone who has achieved the level of success that Cameron had, and anyone who has made the hard decisions about everything, including personnel, has acquired some enemies along the way. Because Cameron was a fair and benevolent boss, he'd made fewer enemies than most, but he had appropriately fired the deadwood that unfortunately but inevitably turned up, from time to time, among his employees. He'd made some people angry. He was cavalier about his own security, but his second wife, Sidney worried about him.

Cameron had married for the first time when he was just out of college, and he'd married a woman several years older than himself. His friends had been puzzled about the union that, to those on the outside, seemed unusual. Were these two well-matched? Did they have anything at all in common? The guys loved their buddy and accepted his marital decision. Sometimes, love is strange. The marriage produced two children but eventually came to an end. The failure of the marriage wasn't anybody's fault.

After being a bachelor for a few years, Cameron met the love of his life. He had made his fortune and his reputation, and he finally had the time to invest in a relationship. Sidney Putnam insisted on it. She let Cameron know that, to make their marriage work, he needed to listen to what was important to her and spend time with her. He was wildly in love with Sidney, but she refused to marry him until he learned that she would be an equal partner in their marriage. She was not a back seat kind of woman.

Sidney's first marriage had also ended in divorce. She had one son, to whom she was devoted, and she'd been able to remain friends with her first husband, her son's father. Most people can't achieve this almost impossible feat, but Sidney had people skills that most people don't. Sidney had been the runner-up in her state's beauty pageant for the Miss America contest. She'd always had the looks, but more importantly, she had the smarts—of all kinds.

Sidney's most exceptional way of being smart was her gift for reading people. Her uncanny ability to know when someone was lying was an asset when she worked as a consultant for the Texas Department of Criminal Justice. She was the prosecutor's secret weapon. She consulted on jury selections and sat in on law enforcement interviews with suspects and witnesses. She was never wrong in her assessments. She didn't necessarily tell the authorities what they wanted to hear. She told the truth. And sometimes, nobody wanted to hear the truth. Sidney demanded that her assistance in criminal cases remain confidential, but she was almost too good to be true. Eventually, what she could do leaked out beyond the walls of the justice department, and she knew being exposed could put her in danger.

Her ability to vet people was invaluable to Sidney when she started her own business. As a single parent, she needed to support herself and her son. With her business, You Are Home, she identified a need that existed and built a business that responded to that need. Her first clients were corporations that frequently moved their employees from place to place. Corporations arranged to move their employee's household goods and paid for the packing and moving and unpacking. The gap in these employee benefits came when the wife, and it usually was the wife back in the day, had to put it all away and set up the new household. The husband, and it usually was the husband, was off doing his corporate thing, and the wife was at home with the kids, trying to find a place to put their stuff in the new kitchen and the unfamiliar closets.

Sidney's company was hired to come in and put their household goods where they belonged. Her well-trained employees would organize the kitchen, at the housewife's direction, but with suggestions from the experts about the best kitchen logistics to make it fully functional. They put shelf paper in the drawers and on the shelves. They put away everybody's clothes—organizing, folding, and hanging everything in the most efficient and easy-to-access way. You Are Home would arrange for a room to be painted, would bring in other professionals to position furniture to its best advantage, and hang art work. Sidney was good at this, and she taught her carefully-selected employees to be good at it, too. She charged high prices for her services, but there was a huge demand for what she was selling. Her company grew rapidly. She was a very successful entrepreneur in her own right when she literally ran into Cameron Richardson in a restaurant.

It was an expensive steak house in Fort Worth, and Sidney was there having lunch and closing a deal with a corporate client. It was summer, and she was dressed in a stunning white designer linen dress. She had a white cashmere cardigan sweater over her shoulders because the air conditioning was turned up so high in the steak house to counter the July Texas heat. She got up to go to the ladies' room, and a tall, good-looking man didn't see her making her way through the tables in the dark, wood-paneled restaurant. The man pushed back his chair and stood up from his table with a large glass of iced tea in his hand. He ran straight into Sidney and spilled the entire glass of tea all over her dress, cashmere sweater, and expensive white high-heeled shoes. They were both stunned. He looked into the bright and beautiful eyes of the woman whose clothes he'd just ruined and couldn't turn away. To say it was love at first sight on his part would probably be the truth. She was angry that her outfit had been spoiled, but Cameron Richardson was very gracious about sending a car to drive her home to change her clothes. He insisted on paying for dry cleaning and replaced the clothes that could not be saved. Sidney had to soften her annoyance.

She had no idea who Cameron Richardson was, and they'd had several dates before Sidney fully grasped the extent of Cameron's wealth and success. Sidney was not looking for a relationship of any kind at this point in her life. She had a business to run and a child to raise. She was incredibly busy. But Cameron always went after what he wanted, and he usually got it. He went after Sidney like nothing he'd ever gone after in his life. Cameron pulled out all the stops to court the independent and strong-willed Sidney Putnam. The more she got to know him, the more she realized that Cameron was not only a success. He was also a kind and caring human being. She finally had to admit to herself that she'd fallen in love with the man.

CHAPTER 8

*Because he had a gunshot wound and was a phy*sician, the staff at the medical center's emergency department took him into a treatment room immediately. Richard did not want to be treated differently or be seen before it was his turn, but he was bleeding. ER nurses don't like to keep people who are bleeding in the ER waiting room as this causes too much anxiety for the others who are sitting there.

Richard was not in a lot of pain. His windbreaker had two holes in it, but he was delighted to learn that the bullet wound to his shoulder had not done much damage. With several stitches to close the wound, he would be as good as new. The ER doctor insisted he use a sling to keep his arm immobilized until the stitches could be removed. Richard would be able to sleep in his bed at the Albergo tonight.

As the young ER doctor put the stitches in his shoulder, Richard explained in detail everything that had happened. He understood that the hospital had to report the gunshot wound. He knew that, at some point, law enforcement would be contacting him for a statement.

When Richard heard the good news that he would not be spending the night in the hospital, he sent a quick text to Elizabeth. He told her he'd been shot but that it wasn't serious. He told her she really did not have to worry and that he would be back at the room in less than an hour. He realized it had been just a little over two hours since he had been helping Brian Ridenour into the back of the town car. He wondered what was going on with Matthew and the Ridenours and was glad he wasn't with them.

Every city, no matter how small and no matter how charming it might be, has street crime. Richard did not have any reason to believe that the gunshots fired at him and the others had been anything other than a random act of violence. Perhaps he and Brian Ridenour had been collateral damage, caught in the middle of a gang shoot-out. Maybe some idiot had intended to hijack the old town car. The gunshots could have been a prelude to a robbery. He did not want to think about the fact that one or more of the people in the group outside Tio Theo might have been an *intended* victim or victims of the shooting, but the possibility continued to niggle at the back of his mind.

Richard called another Uber. While he waited for his taxi outside the hospital's emergency room entrance, he sent a long text to Matthew Ritter, his friend and fellow physician, to let him know that he was all right and what had happened at the hospital. He let Matthew know he'd reported everything to the ER doctor about his gunshot wound. Richard had left the restaurant before Matthew had been able to stop the bleeding from Brian Ridenour's ear. Richard asked Matthew for updates on what was going on. By the time Richard arrived back at the Albergo, Matthew had not responded to his text. Richard was too worn out at this point to hunt Matthew down to find out what had happened with the Ridenours.

Richard went directly to his room. Elizabeth was awake, waiting to hear everything.

Matthew Ritter had his hands full with Brian Ridenour. The doctor knew he ought to call the police and report the shooting. Matthew knew without any doubt that it had been a shooting. But Brian Ridenour kept insisting that there had not been any shooting, that the sound they'd all heard had been firecrackers. Brian insisted that he'd hit the side of his head on the ashtray when he'd scrambled into the back seat of the car. The town car was so old that it still had ashtrays in the armrests. The man refused to let anyone call the police. Nothing to see here, officer, was his attitude. When the driver of the town car had started to protest, Brian had shoved several bills of large denominations into the man's jacket pocket. It looked as if Brian was going to have his way, at least for now.

Matthew knew that sooner or later the truth would come out. It almost always did. He was certain that Richard would report to someone at the hospital ER that he'd suffered a gunshot wound. Whoever treated him would realize that anyway. It seemed ridiculous to try to cover up the whole thing, but Matthew was too worn out to argue any more. He climbed into the back of the town car with his patient who continued to hold the dinner napkin pressed to his bleeding ear. Dana Ridenour sat in the front passenger seat. They drove in silence to the Albergo.

Matthew asked if Brian wanted him to come to his room to take a look at his ear. Ridenour said he didn't want anybody to do anything. It was no big deal. He'd fallen and cut his ear on an ashtray. Matthew let him go to his room. Matthew couldn't wait to get to his own room and go to sleep. He knew he would hear from Richard when Richard had something to tell him.

Cameron had not been able to sleep and was pacing the floor in the living room of his suite. He'd received a text from Matthew Ritter about the shooting outside Tio Theo. He was shocked by the news, but very relieved to hear that Richard had gone to the hospital and was going to be all right. He could not imagine who in the world would want to shoot Richard. Matthew had said he didn't think Richard had been the target, but nobody was certain who, if anyone, had been. Matthew suspected that the shots had been intended for the mysterious Brian Ridenour who was not really Brian Ridenour. Cameron hadn't heard anything more from Matthew. It was late.

Sidney, who was trying to sleep in the bedroom, opened one eye and called out, "What's the matter with you?" Cameron explained to Sidney everything that Matthew had told him about what had happened outside Tio Theo. When Sidney heard the news that Richard Carpenter had been shot and that somebody had also shot the man from the restaurant, she'd commented, "That guy was having a really bad night, wasn't he?"

"I know that guy who collapsed in the restaurant tonight, and it's bugging me that I can't remember how I know him. Now that somebody may have tried to shoot him, I'm even more anxious to figure out who he is. I know he's a businessman, but he also has his fingers in some very creative engineering projects—chemical engineering."

Sidney asked, "Are you trying to think of his name? Because, as it happens, I know his name. His real name is Owen Bruce, and his wife is Alexandra. I talked with her while Matthew and Richard were trying to decide if he needed to go to the hospital, but ..."

Cameron interrupted her before she could finish her sentence. "That's it. Owen Bruce. The man is Owen Bruce. I wonder why he is saying his name is Brian Ridenour. He's a brilliant guy, a really forward-thinking businessman. He has a great crystal ball. I heard him speak decades ago about looking into the future and trying to figure out what kinds of products and materials would be required in our lives—thirty or forty years down the road. He looked at all kinds of trends and knew about the shortages of natural resources and critical metals that we would be likely to face in the future. It was quite fascinating, and thought-provoking... even inspirational. He's a visionary, and I think he is very rich. He may even be a billionaire by now. He's a creative and strategic thinker. At the time, way back then, he had a small factory in some Midwestern state, in Iowa or Illinois or Indiana, someplace like that. His people had invented something revolutionary in the metal-working field, and he was producing as much of his product as he could with his small operation. He must have expanded all over the world by now. He has a first-class mind. Why would anybody want to shoot *him*?"

Sidney knew that Cameron rarely bestowed compliments on people, so his extraordinary remarks about Owen Bruce were close to being a unique observation. Cameron was Googling Owen Bruce, and Sidney was yawning, wanting to go back to sleep.

"Here he is." Cameron had found him on Google. "Apparently, he's within a few weeks of announcing some news about a groundbreaking product or products his company has developed. I need to try to talk to him. I wonder what he's doing here. He hasn't made a public announcement yet, but news leaks out. It always does. When the news goes public, his stock will go through the roof." Cameron continued to do searches on his phone.

"Maybe he's here taking some time off. Maybe he's on vacation with his wife. Some people occasionally take a break from their work once in a while and take their wives on vacation, you know. Well, actually, maybe you don't know that." Sidney realized that Cameron's mind was always on, always planning, always looking ahead to the next thing. She realized it was difficult for him to shut down and relax, but she needed her sleep.

Cameron was texting somebody. Sidney spoke up again. "Who are you trying to contact? Come back to bed. It's the middle of the night."

"It's not the middle of the night in Dubai." Cameron always had an answer. Sidney sighed, let her head sink into the pillow, and turned off her light.

Immediately she sat up and turned the light back on again. "Alexandra Bruce, Owen's wife, introduced herself to me just after her husband collapsed, while she was very upset about Owen. He'd fallen on the floor, and Matthew and Richard had just rushed over to see what they could do for him. I sat with her at their table while they brought him around. She was understandably quite distressed. People always reach out to me and trust me, as you know. I have one of those faces. People tell me things. She didn't know me from Adam... or Eve, but she just began babbling, probably because she was so anxious about Owen. Anyway, after she'd blurted out her name and her husband's name, she grabbed my arm and said she'd made a terrible mistake. She said she and Owen were registered at the Albergo under false names. She begged me to forget the names Owen and Alexandra Bruce. She said their names for the two weeks they would be staying here at the inn were Brian and Dana Ridenour. She said it several times and made me promise not to call her anything but Dana Ridenour. She even got a driver's license out of her purse and showed it to me. It had her picture on it and had been issued to Dana Ridenour. She told me she would explain it all to me some other time. What I gathered from this confused explanation was that, for some reason, she and her husband are hiding out, kind of, under fake names here at the Albergo. So, if you talk to her or to him, please remember they are the Ridenours." Sidney turned out her light again.

Because Cameron was taking this week as a vacation, he'd decided his right-hand man, his main executive assistant, Riccio Murphy, should take the opportunity to go to Dubai to finalize a complicated deal one of Cameron's companies had going with the government in the United Arab Emirates. Cameron had promised not to bother Riccio while he was half-way around the world, but of course, he was going to bug him anyway.

"Riccio, it's Cameron. Yeah, we're fine. The food and wine are fabulous, completely worth making the trip out here. How's it going over there?" Cameron's executive assistant briefly filled him in. "I want you to do something for me. I don't have a computer here because I wasn't planning to do any work while I was on vacation. Sidney only let me bring my tablet and my phone, of course. I want you to run down everything there is to know about Owen Bruce. He's into chemical engineering and metals and probably a thousand other things by now. He has some kind of big deal he's going to announce in a few days or weeks. I want to know all about it. I didn't realize it until I looked him up, but his company isn't public. It's closely held, private, probably just the family owns it. No shares available to buy on Wall Street. Must be nice. Send an encrypted email to my Thibodaux61 email address. I'll print it out here where we're staying. They have an office center with printers, and there's hardly anybody here right now. I don't think anybody will be looking over my shoulder."

Riccio asked Cameron some questions. "Yes, I want to know everything about the guy. He's staying here where we're staying, but he's here under a fake name. Very mysterious. He collapsed in a restaurant tonight, and then somebody tried to shoot him. Or at least I think somebody tried to shoot him. Something weird is going on." Cameron paused. "Yes, ASAP. Thanks."

Cameron knew he had to get some sleep, but his mind was racing. There was something not right about the way Owen Bruce had been taken ill tonight. He hadn't choked, and his wife said he didn't have any heart or blood pressure issues. He looked fit, but of course anyone of any age could have a heart attack or a stroke. Cameron wasn't a medical guy, but he didn't think Owen Bruce had experienced either of those medical emergencies.

CHAPTER 9

Tyler Merriman was a high school football star. The Air Force Academy recruited Tyler to play football, and he played for one year before he was sidelined by a shoulder injury. Tyler stayed on and graduated. He subsequently earned an MBA from Stanford. He became a pilot for the United States Air Force and spent ten years flying military missions for the USA. He never talked about the years he'd spent in the USAF, but his closest friends speculated that he was flying the Lockheed SR-71, "the Blackbird" spy plane that supposedly had the capability to see the numbers and letters on the license plate of a car parked in Red Square. When anyone came right out and asked him if he'd flown the Blackbird, Tyler would hum a few bars of the Beatles' song of the same name and smile his enigmatic smile. If he had flown the Blackbird, he would have been able to see everything and everybody from way up there. But he would never tell.

Tyler had married, briefly, when he was in the military, but his wife was young and somewhat spoiled. She resented the time Tyler spent away from home, and they divorced when they'd been married for less than two years. Tyler moved to

Northern California after he left the Air Force. He built a commercial real estate empire and became a wealthy man. Tyler dated well-known and glamorous women — movie actresses, anchorwomen who appeared on national television, and female politicos. He was a good-looking and much sought-after bachelor, but he successfully avoided the altar for decades after his first marriage ended.

Tyler Merriman had been smart and lucky in his business dealings, and he was an outstanding athlete. He bought a condominium in Telluride, Colorado so he could ski for several months in the winter. Because he was such a skilled and outstanding performer on the slopes, it wasn't long before he was hired as a ski instructor. His time was his own, and he arranged his schedule so he could spend most of the winter in Telluride. He found he loved teaching others to ski. Tyler had his own plane and flew around the country to check on his commercial real estate holdings. He hiked and biked and ran, and when he couldn't be outdoors, he sometimes played squash. Tyler was an active sportsman. He decided he wanted to be closer to his condominium in Telluride and eventually relocated from California to Colorado.

He was in his early seventies when he met the stunning Lilleth Dubois. He first saw her on the ski slopes. Lilleth was skiing The Plunge, the most demanding run on the mountain, with confidence and ease. She was a beautiful and aggressive skier, and her grace and athleticism caught Tyler's attention. He skied close to her and watched her as she turned and handled the difficult moguls and made her way down the slopes. He knew he had to meet her. At the end of the day, he followed her into the ski lodge and wasted no time introducing himself. She did not appear to be with a date, and Tyler moved in to get to know this lovely woman who was at least his equal in the snow.

Lilleth lived in Farmington, New Mexico, and was on vacation in Telluride. Every year, she spent a week of her vacation at a nearby ski resort with demanding runs. She loved the challenge. Lilleth had been married before, but she never talked about her ex-husband. She was not at all interested in a new relationship, but she dated occasionally. When Tyler approached her in the ski lodge, there was something about him that she found intriguing and appealing. She decided to give him a few minutes of her time. As they talked, it became apparent that she and Tyler had much in common in terms of their love of physical activity. She accepted his invitation to dinner, and they drank a bottle of wine and talked late into the night.

Lilleth was a psychotherapist, and her practice consisted primarily of counseling Native Americans who lived on the Navajo reservations in Northwestern New Mexico. Her job was another challenge she enjoyed. A significant percentage of Native Americans have problems with addictions, and Lilleth spent many client hours dealing with these. Her clients spilled the beans to her about who was embezzling money from the casinos, who was cooking meth on the reservation, who was running the bootleg alcohol business, and other confidences. All psychologists hear people's secrets, but because of the particular circumstances of Lilleth's practice, her clients had more secrets to tell.

Lilleth's patients liked her, and most were grateful for her help. Occasionally, one would fall off the wagon, and his or her dark side would take over. He might beat up his wife and children or rob a bank. A client who was polite and meek when sober could turn into a deranged lunatic if he or she indulged in too much alcohol.

Once a client had attacked Lilleth when she was getting into her car. The man had been drinking excessively and was wandering around the parking lot of the community center where Lilleth met with her patients. The man had been in trouble before, and that night he pushed Lilleth down when she tried to open her car door. She hit her head, and the resulting gash required several stitches in her jaw. But Lilleth was tough, and she was able to call 911 on her cell phone while she tried to talk the inebriated man down from his anger and confusion. He was threatening her with a knife when the reservation's law enforcement officers showed up to take him into custody.

Lilleth hadn't wanted to testify against him at his trial, but because, on several previous occasions, he had assaulted other people when he'd been drunk, he was sent to prison. Lilleth visited him while he was incarcerated. She was sorry she'd had to participate in sending him to jail. She had forgiven the man for hurting her. Trying to keep her clients away from the bottle was one of the toughest challenges she faced. She wouldn't allow herself to live in constant fear, but she never knew when someone she was treating would go over the edge.

Lilleth and Tyler dated long-distance for many months. Tyler was in love like he had never been in his younger years. Lilleth was even more wary of commitment than he was, but she had grown fond of Tyler. It was a big step for her when she accepted his invitation to move in with him and live at his house in Bayfield, Colorado.

Tyler had been attending the reunions for years and looked forward to seeing his old friends and their wives and girlfriends. He'd never brought a date or a partner to one of the events. Finally, Tyler convinced Lilleth to accompany him. She'd been anxious to see Maine, and Tyler had assured her that the group was friendly and would welcome her as if they had known her all their lives. Lilleth was skeptical, but she agreed to go to Bar Harbor. Tyler had planned extra days of hiking, biking, kayaking, and other activities. Lilleth knew he liked to show off his vigor to his friends. She suspected he also was proud of how strong she was and that she had the stamina to keep up with the men in the group. Lilleth had attended the Camp Shoemaker reunion in Colorado, and now she was on board for Paso Robles.

CHAPTER 10

The next morning they gathered, masked, in the lobby of the Albergo to wait for the limousine. It was another gorgeous fall day. The sun was pouring down, and there was a delightful breeze. The sky was a cloudless blue. The group of friends decided to walk outside. They stood in a circle around Richard Carpenter, who had his arm in a sling. He told them the sling was just to keep him from moving his arm too much. Richard was making light of his wound and said it didn't really hurt. His friends were asking him about the shooting that had occurred after they'd left Tio Theo the night before. Elizabeth looked upset, even hours after Richard had returned from the hospital. The night before, Matthew had sent a text to everybody about Richard being shot. By the time they had received the information, Richard was on his way back to the Albergo.

Today they were going to visit Winer, one of the most popular wineries in Paso Robles. Winer was situated on a prime piece of property outside of town on Highway 46. In addition to a beautiful stone tasting building that made visitors feel as if they had been magically transported to someplace in Italy, Winer had a spectacular restaurant. It was only open to the public for lunch, and it was sometimes difficult to get a reservation. Occasionally, the winery sponsored special dinners. Places at the table for these events were snapped up so quickly, if you didn't live in the area or have a spy who did, you could forget ever being lucky enough to attend one of those gourmet meals. Winer also did catering, but its primo event for the public was lunch. In these current times of social distancing, few people were allowed to dine inside. Elizabeth and Richard had dined at Winer before. Elizabeth had reserved a table for their large group months ago, as soon as she knew they were going to have a reunion in Paso Robles.

It was such a wonderful morning. Everyone's spirits lifted in spite of the fact that one of their group had been shot the night before. They decided to sit down and wait for their limo in one of the arched colonnades that flanked either side of the entrance to the Albergo. When they headed for the portico, Elizabeth noticed the couple she'd seen in the Albergo's ballroom on their first night in Paso Robles.

The man who had looked so worried and his wife, who'd had tears in her eyes, did not seem as if their lives had improved any since that night. They did not appear to be enjoying their holiday. In her own mind, Elizabeth had dubbed the man "the thinker" because he was so intelligent-looking and so serious. She'd given him that moniker on their first night when she'd seen him in the Albergo ballroom. The handsome older man looked even more haggard now, if that were possible, than he'd looked at dinner two days earlier. Dark rings now completely encircled his eyes. These were the circles a person who is critically ill develops when they are just hanging on to life. He had his head down, and his wife was patting his hand and talking to him with a forced but cheerful smile on her face and a cheerful-sounding voice. She was doing everything she could to keep the man engaged with her and with his surroundings.

Elizabeth was watching the couple from her wheelchair, and Lilleth was seated nearby. Elizabeth asked, "So, my psychologist friend, what is going on with this man and with this couple? I don't know if you noticed them the other night in the dining room, but he is going downhill. He looks even worse today than he did then."

Lilleth had also noticed the couple from the Albergo's ballroom. "Of course, I don't know these people, but this man is definitely in trouble. He is in physical and emotional extremis for some reason. It is as if he has the weight of the world on his shoulders. I'm sure he isn't eating and isn't sleeping. His companion, probably his wife, is making herself sick, too, trying to get him to come back to her, to pay attention to her, to talk to her. I think he has withdrawn into his own world so far that he can no longer respond to her. He is coping with his stress by shutting down and shutting out the world. I have rarely seen a person so worried, so obviously burdened. I might have guessed that he had committed a murder, even a mass murder, but there is no indication of guilt. I can almost always spot psychopaths, and I'm pretty certain he's not a psychopath. So, if he had committed a crime, he would be showing signs of guilt. He shows none of those signs. This is a very puzzling case to me. I can't keep myself from diagnosing people from afar, but I can usually keep from expressing my opinions out loud. Sorry. This man is extraordinarily disturbed about something. He's a good man. He is concerned about something that is beyond his control, and his inability to remedy the situation is taking him down. I wonder where they're going." Lilleth shook her head, and Elizabeth felt for both the desperately worried man and for his despondent wife.

The limo arrived, and it was time to head for Winer. The reunion group planned do a full wine tasting in the winery's large tasting room and then proceed to the dining room for lunch. If they chose to sit inside in the dining room, they could see everything that went on in the kitchen. But it was such a wonderful day, it was difficult to make the decision not to eat outside. In the end they decided to eat indoors so they could watch the kitchen magic. They requested that they be allowed to have dessert and coffee outside on the terrace after lunch.

Winer had an open kitchen, and there was a great deal to see as the chef and many sous chefs moved past and around each other in an intricate kitchen ballet. They expertly danced and swayed back and forth and in and out and around and around, all choreographed to produce their extraordinary dishes. The restaurant was small, and the food was not expensive. Everyone wondered how so many kitchen workers could be supported by the prices listed on the lunch menu. They decided that wine sales must subsidize the restaurant.

The roasted cauliflower soup was seasoned with a touch of thyme and more than a touch of Parmigiano Reggiano. Elizabeth knew there were some other secret ingredients in the soup that the chef did not want to share, but the taste was unique and wonderful. Curry? Turmeric? Saffron? Rolls that were crusty on the outside and yeasty and soft as clouds on the inside were served with what Sidney was certain was hand-churned butter. Sidney liked butter and was something of an expert. Sidney was a very good cook. She made gravy.

The selection of entrees was limited, but each one was unusual and prepared to order. The burger was stuffed with Roquefort cheese and served on a brioche bun with caramelized onions and homemade catsup in which red wine had been incorporated. The French fries were thin and hot and crisp. The seafood tacos were anything but plebian. Filled with Dungeness crab, lobster, and sautéed scallops, they were topped with a creole mustard and remoulade-style salsa, chopped Campari tomatoes, and a finely grated leek and kale coleslaw. The steak frites was tender and rare and sat on top of a toasted baguette that had been generously spread with a layer of wild mushroom puree. Several people ordered the eggplant tower with ripe heirloom tomato slices and slices of homemade burrata. The eggplant was crunchy and sweet with its garlicky panko bread crumb crust. Olivia ordered a second helping of the amazing potato salad that was made without a drop of mayonnaise. Everything on the menu was quite special and had been created and served with tender, loving care. Almost everyone indulged in at least one glass of either Winer's special Sauvignon Blanc or their 2017 Reserve Pinot Noir. Several in the group had helped themselves to a glass of each.

Lunch was long, and they had been so absorbed enjoying their food, no one had noticed the distressed couple from the Albergo at a nearby table. They were seated in a secluded niche, almost hidden from the rest of the room. Elizabeth signaled Lilleth to look in the direction of the alcove. The worried man was half-heartedly trying to get some pasta onto his fork, but he was unsuccessful and finally put it down. His wife had finished her lunch. She looked as if she was losing patience with her spouse. She picked the pieces of grilled salmon and the cherry tomatoes from the pasta dish her husband was not going to eat. Advanced exasperation showed on her face and in her body language. At last, she dug in with her fork to finish the linguini fini from her husband's plate.

The group was finally able to move themselves to a table outside on the terrace. They brought the unfinished bottles of wine with them. No one was really ready for dessert, but they were not going to let one drop of Winer's outstanding wine go to waste. A few ordered coffee. Eventually, Lilleth ordered an

Italian vanilla crème soda milkshake, and everyone had to have a taste. After sampling the delicious ice cream concoction, two more milkshakes and several straws and spoons were ordered. A plate of hand-crafted chocolate truffles arrived at the table. The masked waitress told them that more of these delicious candies could be purchased at SLO Confections, a very special bakery and candy store in downtown Paso Robles.

On his way into the winery, Cameron had spied at least one, maybe two, motorcycles in the Winer parking lot. He could see one of them from where he was sitting on the patio. He'd just watched a motor scooter arrive and go around the corner. He heard the driver turn off the engine. For most of his adult life, Cameron had been a motocross enthusiast and had beaten himself up for many years pursuing the sport. Finally he decided he had worn himself and his body out sufficiently and had given it up. Motocross is the most physically demanding sport in the world. Cameron had loved the rush the dangerous pastime had afforded him, but even more than the risk, he had enjoyed the punishing skill it had required to compete in the top echelon of contenders. Cameron was no longer a participant in the extreme sport, and he no longer owned a motorcycle. But he still loved fast bikes and noticed them whenever he saw one on or off the road.

He thought Bailey and J.D. had, at one time or another during their lives, both owned motorcycles or motor scooters. Cameron shared his love of flying with Tyler, but Tyler had never been able to grasp why the risks Cameron took with motocross were so appealing. Cameron motioned with his head to Bailey and J.D. to follow him to the parking lot around the corner. He knew there were a couple of interesting motorcycles parked there, and he wanted a closer look.

Sure enough, there were not just two but three two-wheeled motorized vehicles in the Winer parking lot. Cameron was betting they belonged to people who worked at the winery. There were two motorcycles and one beautifully-maintained vintage motor scooter. Cameron was drooling over the big Harley that had been fixed up and looked to be in tip-top shape.

The motor scooter was a Lambretta, a style that had been sold in Italy in the 1950s. Cameron knew this particular model had never been for sale in the United States. Many decades ago, the scooter had been purchased in Italy and imported to this country by its owner. Someone might have brought it back with them from a trip abroad. Even this many years later, there was not a dent or a ding on the scooter, and the Lambretta had been painstakingly repainted. The seat had recently been reupholstered. Somebody really loved this creampuff.

The other motor bike was also a beauty, the Interceptor, a Honda sport bike from the 1980s, now a classic. The three once-upon-a-time cyclists were examining and admiring these artifacts from the past, reminiscing, and telling tall tales of their own long-ago exploits, when they heard shouting and screaming coming from the patio where the rest of their friends were sitting. They ran back to the front of the winery to find out what was going on.

CHAPTER 11

*Bailey MacDermott graduated with an engineer-*ing degree from the University of Arkansas. He was hired by IBM directly out of college, and because of his outgoing personality and gift for gab, he quickly became one of Big Blue's best salesmen in his region. But Bailey was an independent guy, and he felt as if he was being smothered in the corporate world. He'd been selling computer systems to the oil industry, to help them with payroll and inventory and to keep track of where their oil was coming from and where it was going. Bailey let a couple of his clients know he was interested in making a change, and within a few weeks he had a job offer from a major oil company. He submitted his resignation at IBM and left his job in Chicago. Houston was calling, and Bailey was ready to conquer the oil business and earn some big money. Soon he was flying back and forth from Houston to the oil-rich kingdoms in the Middle East. Before long, he knew the countries and who the movers and shakers were in the world's wealthiest oil-producing nations.

When the Shah of Iran fell, the world, and especially the Middle East, was turned upside down. Previously ignored actors on the world's political and economic scene were on the march, and a few days after the hostages in Iran were taken, the U.S. Department of Defense was knocking on Bailey's door. He was a patriot and agreed to work with the DIA, one of the pentagon's spy agencies.

At first, he just met with other Americans in Riyadh and other Arab capitals. He carried the packages and papers these agents asked him to take back with him when he flew home to the U.S. Then he was asked to meet with foreign nationals and accompany them to safe houses. Once, in Lebanon, he had to rescue an American who was in desperate shape, running from Hezbollah, and suffering from serious gunshot wounds in his calf and thigh. Bailey drove the man to the airport in his rental car and slipped him aboard the oil company's plane. Bailey's assignments became more and more complex and more and more dangerous. He told himself he was doing all of this because he was helping to fight terrorism, but he also loved the rush he got from taking risks.

After a particularly harrowing mission, Bailey had to take some time off from his regular job with the oil company and from his special work for the DIA. He spent a month recuperating in Paris. He slept late and ate well. He also met and fell in love with an American woman he met at the Rodin Museum. Bailey had gone there to learn more about the sculpture. Marianna Archer was at the museum posing for magazine photographs. She was a gorgeous redhead who earned her living as a highly-paid fashion model. She was doing a photoshoot for an American fashion magazine and was dressed in tight stretch stirrup pants, enormous earrings, and a sexy faux suede off-the-shoulder top. Bailey stumbled into the room where Marianna had her arms draped around *The Thinker.* That day Bailey completely missed seeing Rodin's most famous work of art, but he couldn't take his eyes off Marianna as she pranced and posed around the naked man made out of bronze.

It was the 1980s and Bailey MacDermott decided he had been a bachelor long enough. Marianna was a lonely ex-pat living in France, and she quickly succumbed to Bailey's warm and friendly personality. They spent a lot of time at her apartment getting acquainted, and before Bailey's month of vacation was over, the two were married. It was probably a mistake for them to marry, even under the best of circumstances. The complexity of their work lives and the travel both of their jobs required meant they spent a lot of time apart. Their time together was frenetic, and they never had a chance to really get to know each other.

What Bailey didn't know about Marianna was that she was manic-depressive, a mental illness that has since been renamed "bipolar 1 disorder." If she stayed on her meds, Marianna was mostly fine and a lot of fun. When she went off her meds, all bets were off. When they returned to the U.S., she realized she was pregnant. Bailey and Marianna's son was born in Houston, and Bailey was beside himself with joy. Marianna, on the other hand, lapsed into post-partum depression and a serious depressive phase of her mental illness. She reached the point where she didn't want to get out of bed at all.

Bailey and Marianna eventually divorced. She ceded custody of their son to Bailey, but Bailey was juggling too many things. He told the DoD he wasn't able to work for them anymore, and he quit his job working for the oil company because he didn't want to travel all the time. He began dealing in oil futures and was incredibly successful in this field. He made a lot of money, but the best part of his life at this time was that once he settled down in Dallas, he was able to make a home for himself and his son.

Before he met Gretchen, rumors flew that he had married again in haste twice and then quickly divorced twice! He didn't like to talk about what had happened in his love life during this period, and no one wanted to ask. It was clearly a painful subject for Bailey.

Gretchen Johanssen technically worked in human resources, but she was one of those people who was so competent that, wherever she worked, she eventually took over running much more than the HR department. She was petite and fit, and her good looks and style attracted attention. Once you got to know Gretchen and once you had worked with her for a while, because of her extraordinary competence, you forgot how small she was. Her abilities and her organizational skills belied her size, and she took on a significant presence in any room where she worked or spoke.

Gretchen had married twice and had two wonderful sons. She adopted and raised a foster daughter. When her sons were launched, one into the military and the other to college, and her daughter was in graduate school, Gretchen decided to take a job with an international financial group. She had always wanted to travel and was excited to be sent to run the HR department at her company's office in Zurich.

As always happened when Gretchen arrived on the scene, her ability to get things accomplished was immediately recognized, and she took on more and more responsibilities, above and beyond her HR duties. She always attracted attention at board meetings. When she made an outstanding presentation to a group of international businessmen, the head of one of Switzerland's wealthiest and most secretive banks noticed her. He wanted to date her and wanted to hire her to work for him. He offered her a salary three times what she was earning in her current job. She agreed to take the lucrative position as his special advisor, but she never mixed business and romance.

The Swiss banker was smart enough to agree to her terms, and Gretchen spent several years making top-level decisions in the arcane world of Swiss banking and international finance. She became fluent in German. She met arms dealers, heads of state, assassins, movie stars, Russians and Saudis, and people she was sure were mafia figures or drug dealers or both. She helped her employers invest their clients' riches. She knew the identities of many who had secret money and needed to conceal it.

When one of her ex-husbands was murdered, Gretchen returned to the United States. Her son, who was a Navy Seal, was involved in an almost-fatal car accident, and Gretchen wanted to spend time with him, helping him heal and boosting his spirits as he recovered. She was an accomplished corporate operator, but she was first and foremost a mother. It was while her son was recovering the use of his legs at a rehabilitation center in Texas that Gretchen met Bailey.

Bailey volunteered at the VA hospital where Gretchen's son was going for physical therapy. Bailey still made deals of all kinds. He had branched out from oil futures into commercial real estate, and it seemed that whatever he touched turned to gold. Volunteering to work with military personnel who were trying to get back on their feet was Bailey's way of giving back. He loved his work, but he loved working with the disabled vets even more. He spent time with Gretchen's son on an almost daily basis, and it was the young Navy Seal who introduced Bailey MacDermott to his mother.

Bailey and Gretchen had both been burned in the marriage department. Neither one was looking for a spouse. Each of them was happy living alone, but as they spent more and more time in each other's company, they realized how much they loved each other and wanted to spend the rest of their lives together.

Gretchen had taken a job with a company in Dallas, and in no time, she had, as she always did, made herself indispensable to her new company. She was the kind of employee who quickly became critical to the organization. When she mentioned the possibility of retirement, she was offered a large bonus to stay on for two more years. At the end of those two years, when the subject of retirement came up again, she was offered an even larger bonus, if she would just stay on a little longer. She might never retire because she was making too much money just by mentioning the word "retirement."

Bailey had moved into doing deals in international real estate, and this new clientele sometimes presented challenges. There were language barriers, although most people involved in the upper echelons of the business world spoke English. There were cultural differences, especially when it came to determining what was legal and ethical and what was not. Most of his clients were legitimate buyers who actually wanted to own a warehouse in Hong Kong or Mexico or an apartment building in Singapore. But a few clients who contacted Bailey were interested in buying real estate for the purposes of laundering money.

The schemes the money-launderers devised were complicated and slick. Bailey found himself involved in a couple of these transactions before he caught on to what was happening. When he realized what these faux buyers were up to, he had to say no. He refused to participate in any money laundering intrigue. More than once, a disappointed money launderer had threatened Bailey's life. Bailey loved the rush and the risk of doing high-flying business transactions, but he definitely did not enjoy having a loaded gun pressed against his head. When one of these crooks tracked him to his home and threatened him, Bailey and Gretchen had to move to a different house. Bailey learned to be more discreet, but it was impossible for him to give up the thrill of making a deal. Now he was always wary when he took on a new client. In his early seventies, he was a vital and busy wheeler-dealer in the financial world.

CHAPTER 12

It all happened so suddenly and so unexpectedly, no one was sure, after it was all over, exactly what the sequence of events had been. The reunion goers were lingering over their coffee and chocolate truffles, wondering if they should think about calling for their limousine to take them back to the Albergo. The sun was warm, but not too warm. They'd had a delightful and satisfying meal. No one else was sitting on the Winer's patio, so they were secure in their social distancing protocols. No one had fainted at the table or fallen off their chair. Much was right with the world.

Isabelle and Lilleth looked up when the distressed man and his wife came out the door from the dining room. The woman was literally holding up her husband as they made their way down the flagstone walkway headed for the navy blue town car that was parked at the curb to take them back to the Albergo. They'd almost reached their ride when a white van swung out of a handicapped parking spot, accelerated at full speed across the parking lot, and rammed into the side of the town car. The driver of the sedan, who had just stepped out of the car to go around and help his passengers into the back, was thrown to the pavement.

Two men in ski masks that completely covered their faces, jumped out of the white van and descended on the couple who'd been heading for the town car. But wasn't everyone masked these days? The two masked men punched the woman in the stomach and shoved her to the ground. They grabbed the worried husband and carried him toward the van. Surprisingly, "the thinker" who had appeared to be almost without energy or will up until this point, summoned something from deep down and fought back. He kicked and screamed. He lashed out with his fists and twisted the arm of one of the ski-masked men who were trying to capture him. "The thinker" was, it turned out and when the chips were down, quite a warrior.

His wife had hit her head when she was pushed down on the flagstone walkway, and she wasn't getting up. Her husband was not going to be taken without a fight. And he put up one heck of a fight. Richard was pretty much out of the picture with his wounded shoulder, but Matthew and Tyler rushed to assist the man in his attempts to escape from his abductors. Lilleth was strong and athletic, and she also stepped forward to help … until she saw the long knife that one of the masked men was wielding. She shouted at Matthew and Tyler to step back, "He's got a knife."

No one in the reunion group carried weapons. At least none of the members who were lollygagging on the front patio had any weapons, other than Elizabeth who always carried her potentially lethal cane. She'd tried to get up out of her chair to join the fray, but the men from the van were too quick. They had two extra-large bungee cords secured around "the thinker" and had loaded him into the back of the van before anyone could do anything to stop them.

The three motorcycle enthusiasts had come on the scene late, in time to watch their fellow guest from the Albergo disappear into the back of the van, but not in time to prevent his being taken. Cameron and J.D. were quick to respond, and they both headed back to Winer's side parking lot at the same time. Bailey immediately grasped what they intended to do and hurried to join his compatriots. Cameron was shouting orders as he ran.

"Look under that piece of rubber on the footrest of the Harley. That's where he will have hidden the key, if he hid it anywhere." Sure enough the key was there, just where Cameron had thought it would be. Some things never change. "Toss it to me. I'm going to take the Harley." It was their good luck that the owner of the older Honda had left his key in the ignition. Leaving the key had been a bad choice for the owner but a good one for the motorcycle "thieves."

J.D. was busy hotwiring the ancient motor scooter. "I only had a motor scooter when I was in junior high. I've never driven a motorcycle."

"You can have the scooter, then, if you ever get it going." Cameron had the Harley revved up.

"What if I've forgotten how to ride it? It's been a long time since I've been on one of these things." J.D. was still hesitant.

"It's something you never forget. It's like riding a …." Cameron's words were lost in the roar of the engines as he and Bailey were off and away. They pushed their stolen motorcycles to the limit, chasing the white van down Highway 46. It wasn't long before J.D. and the Lambretta were also in pursuit.

At first the driver of the van did not realize it was being followed, but when he did, he put the pedal to the metal and attained maximum speed. The motorcyclists did their best to keep the van in view. It could turn off at any point along this main road and might disappear forever. If the kidnappers had known they were going to be chased by even a ragtag motorcycle gang, they might have chosen a different vehicle to use for their kidnapping plot. As it was, the van was just barely staying ahead of the motorcycles.

Cameron realized that whoever owned the older Harley he'd chosen to "borrow" had done amazing things to its engine. The owner had "souped it up" or maybe even installed a larger and more powerful engine than this model usually had. Whatever had been done to this Hog had made it possible for Cameron to come close to overtaking the van.

The van finally left the main highway, and this would turn out to be a bad decision for the kidnappers. The road they'd chosen was a winding, twisting, up and down through-the-hills route. It was ideal for those on the smaller, more maneuverable motorcycles and the scooter. J.D. had fallen behind, but he was going fast enough to be able to keep his friends in view.

The van had to slow its pace when it went around the road's sharp curves. It was taking a beating as it bounced hard over the dips in the road. As the van slowed down to make a particularly difficult turn, Cameron pulled around on one side, and Bailey pulled around on the other side. They wanted to force the van to stop, but it refused to pull over. Rather than come to a halt, the van chose to drive off the road. It careened like a drunken sailor as it bounded down a hill and over the rough terrain. Apparently the driver of the van was either incapacitated or had terrible judgment. He refused to slow down. Or maybe the brakes had gone out when the van had traveled off-road, a place where it had never been intended to go. Whatever its problem was, the van never slowed until it rammed at full speed into a large cedar tree. The sound of the impact was deafening. The front end of the van was pushed back, almost into the van's rear cargo compartment.

The pursuers on their motorcycles had never intended for the van to crash. They'd hoped to surround it and force it to stop. In fact, they didn't have a real plan. They just wanted to stop the van that had kidnapped their fellow guest from the Albergo. Beyond that, they'd definitely been winging it.

Now they were worried sick about what might have happened to the man they had gone all out to rescue. Could he possibly have survived the crash and the total demolition of the van? Was it safe to approach the wreck? Would the gas tank explode? Would the van burst into flames at any moment? Would the man with the long knife suddenly come flying out of the crumpled mass of metal to attack them?

Cameron and Bailey got off their bikes and carefully approached the shambles. Fire was always an imminent danger with any motor vehicle accident, and this was a bad one. Vehicles that had been in crashes always exploded in the movies and on TV. When the three had determined that the vehicle was not going to explode, their first priority was to try to extract from the van a man whose name they did not even know. Bailey saw that one of the van's occupants had been thrown clear. He'd evidently not been wearing a seatbelt and was ejected when the van crashed. He had ended up quite a distance away from the cedar tree. It was obvious, even from far away, that his neck was broken. There was no point in checking for a pulse.

Cameron approached the van on the driver's side. When he looked through the smashed windshield, he could barely see the person who'd been driving. The engine of the van now completely filled the space where the front seat of the van had once been. He turned away and could not stand to look more closely at the carnage. His stomach was queasy, but they had to try to find the man who had been kidnapped.

Bailey and Cameron were unable to open the rear doors of the van to get to the cargo area. The entire vehicle was so bent and twisted, it was impossible to open any of its doors. When J.D. arrived on the Lambretta, he shook his head in disbelief when he saw what was left of the van. With a great deal of effort, the three of them were finally able to pry open one of the van's rear doors.

They didn't see the person they had hoped to find there. They did not find any person at all. Two large bungee cords were discarded on the floor of the cargo area. There was a large rug rolled up in the back, but they didn't see the missing guest from the hotel. Had he been thrown out of the van at some point? They briefly looked around the crash site but could not find the kidnapped victim. It was a mystery.

Then they heard small noises coming from inside the rolled-up rug. Muffled cries alerted them to the fact that there was a person in there somewhere. They climbed into the back of the van and tried to unroll the rug in the confined space.

"How did they ever get him rolled up in this thing while they were racing down the road? It probably saved his life, but I can't imagine how they did it. We can't seem to get him out of here even with three of us working at it." J.D. finally pulled the last fold of the rug away.

The rescued nameless one had no idea who these three older men were. He looked up at them and began to mutter some words that were only partly intelligible. "It was a catastrophic accident. They didn't want to unleash it on the world. They were trying to kill off the ones who were being difficult, the ones who were causing trouble and wouldn't toe the line. It was all a terrible, terrible mistake." After he had gasped out this mysterious comment, he passed out.

"I don't know what the heck he was trying to tell us, but we need to get him out of here and take him to a hospital." Bailey paused. "Or, maybe not. Maybe that's not the best idea right now. How badly do you think he's hurt?"

Cameron and Bailey were fully aware of what they had done and what kind of trouble they could be in. Bailey knew they could be in big trouble. "We need to get him out of the van and get ourselves as far away from this place as possible. Someone back at Winer may have called 911. I hope they did. Fortunately, nobody is going to be able to find this mess any time soon. It's way off the beaten track, and there are many small and unmarked roads in the area. I went over several maps, like I always do, before we came to Paso Robles, and this is a rabbit warren of abandoned farm roads and logging trails that are no longer on any map. And every winery has added quite a few of its own roads. Many of those new ones aren't on any maps either."

Cameron was more than ready to get out of the area, too. "We need to get this man out of the van ASAP. It might be a mistake to move him, but we don't have a choice. I wish one of our doctor pals was around to let us know how badly this guy has been hurt, but neither one of them is here. We have to get him away from the scene of this accident, no matter what condition he's in. Once he's out of here, we can try to determine what his injuries are. I don't think we can take him to a hospital. I guess we could drive up to an emergency room and dump him on the ground near the entrance... like druggies do when their friends OD. But, there is no way in hell I am going to do that to this poor guy. He looks more shaken up than hurt to me. I propose we take him back to the Albergo and let Matthew and Richard take a look at him. If they think he needs to be hospitalized, we can call an ambulance from there. Matthew did a heck of a good job taking care of his Uzbek friend from the Hindu Cush last year. And he did all of that in his hotel room. I think that's our smartest bet." Cameron was offering his plan for discussion.

"I agree we need to get away from here, away from this terrible accident, as soon as possible." J.D. had been a prosecuting attorney earlier in his life, and he knew what to do.

"First we need to wipe down the van to be sure our fingerprints aren't anywhere to be found, and I do mean anywhere. Try to remember everything you've touched, inside and outside. There will be rags in the storage compartments of the motorcycles. Find one of them, even if it's dirty, and clean up all the fingerprints. No traces. The state police could very well conclude that this is a one-car accident. Guys took the wrong road and wouldn't slow down. Going too fast, lost control, and ended up driving off the road and into a tree. One of them wasn't wearing a seatbelt. He was thrown out of the van. Very tragic. Terrible. Always wear your seatbelt, etc."

"How are we going to get him away from here? If we had a car …." Bailey was asking.

J.D. had already figured it out. "We have to get our man, whoever he is, tied onto the back of the motor scooter. You will have to lash him to me, with those big bungee cords, so he doesn't fall off. The police will eventually come to investigate this. They may or may not have been told there was a kidnapping. They might assume the guy who is very dead, on the ground way over there, is the person who was kidnapped. Mystery will continue to surround this accident. But we cannot be any part of any of it. We have to get out of here. Now get to work."

Within two or three minutes, they'd erased all traces that they'd ever been at the scene. They scuffed up and smoothed over the ground to try to obliterate the tracks of the motorcycles and the motor scooter. The kidnapped man was still unconscious, and it wasn't easy to get him out of the back of the van and sitting upright on the motor scooter. After much fumbling and falling, Cameron and Bailey were able to repurpose the bungee cords the kidnappers had used on their victim. They secured him behind J.D. on the motor scooter. The bungee cords were tight and uncomfortable around J.D.'s chest, but neither Bailey nor Cameron felt the bungee cords were going to keep the two riders safely on the Lambretta. They looked much too precarious to be allowed on a public highway. What if the bungee cords lost their power or worse, came apart under the strain?

They found a sturdy rope discarded inside the back of the van. They hated to go into the van again, but the rope, which had probably been wrapped around the rug, had possibilities. It took some work, but they were able to use the rope to further secure J.D. and his passenger together onto the motor scooter. J.D. was looking pale and very uncomfortable by now, but he said he thought he could keep his balance and keep the man they'd rescued on the Lambretta's seat with him.

The package seated on the motor scooter was a jury-rigged looking mess. Maybe the two would make it back to the Albergo, and maybe they wouldn't. After one last look around and after a moment lamenting the fact that two people were dead, even if they were kidnappers and probably horrible criminals, the two motorcycles and the motor scooter, carrying two people bungee-corded and roped together, left the scene.

Because he had studied his maps, Bailey could find his way back to the main road. From there it was not too far into town and back to the Albergo. They decided they shouldn't travel together. Bailey would lead alone, and the scooter would follow some distance behind, just close enough that J.D. could see Bailey and stay on the right road. Cameron was heading to Winer to find out what had happened there. He would leave his borrowed Harley in the parking lot, as surreptitiously as he could, and call an Uber to take him back to town. They had to figure out how to return the other cycle and the scooter, and it had to be done without delay. Whoever owned these vehicles would no doubt need them when they'd finished work for the day.

CHAPTER 13

When Elizabeth Emerson was a senior at Smith College in Northampton, Massachusetts, the CIA was actively recruiting from the Ivy League men's schools and from the Seven Sisters women's colleges. The spy agency had decided women had good brains after all and made good analysts. The CIA was especially interested in hiring economics majors because they'd found that people who understood economics had analytical minds, were able to process information in a systematic way, and could reach conclusions and solve problems. The CIA was not looking for covert operatives when they interviewed the college seniors. They were not hiring women to wear the classic fedora and trench coat spy outfit, lean against a lamppost in rainy, post-war Vienna, and wait for a rendezvous with a Russian double agent. The CIA wanted desk jockeys.

Elizabeth, an economics major, was of the duck-and-cover generation and had lived in the shadow of the Cold War all her life. She was intrigued by the pitch from the CIA and decided to look into what would be required for her to pursue a career with The Agency. She went to the initial meeting on the Smith campus and then made the trip to Boston with three other women from her college class. In Boston, the four were given a battery of tests, designed to evaluate their abilities to do the work the CIA would require of them. This was the first step in the application process. Those who passed the initial tests would be given more tests, some interviews, and then perhaps the offer of a job in Washington, D.C.

Elizabeth scored "off the charts" in the inductive reasoning part of the testing. Only one other person in CIA recruitment history had ever scored higher than she did in this one very important area, critical to the kind of work the CIA needed doing. Although she had never realized it before, Elizabeth was told she could read and evaluate vast amounts of material in an incredibly short period of time and come up with an accurate analysis and conclusion. The testing people made a big deal over her, and this embarrassed the somewhat introverted Elizabeth. They singled her out, and she didn't like it. Since she'd never known she had this special skill, she wasn't that impressed with herself. She wondered what all the fuss was about.

Elizabeth had been seriously dating a graduate of Princeton who was now a first-year medical student at Tulane. Elizabeth was in love, and she thought Richard Carpenter was too. It was 1966, and women married young. It was early in the women's liberation movement. Not all women, even well-educated ones, had careers. Many became housewives and mothers. Elizabeth had always been remarkably independent, but she couldn't imagine her life without Richard. Richard was not enthusiastic about her pursuing a career with the CIA. He didn't really understand that she wouldn't be in any danger, sitting in an office in Langley, Virginia, reading newspapers and looking at data sets. He wanted her with him in New Orleans, although he'd not yet asked her to marry him.

When he did pop the question, Elizabeth said yes. They would be married that summer. The CIA was disappointed when Elizabeth turned down their offer of a position as an analyst. They pulled out all the stops and harassed her mercilessly for the remainder of her senior year. They played the "serving your country" card and everything else they could think of. Elizabeth did not waiver, and she and Richard were married in August. She got a job teaching in the New Orleans public schools, and the CIA became a distant memory. But the CIA kept its eyes on her, and years later when she decided to change careers, they welcomed her with open arms.

After she left New Orleans, Elizabeth went to graduate school. After spending two years on the faculty at the University of Texas at El Paso, she took a position teaching economics and economic history at a small college in Maryland. She was pressured to change a grade so that a failing student could become a "C" student. The student, who had not put forth any effort whatsoever in her class, had to have a "C" in order to maintain his eligibility to play basketball for the college team. The academic dean leaned on and threatened Elizabeth. Because she was only a part-time professor, the dean told her she could easily be fired from her position, if she didn't do as she was told and change the grade. Elizabeth refused to knuckle under to the threats and gave the student a "D." He had barely made the "D" and had just escaped failing her class by the skin of his teeth. After she'd turned in her grades, someone went to the registrar's office and changed the student's grade to a "C." The young man never missed a step or a dribble on the basketball court because of his failing academic work. Learning and getting an education had proven to be an afterthought, or given no thought at all, when it came to qualifying for a sports team.

Elizabeth thought she could hang on to her job, but she decided she did not want to be a part of the rotten system any more. She'd always known academia was fraught with politics, corrupted by competition to get ahead of one's colleagues, and filled with bloated and narcissistic egos. She decided life was short, and she didn't have to play the stupid games required to succeed in the university arena. She didn't want to be around the grasping and ambitious meanies any more.

She made some phone calls and began the difficult task of hiring babysitters, drivers, and a housekeeper. She made complicated arrangements for her duties at home to be taken care of when she was gone. She began to build her cover, that she was taking a research position at the Wharton School in Philadelphia. It was a three-hour commute one-way to her new job, and she would be away from home a couple of nights a week, sometimes more. It was a big commitment, but her new boss was willing to work with her to maintain the illusion of the imaginary job she supposedly had at the University of Pennsylvania. She was a valuable commodity, and the CIA helped her manage her home duties and her cover position in Philadelphia, as she committed to the more dangerous job she'd really been hired to do.

Most of her work was in Virginia, using the skills she'd demonstrated when the CIA had wanted to hire her years earlier. Occasionally she had to make trips overseas. None of her family or friends ever doubted for a minute that she was working at the Wharton School. They thought it was odd that she was gone from home so much, but by now, two of her children were away at boarding school in New England. Only one daughter was still at home. No one, not even Richard Carpenter, was allowed to know what Elizabeth did when she was out of town.

It was a rocky period in the Carpenters' marriage. Richard was consumed with his work as head of the pathology department and the clinical laboratory at the local hospital. He participated in the children's activities whenever he could, but he was pretty much oblivious to Elizabeth's needs at this time in their lives. He was angry that she wasn't around all the time, as she had always been before, but he was so preoccupied with his own career, he only noticed she wasn't there when something went wrong.

Richard Carpenter had risen to the top of his career and was the main partner in his pathology group, Richard Carpenter, M.D., P.A. He had done his internship and residency at the University of Pennsylvania, and during those years he'd had the opportunity to work with Philadelphia's medical examiner. In addition to spending his days accompanying the Chief Medical Examiner on his rounds, Richard had done moonlighting for the medical examiner's office to earn extra money. The young doctor became a skilled and convincing expert witness. He was a favorite with prosecutors because juries loved his boyish looks and earnest, honest voice. When he was on the witness stand, members of the jury believed everything Richard Carpenter, M.D. had to say. If he gave evidence against someone in a murder trial, that person was always convicted. Vance Stillinger, M.D. was the Philadelphia Medical Examiner, and Richard Carpenter M.D. became his golden boy.

Carpenter's testimony had sent a number of bad guys to prison. The child molesters, murderers, drug dealers, and drivers who had committed serial DUIs all should have known it was their own behavior that had caused them to be convicted. But bad boys and girls always want to find someone other than themselves to blame. Carpenter became a lightning rod for their anger, and some wanted to blame the blonde, cherub-faced scientist who had so convincingly swayed the juries that had convicted them. Occasionally, a defendant would shake his fist at Carpenter when he was on the witness stand.

Once a man stood up and shouted threats at Carpenter after he'd given his expert witness testimony. The defendant, who had been resoundingly drunk when he'd crossed the highway's median strip and run headlong into a van full of children, said Carpenter had misrepresented his blood alcohol level. The driver of the van and four of the children had died, and the defendant was sent to prison. The drunk vowed that when he got out of jail, he would hunt down Carpenter and kill him and his family.

Elizabeth Carpenter had just come home from the hospital after giving birth to the Carpenters' second child. Law enforcement took the threats against Carpenter and his family seriously, and until the convicted criminal was sentenced and safely locked away, the police kept a guard on Carpenter's rented house in the Philadelphia suburbs. Elizabeth wondered who would be there in a few years to watch out for her family when the man was released from prison.

Stillinger tried to convince his protégé to stay in Philadelphia and become a forensic pathologist, but Carpenter owed Uncle Sam two years of his life to be served in the U.S. Army. Furthermore, Carpenter had educational debts and needed and wanted to earn some money. He wanted more income than the salary of an urban medical examiner would pay him, and he didn't want to live in a big city. The Army sent Carpenter to William Beaumont Army Medical Center in Texas for two years, and from there, Carpenter took a position at a hospital in a small town in Maryland where he built a successful pathology practice. He still testified as an expert witness, but the threats that had come his way when he was at the Philadelphia Medical Examiner's Office were long-forgotten. The question was—had the men he'd helped send to prison forgotten him?

CHAPTER 14

W*hen Cameron pulled into the parking lot at* Winer, he found the space still empty where the Harley had been parked before he'd borrowed it. He turned the bike around so that it was positioned exactly where it had been earlier in the day. He put the key under the rubber mat. No one would ever know.

"If I hadn't been out here to see it with my own eyes, I would never have known that someone had stolen my bike … until I noticed how soon I needed to fill up the tank." Cameron turned around to see an attractive twenty-something young woman with red hair standing half-way across the parking lot. She wasn't accusatory. She wasn't even angry. She had on a face mask. "I am glad you brought it back, though. That bike is an important part of my life. I would have been devastated if you had been a real thief."

Cameron couldn't think of what to say to the owner of the Harley, and he stumbled with his words. "A man was kidnapped, and I took your bike to try to stop the kidnappers. Sorry, I didn't have a chance to ask you if I could borrow it." He took out his wallet and held up several hundred dollar bills.

He tucked the money underneath the seat of the Harley. "This ought to cover the cost of wear and tear as well as the cost of the gas I used. Thanks for letting me borrow the bike."

"I know all about the kidnapping. I don't know how it turned out, but I saw it all as it was happening. I work in the kitchen." She pointed to the money Cameron had left under the seat of her motorcycle and gave him a thumbs up. "Don't you want to know what happened after you left on my bike?"

"Of course I want to know. What happened?"

"The man who was kidnapped was here for lunch with his wife. We heard the van crash into the town car and then we heard the shouting. Some of us ran outside. The wife of the guy who was kidnapped was knocked down when the kidnappers grabbed him. She hit her head on the flagstones when she fell, and she might have been unconscious briefly. Or maybe she was just dizzy. Anyway, lucky for her, there were two doctors having lunch here. They stayed with her until she could sit up. They asked her some questions and determined she didn't have any serious head injuries. They wanted her to go to the ER to be checked out. When they insisted, she refused and was adamant about *not* going to the hospital. She really lost it when they told her that Harrison, that's what she called her husband, had been taken away in the white van. She kept saying that they were going to kill him. She seemed completely convinced of that, but she didn't seem at all surprised that he'd been kidnapped. After she'd calmed down a little, the doctor who had his arm in a sling and the woman with the cane left with the kidnapped man's wife, in the town car. I don't think she knew them. But the guy said he was a doctor, so I guess she trusted them."

Everything the Harley owner had said so far made sense to Cameron. "What about everyone else? Did anyone call the police to report the kidnapping?"

"Yes, one of the women who was with the group sitting on the patio called 911 and reported the kidnapping. I overheard the call. You couldn't miss what she said. She was shouting into her phone. She described the white van and even gave the make of the van and the license plate. I thought she was brilliant to have remembered to get the license number. She told the 911 operator everything, exactly as it had happened. The 911 dispatcher said they were sending someone out here to Winer to interview her and any other witnesses who'd seen the kidnapping. Your friend also told them to 'get their asses out on Highway 46 and go after the van.' She was hot. She told whoever she was talking to that interviewing her would be a waste of time—that she'd already told them everything she knew and everything they needed to know. She told them that finding the man who'd been kidnapped was the priority, not talking to her. She told them about the bungee cords."

Cameron still didn't know whether or not law enforcement would be coming after him. "So, did somebody come out here and interview the witnesses?" He moved away from the Harley and headed toward the front of the winery. The Harley's owner walked over to her bike. She gave it the once-over to be sure it had not been damaged. She took the money Cameron had left for her and stuffed it into the pocket of her jeans.

She continued telling Cameron what had happened. "After the kidnapped guy's wife calmed down and before she got in the town car to leave, she told the woman who'd called 911 that she did not want anyone to know her husband had been kidnapped. The woman who'd called 911 couldn't understand that and asked why she didn't want somebody to try to rescue her husband. They kind of got into it, but the bottom line seemed to be that this Harrison guy, the woman's husband, is working on some kind of secret something. The wife doesn't want law enforcement involved because she doesn't want the press involved. I couldn't hear everything they were saying at that point, but what I heard sounded pretty complicated. I don't think the woman who had called 911 was happy with the wife of the kidnapped man. And then the wife left, with the doctor and the woman with the cane. The three of them just got into the sedan and drove away."

The owner of the Harley continued her account of the drama. "The driver of the town car was knocked down when the van rammed into it. There was so much other stuff going on, nobody paid any attention to that poor guy. It turns out he was okay. The van didn't actually hit him. He fell down because of the huge impact the town car took when the van hit it. Even though the van didn't hit him, he was really shaken up. Once the other doctor checked him over, he was reassured and was okay to drive the town car. He's going to have some big bruises, but he's not badly hurt. The town car had a giant dent in the side, but it was drivable. They had a little trouble getting the doors opened, but those old cars are tanks. That thing must weigh several tons. It took a tremendous hit, but it had no trouble driving out of here.

"The rest of the people in your group got into their limo and left, too, except for the woman who'd called 911 and another couple. Two friends of the 911 caller stayed behind with her to talk to the sheriff. It was the sheriff who eventually showed up. The woman who'd called 911 was pissed. She wanted to leave, too. The couple that had stayed with her were pretty good about keeping her calm. I had to go back inside to help clean up from lunch, so I didn't hear what the woman told the sheriff. I don't know when she left. When I came back out for my break, everybody else had gone, and here you are, bringing my Harley back to me. I hadn't even noticed it was missing. So that's on me. I was so caught up with the kidnapping and all the rest of it, I didn't notice you'd stolen my bike. I'm Petra, by the way." She smiled and patted the pocket where she'd put Cameron's money. All was forgiven.

Cameron was not about to give Petra his name. He had on his mask, so Petra, who worked in the Winer kitchen, hadn't really seen much of his face. She'd only seen the upper half. He'd left her with enough cash that he didn't think she would squeal on him. She hadn't noticed that her bike was missing from the parking lot until she'd caught Cameron bringing it back. He was betting she hadn't noticed that any other bikes were missing. The kidnapping had been a great diversion. Everybody had been paying attention to that and watching the action. Nobody had been looking in the direction of the parking lot.

Cameron didn't want to hang around a place where he had borrowed something that did not belong to him. He wanted to call an Uber and get back to the hotel. When he'd arrived at Winer, he'd sent texts to J.D. and Bailey and told them to get themselves and their two-wheeled vehicles back to the parking lot of the winery as quickly as possible. He told them to stop and get gas to fill up the motorcycle and the motor scooter before they arrived. He didn't like the idea of waiting any longer than he had to for J.D. and Bailey to return to Winer. But he also didn't think it was right for whoever owned the bikes to run out of gas on their way home tonight. Cameron was nervous about waiting around at the scene of his "crime," and he hoped his friends would hurry. What if the owner of the other motorcycle and the owner of the Lambretta were not as understanding as the owner of the Harley had been? Cameron didn't want a confrontation. The fewer people who knew about the borrowing they had done, the better.

Cameron wasn't really worn out from the motorcycle rescue, but he needed some down time, time to think and figure out where they were going to go from here. They'd been in Paso Robles for less than forty-eight hours, and one of the Camp Shoemaker boys had already been shot. It was a minor flesh wound to be sure, but there was no getting around the fact that Richard had sustained a gunshot wound. And nobody had any idea why he'd been shot.

They had witnessed a violent and brutal kidnapping of someone who was staying at their resort hotel. Cameron and his friends had taken, without permission, two motorcycles and a motor scooter. They'd always intended to return the bikes and the scooter, but still.

Other than stealing the motorcycles, had they actually broken any laws? Had they caused the car accident in which two people had died? Cameron decided they definitely had not. The criminals driving the van had made choices, even after they had made the very bad choice to kidnap a man. They could have chosen to slow down. They could have pulled the van over to the side of the road and stopped. They could have fastened their seatbelts. But the two men had chosen to continue speeding on a dangerous road, and they had both died as a result. They were criminals—kidnappers who had failed to use good sense when they could have saved themselves. They had chosen not to save themselves. No one else was responsible for their deaths.

Cameron could not believe their reunion trip had once again been overtaken by so much unwanted excitement. This time it seemed to be other people's turmoil, but he and his friends were definitely involved ... up to their armpits and their eyeballs. He couldn't blame it all on his doctor friends this time, trying to save the world. He'd been just as complicit as anybody else. He didn't feel as if he'd had a choice. If you witness a kidnapping and think you might be able to save the victim, you try to save him. It's not rocket science. It is an automatic reaction, not even a conscious decision.

Cameron was certain it had been Gretchen who had called 911 about the kidnapping and had been forced to stay behind and give a statement to the sheriff. So much for having a good deed rewarded. So much for doing the right thing and then being punished for it. He sent a text to Gretchen to let her know the man who had been kidnapped had been rescued and had probably already arrived at the Albergo. He told her not to ask any questions and not to inform law enforcement. He said he would tell her all about the rescue when he could.

But Cameron had some questions for himself. How were they going to explain the rescue of the kidnapped victim? He didn't have a good answer for that one. He didn't even know if J.D. had been able to successfully deliver his passenger back to the Albergo. Bungee cords and rope? Really? They'd looked pretty treacherous perched on the Lambretta. The extra weight would have caused the motor scooter to be very unstable and forced it to go even more slowly. What if someone had seen the bizarre Siamese twin-like bundle of two human beings on the motor scooter? Would Cameron have called the police if he'd been driving down the road and spotted such a sight? What if the sheriff himself, or one of his deputies, came across J.D. making his way into town with an unconscious passenger lashed to his body? What if the passenger had regained consciousness and become combative? Or worse, what if one or both of them had fallen off the motor scooter.

Should he call and report the accident? Anonymously? Cameron was leaning in the direction of not reporting it. He wondered if they had left any motorcycle tracks at the accident scene. Even if law enforcement did a really thorough investigation, they probably would not be able to trace the bike tracks, if any had been left behind. Cameron doubted anyone would spend a lot of time looking into the accident. If they did investigate, he doubted they would go to the trouble of bothering with any tire tracks they might find. The scene was a mess. There were more immediate and pressing things for investigators to look at than some tire impressions that might have been left in the dirt.

Cameron was a straight shooter, as were all of the Camp Shoemaker group. He did not want to break the law. He did not want to steal or borrow, without asking, anyone's motorcycle or motor scooter. Under normal circumstances, hewould never have done any of this. But, he wondered, when would normal circumstances return?

Finally, Bailey and J.D. arrived. Before they even talked about what had happened with the trip back to the Albergo or with their kidnapped man, they returned the Lambretta and the other motorcycle to their original spots in the parking lot. J.D. tucked the wires he'd used to hotwire the motor scooter, up under someplace where he though they wouldn't be noticed. They had filled the gas tanks of the cycle and the scooter. The owners would not be stranded as they drove the Honda and the Lambretta home from work today. Now that the bikes and the scooter were all back in their parking spots, the three wanted to get away from the Winer property as quickly as possible.

Cameron called an Uber to pick them up, and the three bikers left the parking lot to wait in front of the winery. Hopefully, whoever owned the Honda and the Lambretta would never know about the adventure their bikes had taken part in while their owners had been at work.

CHAPTER 15

They had to talk, but the Uber arrived before they could say too much. They knew they couldn't discuss what had happened in front of the driver. He dropped them off at a coffee shop a few blocks from the Albergo. They found an open outdoor table, a good distance from any other masked customers and any eavesdropping ears. Bailey placed their order with his phone, and they tried to focus on deciding what to do next.

J.D. was the first to give his report. "Of course I was terrified the whole time I was driving the scooter close to town, that somebody would look at me bundled up with an unconscious person on the back and call the cops. I tried to avoid busy streets where I thought there would be a lot of people. When I was stopped at a traffic light, I sent texts ahead to Olivia and Tyler to meet me by the patio next to the swimming pool, the place where we had drinks last night before we went to Tio Theo. Was that just last night? Olivia was pretty angry with me for taking off on the motor scooter like I did and leaving her at Winer without any explanation. But when she saw I had the kidnapped guy on the scooter with me, she was so shocked, I think she forgot to be angry. His name is Harrison Davis, by the way. He's a scientist. That's all I know about him. He was just beginning to regain consciousness when we arrived at the Albergo. The kidnappers must have drugged him with something, for him to stay out that long. In a way it's a blessing he didn't wake up while we were on the motor scooter. Lilleth came to the pool area with Tyler, and thank goodness she did. We needed her. The three of them had a tough time taking those bungee cords off from around the two of us. The cords were so tight; I could barely breathe. They had to cut the rope away. It was all really uncomfortable, but it did the trick. Harrison Davis did not fall off the scooter, and he didn't bring me down. We made it. But, I will tell you, it was a huge relief when those enormous rubber bands and all the rest of it was gone from around my chest."

J.D. continued his part of the story. "We got him into a lounge chair, and that wasn't easy either. We didn't want to injure the guy any more than he'd already been beaten up. At this point, Davis was conscious on and off, but he didn't know where he was. And, of course, he didn't know who we were. He kept asking for Rosemary, his wife. Olivia called Matthew to come and take a look at him. We hoped no other guests would arrive, wanting to use the pool, while Davis was lying there. I told them all, Olivia and Tyler and Lilleth, right up front, not to ask any questions about how we'd rescued the man. Harrison probably won't remember anything, and nobody else really needs to know. Everybody always wants to know everything, and Olivia won't give me any peace until she has the whole story. But for now, only the three of us can know anything about how we rescued Harrison Davis."

Bailey was nodding his head. "We need to discuss what we're going to do about the fact that we chased down the van and it crashed. I'm in favor of never telling anybody anything about what happened. I know you said you're going to tell Olivia, but I'm not sure I'm going to tell Gretchen. She is pretty angry with everybody right now, especially with me, of course. She did the responsible thing, like she always does, and called 911 to report the kidnapping. She even got the license plate of the van. Of course, when she was doing all of this, I was nowhere to be found. I'd taken off down the road with the two of you. She said ... well, you know, she wishes I would stay around sometime and keep her company, give her some moral support. She says I never do.

"She said that everybody, except for Tyler and Lilleth, left to go back to the Albergo. The two of them waited with her for the sheriff to arrive. She couldn't understand why the kidnapped guy's wife wasn't willing to wait and give a statement to the sheriff. The wife, Rosemary, was very upset and told Gretchen that her husband was doing secret work of some kind. She was frantic that he not become involved with the police. She wouldn't even tell Gretchen his name ... or her name. Gretchen couldn't understand how a wife could just drive away after she'd seen her husband being kidnapped. Gretchen wondered why the woman didn't want her husband back. And, the people who had kidnapped him had also assaulted her. They pushed her to the ground and left her with a seriously bleeding scrape on the side of her face. Gretchen couldn't understand why the woman didn't want those people caught. Gretchen was furious when Rosemary got into the town car and left the scene of the kidnapping to return to the inn.

"When I got back to the Albergo, I made the mistake of going to our hotel room. I should have gone to the pool and waited for the rest of you. Or, I should have hidden out in the bushes. I should not have gone back to the room. Of course, Gretchen wanted to know where I was going when Cameron called and I left again. I was just thankful she hadn't seen the motorcycle. At least I had the smarts to hide that in the back of the parking lot behind some trees. Thank goodness she didn't ask how I got back to the Albergo." Bailey was always in trouble with Gretchen. He couldn't seem to help himself.

"Elizabeth and Richard rode back to the Albergo with the wife, Rosemary Davis. Richard was concerned because she'd fallen and hit her head. She'd been on the ground for several minutes and had a lot of blood on the side of her face. Richard and Matthew didn't think she was making a lot of sense with all the talk about secret work. It didn't seem right to them either that she wouldn't want to call the authorities to report that her husband had been kidnapped. They were afraid she'd suffered a concussion and was talking gibberish. Richard offered to accompany her back to the hotel to be sure she was going to be all right. The woman was in a very big hurry to get away from the winery and definitely was desperate to get out of there before the sheriff showed up.

"The three of us had taken off after the van, and then Elizabeth and Richard were gone. A few people from our crowd were still there. They left in the limo to return to the Albergo, except for Gretchen who couldn't leave. Thank goodness Lilleth and Tyler stayed with her." Bailey continued. "That left Gretchen to talk to the sheriff, without the kidnapped man's wife to back her up. I'm sure the sheriff thought it was very odd that Gretchen was there to make a statement, but the wife of the man who had been kidnapped had neither called 911 nor cared to stick around to report her husband missing. No wonder the sheriff was skeptical of Gretchen's statement and the 911 call. She didn't think the sheriff quite believed her... that anyone had been kidnapped. The sheriff even had the nerve to tell her she could be prosecuted for filing a false report with law enforcement. You can imagine how that burned her up. She gave the sheriff the names of everyone she knew who had witnessed the kidnapping. At that point I think she just wanted to have somebody verify that the kidnapping had actually occurred. Tyler told the sheriff it had all happened so fast, he wasn't sure what had happened. He said he'd seen a white van take somebody away, but it had been chaotic. And there really was a lot of confusion... obviously, about everything."

"What about the people who work at the winery? Didn't the sheriff want to ask them about the kidnapping?" Cameron knew for a fact that at least one person on Winer's kitchen staff had seen what happened.

"Gretchen said it was more than an hour after the guy was taken before the sheriff showed up. I don't think they'd sent anybody to go after the van. Stuff like kidnappings... well, those things don't happen around here. It's a quiet town. They aren't used to car chases and running down criminals. I think they may be out of their depth with a kidnapping. Several of the staff had come out of the winery when they heard the yelling, but they'd disappeared back inside and gone back to work long before the sheriff arrived. Quite a few of them had already left for the day. The sheriff said he was going to track them down and ask them about it. I guess it was kind of a big mess. Most of the other witnesses had left the winery before the sheriff got there. The wife of the kidnapped man didn't seem to care enough to stay long enough to give a statement that her husband was gone. It's no wonder the sheriff was suspicious. Gretchen is angry as a hornet. She did the right thing by immediately calling 911, and now she feels as if she's being made to look foolish. I think she's even a little offended, miffed is maybe a better word, that we actually recovered Harrison Davis. She's angry with me because I won't tell her anything. She thinks we ought to call the sheriff and tell him everything that happened. She doesn't understand why that absolutely cannot happen." Bailey put his hands on the table and put his head down in his hands. Bailey was always in trouble for something.

J.D. knew Gretchen was on the hot seat with the sheriff, and he didn't blame her for being angry. "When the news reports link the two dead guys from the accident to the possible kidnapping, she will be angry all over again. She will probably go to the sheriff and tell him that the kidnapped guy is safe. And, she will probably turn the three of us in to the sheriff for questioning. Maybe you should just tell her everything that happened and try to talk her out of going to the sheriff with her information."

Cameron added his two cents. "I plan to tell Sidney everything, eventually, but Sidney is another straight shooter. She will also want us to tell law enforcement all about it. So, I'm going to hold off telling her about the accident, at least until we can find out how much law enforcement knows. I have to admit that I'm also very curious about why Harrison's wife didn't want his kidnapping to be reported to the cops. That is very odd. Do you think she might have had a worse bump on the head than anyone realizes?"

"Yeah, that bothers me, too. All this stuff about top secret work and refusing to speak to the sheriff… it is bizarre, really." J.D. knew that if he had been kidnapped, Olivia would have raised the alarm at once and with everybody, and she would have left no stone unturned until she'd found him. He knew this to be a fact because he'd been kidnapped two years earlier in Maine and had been missing for more than twenty-four hours. Olivia had made a huge fuss with the local law enforcement people because they wouldn't look for J.D. When she'd reported him missing, they told her he'd probably run off with a younger woman. Olivia ended up hiring a private investigator who'd uncovered facts that had eventually led to J.D.'s rescue and that of Isabelle Ritter.

Cameron had more questions. "Tell me, did Harrison finally wake up, and was he okay? What did he have to say? Does Rosemary know her husband has been found? What happened while he was recovering by the pool?"

Bailey still had his head in his hands. J.D. continued the conversation. "Matthew showed up and gave Harrison a quick examination. I think our doctor friend is pretty tired of taking care of people in hotel rooms. He kept shaking his head, but he did all the right things for Harrison Davis. He asked Harrison a few medical questions and told him that, except for some cuts and bruises, he would be fine.

"Then he asked him what he remembered about the kidnapping. The poor guy remembered being trussed up with bungee cords at the winery, but he remembered nothing after that. He didn't remember being put into the van or anything at all about the crash. He didn't remember the ride on the back of the motor scooter. The next thing he remembers is waking up beside the Albergo pool. So the entire episode is a blank for him. I wonder if the kidnappers knocked him out with something before they wrapped him in that rug. They apparently didn't hit him on the head, but something made him unconscious and caused him not to remember anything. He put up such a fight at the winery, I don't think he would have allowed them to roll him up inside a rug, if they hadn't sedated him with something first." J.D. was a former law enforcement person, and he looked at all crimes from that point of view.

"When he woke up, I guess he just kept asking for his wife, Rosemary." J.D. continued. "From what I could gather, when the town car delivered the three of them back to the Albergo, Richard and Elizabeth took Rosemary to her room. They did their best to clean up the scrape on the side of her face, and Richard decided she was not delusional as a result of her head injury. Elizabeth believed the things Rosemary was saying about secret work and all that, but the woman refused to give them any real explanation. She was devastated that Harrison had been taken, but she seemed more frightened than anything. Richard and Elizabeth tried to get her to talk to them about what was going on, but she was still saying weird things. I'll leave it to them to tell you about it tonight."

"So, did Rosemary and Harrison ever get back together? And where are they now?" Cameron wanted to know what everyone's current status was at this moment.

J.D. filled him in on the Davises. "We received your text about that time, and we were getting ready to leave anyway. Tyler and Matthew got Harrison on his feet, and they helped him walk to his room. We followed along in case they needed extra help. He was woozy and unsteady. He really couldn't walk on his own. I'm sure he'd been drugged. He had to have someone on either side of him to hold him up. They almost had to carry him to his room. Olivia and Lilleth opened doors.

"Harrison had lost his mask somewhere between the bungee cords and the accident. The rest of us were all masked, but when we got to their room, it was clear Rosemary didn't want to let any of us into their suite. Four of us stayed out in the hall, but Tyler and Matthew delivered Harrison to the room and put him on the couch. Rosemary was both shocked and overjoyed to see him, as you might imagine. She nearly fainted when she saw him at the door. He was still pretty out of it but seemed glad to see her, too. She thanked us profusely, but then shooed us all away. Matthew said he thought Rosemary was still in a state of shock from the kidnapping incident. He was worried that she wouldn't be able to get Harrison to the bed by herself and wanted to stay around to help her. The guy did not have any obvious injuries, but he was not really all right by any means. Matthew said something about following up on his health, but the wife pretty much slammed the door in our faces. Bailey and I left to get our bikes back to the winery. That's all we know."

CHAPTER 16

M*atthew was determined to finally be able to* present some movie montages that night before dinner. He'd arranged with the Albergo to have a special room set up for the showings. It was a relief to everyone that the electronics seemed to be working. The group of friends was happy to be doing something they all enjoyed and something that was familiar. Movie montages were fun. Any controversy that might arise from watching Matthew's film clips would not be taken personally.

There had been too much excitement that day, and they didn't want to talk about any of it. Feathers were ruffled, and everybody felt as if they'd been left out of the information loop. The fact was that nobody really knew much of anything for sure. Harrison Davis had been rescued and reunited with his wife. But none of the Camp Shoemaker crowd had any idea what was going on with those two. The people in the reunion group, who were not in the know, were very curious to learn exactly how Harrison's rescue had been accomplished. Those who had effected the rescue were emphatic that no absolutely no details would be forthcoming—at least for the time being.

Matthew had selected segments from films that were pertinent to epidemics and pandemics. These included *Outbreak*, *Contagion*, *Pandemic*, *The Andromeda Strain*, and *The Twelve Monkeys*. He also had several long pieces taken from *The Good Earth*, a 1937 film based on Pearl Buck's book about China that had won a Pulitzer Prize for Fiction in 1932. Buck won the Nobel Prize for Literature in 1938.

But the real coups that night were clips from three documentaries about Tiananmen Square, the place where hope for democracy in China had been crushed more than thirty years earlier. The slaughter had occurred on June 4, 1989. Elizabeth had asked Matthew to try to find these controversial documentaries. Matthew had gone to a variety of sources to obtain copies of the films about that day. His finale for the evening was a comparison of three documentaries—*Tremble and Obey*, *It Happened in Tiananmen Square*, and *The Gate of Heavenly Peace*. He recommended that everyone see the full-length movie *The Tank Man*. Olivia proposed renting *The Good Earth* on Netflix so everyone could watch that movie together.

Because they'd had such an elegant and filling lunch at Winer, they'd planned to order a couple of pizzas delivered to the media room where they were watching montages. They would order wine and beer and snack on pizza while they watched the movie clips, and that would be dinner. But so much had happened since they'd eaten lunch. There had been a kidnapping. Some in the group had tried to prevent the kidnapping, and a motorcycle gang of sorts had chased and tried to bring down the kidnappers. There had been a very serious motor vehicle accident. A man had been rescued and returned to his wife. One of their members had driven from the countryside into town on a motor scooter with a man strapped to his back with bungee cords. The sheriff had been called, and statements had been given. Two motorcycles and one motor scooter had been stolen and then returned. Cover-ups had been planned. It had not been a quiet afternoon. A couple of pizzas were not going to suffice for this active crowd. They ordered five extra-large pizzas, several large salads, three orders of pasta, and two loaves of garlic bread to be delivered from Cucina Italia. Additional bottles of wine were ordered and opened.

All three documentaries that Matthew shared that evening were controversial. Some of the people who had experienced the events at Tiananmen Square claimed that *The Gate of Heavenly Peace* was an attempt to whitewash the horror ofthe day and to portray some Chinese Communist officials in a positive light that they did not deserve. The documentary had been controversial before it was ever made available to the public. Some reviewers claimed that this three-hour long documentary, which eventually aired on PBS in the United States, was too considerate of the Chinese Communists and their brutal ways. *Tremble* and *Obey and It Happened in Tiananmen Square* had both been produced by outsiders who were not sympathetic to the Communist government. Because of the length of these documentaries, Matthew could not show his audience everything they needed to see. But he had meticulously selected segments from these documentary films that he felt represented the tenor of each one. The Camp Shoemaker group could easily see how the same event, and ostensibly the same facts, could be edited and interpreted, slanted and twisted to tell very different stories. A highly-motivated discussion accompanied the pizzas.

These movie and documentary montages added to Olivia's discussion from the previous evening about the difficulties the Chinese Communist government faced as it struggled to keep the country under control. Several in the group wondered aloud, given the chaos and the repression that reigns inside China, why it had taken so long for the Chinese to unleash a terrible plague upon the world. Their incompetence, their brutality, their inability to govern their country, and so many other things were obvious harbingers of disaster, no matter how you looked at it.

The group was worn out from the day and worn out from the impact of the powerful stories Matthew's montages had to tell. They were ready to go to bed. They'd been warned emphatically that they would not be told any details about the rescue of the kidnapped Albergo guest, so no one brought up the subject of Harrison and Rosemary Davis—two enigmatic people who had been thrust upon the group of friends today without warning.

No one asked about the Ridenours who had dined at Tio Theo the night before. Richard's gunshot wound would eventually heal, but he hoped that one day he would have an explanation about why he'd been shot. He had been completely honest when he'd told his story to the emergency room doctor, but so far, no one from law enforcement had contacted him for a statement. Richard found that puzzling.

In spite of not talking about their fellow guests at the Albergo Riposante, everybody in the reunion group was wondering what the heck was going on with them. Both the Ridenours and the Davises had to be well-known at the Albergo. Being a previous and frequent client was a minimum requirement to have been invited to participate in Quandanche Quarantena. Everyone who was currently staying at the inn had been asked to join the week's activities by special invitation only.

But, the Ridenours were not really the Ridenours. They were staying at the hotel under an assumed name. And the Davises had secrets. Rosemary Davis had said so. The Ridenours would not go anywhere near a hospital—even after

Brian had a suffered a severe allergic attack and a gunshot wound which he swore was not a gunshot wound. Rosemary Davis would not allow either of the doctors in their group to do anything but superficially check out her husband to see if he had been injured during his violent abduction. Harrison Davis had suffered two painful encounters with bungee cords and been involved in a horrible van accident that had proven fatal to two people. Neither couple would allow anyone to even think of calling law enforcement... in spite of a shooting on a public street and a very public kidnapping. What was going on with these people?

Even within the reunion group, their own friends and husbands refused to talk about or even allow any of them to ask questions about the heroic rescue of Harrison Davis. The fact that the man had been saved from who knows what was an accomplishment to be lauded and celebrated. Why was this amazing and successful act of courage being treated as a big secret?

The group was scheduled to visit the Hearst Castle the next day. Public tours of the castle had been suspended in mid-March due to COVID-19, but Tyler knew the people who ran the tours and took care of the castle. He'd arranged for his friends to have a private day-long tour with the castle's best guide. The guide would be masked and would stay six feet away from his tour group. The members of the reunion group would all wear masks. The Albergo would send another wonderful boxed lunch from Rialto which their group would enjoy outside on the castle grounds.

The Hearst Castle was located in San Simeon, California which was about a forty-five minute drive from Paso Robles. Their limousine would drive them north on part of the Cabrillo Highway which ran along the Pacific Coast through Cambria, California and the Hearst San Simeon State Park.

This was one of the most breathtaking scenic drives in the United States, and they were all thrilled to be able to make the trip and to have the specially arranged tour of the castle. They put aside their worries about kidnappings, shootings, and the secrets of their fellow guests at the Albergo. The day would be a fantasy adventure. They would imagine they were living at a different time in history and having a glimpse into the lives of the very rich and very infamous.

Everyone was going on the tour except Elizabeth and Richard. They'd been through the castle several times in the past. Under different circumstances, they would have enjoyed today's special tour with their friends. They would have particularly enjoyed the drive along the Pacific coast. But Elizabeth would have to be in a wheelchair to make the castle tour, and that would slow everybody down. Richard was worn out trying to do everything with one arm, while his other arm was in a sling. There were ten wonderful friends who were willing and able to push Elizabeth's wheelchair because Richard was unable to do it, but Elizabeth said she wanted to stay home and keep Richard company. Every so often, she needed a day off from the scheduled activities. They would order lunch from room service, and if nobody else was around, they might sit by the pool in the afternoon. Richard liked his daily naps, and these were few and far between on the reunion trips. He would have at least one nap today, maybe two.

After lunch, while Richard was sleeping on the couch in their suite, Elizabeth took her cane in hand and made her way to the patio beside the pool. She had on her mask, as required, and didn't meet anyone on her short trip to the beautifully landscaped outdoor pool area. When she arrived, she saw another guest sitting at a table shaded by an umbrella. As Elizabeth moved closer, she saw that it was Rosemary Davis. Rosemary had a glass of iced tea in front of her, but she had not touched it. The ice had melted, and Rosemary was staring off into space.

The previous day, after Harrison had been kidnapped and Rosemary had been pushed to the ground, Elizabeth and Richard had accompanied Rosemary back to the Albergo. She'd not been badly hurt when she fell, but she had scraped her face when she'd collided with the flagstone walkway. Rosemary had been in shock on the drive back to the inn. She hadn't cried and had not uttered a single word to either Elizabeth or Richard during the entire ride. She had been terribly upset when Gretchen had called 911. The Carpenters had decided not to question Rosemary or try to coax her into speaking. They accompanied her to her room at the Albergo, and she had remained silent as she'd opened the door and entered her room. She hadn't wanted to admit them, but Richard pushed his way in and said she needed to clean the blood off her face. He said he wanted to take a look at her injury.

Elizabeth brought a warm wash cloth and found a bottle of hydrogen peroxide. She gently washed the blood from Rosemary's face. Because Rosemary was so paralyzed with shock, she was unable to wash her own face. Richard examined the wound and made a recommendation about using an over-the-counter antibiotic ointment. They'd hated to leave her in her shell-shocked condition, but they could tell she wanted them to go. After they'd done all she would let them do for her, they left, and without a word, she closed the door behind them.

Elizabeth hesitated to speak to the woman now, considering how closed and defiant she had been during their encounter the day before. Elizabeth knew Rosemary had been seriously suffering for some time, and she didn't want to cause the poor woman more distress. Elizabeth took a seat at another umbrella-shaded table that was positioned several yards from where Rosemary was sitting. When Rosemary looked up, Elizabeth smiled and waved briefly. Rosemary looked as if she might say something, but she didn't. A masked waitress approached Elizabeth's table and took her order for a carafe of red zinger tea with mint, orange slices, and extra ice.

Rosemary spoke up, loud enough for Elizabeth to hear her at her table a safe distance away, "Thank you for bringing me back to the Albergo yesterday. Please give my thanks to your husband, too. I appreciate it that you made sure I was all right. Please thank your friends who rescued my husband. I am forever in their debt." Rosemary's voice was full of emotion, and she paused to recover her composure. "He doesn't remember much of anything about what happened. He remembers having the bungee cords put around him and being loaded into the van, but he doesn't remember anything else after that... until he woke up here beside the pool. I never thought I would see him again." Tears began to roll down her face.

"Is he all right? Does he have any injuries as a result of the kidnapping or the rescue? Our friend J.D. used the bungee cords to strap Harrison to himself so they could both ride safely on a motor scooter. He must have had some bruises from all of that." Elizabeth waited for Rosemary to respond.

Rosemary brushed the tears away from her face. "Oh, he has plenty of bruises all over him. The kidnappers must have rolled him around a good bit in the back of the van. You can see bruises where the bungee cords were around his chest. But he doesn't seem to have any really bad injuries. He didn't have any open wounds and wasn't bleeding. I think he was drugged with something, though. He wasn't himself at all last night. He didn't know what had happened and seemed very confused. He's better this morning. His brain seems to be back to normal anyway. He still doesn't remember anything after they put the bungee cords around him. He's very traumatized, of course, and it will take a while for the bruises to go away."

"I'm so glad he wasn't badly hurt." Elizabeth wanted to reassure Rosemary and let her know she was there to help. "Our friend Dr. Matthew Ritter would like to have had a chance to examine him, but it doesn't sound like your husband needs a doctor. I hope the bruises aren't too painful. And, if you do need a doctor, we have two doctors in our group. You know my husband Richard. Dr. Matthew Ritter is also a physician. He took a look at you when you were pushed to the ground by the kidnappers. You may not remember any of that. Both doctors are retired, but they still know their stuff. We're in room #114 if you need us. And Dr. Ritter and Isabelle are in #118." Elizabeth hoped Harrison Davis really was all right. If he'd been thrown around in the van as it made its escape, and he certainly must have been, he could have internal injuries that were not immediately apparent.

Rosemary was wondering if she had revealed too much. "I wish I could tell you more, but I have already said more than I should have. My husband is in great danger. He knows things people don't want him to know. We came to the Albergo partly so he could take a break from his work. He was on the verge of collapsing from exhaustion. He's supposed to be resting and getting away from his research. He is not supposed to be thinking about work for a while, but of course, that's impossible. He isn't sleeping and he isn't eating. And I'm not doing much better. Last night was the first good night's sleep he's had in months. I'm thankful for that. Please, please don't tell anyone I spoke with you. I shouldn't have said anything, but I wanted to thank you for your kindness. I don't know how your friends did it, but I will always be grateful that they saved his life and rescued him from the van." Rosemary paused. "And they really did save his life, you know. Make no mistake about that. The men who took him intended to kill him. I thought he was gone for good."

"Are you in danger, too? Can't you get some help from law enforcement or from somebody to keep yourselves safe?"

"I am only in danger because Richard cares about what happens to me. Someone could threaten to do me harm, and they would have that to hold over Richard's head. He wants nothing to do with law enforcement. There are too many leaks to the press at all levels—with the sheriff all the way up to the FBI. That absolutely cannot be allowed to happen. My husband, for all intents and purposes, does not exist. We are planning to disappear. We have to disappear. We are in hiding here at the Albergo. Please don't say anything about any of this to your friends. No one must know. Please respect my wishes. Our lives depend on your silence. Our lives are in your hands." She stood up and started to leave, but then she turned around and spoke again. "I should not have told you any of this." She turned her back on Elizabeth and abruptly walked away.

Elizabeth finished her red zinger and went back over everything Rosemary Davis had said to her. Richard would be waking up from his nap soon, and Elizabeth grabbed her cane. She walked back to her suite. She liked Rosemary Davis. The woman was obviously smart, well-educated, and devoted to her husband. She was terrified of something or somebody. The woman really believed that she and her husband were in danger of being murdered. Even though she showed obvious signs of extreme fatigue and stress, she was such an attractive woman. She had gorgeous hair and looked wonderful in pink.

What in the world could have happened to the Davises that they could not call on law enforcement to protect them? Why did they feel they had to disappear? He'd been kidnapped right in front of Elizabeth's eyes, so she believed Rosemary when she said Harrison's life was in danger. It was true, no question about that. Elizabeth always wanted to help, but in this case, apparently all she could do to help the Davises was to keep her mouth shut.

CHAPTER 17

The trip to the Hearst Castle was a huge success. When they met for cocktails beside the pool that evening, the others were eager to share their stories with Elizabeth and Richard. The drive had been magnificent, and the personal, private tour of the castle had dazzled them. They were grateful to Tyler who had set it all up. The tour guide had shared with them quite a few personal anecdotes about the Hearst family. He'd told them inside information about Patty Hearst's kidnapping—things nobody outside the family had ever been told.

Their lunch had been another spectacular achievement from Rialto. They'd had a curried chicken salad made with currants, yogurt, almonds, and Major Grey's chutney. That was everybody's favorite. They'd also had a shrimp salad made with capers and celery. Lilleth had decided the sauce for the shrimp salad tasted a little bit like McDonald's special sauce, but was more lemony and so much better. The olive and pasta salad in a red wine vinaigrette had been the perfect side dish. The thin cheddar cheese biscuits were crisp and addictive. Olivia was going to try to bribe Rialto's chef for the recipe.

She had to have more of those. They'd had chocolate and raspberry napoleons with whipped cream for dessert. It had been a very fun day for everyone.

They knew they would be late returning, so they'd decided there would not be any salon tonight. Cocktail hour with movie montages and talks by their friends would resume on Friday evening. They were dining at Rialto again tonight. The Albergo focused on Italian food, but tonight was Rialto's one-time special "International Night." The group put on their masks and again made their way to the ballroom that had been turned into the Albergo's dining room. The Ridenours were seated at a table in the corner. The Davises did not make an appearance at all. Elizabeth was sorry they were not up to it. She wondered if everything was okay with them. Of course, she knew it wasn't. She wondered if the Davises had already disappeared.

The masked waiter arrived pushing a trolley with several open bottles of champagne on it. Also on the trolley were a dozen champagne flutes and an envelope with a note inside. They looked at each other, and shrugged or shook their heads. No one at the table had ordered the champagne. The waiter told them that Mr. and Mrs. Ridenour had ordered the champagne for them as a thank you and an apology. Mr. Ridenour had written them a note. They waved and smiled their thanks across the room. The Ridenours waved back, very friendly now. They noticed that Brian had a sizeable bandage on the side of his head.

Matthew, who had spent the most time with the couple, opened the note and read it aloud to the group. Brian Ridenour graciously apologized for his insolence at Tio Theo. He said he wasn't usually so grumpy, and he blamed the allergic reaction for his unusually belligerent attitude. He hoped the doctors in particular would excuse him for giving them such a hard time. He was very grateful that they had treated him in his distress and that they had respected his wishes not to call the EMTs.

He did not mention the gunshot wound, or the supposed fall against the ashtray in the town car, that had left him with the very noticeable bandage. The champagne offering turned out to be several bottles of the best vintage the Albergo had to offer. The Camp Shoemaker group waved again, raised their glasses in a toast, and communicated their appreciation to the Ridenours. All was forgiven ... kind of. The Ridenours and their names and their secrets were still a mystery.

Lilleth loved Chicken Kiev, so she went Russian/Austrian with homemade spatzle on the side. Several in the group ordered the German pork schnitzel with cucumber salad and potato dumplings, and everyone who ordered this one raved about it. Elizabeth ordered the cream of mushroom soup which was said to be Hungarian. It had a large dollop of unsweetened whipped cream on top of the rich mushroom concoction, and it was heavenly. She followed with the veal paprikash and buttered hand-made egg noodles. Two people ordered stuffed cabbage in a sweet and sour sauce. No one chose the Chinese option. The dessert trolley arrived with sweets selections from around the world. The Hungarian sponge cake stuffed with ground almonds and vanilla pastry cream was an especially popular choice. Homemade Italian chocolate gelato had a cult following.

A tour at the Hearst Castle, the dessert trolley, and glasses of top-shelf champagne had returned the reunion group to the happy campers they were most of the time. Whatever secrets individuals might be keeping had been put aside for the evening. In spite of a pandemic and the fact that one of their own was sporting a gunshot wound, they were laughing and enjoying their time together. Quandanche Quarantena!

Maybe the drama of the past two days had finally come to an end. More winery tours were scheduled for the next day. Everyone slept well that night.

There had been nothing on the evening news the night before about the van accident, and the three friends who knew what had happened, wondered if law enforcement had even found it yet. They decided that the longer it took for anybody to discover the accident scene, the better it would be for them. They would keep checking the online *Paso Robles Press* and the printed daily newspaper from San Luis Obispo.

Finally, on Friday morning, there was an article in the online editions of the *Paso Robles Press* and the *SLO Tribune*. Sometimes press reports tell the reader what the authorities actually know, but there is not perfect congruence by any means. With law enforcement keeping their investigation close to the vest, it was the best reporters could do. Bailey always got up early, so he was the first to find the article.

Paso Robles... Two men are dead after the stolen van they were driving crashed head-on into a tree in rural San Luis Obispo County. The one-car accident went undiscovered for at least twenty-four hours and is believed to have occurred sometime Wednesday night. The crash site was discovered about seven miles south of Highway 46 on a little-used farm road that is believed to be part of the old Devages Ranch property. The identities of the deceased have yet to be determined. Their names will not be released until the next of kin have been notified.

The white Ford Econoline van was traveling at a high rate of speed when it struck a tree. Why the van was on the remote road and why it was speeding are under investigation. One victim, believed to have been a passenger in the vehicle, was thrown more than fifty feet from the point of impact. This man, who had not been wearing a seat belt at the time of the collision, died of multiple injuries, including a broken neck. The driver, who also died instantly, was pinned under the dashboard.

The utility van with a California license plate had been reported stolen on Tuesday afternoon from a Templeton parking lot. The van may have been involved in an alleged kidnapping that is said to have occurred outside a Paso Robles winery. The van's connection to the possible abduction has not been confirmed and is under investigation.

Neither of the accident victims was carrying any identification. If anyone knows anything about the accident or about the identities of the deceased, please contact the SLO Sheriff's office in Paso Robles.

When Bailey read the news item, he was mostly relieved. He was relieved that apparently no one had reported seeing any suspicious motorcycles or a motor scooter near the accident scene. He was even more relieved that the events at Winer were being referred to as an "alleged kidnapping" and a "possible abduction." He sent texts to J.D. and Cameron to tell them to check out the online story.

The SLO County Sheriff's Office would initially be tied up investigating the accident and trying to figure out who the victims were. But eventually they would go after the connection between the van accident and the report of a kidnapping. At first they might assume that the man who had died as a result of being thrown from the van was the kidnap victim. But, at some point, they would realize that witnesses to the "possible abduction" had reported there were two kidnappers in addition to the victim who had been taken away wrapped in bungee cords. The authorities would realize that there should have been three people in the white van and three people to be accounted for. They would realize that someone was missing, and they would begin looking for that missing person.

Bailey had his fingers crossed that no one in the reunion group, other than himself, Cameron, and J.D., would be interested in the online daily news articles from the local paper. The fewer people who might ask uncomfortable questions about the accident, the better. Unfortunately, Bailey was not going to get everything he wished for.

A car from the sheriff's department pulled up at the Albergo just after eight o'clock that morning. They parked right outside the front entrance, and two masked deputies asked at the reception desk to speak to Dr. Richard Carpenter. The front desk called Richard's room to let him know the sheriff's deputies had arrived to talk to him. Interviewing the doctor was going to be difficult, given social distancing requirements, and would require special handling. The Albergo was gracious and allowed the representatives of law enforcement to interview the guest in one of the hotel's meeting rooms.

Richard had known that someone would show up sooner or later to ask him about his gunshot wound. His instinct and his initial intention were to tell them everything he knew. He would never have told anything but the truth, anyway, but he knew he was treading on dangerous ground. He knew Brian Ridenour did not want to be involved in any part of this story. It would be tricky.

Richard wore his mask to the interview, and both deputies also wore masks. One of them was short and one was tall. Other than that, Richard could not see their faces, only their eyes. They introduced themselves, and both of them sat down across the table from where Richard was asked to sit. "How is your shoulder, Dr. Carpenter?" The tall deputy spoke. "We have the physician's report from when you were treated at the Central Counties Medical Center emergency room on Tuesday night. You gave a statement to the doctor who treated your gunshot wound, and we are here to follow up on that report. Paso Robles has a reputation as a quiet town, a peaceful town, a family town. We take seriously any and all crimes, especially crimes that are committed with guns. We cannot have people shot on our streets. We are very concerned that no one called the police when this incident occurred."

"My shoulder is fine and healing quickly. I get rid of the sling tomorrow when the stitches can be removed." Richard didn't think the men really cared about how his shoulder was doing, but he was going to tell them anyway. "If you've read what I told the ER doctor, you already know everything I know. My friends and I had eaten dinner at Tio Theo. A man who was a guest here at the Albergo was also dining at the Mexican restaurant. He had a serious allergic reaction, and a fellow physician and I went to his rescue. We got an Epi Pen from one of the waitresses and gave him a shot of epinephrine. He refused to go to the hospital to be checked out. We respected that decision. When he seemed to have recovered from the allergic attack, we escorted him outside to get into the car he'd hired to drive him and his wife back to the hotel. As I was helping him into the back of the town car, we heard what sounded like firecrackers. We had no reason to believe they were anything but firecrackers, until I realized I'd been hit. I had no idea where the shots had come from or why someone was shooting at me. I knew I'd not been badly hurt—that the shot had just grazed my shoulder. My windbreaker, a favorite of mine for many years, was ruined. But I was extremely lucky that the injury was not a serious one. I realized I was going to have to go to the hospital and have the gunshot wound taken care of."

"Did you tell anyone else that was there with you at the time that you'd been shot?"

"I did, but they all thought the shots had been firecrackers. That's what they sounded like to all of us. If they hadn't seen the blood on my shirt, they would probably have sworn I'd imagined being shot. It was such a minor injury, I didn't want to make a big thing out of it. The guy who'd had the allergic reaction was in much worse shape than I was. I told them to go ahead and leave, that I would be fine. I'd called an Uber, and it had already arrived. I got into the Uber and told the driver to take me to Central Counties. I didn't have to wait long at the ER. I told the doctor who treated me everything about the shooting. We talked a little bit about it. I wondered if I'd just been in the wrong place at the wrong time. My best guess was that a random shot from some gang battle had dinged me. It was bad luck that I was there, but it was good luck that I had such a minor injury. A few stitches, and I was on my way. I also wondered if whoever had shot me might have planned a carjacking and then changed his mind."

"Who were the other people who witnessed the shooting? We want to talk to them. What about the guy who had the allergic reaction? You said he was a guest here. We need to talk to him."

"They may have left the Albergo by now. This all occurred on Tuesday night. Today is Friday. I don't really know the name of the man who had the allergic reaction. I was just kind of doing my Good Samaritan thing, you know, trying to help the man who'd fainted." Richard was telling the literal truth when he said he didn't know the names of the people who were guests at the Albergo. They might be the Ridenours. They might be the Bruces. They might be somebody else entirely. Richard honestly did not know for sure.

"For somebody who's received a gunshot wound, you don't seem to be very upset about it. And you say you don't know much. What about the driver of the car? Who is he?"

"There were two drivers there, and I don't know either of their names. One was an Uber driver, and I'm not sure he heard or witnessed anything. I didn't hire the other driver, the driver of the town car, so I don't know anything about him." Richard realized he'd not yet mentioned that Matthew was anywhere around when the shooting occurred. He wanted to protect his friend, but he also didn't want to lie. He realized he needed a diversion. If he was not going to make a full disclosure, he needed to segue to another subject.

"I'm a retired pathologist, and when I was doing my residency, I worked for a while at the office of the Philadelphia Medical Examiner. I saw quite a few gunshot wounds every day, and every one of them was worse than the one I sustained the other night. Philadelphia is a big city with a lot of crime, like every other big city. I guess I didn't think it was that big a deal to be shot at. I have to add that I was surprised it happened here. I was never shot at when I lived in Philly, but I was mugged several times. My inner-city apartment was broken into twice before I moved to the suburbs. When I lived in the city, the guy who lived in the apartment across the hall from my wife and myself was murdered. He was not murdered in his apartment, and I never found out any details. So, you see, hearing gun shots, that everyone else thinks are firecrackers, is not a shocking occurrence to me. I am used to gunshot wounds, and I am used to murder. I am absolutely certain that someone shot me by accident, and that's all there is to it. I was very lucky it wasn't worse. I really don't have anything else to tell you."

Richard wanted the deputies to leave. He didn't want to talk about the incident any more. He had the feeling these two had come to ask him questions because they were expected to investigate and follow up on the statement he'd given at the ER. "Don't tell me that in this cowboy town, people don't get crazy with their guns some nights when they've had too much to drink or get into an argument with somebody. This is not a big deal and not really worth your time."

"Paso Robles is no longer really a cowboy town, Dr. Carpenter. We are more of a wine town, now. We have gone upscale, and taking pot shots at either our citizens or our visitors has never been acceptable. I think you are not telling us everything you know, and I can't figure out why that is. We are leaving for now. If you think of anything else you want to tell us, here's my card. Please call me." Both policemen stood up, and the tall one left his card on the table.

Richard knew he was off on the wrong foot with the sheriff's deputies and had offended them with his comments about Paso Robles being a cowboy town. He'd actually meant it as a compliment. He liked the idea that it might mostly still be a cowboy town rather than a wine town. He was uncomfortable because he hadn't told the deputies everything he knew. He hadn't wanted to bring his friend Matthew into the mess, but he couldn't figure out exactly why he was protecting Brian Ridenour, or Owen Bruce, or whatever the guy's name really was. He realized, by leaving out parts of the story, he had made a choice to protect this man who had multiple names.

Richard decided he wouldn't say anything to Elizabeth about his visit from the sheriff's department. She would only worry, and there wasn't anything she could do to help him get out of his tangled web.

CHAPTER 18

The group was scheduled to go on another wine tour that morning and then have lunch at the Pacifica Winery Bistro. Richard Carpenter was definitely not in the mood to taste any wine right now. He felt as if he'd been put through the wringer with the sheriff's deputies. He was not used to being grilled by the authorities, and he was not used to being duplicitous. So the interview had been especially hard on him. It was only 9:30 a.m., and he felt as if he'd already put in a full day's work. Who wanted to drink wine in the morning anyway?

In fact, he had to admit that he'd been the one who had wanted to go on the winery tour this morning. He had arranged for today's wine-tastings and made the reservations for lunch. That had been weeks ago, when this trip had been theoretical, before he'd been shot and before he'd decided not to tell the whole truth to the police. He hadn't gone to the Hearst Castle the day before, so he felt he had to go with the group today. He knew he could always say his shoulder was giving him problems, but he felt guilty begging off again. He should have urged Elizabeth to block off more unscheduled days for the trip.

As it turned out, he wasn't the only one who wanted to be excused from the winery tour. J.D. and Tyler intended to play golf, and they were probably already on the golf course. They had tried to schedule their golf game for the following morning, but all the tee times were taken for Saturday. Golf was one of the few sports that people could still safely participate in during the pandemic.

Isabelle and Olivia were going to try out the spa at the Albergo. Special regulations were in place because of COVID, so only a few people could have spa appointments each day. Because special Plexiglas screens had been erected to keep clients' faces separated from those of the nail technicians, pedicures and manicures were possible. Facials were no longer being offered. Massages could be arranged, but with limitations.

Gretchen and Sidney, after what had happened at the Penmoor Resort's spa the year before, were not especially eager to sign up for any spa appointments this year. It wasn't that they were really afraid, but there probably was some small amount of PTSD going on. With all the social distancing rules, it wasn't worth it to risk the exposure. They would be joining the wine-tasting trip and the lunch at the Pacifica Winery Bistro. Elizabeth craved a therapeutic massage. Her creaky joints and the muscles that surrounded them always sang with joy after she'd indulged in a vigorous professional pummeling. COVID-19 had put the kibosh on massages for months, but spas were gradually figuring out how to take care of their customers without subjecting them to unnecessary health risks.

Elizabeth and Lilleth were going to skip the wine tasting but meet the group for lunch. They had planned their own mini-tour of the art work that hung everywhere in the ground floor hallways of the Albergo. The owner of the inn periodically selected a theme or an artist and displayed art accordingly. Even without any organized tours, there were enough interesting paintings to keep them busy for a couple of hours. Elizabeth briefly considered asking Rosemary Davis to walk around the Albergo's halls with them, but decided contacting Rosemary would not be a good idea.

Whoever had designed the Albergo Riposante's reception area and main building had already been collecting beautiful small chests for quite a long time. The collection of chests was remarkable and varied. The hallways of the Albergo had many niches built into the walls at intervals, and each niche contained a unique and interesting chest. The volume and variety of the chests was remarkable. They came from all over the world, and each one was a work of art. Just walking down the halls and looking at the chests was akin to taking a tour in a special furniture museum. Between the art work on the walls and the magnificent collection of artifacts, Lilleth and Elizabeth spent a delightful morning. Lilleth pushed Elizabeth's wheelchair. Elizabeth called an Uber, and they headed out to meet the rest of the group at the Bistro.

Today's lunch would specialize in fresh, farm-to-table offerings. Lilleth tried to stay away from too much meat. Elizabeth was an unabashed omnivore. A rare roast beef sandwich with coleslaw and Russian dressing was calling her name. The Bistro menu promised something for everybody. After lunch, the limo would make another trip along the Cabrillo Highway. It had been such a magnificent drive the day before, they wanted to see it again. Elizabeth and Richard had missed the trip to the Hearst Castle, so they were particularly thrilled to be able to participate in today's scenic tour.

Every morning since the accident, Bailey had checked the online local news, and this morning he'd read a follow-up report on the accident that puzzled him. J.D. was playing golf and had skipped the winery tour. Bailey had not yet had a chance to speak with Cameron confidentially. The short news item referenced the van accident that had killed two people and was believed to have occurred on Wednesday night. Today's report said the two deceased victims' names were still not known, but their DNA indicated that they were both of Russian descent. The public was once again urged to contact the sheriff's office with information about the accident or the victims.

Bailey had wondered why anyone wanted to kidnap Harrison Davis. Now he wondered why in the world the Russians had tried to kidnap him. Bailey was always worried whenever Russians entered the picture. Because of work Gretchen had done at a bank in Switzerland more than a decade earlier, she'd been targeted by Russian assassins in both Bar Harbor and in Colorado Springs. Gretchen and Bailey had trusted the agents from the FBI a year ago when they'd told the MacDermotts they didn't need to worry any more, as they didn't think Gretchen was in danger from further Russian attacks. Gretchen and Bailey wanted to believe them, but there was always that lingering fear that somebody would again decide that Gretchen was a threat. Whenever Bailey read that Russians were involved in a crime that occurred anywhere close to Gretchen, his blood ran cold.

There was no question in anybody's mind that the recent kidnapping incident at Winer had targeted Harrison Davis. And they'd been successful in abducting him. Gretchen had been sitting on the patio at Winer, enjoying the sun and the chocolate truffles, and no one had approached her or threatened her in any way. Bailey did not know anything about Harrison Davis, so he could not possibly know why he was in the sights of the Russians. But Bailey did have a better understanding of why Rosemary Davis had refused to speak to law enforcement about her husband's abduction. If the Russians were involved, no wonder Rosemary had refused to talk to anybody about anything. No wonder she'd said she didn't think she would ever see her husband again. No wonder Harrison always looked worried and depressed. Bailey wished he could explain this to Gretchen. She might find it in her heart to forgive Rosemary Davis for her adamant refusal to involve the authorities. But, of course, Bailey couldn't tell Gretchen anything.

Bailey felt guilty that he was somewhat pleased to hear that the people they'd pursued in the van were Russians. The two Ruskies had stolen the van, and Bailey could only assume that they were Russian Mafia. These people were ruthless, and being taken by one of them would have inevitably ended in death. He absolutely forgave himself and his friends for borrowing the motorcycles and the motor scooter. They had, without question, done the right thing. If they hadn't done what they'd done and chased down the Russians in the van, Harrison Davis would definitely now be dead.

One of the two Russians had been a very bad driver, or they'd stolen a van with bad brakes. For whatever reason, they'd not slowed down when they'd left the pavement. Bailey had never really felt guilty that the kidnappers were dead, but now he felt just slightly elated that two bad Russian dudes had been taken out. There was a little bit of convoluted retribution and retaliation for what Russian assassins had put Gretchen through. Bailey couldn't wait to give J.D. and Cameron the latest news about the ethnicity of the kidnappers.

After their golf game, J.D. and Tyler had lunch in the Albergo's regular dining room. Rialto was open for lunch just three days a week now. The few tables and a limited menu were available on a first-come-first-served basis. J.D. loved club sandwiches, and there was an Italian version, called the Caprese Club, on the Rialto lunch menu. The sandwich arrived on toasted Italian bread with sliced turkey, layers of crispy pancetta, heirloom tomatoes, and slices of homemade mozzarella cheese. The homemade basil and garlic flavored mayonnaise slathered on the toasted bread was served up as a mouthwatering combination. Tyler chose the Caprese Capppellini. The angel-hair pasta was smothered in cherry tomatoes that had been sautéed in olive oil and fresh garlic. Small pieces of burrata had melted into the sauce. It had all been topped off with ribbons of fresh basil, grated Parmigiano Reggiano, and a splash or two of balsamic vinegar. The two friends were in Caprese heaven and not a bit sorry they had skipped lunch at the Pacifica Winery Bistro. They carried their glasses of iced tea to the pool and fell asleep on lounge chairs.

Tyler was the first to open his eyes. There was an argument going on. It was so loud, it had awakened him from his nap. He couldn't see who was arguing, but he could hear what they were saying. He didn't really want to eavesdrop, but there was no way he could avoid overhearing these two. He nudged J.D. to wake up and listen. They determined, after listening for a minute or two, that it was the Ridenours who were arguing. They were arguing about lawyers. Dana Ridenour start to cry, and Brian Ridenour began apologizing. Minutes later, the two of them came around the corner of the patio holding hands. The argument was over, and they'd made up.

Brian Ridenour's face lit up when he saw Tyler and J.D. "I think you guys, or at least one of you, are just the people I've been wanting to talk to. Somebody told me that one of you is a lawyer. Is that right?" Brian Ridenour was asking.

"That would be me." J.D. confessed, although he was afraid of what he might be getting himself into by admitting to this fact. "I actually haven't practiced law for many years, but I keep my law license up to date. I now own a trucking company. Knowing the law is very useful when you are the CEO of any business. There's not a day that goes by when I don't call on my legal expertise to understand or solve a problem."

Brian sat down at the next table. The table was sufficiently distanced, and he was wearing a mask. Dana, who was also wearing the mandatory mask, was polite and excused herself. She said she was going to her room.

Brian Ridenour began his story. "I heard you were a crackerjack prosecutor in Ohio or Oklahoma or Iowa ... someplace in the middle part of the country. I'm from Indiana, so I ought to know which state you're from. Sorry. I Googled you, and there was so much about you in the biography, I forgot where it said you were from originally."

"Oklahoma. I was a prosecutor in Oklahoma." J.D. filled him in.

"Then you are definitely my man. I need to talk to somebody who knows about criminal law but isn't currently connected with law enforcement. I would like to talk to you about a case, but I don't want you to have to report anything about it to the authorities. I want everything I say to you about 'my case' to remain confidential. Attorney-client privilege and all that. I insist on paying you for your time."

J.D. was intrigued, but he didn't need or want any money. He did want to hear more about what this interesting and mysterious fellow had to say. "I am happy to talk to you anytime. No need for a retainer ... or an appointment. Go ahead. Shoot."

CHAPTER 19

“W*ell, that’s partly what this is about… the* shooting. But let me start at the beginning.” J.D. and Tyler were giving Brian Ridenour, or Owen Bruce, or whoever he really was, their full attention. “I am a successful businessman and own several companies. I’ve made a lot of money.” He paused. “The reason I’m telling you this is because my wife and I have been threatened, and I am certain the reason for the threats is money. Anyone who does business aggressively, and I do, makes themselves a target for competitors—at home and abroad. There are groups and individuals who might want me eliminated, for professional reasons. I have taken more than a few contracts away from people during my career. I have leveraged some unfriendly takeovers. I admit these things have happened. There probably are people who hate me enough and would like to see me dead.”

“What kinds of threats have you had? Written? Over the Phone? Emails? What?” J.D. wanted to know.

“All of the above. We have had threats in the mail. We have had vicious phone calls that could only be traced to pay phones in big cities. We have had email threats. We have had our houses and cars vandalized. The most recent thing was that somebody killed my wife's cat. The cat was very old, almost twenty years old, but Alexandra adored Mathilde. They killed the cat and left her on our front doorstep. It was a horrible scene. That happened two weeks ago, and it was the final straw for her. We had to get away. Some of the people in your group know that we are staying at the Albergo under assumed names. We've had to resort to that to protect ourselves. We have stayed here many times using our real names, and the management has been very understanding about our current situation. We're good and long-time customers, and they are allowing us to stay here registered under false identities. Somebody is very angry with me and wants to hurt us."

Tyler and J.D. waited. Brian Ridenour had much more to tell them. "I've thought a lot about it, and now I am convinced, in fact I know, it's not a business competitor. I hate to say this, but I fear it's someone much closer to home. By home I mean, someone who works for me in my immediate headquarters or one of our house staff, or a friend, or someone in the family. It is such a distressing situation anyway, and then to think that someone who knows us well wants us dead. My wife is very frightened, and I am very angry."

"What makes you think it's someone close to you rather than a business competitor?" Tyler wanted to understand how this man was thinking through his situation.

"I had no idea who it might be that was targeting us, until the other night when I was shot at outside the Mexican restaurant."

"Matthew said you swore you hadn't suffered a gunshot wound. He said you were adamant, in spite of Richard Carpenter being shot in the shoulder and going to the hospital, that there had been only firecrackers." J.D. was checking his facts.

Brian Ridenour had the grace to hang his head. "That was me whistling past the graveyard, I'm afraid. I'd just had an allergic reaction and made a fool of myself by fainting and vomiting in a public place. Then someone started taking pot shots at me. I tried to pretend it wasn't happening. Of course, that never works, to pretend anything, does it? I did get shot... in the ear. But then, you all know that, don't you? I feel doubly foolish for putting up such a protest, saying that there'd been no gunshots and all of that. You must think I am a complete and utter chump to say something so stupid."

"People say stupid things when they are frightened. And I know you aren't stupid. I Googled you, too, so I know you are smart and successful and very competitive. I also know you are worth a great deal of money." J.D. wanted Brian to know he'd been checking up on him as well. "Of course, I Googled Owen Bruce."

"Of course."

Owen Bruce continued. He seemed relieved to finally have somebody to talk to. "I had no idea who might be after me until a couple of days ago. Let me explain. The other night, when I was so vociferously claiming that those gunshots were firecrackers, I found two spent rounds on the floor of the town car. One of those was undoubtedly the bullet that took off the top of my ear. The other one must have hit something in the interior of the car and bounced onto the floor. I picked them up off the floor of the car and looked for more. I stuck them in my pocket. At the time, my intention was to hide them. I was still telling the firecracker story, so no one could be allowed to find any used bullets in the car, could they? But, I was shocked when I examined the bullets later. I'll tell you why in a minute. The next day I went back to the scene of the shooting outside Tio Theo to see if I could find any more rounds. I searched all over the ground and the street, and I finally found one more bullet that had been fired the night before. I knew it was one of the bullets that had been fired at me because this particular ammunition is unique. At least it becomes unique after it is fired from a particular and unique gun."

Brian took a deep breath. "The shots that were fired at me, the shot that hit Dr. Carpenter, and the round I found on the ground outside Tio Theo—all of them were fired from a gun that belongs to me. The bullets were shot using a gun from my own gun collection. As preposterous as this might sound, I know it to be an irrefutable fact."

"How could you possibly know what gun was used to fire those bullets?" J.D. had become once again the criminal lawyer and was on the case. He also knew about guns.

"I'm a gun collector, and I have a very extensive and valuable collection of all kinds of guns. I used to be a hunter, although I don't do that anymore. I love guns, especially antique guns. I've spent more money on them than I should have, but it is my passion. Maybe it is my obsession. The gun that was used in the shooting the other night belonged to my grandfather. It is one of my most prized possessions. The antique gun is a handmade revolver, and it is a beauty. It has a magnificently hand-carved wooden handle. Someone who was important to my granddad made it for him. But my grandfather could never get the gun to shoot straight. He showed the gun to me when I was a boy. We set up targets and fired the gun. No matter what we did, the gun never put the bullets where we wanted them to go. We took the gun apart, and he showed me what he had found years earlier, that there was a fundamental flaw in the barrel of the gun. It was never going to shoot straight. Another thing we discovered was that every bullet that was fired from that handmade gun had a distinctive groove down the side. This was part of the reason the gun would never shoot accurately. The barrel of the gun had a tiny protruding point of metal that put the gun off and left the distinctive mark on each bullet that was fired from it."

"The bullets you found in the car and outside the restaurant had this distinctive mark? That's how you knew they were from your grandfather's gun?"

"Yes, I knew, without a doubt, when I looked at those rounds I found in the car and on the ground that they had been fired from my grandfather's gun."

Both Tyler and J.D. said, almost simultaneously, "Are you absolutely sure?"

"Oh, yes, I am absolutely sure. I was taken totally off guard and could scarcely believe it myself. I didn't think there was any possible way that someone could have possession of my grandfather's revolver. It just could not have happened."

Owen Bruce shook his head in disbelief and continued. "I called the houseman who takes care of our farm in Indiana the next day and had him check my gun room. The farm is where I keep my gun collection. He checked, and sure enough, he confirmed that the handmade revolver was gone. He knows the gun and knows how important it is to me. I have no idea who could have stolen it or when it was stolen. We have lots of parties, large and small, at our house. Alexandra loves to entertain."

Bruce continued. "But no one, and I mean no one, ever goes into my gun room. All the guns inside the room are locked away in cabinets, anyway, and the door to that room is always locked. When we have guests, I hire a special guard to stay in that room. When the boys were little, I wanted to be sure none of their young friends wandered into that room by mistake and got hurt. Likewise, I don't want any of my dinner guests to wander in there by mistake. The guard stationed there is stern and escorts unexpected snoopers away from the door immediately. I wracked my brain to figure out who could have gone in there and taken the gun. And why would they? And why that gun? It doesn't even work right. If someone is trying to shoot me, I can only be thankful that the person who crafted that gun for my grandfather made a beautiful gun that doesn't shoot straight."

"Who benefits when you die? To whom have you left your fortune?" This was always the question the lawyer had to ask, so J.D. asked it.

"My wife and I have two sons. They are our heirs. If I predecease my wife, everything goes to her. Upon her death, everything goes to our boys. They already have trust funds that allow them to live very comfortably. They don't spend all the income they receive from their trusts, and neither one is into gambling or anything like that. Neither one lives beyond his means. One of our sons is an artist, quite a good one. He actually makes money from his art work. He has no interest in being a part of any of my businesses. Our other son is a businessman and is an important part of my company. He will run the company when I retire or die. We have divided things very equitably between the boys, and they know all about the trusts and our wills and everything. Because one of ours sons will continue to run the businesses and the other one wants nothing to do with any of that, it was complicated to arrange everything. We wanted it to be exactly fair, in terms of dividing up the large estate we are leaving. But we came up with an arrangement that suits both of them. Neither one needs the money. Neither one of them tried to shoot me."

"What about other people who might think they deserve something from your estate? Do you have any other relatives waiting in the wings?" J.D. was asking all the right questions.

"Just my sister. She's my only living relative, other than our boys. She's a good bit older than I am. She's in her late seventies. She had just gone off to college when I was born.

I was kind of an afterthought, or maybe just an accident. When our father died, the family business was quite small. Our mother was already gone, so Angela and I inherited the business. She received fifty percent of the shares, and I received fifty percent. She had no interest in the company. I did. So I bought her shares. I wanted to run the company and take it in new directions. To be in control, I had to own more than a fifty percent share. Right before our dad died, my sister divorced her alcoholic husband. She wanted the cash rather than any shares in the family business. I was able to buy all of her shares from her over a period of several years. She was delighted with the arrangement at the time, and she's never regretted selling her shares to me. She lives very well and doesn't need money either. We're close and spend every Christmas together. She knows that if she ever needs anything at all, she can come to me. She's seventy-seven years old. She hates guns and has never had one in her hand as far as I know. She is not behind this. And I cannot imagine who is."

"Does she have any children?" J.D. asked the obvious next question.

"She had a one son who died in a car accident many years ago. He was only sixteen. Her marriage and her husband fell apart after their son was killed. It was tragic and a very rough time for her. It was a terrible time for all of us, but she was better off divorced. Her ex-husband has been dead for years, for twenty-five years or more. It isn't him either."

"Well, you certainly have a puzzle on your hands with this one, don't you?"

"I certainly do. What would you do if you were in my shoes? I have considered hiring a private investigator, but I have never had to do that before. I want to be sure that, if I decide to hire a PI, I hire someone who is both competent and discreet. Too many times, when I hire somebody to do something for me, they find out how much money I'm worth. Armed with this knowledge, some of them literally hold me up by charging outrageous fees. I don't mind paying, but I hate being taken advantage of and stolen from."

"Can't blame you for that." J.D. hadn't been connected with law enforcement for two decades or more. He was at a loss about how to advise this man.

Tyler spoke up. "It's a pretty dead end, I agree. I do, however, know of a dependable and fair PI who is quite brilliant at figuring out the impossible. I will give you his phone number and email address. I know he won't rip you off. Jack is semi-retired, and he's made his money. Now he only takes cases because he finds them intriguing. I think he will be very interested in this one and will want to take it on. Tell him everything you've told me, and tell him I referred you to him because I thought the case would challenge him. Let me know what happens. Give me your email address, and I'll send you his contact information."

"I appreciate it. I'm desperate. The shooting points to some kind of an inside job, but there isn't anyone on the inside who could either get to the gun or who would want to shoot me. Really. I am stumped." Bruce wrote down his email address and handed it to Tyler. "My wife is beside herself. She is furious with me… for several reasons. I deserve her fury. I need help to get us out of this mess, but even with all of my financial resources, I don't know if I can trust anybody I know. I don't know you guys. The two doctors in your group came to my rescue and may have saved my life when I had the allergic reaction. I figure you could not possibly be connected in any way to whoever is trying to kill me. So, I trust you."

CHAPTER 20

S*ui Wai Cheung knew it was past time to leave* Hong Kong and go into hiding. The problem was, in a country like Communist China, it is almost impossible to hide, especially if you are trying to hide from the government. It is also pretty difficult to leave the country without the government knowing about it. Sui Wai was a well-respected physician. She was a brilliant scientist, a highly-trained virologist who was married to another highly-trained virologist. Sui Wai's husband had always been more of an enthusiast, a cheerleader even, for the country's Communist regime. Sui Wai was an iconoclast. She was more critical of the repression and the human rights violations. She didn't talk about these things out loud.

Now she found herself completely at odds with her husband's political point of view and with his scientific point of view. They had both been totally committed to their work. They spent long hours in the laboratory and had very little life outside their love of science. From the beginning, their marriage had been more of a convenience than a love match. Now the marriage was over. Sui Wai's career as a virologist was over.

She feared not only for her own life, but for the lives of the Chinese people and the people of the world. She had worked with SARS viruses in the past and had been asked specifically to study this novel coronavirus. Although she had a high-profile public health position in Hong Kong, she also had a wide network of friends and family and colleagues in her field throughout mainland China. She had confidants who worked at the Wuhan Institute of Virology. She'd heard from some of them, and the news was grim. In December, she began hearing from other physicians and fellow-scientists that big trouble was on the horizon. Something had mutated and escaped from the lab in Wuhan. It was a military project that had gone bad—very bad. Sui Wai went to her supervisor and was told to keep quiet and keep working. By January, her supervisor was in a panic. It was a well-concealed, even secret panic, but Sui Wai recognized panic when she saw it.

She realized now that she knew too much, and her conscience would not allow her to remain silent. The Chinese government was lying to its people and to the world. They were attempting to cover up the virology research in Hubei Province, the research that had gone so terribly, terribly wrong. The government had tried to hide the fact that this research in Wuhan was in fact being conducted by the Chinese military. Things were out of control. Because of what she knew about the research, she felt compelled to become a whistleblower. But, if she spoke out and tried to be a whistleblower in China, she would be imprisoned and killed or otherwise made to disappear. She knew she had to leave China if she ever hoped to speak out.

As a physician and a respected researcher, she had enjoyed a position of privilege in Communist China. That was all in the past now. She needed to make plans to leave Hong Kong, and she would leave everything else that she'd worked so hard for, behind forever. There would be no going back, no returning to China. She would never see her friends and family again. But she felt she had no choice.

Sui Wai lived in a luxury, high-rise apartment building in Hong Kong. Because of her prestigious position in the medical community of the city, she and her husband had been allowed to live in the high-end, government-owned condominium, in one of the best buildings in one of the best neighborhoods in Hong Kong. Of course in a Communist country, almost everything is owned by the government.

Her neighbors in the high rise were mostly wealthy people from countries around the world, Americans, Brits, Japanese, Indians, non-Chinese citizens who still had businesses in Hong Kong. Sui Wai had become friends with the American couple who lived next door. Sue and Walter Keely entertained often because of their business connections, and they always invited Sui Wai and her husband to their parties.

Sui Wai's spouse did not like Americans, or any foreigners. He was suspicious of them and their motives. He did not like the private enterprise system to begin with. He mistrusted that, too. He did not want to associate with any businessmen or women, especially from the West. Sui Wai had often wondered why she'd ever married such a sourpuss.

Sui Wai Cheung and Sue Ann Keely laughed about their first names, pronounced the same way but spelled differently. The two women had lunch together when Sui Wai could get away for an hour from the laboratory and her public health responsibilities. Sui Wai's English was perfect, and she spoke it with a delightful British accent. The women had waited three weeks for a lunch reservation at the Polo Club Restaurant, a traditional British establishment that still served a lavish afternoon tea and a dinner menu of typical English food. If you did not know any differently, when you were in the dark wood-paneled dining room, you might think it was 1910 and the British were in charge in Hong Kong and in the rest of the world. The Polo Club Restaurant also served the best dim sum in Hong Kong. It was the excellent dim sum that made it so difficult to get a lunch reservation.

Sui Wai and Sue Keely both loved dim sum, so it worried Sue Keely when her friend wasn't eating. Sui Wai had a voracious appetite and an amazing metabolism. She usually ate everything on her plate and then ate everything from everybody else's plates. Today she was just pushing the food around, and she wasn't talking. Sue Keely knew something was very wrong. "Okay Sui Wai, tell me what's troubling you. And don't say, it's nothing, because I know for a fact that it's definitely something."

Sui Wai lowered her voice so she was barely whispering. Sue Keely had to lean forward across the table to hear what she was saying. "I can't really tell you. If I do, your life might be in danger. I know mine is in danger."

Sue Keely was stunned. What could Sui Wai possibly mean? How could this small, lovely, brilliant scientist be in danger? She was not a political person. She was a scientist, and a very highly regarded one. The Chinese government had given her a luxury apartment to live in. Sue Keely knew Westerners were living on borrowed time in Hong Kong. There had been serious protests about self-rule in Hong Kong. The Chinese government had promised to honor private enterprise and capitalism for several more decades before they could turn this magnificent city state into another failed "socialist paradise." But who knew if the Chinese Communists would continue to honor their agreement?

"What are you talking about? Why would your life be in danger? Please tell me. I want to know." Sue Keely was insistent.

"You are my friend, and I care too much about you to put you in danger. I am being watched and followed. I should not have met you for lunch today. In fact, I tried to make sure I lost my watchers before I came here. I'm not sure I was successful. You see, I have already 'put my foot in it.' I am trying to figure out how I can leave China and get to the United States or to Great Britain. I've decided to become a whistleblower. If I want to tell the world the truth, I must leave Hong Kong before I can speak out. If I speak out in China, I will be arrested and killed outright, or I will be made to disappear. That happens here more than anyone realizes. People are here one day, and then are never seen again. There is no due process in China. But you know all of that."

"You won't tell me, will you? I can see it in your eyes that you will not tell me anything about why you are so frightened. That's okay. I respect your judgment and your right to be silent. But if you are sure you want to do this and if you'll let me, I can help you get out of Hong Kong. My husband and I know people. We can arrange for you to get out of the country. I don't want anything to happen to you. I hope you know you can trust me. "

"I won't do anything to put you at risk. I am on my own in this, but I appreciate the offer of help. I have relatives in Malaysia, but that is just too close to China for comfort."

"You are determined to do this ... to leave, aren't you? Please let me help you. If you really want to leave the country and you don't think you can do it safely, I have an idea." A glimmer of hope had briefly sparked in Sui Wai's sad eyes. Sue Keely could see she might be able to convince her friend to go along with her plan. There would be some risk, but it would probably work."

"Please, tell me your idea. I am in despair."

"My husband and I have plane reservations to return to the United States in two weeks. We own a house in Southern California, and we are way overdue to make a trip back to the States to check on it. We haven't been there in several years and need to have workmen in. I need to get to California to organize people to make repairs and fix things up there. There's a roof issue, and we had several plumbing problems in the house this winter. There are a bunch of other things on the property that need to be taken care of. We have a caretaker who does a very good job for us, but we need to be paying more attention. Our caretaker has a lot of interest in the grounds and the outbuildings. It's a farm, and he pays a great deal of attention to the farm part of the property. He doesn't seem to be as interested in the house. I ought to go back to the States more often, but we get busy here and don't make the effort. We'd both intended to make this trip, but Walter just told me two days ago that he's not going to be able to go with me to California. He wants me to go without him. One of us has to go to take care of the house repairs, and I am the one who is going. I haven't cancelled his reservation yet, so right now, I have two first-class plane tickets to Los Angeles." Sue Keely paused and looked at Sui Wai. There was another flicker of interest on the distraught woman's face.

Sue Keely continued. "I also have a passport that belongs to my daughter. She was married three years ago and decided to take her husband's name. She applied for a new passport in her married name. The passport never arrived, and she had to apply for a second passport. Then the first passport arrived in the mail. It was a mess. It was a big mix up and more than you want to hear about. Anyway, I still have her old passport that was issued to her in her maiden name. Because she doesn't use her maiden name anymore and has a new passport, the old passport was cancelled electronically in the

United States. Because it has been cancelled, she can't use it to get back into the U.S. But I happen to know for sure, from personal experience, that her passport can still be used to leave Hong Kong."

Sui Wai was now hanging on every word that Sue Keely spoke. Sue continued. "But, we have to put your photo on my daughter's passport. I'm going to need a passport-size photo from you, and I need it as soon as possible. I've traveled back and forth between Hong Kong and the U.S. for years. I know exactly when they will look closely your passport and when they won't. I know exactly when they will scan it to see if it is valid. The airlines just look at your passport when you are checking in for a flight to leave Hong Kong to go to the United States. They don't scan it or check it carefully. On the other hand, when you arrive in the United States, immigration and passport control will *definitely* scan your passport electronically. When we get to that point, you will no longer be able to pretend to be my daughter, and you won't be able to use her passport. As soon as we get off the plane in Los Angeles, you will have to use your own valid Chinese passport to get into the United States. I have connections in the consulate and can arrange for you to have ninety-day tourist visas to visit the United States. I will have those visas in hand for you before we leave. So, you will have two official tourist visas with you. You will present one of them, the one that has my daughter's name on it, when you use my daughter's passport to leave Hong Kong. You will use the other one when you present your Chinese passport to enter the United States. That tourist visa will be in your real name."

Sue Keely paused to be sure her friend was following all of this. "You will be able to use my daughter's old passport to get out of Hong Kong, but I need that passport photo ASAP. I have somebody who can put your photo on my daughter's passport, no questions asked. She does beautiful work. Don't worry. Only the people at the airline check-in desk will ever look at that passport and at that photo. They are always rushed. They don't give first-class passengers much scrutiny anyway. They want to keep us flying first class and paying them a bundle to do it. It will be fine. Once we are in Ojai, I will work on getting you a visa that will allow you to stay long-term in the United States... as a political refugee."

"Do you honestly think I can leave China using your daughter's passport with my picture on it? You are American. I am Chinese. No one will believe that I am really your daughter."

"Her name is Emily. There are plenty of women who live in Hong Kong who have the first name of Emily. There are plenty of Chinese women in Hong Kong who have the first name of Emily. It is a very English name. This used to be an English colony. You could be my adopted daughter. My husband could be Chinese, and you could look like him. You could be his daughter by a first marriage. There are many reasons why I might have a Chinese daughter. Who will know?"

Sui Wai began to cry. Sue Keely had never seen her cry before. "Oh, yes. If you are willing to do this for me and take this chance, I will go with you to California. I just wish it could be tomorrow and not in two weeks."

"Are you sure you are willing to give up your family and your friends and your position in the medical community here and everything else you will be giving up? It is a big decision. Of course, I can arrange everything for you, but you must be absolutely certain you want to do this."

"I came to that decision some time ago. I want to leave China. I must. Tell me what you want me to do?"

"Do you have any money? What do you absolutely have to take with you when you leave? If we show up at the airport with twenty-five cardboard boxes packed with clothes and dishes, someone will become suspicious." Sue Keely smiled, hoping to lighten the mood a little bit.

"I have my research that will support my claims. I need to have these papers with me to be a convincing whistleblower. I have a few personal things I want to take. I will have to take some clothes." Sui Wai was already making plans. "My cousins in Singapore are ardent capitalists. They despise communism. They are rich. They convinced me years ago to send some of my cash out of the country with them when they came to visit. They set up investment accounts for me, and they've made me quite a substantial nest egg. It is not a huge fortune, but it is outside of China. That's the important thing. My husband knows nothing about my funds in Singapore."

"Good for your cousins. I would like for you to bring the things you want to take with you to the United States to my apartment, discreetly, over the next two weeks. Bring a few things at a time. Call me first to be sure I'm at home. Leave a bag or box outside my door. Call me again as soon as you've left something. I will retrieve it from the hall. Can you do that? Can you get your clothes and the other things you want to take with you out of your apartment without your husband knowing? My door is just down the hall from yours, so it isn't like you have to travel very far. Through Walter's business, I can arrange for your things to be boxed up and shipped to our house in Ojai. I do this all the time. I send things of my own back to the United States. No one will be suspicious. You just have to bring me what you want to send. You can't take everything, or your husband will suspect something. When you and I get on that plane in two weeks, you will be able to bring only one large suitcase to check and your carry-on plus your briefcase. I suggest you buy a new piece of luggage, a large one you will check through to Los Angeles. Do you think you can buy a new suitcase and hide it in your apartment so your husband doesn't suspect anything? When he realizes you are gone, he will check to see if you have taken any of your luggage. If he sees your luggage is still in the apartment, he won't suspect you have gone very far. It's just a delaying tactic. If you can't get another suitcase, don't worry about it."

"I understand. My husband doesn't notice anything. He is so tied up in himself, he doesn't even notice me anymore. I know what to do. He will never suspect a thing, even after I am gone. Even then, I wonder how many days, or weeks, it will take before he notices that I've not come home."

"We have a plan. I need to make a few phone calls. I am going to write down our flight number to Los Angeles on this piece of paper. Memorize it and give the paper back to me. It's a non-stop flight. The plane leaves at 9:00 in the morning on March 3rd. Bring your suitcase to check and your carry-on to my condo the night before. Call me before you come and again when you've left them. I will take them to the airport with me. I will arrange for someone to meet you at the airport ticket counter with your bags. When you leave your apartment the morning of our flight, you will have only your purse and your brief case, as usual. You will be pretending to go to work. You will be long gone before your husband realizes you have left the country. Now, tell me when you think you can start to bring your clothes and other things to my condominium."

"Where will I live? Where will I stay when I have arrived in the United States? I know no one there."

"You will stay with me, of course, as long as you want to. Our house in Ojai is large. We have plenty of bedrooms and plenty of bathrooms. We have completely renovated the old farm house, and it is on quite a few acres of land. You will be safe there. I will be there for several months, tending to the house repairs. I will visit my children and grandchildren and some other friends while I am in the U.S. Once we are in

California, I will arrange for you to be granted a permanent visa. You can hide out in Ojai and talk to a reporter or a ghost writer or whoever you want to talk to."

The two women discussed the details of their plan. They agreed it would be best if they did not see each other again before the morning their flight was scheduled to leave Hong Kong. They would take separate taxis to the airport. Sui Wai would arrive at the last minute. Sue Keely would arrange for someone to meet Sui Wai at the airline ticket counter. This person would give Sui Wai her luggage to check and her carry-on. Sui Wai would check her large suitcase and then go through security. She and Sue Keely would sit together in the boarding area, as people would expect a mother and daughter to do. Once they were on the plane and the plane had taken off, Sui Wai would be safe. She reached out and squeezed Sue Keely's hand in gratitude just before they left the Polo Club Restaurant.

CHAPTER 21

C*ameron had a short speech to deliver at the salon's* cocktail hour that evening. He always had something interesting to talk about, usually something one of his companies had invented or was in the process of inventing. This year his pre-dinner salon presentation was about voter fraud. He'd told his friends that his company was developing some kind of software that had to do with making sure nobody voted more than once. Cameron implied that it was foolproof. Most in the group were skeptical of his use of the word "foolproof." Nothing was foolproof. But they were eager to hear more about Cameron's latest computer adventure.

To introduce his talk, Cameron had asked Matthew Ritter to find some movie clips about elections, specifically about election fraud, to play for the group. Matthew had discovered that voter fraud was not a hot topic of interest for movie makers. Hollywood seemed a little bit more interested in shining a light on voter suppression and ignoring voter fraud. The truth is that Hollywood finds both voter suppression and voter fraud pretty boring. They don't make movies about either subject.

Cameron had done some research on his own and had found some true stories about voter fraud—real "doozies" to tell his friends. Cameron believed in one person, one vote. He did not believe in voter suppression, and he did not believe in voter fraud. He wanted *everyone* who was eligible to vote to be able to cast a ballot. But he also wanted to be sure that nobody cheated, that nobody voted more than once, and that no dead people voted.

Finding a bag full of fraudulent votes in the closet after the election was over was wrong, no matter which party found them. Having a van drive up in the middle of the night and dump thousands of questionable absentee ballots at a precinct was cheating, no matter which party was doing it. Allowing a dead person to cast a ballot would not be allowed anymore. Illegally stuffing the ballot box for any candidate in any way would not be tolerated. For quite a few months, Cameron had been working with several other companies, to guarantee that every eligible voter was allowed to vote—but only once.

"We have the full spectrum of political opinions in this group. We have social justice warriors and climate change enthusiasts on the left. We have independents and some middle-of-the-road Democrats and Republicans. We have right-wing conservatives. I want to be even-handed. In the interests of full disclosure, I will tell you that I am a registered Republican. Most of you already know that. However, I do not always vote for Republican candidates. I often vote for Democrats. I really vote for the person, not for the party. In fact, in several elections recently, I have not voted for the Republican candidate for President. I probably should be registered as an Independent, but I like the idea of the Republicans being in charge of the Congress. Democrats love to give money away. They love to give away my money. It's my money, and I want to decide who gets my money. I do not want to have some fat cat who has had a bunch of facelifts and has lived in Washington D.C. all of his or her life, to decide who to give my money to. Anyway, those of you who are fans of Richard Daley, a former Mayor of Chicago, a man who urged his supporters to 'vote early and often' will probably want to leave the room now. My talk is only going to make you angry. Oh, that's right. Richard Daley's dead. But, you know, he might still be voting. Lots of dead people vote. Some of them vote twice.

"I happen to believe in one person, one vote. I do not believe that the ends justify the means. I respect the process. I don't agree with Vince Lombardi that winning is the only thing. It is important to me that whoever wins, wins honestly. That makes me pretty old-fashioned, I guess. Republicans are always crying about voter fraud. Democrats are always crying about voter suppression. I am not in favor of either suppression or fraud. I want every person who is eligible to vote to be able to vote, and I don't want anybody who is not eligible to be able vote to vote at all.

"I have stories. The guy in Los Angeles County, who was recently arrested for voter fraud, keeps voting twice in every election. He casts a vote in his own name. He also sends in an application for an absentee ballot for his mother and casts an absentee ballot for her. She died in 2006. I have no idea what party he belongs to or what party his mother belongs to, I mean belonged to. I don't know or care for whom he votes or for whom his mother votes. When he was caught, he said a number of things in his defense. He has said his mother loved to exercise her patriotic duty to vote, and he is just carrying on that tradition. He has said he is 'keeping her memory alive.' He has said that she didn't get to the polls a few times in the 1980s and the 1990s, so he is just catching up for those times she missed getting out to the polls. Either this guy is a not very funny comedian, or he has some serious mental health issues. Who does he think he is —Tony Perkins in *Psycho*? Or maybe this is his way of pretending to be Miss Emily Grierson in William Faulkner's *A Rose for Emily*. Did Emily cast an extra vote as Homer Barron? Who knows?

"Democrats ask, 'Why do Republicans want to keep minorities from voting?' Republicans ask, 'Why do dead people always vote for Democrats?' Everyone has heard the stories of vote harvesters who go into nursing homes and memory care units with ballots and come out with stacks of votes for *their* own favorite candidates.

"One of my personal favorites is the mailman who delivers mail in a neighborhood where almost everyone is registered to vote for candidates who belong to the party that is not the mail carrier's party. When he picks up an absentee ballot out of a mailbox from that neighborhood, he knows with 95% certainty that the votes on the ballot inside that envelope are going to be cast for candidates he does not like. If a particular candidate's sign is in the yard, the mailman can be 100% certain for whom the absentee ballot sitting in the mailbox has been cast. That absentee ballot will go directly into the dumpster. It will not pass go. It will never make it to the post office. It will never be counted. It will never be seen again.

"The very best story, however, is the woman from Baltimore who pushed the envelope way too far and busted that envelope into a thousand pieces. She is the ultimate poster child for voter fraud. She owned a home in Baltimore County, Maryland, and she owned a second home in Citrus County, Florida. She registered to vote in both states. When she was arrested, it was discovered that she had voted in primary elections and general elections—in both states in the same year. And, this had happened on more than one occasion. This is voter fraud, and it is illegal. She might have been able to get away with her 'double down double trouble' voting scheme if she had laid low, but she was not able to do that. She was not able to keep herself from being the flaming fraudster of the year. Her hubris, her arrogance, and her stupidity led her to make an embarrassing public spectacle of herself. This idiot had the audacity to seek and to win her party's nomination as their candidate for United States Congress in one of the Congressional districts in the State of Maryland. You've got to admit this takes really big balls—to be a vote fraudster and then to run for Congress with a straight face. Yikes! Call the cops!

"She was investigated, arrested, and charged with fraud. But, not in time to have her name removed from the November ballot. Her party nominated a new candidate to run for the Congressional seat, but to vote for him, you had to write in his name. He lost. The Fraudster Candidate, in spite of the fact that she was a criminal, had been declared ineligible, and was no longer 'officially' on the ballot, received somewhere in the neighborhood of 35,000 plus votes. She was still on the ballot, albeit erroneously. She received thousands of votes because those who voted for her were either voting a straight political ticket, or they were dumb enough to vote for a candidate who had been disqualified and was no longer running for the office.

"She paid a small fine. She had plenty of money, and a smart lawyer got her off with a plea deal and a few hours of community service. Really?? I hope they didn't let her do that community service counting ballots or serving as a poll watcher. Yikes again! This is a very scary person. I know it sounds preposterous, but this is all true.

"It's a problem. Political parties hire buses to drive groups of people from precinct to precinct to cast multiple votes on Election Day. That guy who votes as himself and also votes as his mother, is a piker compared to these people. Then there is the problem of the voting machine that is programmed to change votes from one candidate to another. That is several volumes worth of lectures that I am not going to go into tonight. I would like to put all of these people out of business. Finding a bag full of uncounted votes in the closet, hours and days after the election is over, is not acceptable. Programming a voting machine to change votes for either political party is against the law."

Bailey had heard enough about voter fraud. "Okay, okay. We know voter fraud exists. Some of us will take exception to the fact that it is as big a problem as you are implying. Some of us might want to offer a rebuttal in the form of all the ways voting is suppressed in this country, but I want to know what you and your company have to do with any of this."

"There is one thing that is unique to every human being. It can't be stolen, and it can't be faked. That is your DNA. With the exception of monozygotic identical twins, no one in the world has anybody else's unique DNA, except for you. DNA will become the basis for voter ID verification in the future. The process has not yet been perfected. We still have a ways to go, but DNA will determine how we prevent duplicate voting in the future. Driver's licenses as ID, fingerprinting, retinal scans ... all will be obsolete. Even the Baltimore Fraudster, voting in two different states, will be found out.

"Depending on the lab, it takes at least a day for somebody's DNA to be tested. How can this possibly work for voting? Submitting a DNA sample and waiting for the results will bring the voting process to a grinding halt." Richard knew about DNA, and although he might have liked Cameron's idea in theory, he knew it would never work in the real world.

Cameron had anticipated this objection. "I am not at liberty to reveal everything I know, but I will tell you that very recently, there have been some revolutionary advances in DNA testing. This is not my area of expertise, and other companies are working on this critical piece of the project. But, I will tell you that soon there will be a way to test DNA instantaneously. The DNA result will be recorded more quickly than the ballot can be counted."

"How will they collect the DNA?" J.D. was a logistics expert and a very practical guy. His skepticism centered around how DNA samples could possibly be collected in the voting booth.

"I don't know exactly how it works, but I have seen the very nifty and easy-to-use swab that will be handed out with each and every ballot. It is small and flat and looks like a piece of litmus paper. You peel off the back of the litmus paper thingy, lick it like a postage stamp, and then stick it on the ballot. It's quite ingenious. It takes less than two seconds to put the little paper into your mouth and attach it to the ballot. The DNA is read by a scanner at the same time the ballot is read. I find the technology to be amazing. I am not amazed by very many things, but I have to admit, I am amazed by this."

"Isn't collecting DNA a violation of a person's right to privacy?" Gretchen worked in HR, and because of her job, she had to be aware of everything that could possibly be construed as a violation of a person's rights. Her days and her nights were consumed with trying to stay ahead of that game.

"There will be no names attached, to either the DNA or to the ballot. Those details are all being rigorously discussed and ironed out by others. I want to tell you how my company's part of it will work."

"That's what we've been waiting to hear." Tyler always wanted speakers at the salon to cut to the chase and get to the point.

"All of you know that I have made my fortune by using computers to crunch enormous amounts of data. Because of my success in the arena of big data, I was invited to participate in this effort to make voting more honest and more accessible. The challenge for my company was to write software that is able to instantaneously compare the DNA results. If each ballot is submitted with a DNA swab, there should be one and only one example of each DNA result entered into the database of the entire United States. That is where my software comes in, to provide that instantaneous comparison of DNA results across every precinct in every state on Election Day. If no one else has submitted a ballot that has a swab with your DNA on it, your ballot will be counted. If you try to vote more than once and more than one sample of your DNA shows up, your vote will be tossed out. It is simply a matter of collecting the results of the DNA samples and making sure nobody submits more than one."

"What about monozygotic twins, identical twins? Will their votes be tossed out?" Richard was a scientist.

"That's being addressed and sorted out. That's not the area I have to worry about. This is still in its experimental stages, of course, but we will be doing a few practice runs this November. There are some places that have had problems in the past with over-voting. A person in New Jersey, who was previously in charge of manipulating the system so that certain candidates would win in some very close elections, has seen the light and has confessed to his past misdeeds. We are trying out our technology in some of those precincts where he's had his finger on the scales in the past. There are a few other troublesome places that we are using as trial laboratories. This year our experiment will happen alongside the regular voting process in these places. The results from the traditional method of ballot counting will be compared to our DNA-verified ballot counting results. We will be able to see how congruent the results are. Eventually, when all the kinks have been ironed out, DNA-verified voting will take the place of voter registration cards, driver's licenses, and everything else as proof of identity. There will be no more dead people voting. There will be no more buses making the rounds to multiple precincts. There will be no vans full of votes arriving in the middle of the night. Those wacky vote-changing machines will be on the scrap heap along with buggy whips."

"This all sounds way too futuristic for me. Even if everyone agrees to contribute their DNA, it seems cumbersome. In our instantaneous gratification culture of today, who is going to want to wait this out?" Bailey was skeptical. "I don't think people will agree to give up their DNA."

"A few people won't, but I suspect that most people want the system to work, and work honestly. It's only a few criminals and cheaters who are trying to game the system so that their own personal choice of politician wins. Those charlatans might not even try to continue to stuff the ballot boxes. They may decide it isn't worth it to try to 'Fool Mother Nature.' If the crooks and cheaters decide it isn't worth it to continue their schemes, that's a win, too."

"I want equal time tomorrow night to talk about voter suppression. In fact, I want to bring that important topic up right now for discussion." Bailey had his soapbox ready. The Camp Shoemaker crowd was off and running again. They had vowed not to discuss politics during their reunions, but the door had been opened and everyone was rushing through it.

CHAPTER 22

Tonight they were going to La Buona Ricetta, perhaps the best known restaurant in Paso Robles. La Buona Ricetta catered to locals, to families, to tourists, and to the fancy pants people who flew up from L.A. to dine at this wonderful place. Here food was not just the most important thing; it was the only thing. The Carpenters had eaten at La Buona RIcetta quite a few times. Elizabeth had called for reservations as soon as she knew there was even a modicum of interest in having the reunion in Paso Robles. She had always enjoyed the extraordinary "people watching" the restaurant provided and wondered how different the place would be tonight because of COVID quarantines and social distancing. There would definitely be fewer patrons dining at La Buona Ricetta.

The restaurant was not large, and the management was adhering strictly to COVID rules. There were only five tables set in the entire restaurant. The largest was for their reunion group, a table for twelve along one wall. The next largest table was a round table set for eight in the center of the room. At the table set for five, a group of Japanese businessmen was already seated and had begun eating. There was a still-unoccupied table for four in the corner. A table for two was tucked into the other corner, away from the door.

The Camp Shoemaker group was a little late, as discussions about voter fraud versus voter suppression had become heated and prolonged. Finally they had looked at the time and realized they were going to be late for their dinner reservation. Elizabeth called the restaurant to say that they were on their way. They'd worn their masks from the limousine into the restaurant, and removed them only when they were seated. They had looked at the menu online, but there were specials. Their waiter brought disposable paper menus for them to look at, and he went over the specials.

They'd not had hors d'oeuvres earlier when Cameron gave his DNA talk because they were saving themselves for the delights of La Buona Ricetta. Whenever Elizabeth dined at this favorite restaurant, she promised herself she would order something different, something she'd not ordered before. But the minestrone was so delicious, she always had to order it. The vegetables were crisp and the broth was rich but light. The cheese the waiter grated into the large soup plate yielded a helping of ambrosia that was food fit for the gods. Elizabeth ordered the minestrone; she couldn't talk herself out of it. Olivia loved soup and also ordered the minestrone. With a table for twelve, it seemed their group ended up ordering one of almost very appetizer on the menu.

Elizabeth always chose the angel-hair pasta with fresh tomatoes, garlic, olive oil, fresh basil, and pecorino Romano cheese for her entrée. But tonight there was a special of beef braciole in a tomato and red wine sauce. When the waiter described it, Elizabeth could not resist the special, and several others in the group could not resist it either.

Just after they'd placed their orders, the table for eight arrived. Elizabeth had seen this crowd at La Buona Ricetta before—twice. Did these people eat here every night? They all wore masks which they removed as soon as they were seated. This was a group that Elizabeth, who was usually very good at figuring people out, had not been able to decipher. The older woman in cowboy boots and a cowboy hat was clearly the grande dame of the table. Although she looked nothing at all like the usual grande dame, she was definitely in charge. Elizabeth was certain she was the one who paid the bill. She was a real cowgirl, a real horsewoman. Her hair was grey and long and frizzy and stuck out at odd angles from underneath the beat-up felt hat which she never removed from her head during the entire meal. She wore old, baggy jeans that hung loosely on her wide and ample rear end. She looked as if she had come directly from the stable at the ranch. There was no pretense whatsoever here. Elizabeth suspected that inside the wrinkled leather, saddlebag purse that hung on her chair, there was some kind of firearm. And it would be loaded. This woman was not fooling around. A long and elaborate concho belt with magnificent silver and turquoise medallions was her only bow to fashion. Curious.

Also at the table were a younger Anglo woman, maybe a daughter, and two pre-teen girls. Granddaughters? All wore jeans but were very well groomed. There was a young Hispanic man who was "dressed to the nines" to go out for dinner. His black pants were skintight, and his black hair was carefully combed straight back with some kind of hair product. There was an elderly Hispanic woman who might have been a housekeeper, and there was a very old Hispanic man who used a walker. He had to have help sitting down at the table. There was one empty seat. The old man always sat by the grande dame. Elizabeth had noticed this before. The cowgirl spoke with him continuously throughout the meal. He was obviously very dear to her. This group always ordered lots of food, and they passed it around the table family style. They packed up and took away with them everything that was left over. They were a family. Elizabeth promised herself that one of these days she was going to ask her waiter about them. She wondered if the woman might own part or all of La Buona Ricetta.

The Camp Shoemaker group's food arrived. The portions were generous, and the rolls of steak stuffed with herbs, cheese, and breadcrumbs were fork tender. The aromatic tomato broth, made with pureed San Marzano tomatoes and Paso Robles red wine, was to die for. The braciole were served on a bed of angel-hair pasta, so Elizabeth did not feel pasta deprived after all. The veal offerings were perfectly cooked, and the linguini dish with clams and mussels in a garlicky, buttery sauce was a particular hit.

While the table for twelve was devouring their entrees, a group arrived from L.A. Their obviously expensive and outrageous clothing let everyone know they were in the entertainment industry. One of the four, a young man dressed in posh and trendy leather pants, looked familiar to Olivia. She knew all about the rich and famous who hung out in Hollywood. Matthew agreed that the one Olivia had pointed out was a well-known face. But nobody could think of his name. The women were gorgeous, and the other man at the table had obviously had some major plastic surgery. He wasn't as young as he wanted you to think he was. It was a typical group from Los Angeles. They were regulars at La Buona Ricetta, and the wait staff greeted them with much fanfare. The L.A. contingent dined here often. Olivia assumed they'd flown in someone's private plane to Paso Robles to have dinner.

The Camp Shoemaker crowd never tired of Italian food in all of its many varieties. The wines of Paso Robles contributed to their wonderful meal. La Buona Ricetta offered homemade gelato in several enticing flavors as well as flourless chocolate cake, tiramisu, and a cherry turnover made with puff pastry and served with almond-flavored mascarpone on top. The reunion group had enjoyed an entire meal during which no one had fainted or been shot, poisoned, or kidnapped. No one had died. What a successful evening it had been.

They all were sated and tired and went to their rooms as soon as the limo returned them to the Albergo. Matthew and Isabelle had just closed the door to their room when someone began banging on it and screaming. They were tired and wanted to go to bed. Who in the world could be screaming in the hall outside their door? They'd just been with all their friends, so they knew it probably wasn't one of the reunion crowd. Isabelle looked at Matthew, and Matthew looked at Isabelle. It had been such a nice evening, such a peaceful evening. She shrugged her shoulders, and Matthew went to open the door.

Rosemary Davis stood outside the door. She stopped screaming when she saw Matthew's face. She was covered with blood. Her clothes and her hair, from head to toe, were soaked in red. Even her shoes were bloody. She took a step forward, stumbled against Matthew, and blurted out, "He's been kidnapped. My husband ... Harrison has been kidnapped ... again." Then she collapsed on the floor.

Matthew pulled his gloves from his pocket and knelt on the floor beside Rosemary. Isabelle found a small basin and went to the bathroom to fill it with warm water. She collected towels and washcloths. She realized that no evaluation of Rosemary's condition could even be attempted until some of the blood had been cleaned up. Isabelle wiped the blood from the woman's face, as Matthew tried to find a pulse. Rosemary's heart was racing, but her pulse was strong. Matthew could only assume that she wasn't bleeding out and the blood that soaked her clothes had come from someone else. He hoped the blood had not come from Harrison Davis. He wished, just to himself, that a person who needed medical care would, just once, knock on his friend Richard Carpenter's door instead of on his door. Matthew had been retired for more than six years and no longer had a blood pressure cuff or a stethoscope. He wondered if he had a sign on his forehead that said, "I am a real doctor. Kick me!"

When Rosemary had collapsed on the floor, she'd not really fainted or fallen unconscious. She'd been running from somewhere all the way to the Ritter's room, and she was out of breath and terrified. Isabelle cleaned the blood off her face, and Rosemary tried to sit up. She was speechless and was gasping for breath. Matthew figured she was having a massive anxiety attack and told her not to try to sit up.

"Just lie there for a few minutes. We will help you sit up when you are breathing more easily. You've obviously had something terrible happen. All this blood? Where did it come from? Tell us about Harrison. Who has taken him?"

"They knocked on the door. We never answer the door unless we've ordered room service or called housekeeping. But these people just kept knocking. They said they were hotel management and needed to speak with us immediately. They said it was an emergency. I went to the door and opened it just a little bit. That little bit was too much. I kept the security chain on, but they pushed against the door and broke the security chain. Three of them burst into the room. They were Chinese. I could tell they were Chinese even though they had masks on. Of course everyone has masks on these days. Two of them began to secure Harrison's hands together with those plastic ties. You know, the ones you see on television cop shows. Harrison fought back. I got the iron out of the closet and attacked one of the guys with the iron. We don't own a gun. The iron was the only weapon I could find in a hurry. I just kept bashing him on the head with it. That's where all the blood came from. I actually knocked him out. He fell —don't know why they didn't shoot me. At that point, I didn't really care. For some reason, these men did not want to take me with them. They only wanted Harrison. They tried to tie me up, but I wouldn't stay still long enough for them to do that. They put a cloth soaked with chloroform or something over Harrison's mouth and nose. He went limp. One of them tried to put the cloth on my face to knock me out, too. I bit his hand. Hard. The other man shouted to him, and he left me alone. One of the men dragged Harrison out of the room. The other guy who was still standing dragged the one I'd clocked with the iron out into the hall. These men were big, and they were strong. They were gone in less than five minutes from the time they broke into the room—start to finish. I really don't understand why they didn't just shoot both of us."

"I hesitate to ask because I already know you don't want me to do it, but will you let me call the sheriff's department or the state police?" Matthew thought he would try again to talk Rosemary into calling the authorities.

"You're right. The answer is definitely no. You cannot call the authorities. I came to you because I knew your room number. Elizabeth Carpenter gave me your room number and hers … because you and her husband are both doctors. I got to room #118 first, before I got to #114. Your friends found Harrison the last time and saved his life. They brought him home to me. I was hoping they could find him again, although I know in my heart that's a ridiculous request. "

"I didn't have anything to do with the motorcycle rescue. In spite of the fact that my friends were the heroes and succeeded in saving Harrison, they won't tell us anything about how they were able to rescue him. They've refused to say a single word about what happened. They've said they will eventually tell us everything, but for now, we know nothing. They won't even tell their wives about it."

Rosemary wanted to clarify something about this most recent group of kidnappers. "These three were a completely different group of people. I mean, the last people who took him from the winery were Russian. At least I heard them shouting at each other in Russian while I was lying on the ground at Winer. I don't speak Russian, so I didn't know what they were saying. But I know what Russian sounds like. The people who took Harrison tonight are Chinese. They had on masks and black windbreakers, but I recognized the language they were speaking. I don't know how to speak Mandarin or any of the Chinese dialects, but I think these three were speaking Mandarin."

"How can you be sure it was Mandarin? How did you even know it was a Chinese language?"

"For twenty years, I taught at an international school in New Jersey. The kids came from all over the world. Their parents mostly worked at the United Nations, and the school where I taught was right across the river from Manhattan, close to the entrance to the Lincoln Tunnel. Lots of the U.N. people lived in the suburb where the international school was located. Their kids came to our school. I taught general science and advanced chemistry there for twenty years, so I recognize what lots of languages sound like. They were definitely speaking Mandarin." Rosemary Davis was in shock. Some people become completely silent, almost catatonic when they are in shock. It's often difficult to get them to say one word. Others blabber incessantly. Rosemary was a talker.

Isabelle asked, "Is there blood all over the room? Will housekeeping become suspicious? If there is blood all over the place, the Albergo management will definitely bring law enforcement to investigate. Then you would for sure have to deal with them and tell them about Harrison." Things were getting complicated.

"Our room is like yours. The floors are all dark red tile, thank goodness. There are nice rugs on the tile floors in the bedroom. But the entryway to the room, right inside the door, doesn't have a rug... just like this room doesn't. It's just the tile. Most of the blood got on me. I can wipe up the blood that got on the floor. There may be blood in the hallway or in the parking lot somewhere, but there isn't much blood in our room. I can clean up the blood so housekeeping doesn't suspect anything. I will wash my clothes and throw away whatever won't come clean."

Rosemary almost seemed more worried about how to get rid of the blood evidence than she was about how to rescue Harrison. That was the shock talking. She couldn't bring herself to talk about what really terrified her, that she would be unable to save her husband, that she might never see him again. So she was preoccupied with something she could control—cleaning up the blood.

CHAPTER 23

S*ui Wai's taxi was caught in the inevitable Hong* Kong traffic jam. Usually she accepted this with only a slight rise in her blood pressure, but this morning she was frantic to make it to the airport on time. Her life depended on it, but there was nothing she could do to make the taxi go any faster. There were entirely too many people for the number of square miles in Hong Kong, not to mention roads. Everybody lived in high-rises. Everybody was constantly caught in traffic, even in the middle of the night. But today was critical for Sui Wai. Today she was leaving Hong Kong forever. Today she was escaping to the United States where she would be able to tell her story about the Wuhan virus. She could not miss the plane today.

As she waited for her taxi to make some progress, Sui Wai went over everything she'd done and said in laying the plans for her escape. This morning, after she'd called in sick to work, she had taken her phone apart, just as Sue Keely had told her to do. She'd taken off the protective case and removed the various tiny cards from the inside. She'd been able to stuff all the parts of the phone down the garbage disposal. She'd thrown the rest of her uneaten breakfast in after the phone. It was incredibly loud as the disposal chewed up the phone. She ran the disposal until there was no longer any noise coming from the sink. No one would ever find her phone, and no one would ever use that phone to track her. She was sure she had disabled all GPS and tracking devices on her computer. She had uninstalled her internet services and email accounts. She would never again receive an email on that computer. All that remained on it now were her research files. She was an electronic ghost, or at least she hoped she'd done everything she could do to make herself invisible.

The taxi finally made it to the airport, but there was another traffic jam around the United Airlines curbside baggage check-in. Sui Wai grabbed her briefcase and her purse. She threw money at the driver and exited the cab. She ran the rest of the way to the United Airlines ticket counter inside the terminal. A man carrying her luggage approached her. He didn't say a word but handed over her large suitcase and her carry-on bag. Sui Wai stuffed her purse into her carry-on and got in line.

Thank goodness for first class. She presented the boarding pass Sue Keely had printed out for her. She handed the ticket agent Emily Keely's American passport and the visa in Sue Keely's daughter's name. She checked her large piece of luggage. She was late, and the agent who was looking at the documents realized she was in a rush. He gave the passport only a glance and told Sui Wai she'd better hurry to get through security. Fortunately her boarding pass had a TSA-preferred stamp on it, so she was able to go through a special line. Whoever was checking identification, again gave the passport only a cursory look. Sui Wai raced to the gate as it was boarding. First class had already boarded, but she was bold and pushed herself in at the front of the queue. She was desperate to get on the plane. She would not relax until the plane was in the air.

She found her seat next to Sue Keely who was visibly relieved when she appeared. "I was worried. I was afraid something had happened to you."

"It was just the usual Hong Kong traffic. I thought I'd allowed enough time. Thank goodness the man with my luggage was standing right next to the check-in counter. Besides the taxi driver, he's the only person who saw me, I think."

"You can trust him. He works for me. I was afraid your husband had become suspicious and realized you were leaving him. Then I worried that the passport hadn't passed muster. Then I worried you had been arrested or worse. I can always find something to worry about." Sue Keely sighed and smiled with relief that Sui Wai had finally made it onto the airplane.

The flight attendant came around and asked if they wanted something to drink. Sui Wai and Sue Keely both ordered tomato juice with lemon and extra ice. Sui Wai allowed her shoulders to relax a little as she fastened her seatbelt. She could scarcely believe she was about to leave China. She could scarcely believe she was leaving her husband, a man she had married in haste and had never really loved. She was also leaving her successful career. She had worked hard to reach the top of her field, but she had already more than come to terms with leaving everything behind. Her adventure was beginning. She had a new mission. She wondered if what she had to say would be believed.

She wondered if the Chinese government would look for her. She wondered if they would be able to find her while she was hiding out at the Keely's farm in California. She knew there were thousands and thousands of Chinese spies in America. They were everywhere—in every major university, in every major corporation, and in every major city. She knew that a few Chinese spies worked for people in the United

States Congress. Sui Wai had never tried to hide herself before. Could a Chinese person hide in the United States? She knew she would stick out, but maybe not so much in California. Many Asians lived there. Sue Keely reached over and squeezed her arm in reassurance.

"It's going to be fine. Take a deep breath. Drink your tomato juice. Enjoy the flight." Enjoy the flight." Sue Keeley smiled. Sui Wai knew she was in good hands. Finally the plane finished boarding, and they were speeding down the runway. As soon as the plane lifted into the air, Sui Wai leaned back in her first class seat and closed her eyes. The knot in her stomach disappeared. It was a long flight to California. She slept.

The next hurdle was getting into the United States. Sui Wai didn't think anyone in Hong Kong would have noticed yet that she was gone. She had to use her Chinese passport to enter the United States. She had called in sick where she worked. She had said she would be out for at least two days, so no one from work would be looking for her until she failed to show up after her sick leave. She'd told her husband she had to travel for business. She wondered if he had even heard her. She hoped she'd covered all the bases. She didn't think anyone would have put a hold or an alert on her Chinese passport. She wanted to be able to complete jumping through all the immigration and customs hoops and be on her way to Ojai before anyone realized she'd ever left Hong Kong. If she made it to the Keely's farm before anyone began to look for her, she felt she would be safe.

She tried not to appear to be nervous as she presented her passport, visa, and other papers to U.S. immigration officials. The visa worked. Her Chinese passport in her own name worked. This would be the last time Sui Wai would ever use that name, that visa, or that passport.

Finally, she'd cleared all the hurdles and found Sue Keely. She saw a man in a cowboy hat standing with Sue just as Sui Wai overcame her final challenge and walked away from agriculture control. The man in the hat took her suitcase and her carry-on and put them on a luggage trolley with Sue Keely's luggage. Sui Wai kept her briefcase in her hands. Sue Keely took Sui Wai's arm and led her out of the terminal. They walked toward a white Range Rover. The cowboy, who was introduced to her as Reggie, loaded their suitcases into the back of the SUV and handed Sui Wai her carry-on. Sui Wai was in another world. She allowed herself to be led and taken care of. Even though she had slept much of the way on the airplane, she fell asleep again on the drive to Ojai.

When Sue Keely roused her, Sui Wai looked out at a world of green around her. She was in the countryside. For an urban woman who had spent most of her life in Hong Kong, she believed for a few seconds that she was inside a picture postcard. She had never been in a place that was so green. She tried to say something, but was too tired to speak.

Sue Keely was talking to her. "We're here, Sui Wai. We have arrived at White Fox Farm. You are home now, and you are safe here. You are going to have the guest house all to yourself. As we discussed, you will join me in the main house for meals when you want to, and you will have the run of the farm. I thought you would like to have your own space. The guest house is very comfortable. We call it a casita in California. Casita means little house. You will need to rest and regroup. I promise to respect your privacy and your need to be alone," Sue Keely seemed to understand that this enormous transition was traumatic and exhausting for Sui Wai. Her friend knew exactly what to say.

They went into the main house to have lunch. Sui Wai was in a daze. She drank her iced tea and ate her chicken salad sandwich. She almost fell asleep in her plate. She claimed jet lag, thanked Sue Keely, and walked to the guest house, to her casita. Her luggage was there. The belongings she had delivered to the Keely's condominium in Hong Kong to be boxed up had already arrived at the guest house. She was too tired to unpack anything. She shed her clothes and stepped into the large shower. Everything was bigger in the United States, it seemed, or at least things were bigger in California. She pulled on the terry cloth robe she found on a hook behind the bathroom door and fell asleep on the king-size bed.

The coronavirus would soon be on the doorstep of every person on the planet. Sui Wai and Sue Keely would be relatively safe from contamination because they were on a farm with lots of space, acres of space. Face masks would become the norm. New vocabulary words would become commonplace in the lexicon of the human race—social distancing, COVID hair, pangolin, wet markets, Wuhan. Even though she had anticipated what would happen, Sui Wai was surprised at how quickly the virus was spreading around the world.

Sui Wai had a lot she wanted to say. She was ready to tell her story. How long would it be before anyone realized she was gone? Did anyone suspect what she intended to tell the world? Would the Chinese try to discredit her before she was able to speak out? Would their spies find her?

CHAPTER 24

H*arrison Davis once again fought hard to keep* from being kidnapped. But his luck had run out. Rescued from his first kidnapping by a trio of senior citizens on motorbikes, he could not believe he was being kidnapped for a second time. The last thing he remembered, as the second group of kidnappers pressed a cloth over his nose and mouth, was the sight of Rosemary covered with blood. She was banging an iron against the face of one of the three men who had forced their way into their hotel room. She was fighting hard with the iron, but Harrison was panicked that some of the blood might be Rosemary's.

When Harrison woke up, he immediately realized he was in the trunk of a moving car. His wrists were secured with plastic ties. Whatever this group had used to drug him had made him feel sick to his stomach. He wondered how long they would keep him alive before they killed him. He hoped they'd not hurt Rosemary, but he was almost certain they had. He tried to stay awake and alert, but he passed out again.

He had no idea how long he'd been in the car or how long the car had been on the road. His usually sharp brain was muddled. He wasn't thinking clearly. He knew why he'd been kidnapped, but he didn't know who had taken him this time. He thought they were Chinese. Rosemary would know. She knew what all the languages sounded like. It made sense to him that the Chinese would kidnap him, although right at the moment, he couldn't put his finger on exactly why it did make sense. He decided he would try to save his strength and not put up a fight until he thought he had a chance to get away.

His sense of time was confused. It seemed as if he had been in the trunk of the car for a very long time. Was it hours or days? Had his kidnappers driven him to Arizona or even to Texas? How would anyone ever find him now? As his mind began to clear from whatever drug he'd been given, he grew more and more depressed. He felt as if he had no chance at escape this time. He was outnumbered. He was doomed. The only thing he could hope for was that they hadn't harmed Rosemary. She had put up with him for all these years. He had worked too much. He had neglected her, but she loved him still. He had given up on himself, and all he could think about was Rosemary. Could she hide out and disappear? Could she save herself and have a life?

Finally the car stopped, and someone came to the trunk. He thought they were speaking Chinese, but he knew there were many Chinese dialects and many Chinese languages. The three men were wearing masks, but from what he could see of their faces, they looked Chinese to Harrison. These men were big—bigger than he would have expected Chinese people to be. They jerked his head around when they put a blindfold over his eyes, but didn't seem to care that he didn't have a mask over his nose and mouth. They lifted him out of the trunk of the car and marched him forward through rough terrain. He stumbled over tree roots. The air felt damp. He was in a forest of some kind. It seemed as if they walked a long way in the woods, but Harrison's sense of time was distorted. Maybe he hadn't walked that far. He didn't know. His abductors were forceful and pushed him along quickly over the uneven ground.

The air smelled of pine trees. Harrison had an acute sense of smell. He thought he also smelled the ocean—the briny, slightly fishy smell of salt water and the smell of surf breaking on the beach. He was certain he smelled pine, but maybe the smell of salty water was just wishful thinking. If the car had been traveling for days, they had to have been heading east. The Pacific Ocean was west of Paso Robles, and the coast was less than an hour's drive from the Albergo. Maybe they had driven up or down the coast? Maybe he was hundreds of miles away from Rosemary and his room at the Albergo? He had no idea where he was, but he was sure he was some place where no one would ever find him.

His captors pushed him into some kind of structure. There was a lot of noise and a great deal of screeching and creaking of metal, like old metal doors opening and closing. There was a lot of banging against things. It sounded as if they were trying to close the doors and lock them. It was not going well for them. They were muttering, maybe even cursing in Chinese. When they'd carried him away from his room at the hotel, they had insisted he bring his briefcase with him. He'd left it in the trunk of the car. Had they forgotten it? There was not much in his briefcase anyway. There wasn't anything these men wanted inside his brief case. All the really important stuff was in his own head. They had insisted on bringing along the briefcase, and then they'd left it in the car. Maybe they were not the professional kidnappers or killers Harrison feared they were.

They left him in the structure with the metal doors. His hands were still secured with plastic ties, and he still had the blindfold over his eyes. He could tell there was a concrete floor in the place where he'd been dropped. It smelled musty and like old turpentine and old paint. Harrison's mother had been an artist, and this place smelled a little bit like her studio had smelled. But no one had painted anything in here for a very long time. This was an abandoned shed of some kind, and it was in the woods.

Harrison knew two things, one or both of which were probably the reason or reasons he had been taken. He knew without a doubt that the coronavirus had been genetically engineered in a laboratory. He also knew that the virus had been designed to attack and kill people with a certain genetic makeup. He could not possibly know exactly what particular genetic groups the virus had originally been intended to attack because the laboratory development of the virus had been cut short. Because the virus had somehow accidentally escaped the laboratory, perhaps through the research animals the lab was using, and had prematurely run rampant in the population, no one might ever know exactly what genetic group or groups had been the original targets of the virus. The virus had mutated and was continuing to mutate. The original intent for the genetically engineered virus might forever remain a mystery. It was all too out of control now to know anything for sure.

Harrison could speculate endlessly about what particular genetic groups the virus had been developed to attack, and based on what he knew about China, he had a pretty good idea which groups those were. China had segments of its population that were causing the central Communist government a great deal of difficulty. Harrison could imagine that it might be a tremendous advantage for the leaders in Beijing to be able to reduce the size of these noncompliant populations so that there were fewer ethnic trouble makers to contend with.

It could never be said to be genocide if a terrible virus decimated certain populations within the country. These would all just be tragic natural deaths, due to a strange disease. If these natural causes happened to wipe out very specific ethnic groups within China, how could any of that be blamed on the government? It would be deemed bad luck, or bad genetics for some of China's people.

One thing Harrison knew for sure was that the Chinese Communists and the World Health Organization had lied and had done everything they could to try to cover up the truth about what had happened.

Harrison worked for an independent research laboratory. Through his research into the genetics of COVID-19, he had also come close to discovering a way to block the virus from being able to latch on to the human immune system. His discoveries were complex and would only be understood by another geneticist or virology researcher. And, he had not verified what he had discovered to his own satisfaction—to the point of being able to be completely certain of his information.

When he had made his critical breakthrough discovery, he had approached his superiors with the information. That was when his troubles started. Someone in his laboratory had given his name to somebody or some group who didn't want what he had discovered to become known to the public or to anybody. The threats had begun. Someone had broken into his lab and destroyed all of his work. They had started a fire that wrecked parts of the lab. Harrison had not been in his laboratory that evening. Normally he would have been there, and whoever had broken in and set fire to his work space might have correctly assumed he would be working that night. If he had been there, Harrison was certain he would have been killed. But he hadn't been there, and he hadn't been killed. Those who had come after him had to figure out another way to keep him quiet. What they couldn't destroy was what was inside Harrison's head. They only way they could destroy that was to destroy Harrison.

After his laboratory had been ransacked, wrecked, and set on fire, Harrison realized he was in serious danger. He knew he had to disappear. He did not know if he could trust anybody he worked with. He and Rosemary had packed their car with as many of their clothes and belongings as they could fit into the small SUV. They had driven several hundred miles south from their home in Seattle. They checked into to a Holiday Inn Express in southern Oregon, close to the Nevada border.

While they were there, Harrison became obsessed with trying to preserve his research. He wrote down everything he had discovered, everything he knew to be a fact. He also wrote down his hypotheses and everything else that was in his head but had not yet been tested and confirmed to his high standards of proof. He assembled a lengthy and detailed report and made multiple copies. He rented a safety deposit box at a local bank and put several copies of his work there. He sent a copy to his brother who lived in Wisconsin. He sent other copies of his report to long-time former colleagues and friends he thought he could count on. Most of them would not understand anything about what he had written down, but he knew he could depend on them to come forward and do the right thing if something happened to him. He hoped he had not put his brother and the others in too much danger.

Harrison had been working to the point of exhaustion in his laboratory before he'd made his discoveries. Burning his laboratory had been the final straw. He had been at the edge of a physical collapse when he and Rosemary had packed their car, left Seattle, and driven to Oregon. He pushed himself even harder to record the findings of his research and disseminate copies across the country. After he had sent these copies of his work to people he trusted, the couple left the Holiday Inn Express and drove to rural northern California. Harrison was at the end of his rope and unable to concentrate enough to drive the car, so Rosemary was at the wheel.

They drove around the remote towns and mountain resort areas in northern California until they found a motel that had small individual cabins, each with a kitchenette, the kind of motel that harkened back to the 1940s. Harrison had collapsed in the passenger seat of the car. His face was gray with exhaustion. He couldn't or wouldn't eat. Rosemary was frantic, but she knew she couldn't take him to a hospital or to a doctor. She knew they had to find somewhere off the grid where he could rest. She knew somebody from Harrison's laboratory would soon be looking for him, if they weren't already. If they were serious about finding him and killing him, being in the database of a major hotel chain would for sure let whoever was after him know exactly where he was. They had taken a big risk when they'd stayed at the Holiday Inn Express. They couldn't take that chance again.

Rosemary could only hope that whoever operated the motel with the old and musty-smelling cabins did not have a computerized reservation system. When she had checked in and paid for a week's stay in cash, she'd tried to nose around and see if there were computers in the office. She didn't see any, but that didn't mean there weren't any. The manager of the motel was a back-to-nature type—an older man with long hair and a beard who might not know how to access the internet. Or he might just want to pocket the cash and forget the IRS. The kitchenette in their cabin hadn't been updated for decades. There was no washer or dryer, and it was in the middle of nowhere. It was perfect.

After checking in, Rosemary drove to the closest town which was fifteen miles away. She found a reasonably adequate grocery store and bought groceries for the week. She hated to leave Harrison in the car, but he was in no condition to go into the store with her. She bought all of his favorite foods, or as many as she could find in this small town, hoping she could convince him to eat something. In spite of her best efforts, he was unable to eat or sleep. He paced the floor of the cabin.

Rosemary did not know what to do. She seriously considered calling a doctor, but decided that would only lead to more trouble. Then she received the email from the Albergo on her phone, and she saw the chance to spend some time there as a lifeline for herself and for her husband. They had been hesitant to leave their cabin because of the coronavirus quarantines and because they didn't know who was trying to track them.

Hiding at the cramped, smelly Northern California motel was driving them both crazy. Their experience literally defined "cabin fever." Rosemary was unable to distract Harrison from his melancholy. The dreary weather was also getting to Rosemary. Mold was growing on their shoes. After three hot and mosquito-filled weeks in the cabin, punctuated by sudden and violent thunderstorms, it was time for a change. They both desperately needed to get out of there and sleep in more pleasant surroundings.

They had stayed at the Albergo Riposante in Paso Robles a couple of times on vacations. They both loved the place. Rosemary had become friends with the manager of the inn. That was why the Davises had received the invitation to Quandanche Quarantena. Rosemary accepted the Albergo's invitation, and she didn't care how expensive it was going to be. Harrison needed to be someplace where he could rest, where the food was good and the weather was nice. He had to be distracted from worrying about his research and who was trying to kill him. Rosemary thought the elegant Albergo Riposante located in Paso Robles, California might be just the place for that.

The manager at the Albergo had agreed to register the Davises under Rosemary's maiden name of Schaeffer. Rosemary had explained that her husband was trying to avoid the press and needed a rest. He didn't want to be registered anywhere under his own name. The manager of the Albergo had accepted this explanation from Rosemary, and the couple had driven their car to the long-term parking lot at the Los Angeles Airport. For anyone who might have been following them, Rosemary hoped it would appear they had flown someplace, perhaps out of the country, from Los Angeles. The couple hired a very expensive taxi to drive them and their car full of belongings from L.A. to Paso Robles.

Rosemary hoped they would be safe, at least for a little while. She realized that whoever was after Harrison would be able to hunt him down eventually, but she was at her wits end and needed a relaxing place to rest and gather her thoughts. She hoped she could nurse her exhausted and depressed husband back to health with a luxurious room, a swimming pool, and wonderful food. They had both loved staying at the Albergo in the past, and she hoped being there again would bring back nice memories for Harrison, as well as for herself.

Things had worked out for a few days, but the bad guys had found Harrison much sooner than either Rosemary or Harrison had expected. Harrison didn't know for sure why Russians had kidnapped him from the Winer Winery, but he suspected it might have to do with the fact that he was close to finding a way to prevent the virus, close to finding the key to developing a vaccine. He had no idea how in the world the Russians had discovered that he was close to success. He knew, along with everybody else who listened to the news, that the Russians were touting the discovery of their own vaccine. Everyone in the world was working as fast as they could on finding a way to inoculate against the deadly scourge.

The two guys the Russians had sent after him had definitely not been their A-Team. This made Harrison question who those Russians, the two men who had kidnapped him the first time, had actually been working for. Had the Russian thugs been hired by the Chinese to do their dirty work, or had the Russian mob come after him at the direction of their mobster president, Valdimir Putin? Because the first two kidnappers were now dead, no one would probably ever know who had paid them to come after Harrison. It was puzzling.

Harrison knew why the Chinese wanted to kidnap him. He knew they wanted to keep his discoveries about the genetic engineering of COVID-19 from becoming public knowledge. His research, that the virus had been targeted towards certain genetic and ethnic groups, would be damning to the Chinese government. It would give the leaders in Beijing a terrible black eye and make them pariahs in the eyes of the entire world. In a desperate attempt at damage control, politically correct pundits worldwide were already becoming apologists for the Chinese and were bizarrely trying to pretend the virus had not come from China, as if anybody with half a brain was going to be fooled about that.

Harrison's research had exposed the Chinese Communist government for the genocidal murderers they had always been but had tried to pretend they were not. He knew they would keep on trying to kill him until they were successful. Now that they had him again, Harrison wondered why they were continuing to keep him alive. Why didn't they just kill him? He could only guess that they intended to torture him to find out what he knew. They would torture him to try to find out if he had told anyone else about his discoveries.

He had sent multiple copies of the report about what he had discovered to several people. He did not want to think about what his captors might do to try to get the names of those people from him. But in the end, he realized that the only way for the Chinese to keep his information from the public was for him to die. He knew he was doomed. He feared that involving others by sending them his shocking research results might have sentenced them to death as well. All he could hope for was that Rosemary would be able to escape, to stay alive, and to make a new life for herself.

The Davises intended to find a way to hide by purchasing new identities and relocating. They knew their old selves had to vanish completely, and they had to become other people. They would have to disappear on their own. Rosemary and Harrison Davis would cease to exist. Harrison intended to have his brother sell their home in Seattle. The Davises hoped to find some place where they could live quietly and remain obscure, lying low under new names. They had some family money and had been careful with their savings. They could afford to live comfortably in their retirement. Rosemary might be able to get a teaching job to help with their finances. It was not the life they had planned for or hoped for, but it was the life they now were desperate to achieve.

But the dream of that future life had been destroyed. Harrison had been found and kidnapped a second time. Harrison was resigned to his own death, but he was determined to protect Rosemary. Who knew what this gang of kidnappers might have done with his beautiful wife? He would try to escape, but realized his efforts would probably be futile. All he could hope for now was that Rosemary would survive and live on for both of them.

CHAPTER 25

Sui Wai was so exhausted after arriving in Ojai that at first she was afraid she had contracted the coronavirus. She wanted to sleep all the time and barely had the strength to make herself drink water and take a bath. She struggled to get dressed each day and go to the main house at White Fox Farm to eat a meal with Sue Keely. Sue Keely seemed to understand, almost better than Sui Wai herself did, that she needed time to adjust to her new life.

Sui Wai finally decided that she did not have COVID and was just worn out by circumstances—abruptly leaving her old life behind and making the transition to an unfamiliar existence. She was eager to reveal to the public the information she had. But she had not yet summoned the energy to think through how and to whom she was going to tell her story, let alone get herself together enough to actually do anything about it.

By April, everyone in the world knew a terrible pandemic was sweeping the world. Stories about the origins of the Wuhan virus were constantly coming out of China and from the World Health Organization and every news outlet on the planet. Some politicians had even called for making it a crime to say out loud that the virus had come from China. What was wrong with these people? Were they crazy? Everybody knew the Wuhan virus had come from Wuhan. To pretend otherwise was ridiculousness.

Sui Wai watched the TV in the guest cottage as news commentators, doctors, politicians, and everybody else in the world blabbered on and on about where the virus had come from and where it was going. The fact was that it was going everywhere. It was so highly contagious, even casual contact could mean death to an older person. The disease devastated nursing home populations where people were in close quarters. Many people, especially children, who carried and infected others with COVID-19 were asymptomatic. They spread the disease far and wide without even knowing they had it.

Nothing quite like this disease had ever before been let loose in the world. It took a long time for health officials to figure out what to say and what to recommend that people do. It was all ad hoc and by the seat of the pants. The world had never been presented with a global catastrophe like this was turning out to be. Sui Wai wanted to do something, but she didn't know what to do. She wanted to speak out and correct the erroneous reports about wet markets and other outrageous and misleading stories and absurd cover-ups. She found herself paralyzed to move forward or to take any action.

She knew, after she'd been in California for a few days, that her colleagues at work, her husband, and officials in Hong Kong must realize that she was gone. Sui Wai didn't know if the Chinese government would expend any resources to try to track her down. Maybe they would assume she had succumbed to the virus and died unknown in one of the many distant Chinese provinces. Sui Wai did not think the authorities would be able to find her. She had left Hong Kong using another woman's identity, passport, and airline tickets. The reservations to fly to Los Angeles had no link to Sui Wai.

If the United States immigration service was cooperating with the Chinese or if Chinese hackers could get into U.S. government databases, they would eventually discover that someone using Sui Wai's Chinese passport had entered the United States in early March through Los Angeles, California. That was as far as anyone would be able to trace her. From that point, Sui Wai believed she was a ghost. They could not track her on her cell phone. That phone was long gone.

If no one was ever made the connection that Sui Wai and Sue Keely were friends, they would never find her. Sui Wai was worried that somebody would become suspicious when they realized Sui Wai had disappeared at the same time Sue Keely had left Hong Kong to return to the United States. Sui Wai's husband knew she was friends with Sue Keely. If hackers discovered that the last day Sui Wai had been seen in Hong Kong was the same day Sue Keely had flown to Los Angeles, Sui Wai could be in trouble. Sue Keely had called her husband Walter to let him know she'd arrived in Ojai. No one had been to their Hong Kong condominium asking questions about Sui Wai. Maybe she was safe.

An ophthalmologist from Wuhan had been one of the colleagues who had alerted Sui Wai about how deadly the coronavirus was. Dr. Li Wenliang had sent Sui Wai a long email describing what he knew to be true as well as what he suspected. He had known this was a disease unlike any other. When he had tried to speak out, he was put under house arrest by the Chinese Communist authorities. Sui Wai had begun to investigate the things Li had told her. The attempts to muzzle the doctor and keep him from telling the truth to the world were to be expected from the repressive Communist regime. This was the way the Chinese government treated everything and everyone who tried to speak out. This was standard operating procedure. Never let the public know the truth. This was the Communist way.

When Li Wenliang died in early February, Sui Wai knew she had to do something. She was determined to become the whistleblower that Li had tried to be. The pandemic had already been unleashed. It was about to run rampant throughout the world. It was too late to stop it. The Chinese government had lied, and the World Health Organization had lied. An organization that had once engendered trust and respect had been co-opted and corrupted by the Chinese Communists. They had put their man in charge, and to protect them, he had willfully and intentionally lied to the world. He was responsible for many deaths. The world would be faced with that truth all too soon.

Sui Wai was committed to telling the world what she had discovered. She wanted the world to know what the military research scientists in Wuhan, China had been doing when they'd lost control of this deadly scourge. She wanted to expose the motives of the murderous Communist criminals who were attempting to control China from Beijing. She wanted everyone to know where COVID-19 had come from and why it had been developed in the first place. She wanted to put the blame where it belonged.

She knew these military researchers had not intended to spread their deadly discovery all over the world. This disease had been intended for very specific ethnic groups with very specific genetic make-ups. Sui Wai knew something terrible had happened at the laboratory in Wuhan. She didn't know exactly how the virus had gone rogue, mutated out of control, and escaped from the laboratory. She suspected that laboratory animals had somehow escaped from their cages and from the laboratory building. She didn't know the details about how all of these things had turned into a world-wide tragedy, but she did know that the original plan had gone completely haywire.

Sui Wai knew the science, and she had inside information about the origins of the virus through her network of scientific colleagues. She knew she had a responsibility to speak out and tell the world what she knew. The American press would try to discredit her, in their politicized attempts to be apologists for the liars in the Chinese Communist government. The press would call her a racist because that was what they always did when they wanted to smear somebody. Even though she was Chinese herself, she knew they would try to find a way to cast doubt on whatever she said. She knew many who heard her voice would not believe her. She knew that by going public with what she knew, she would be making herself a target for the many agents of the Chinese government who lived and worked in the United States. She knew that speaking out could sign her death warrant.

The relief she had experienced after escaping out from under the rigid control of the Communist system had been enormous. Her new freedom had also been challenging. Sui Wai had not fully realized the terrible toll the years she had lived and worked under such a regime had taken on her psyche and her spirit. To find herself free of the Chinese Communists and from her husband had temporarily stunned her.

She had not been raised or educated to think and feel like a free person—a person who had options and choices, a person who could speak out. Sui Wai had been brought up to be guarded about everything she did and said. Her brain had been wired to take orders and obey. She realized that, having been transported to a free society, her entire personality was undergoing a transformation. She had physically left behind the repressive regime, but allowing herself to think and feel like a free human being was going to take a great deal more time than the plane flight from Hong Kong to Los Angeles had taken.

Sui Wai realized one of the reasons she had not been able to take any action to make public her knowledge about the Wuhan virus was because of fear. She was terrified that the Communist government in China would send one of its agents who worked in the United States to find her. She did not trust the journalists she saw on television or the ones who wrote in any of the newspapers she read online. Every journalist she looked into and researched seemed to have some kind of political axe to grind. She didn't feel as if she wanted to reach out to or confide in any of them.

She rationalized her lack of initiative and chose to stay in hiding. She knew she would have to speak out publicly at some point, but while she continued to be afraid for her life, she stayed silent. She knew that her hostess and protector Sue Keely was concerned, but she never put any pressure on Sui Wai. She was happy to provide Sui Wai with a safe haven, a sanctuary, where she could rest and recoup.

When Sui Wai woke up one morning in the guest house at White Fox Farm, she was having difficulty breathing. She felt as if she had a terrible case of the flu. She ached all over. She could barely get out of bed to search for a thermometer to take her temperature. She stumbled into the bathroom and fainted. Grabbing hold of the side of the shower, she kept herself from hitting her head as she went down. She didn't know how long she lay unconscious on the bathroom floor. She regained consciousness from time to time and tried to pull herself up by grabbing onto the sink vanity. She knew she'd come into the bathroom for a specific and important reason, but her mind was foggy. She couldn't remember what it was that had been so crucial. She passed out again.

When Sui Wai did not show up for lunch, Sue Keely sent her a text and asked if she was all right. Sui Wai didn't answer. Keely became concerned. She knew the young doctor from Hong Kong had been struggling with the enormous upheaval in her life that leaving her old existence behind and becoming a free person for the first time had brought about. She'd tried to respect her friend's privacy. But when Sui Wai had not answered any of her texts and did not arrive to have dinner, Sue Keely walked to the guest house to check on her. Sui Wai always kept the doors locked. Keely knocked and knocked. She called out to Sui Wai to answer the door. When there was no response, she became frantic. She ran back to the main house to find a key so she could let herself into the casita.

She found Sui Wai lying unconscious on the bathroom floor. Sui Wai was burning up with fever. Sue Keely couldn't rouse her and was very frightened. She knew she couldn't call an ambulance or take Sui Wai to the hospital. Sui Wai had a visa to be in the country, but she did not have a passport that was safe to use. She didn't have any health insurance. Sue Keely could afford to pay for a hospitalization for her friend, and she would be more than willing to do that. But she knew Sui Wai would not want to be taken to the hospital because she would have to take the risk of using her real name.

She'd talked about getting a new identity and a new passport. Sue Keely had volunteered to help with this, but Sui Wai had been almost paralyzed by the trauma of acclimating to her new environment in the United States. She'd not been able to take the necessary action to secure a new identity for herself.

And now the woman was critically ill and unconscious in the Keely's guest house. Sue Keely had to do something. She didn't think it was possible that Sui Wai could have COVID. She'd stayed inside the casita all day almost every day for the past three months. She had only come out to have meals with Sue at the main house and occasionally to take a walk around the farm fields. She'd had no contact with any outsiders, or so Sue Keely thought.

Keely knew she had to bring a doctor to the farm to see her friend. Sui Wai was having difficulty breathing. She needed oxygen. Sue Keely was not a nurse and had no medical training. Were there any doctors anymore who would even think about making a house call? Sue Keely texted Reggie, the farm foreman, asking him to come and help her. She was so certain that Sui Wai did not have COVID, she did not think she was risking exposure for anyone, herself included.

Reggie arrived at the guest house and helped Sue get Sui Wai back into bed. Reggie knew the young woman was hiding at White Fox Farm for some reason. He didn't know what that reason was, and he saw her so infrequently, he'd almost forgotten that she was staying at the farm. Keely dispatched Reggie to find an all-night pharmacy where he could buy a portable oxygen machine, a blood pressure cuff, and a new thermometer. Sue Keely knew that this very ill young woman needed oxygen, but that was about all she knew. She tried to get Sui Wai to drink some water.

Sue Keely had consulted a nurse practitioner a few years earlier when she'd had a bad case of bronchitis. She had liked Ann Lemoine who'd taken care of the bronchitis with one office visit and one prescription. Ann and her husband lived in the area, and Sue Keely had seen her at neighborhood get-togethers ... in the past when people still socialized and went to parties, before COVID had driven everybody into their homes to hide. She still had Ann's cell phone number programmed into her phone. Lucky for Sue that Ann answered right away. Hardly anybody answered their phones any more, it seemed. Ann remembered Sue Keely.

"Tell me about her symptoms again. Slowly this time. I hate to say this, but I think she might be infected with the coronavirus, COVID-19. If this were last year and if she wasn't so severely ill and unconscious, I would not jump to that conclusion. We did not have COVID last year. Now we do. I have seen quite a few cases of COVID in my practice, and this sounds like one. In spite of what you hear on the news, young people can get this disease. Many who test positive are asymptomatic, but I have had several young patients who have had to be hospitalized. Nationwide, quite a few people, even in this age group, have become infected and have died."

Sue Keely carefully described Sui Wai's symptoms again for the nurse practitioner. "I don't think she could possibly have COVID. She has not been anywhere or done anything. She's stayed in my guest house almost twenty-four hours a day. Where would she have caught it? If she does have COVID, I've just exposed myself, and I've also exposed Reggie. I sent him to the pharmacy to get an oxygen machine. I also told him to buy a blood pressure cuff. I have no idea how to use one of those or if I will even need it. I am a medical nincompoop, Ann. I know nothing."

"Why can't you call the EMTs? It sounds as if your guest needs to be hospitalized, or at least seen in the hospital ER. I can't do much for her over the phone."

"It's complicated. She can't go to the hospital. She's not exactly in the country illegally, but she is kind of hiding out here with me at the farm."

"Is she Hispanic? In California, we give medical treatment to illegals without asking any questions. Some states do and some states don't. The immigration situation is a mess, but we don't deny care to people because of their immigration status."

"She's not Hispanic. She's Chinese. She is a physician and a scientific researcher from Hong Kong. She was my next door neighbor in Hong Kong, and I helped her escape from Communist China in early March. I don't want to get anybody into any trouble, but she can't go to a hospital. There can be no record that she is at White Fox Farm or that she is in the United States."

There was silence at the other end of the phone line, as Ann Lemoine tried to figure out what to say in response to this unexpected disclosure.

Sue Keely took a chance. She was already knee deep into it, so she decided to jump in all the way. "She left Hong Kong so she could be a whistleblower. She's a virologist who knows about the origins of the virus from the laboratory in Wuhan. She knew people who worked there. I don't understand any of it. It has to do with genetics and virology and I don't know what all. But she has proof of what was going on there in Wuhan, and she wants to find a way to tell the world about it. She's a friend of mine, as well as a neighbor. I wanted to help her. She was desperate to get out of China. I made that possible and offered her a refuge here at the farm. She's had a hard time making the transition to living in the U.S."

"Wow! That's some story, Sue." There was more silence on the line. Sue waited. Ann made a decision. "I will be right over. I will help you. We will save this brave young woman so she can tell the world the truth."

"It might be dangerous for you to associate with her, Ann. I don't want you to take any unnecessary risks."

"Like Air Force Major General Frederick Corbin Blesse said, 'No guts; no glory!' What drugstore is Reggie going to? I want to call in a prescription for oxygen that comes in a tank. He can buy an oxygen concentrator without a prescription, but to get a tank, he has to have a prescription. I also want him to buy a pulse oximeter."

"I have never heard of that. What is it?"

"When you go to the doctor and they stick that clip on your finger, that's the pulse oximeter which measures the oxygen saturation in the arterial blood. We need to keep track of your friend's oxygen levels, and the oximeter is a non-invasive way to do that. I will call the drugstore and tell them to be sure Reggie gets a good one. I'm going to make that phone call now. I will be at your house in about ten minutes."

"Thank you, Ann. I am forever in your debt. Should I be doing anything right now to help her?"

"Are you wearing a mask?"

"I don't usually wear one at home. I always wear one when I leave the property."

"Put on your mask. I will be wearing mine when I get there, and I want you and Reggie to be wearing yours as well."

CHAPTER 26

Sui Wai tested positive for COVID-19. Sue Keely and Reggie also tested positive. Sue Keely was sick for two weeks. Reggie spent six weeks in the hospital and almost died. He discovered he was prediabetic which he had not known until he was hospitalized. The predilection for diabetes had made his disease much more severe. All the employees at White Fox Farm were tested for COVID-19.

The Keelys' housekeeper turned out to the source of the infection. The housekeeper's grandson had been to a birthday party where he had contracted COVID. He was completely asymptomatic and had no idea he'd been infected until his test came back positive. In the meantime, he had transmitted the disease to his mother who had also not noticed any symptoms and had not suspected she was infected. But the housekeeper's daughter had infected her, and she became ill. She'd not been to work for several days because she wasn't feeling well. But before she'd begun to feel the effects of COVID-19, she had already infected Sue Keely, Sui Wai, and Reggie. All three had daily contact with the housekeeper. She cooked and served their meals and did their laundry. She was around the house and the guest house almost every day. She interacted with Sue Keely and with Reggie every day. The housekeeper wasn't very sick at all, mostly just too tired to get out of bed.

Sue Wai's disease, for whatever reason, turned out to be much more severe than Sue Keely's disease. Sue Keely recovered from her acute illness after two weeks. Then she endured weeks of lingering fatigue which kept her from completely resuming her normal activities. Determined to keep Sui Wai out of the hospital, Sue Keely and Ann Lemoine had nursed her back to health. Ann Lemoine had set up an IV in the guest house to be sure Sui Wai stayed hydrated and to facilitate administering her medications.

Sue Wai was also overcome with debilitating fatigue as she struggled to get back on her feet. Since she had now experienced the wrath of the virus for herself, she was more determined than ever to tell the world about this terrible illness. She had languished long enough, and as she regained her strength, she was increasingly motivated to find a way to tell her story.

Her new-found burst of enthusiasm probably caused her to be somewhat careless. Anxious to communicate her information to the public, she contacted a writer she had researched over the internet. On paper, the woman's credentials were first rate. She sounded almost too good to be true. Sui Wai began an email conversation with the journalist. Little by little, Sui Wai revealed to the journalist who she was and why she wanted to be, and was qualified to be, a whistleblower.

Sui Wai had hoped she could tell her story without actually having to leave White Fox Farm or go on television. In spite of having lived in a repressive Communist country all of her life, the young doctor was too trusting on a personal level. She had never trusted the totalitarian government, but she trusted individuals. The journalist said all the right things in her emails, and over a period of several weeks, she built trust with Sui Wai.

The journalist insisted that they meet in person. She wanted Sui Wai to tell her story on video. She told Sui Wai that her statement would have much more impact if she told the story in her own words. Sui Wai agreed that this was true, and they made plans to meet at an office building in San Bernardino to record the video of her statement. Sue Keely agreed to drive her to the meeting. Sui Wai had never learned to drive. They thought they would be safe.

The big day arrived. Sue Keely helped her friend dress for the video camera. She helped her apply the right makeup so Sui Wai would look her best. They drove to the building in San Bernardino. The journalist had asked that Sui Wai come alone. She said she didn't want the distraction of having anybody else in the room when the video was being shot. This did not seem like an unreasonable request. Sue Keely didn't like it that she was being kept away from the action, but she told herself not to pout because she wasn't going to be able to observe first-hand what was going on. Both women thought they would be seeing the video immediately on every cable news channel and every news outlet in the country. This was big news and would be a national headline for days. Sue Keeley waited in her car while Sui Wai was inside, supposedly being interviewed.

When Sui Wai did not return after two hours, Sue Keely began to get worried. After three hours, she began to send texts to Sue Wai's new cell phone. When she received no replies, Sue Keely decided to go to the office where she thought the video was being shot. She took the elevator to the seventh floor. She found room # 7049. Sue Keely was shocked to find that it was a completely empty office. There was no sign on the door. There was no one anywhere around. The door was locked. The entire appointment to record Sui Wai's whistleblower statement had been a hoax.

Sue Keely was frantic. She sent several more texts to Sui Wai but did not receive any replies. Sue Keely didn't know what to do. She couldn't call law enforcement and report a kidnapping or a disappearance. Sui Wai's status in the country was questionable. She had a visa so she was legal, but Sui Wai had never bothered to get a new identity or a new passport.

Sue Keely was inconsolable. She didn't know where to turn. She felt responsible for what had happened to her naïve scientist friend and imagined the worst for poor Sui Wai. The doctor from Hong Kong had often spoken to her about the many Chinese agents who had worked their way into every facet of American life. Sue Keely had listened but had thought to herself that Sui Wai was exaggerating and perhaps even engaging in some paranoid thinking. Of course, there would be Chinese agents in the United States. Everybody spied on everybody else. She had dismissed Sui Wai's concerns. She had not taken Sui Wai's fears seriously enough.

Back in Ojai, Sue Keely decided to hire a private investigator. She hired a good one. He agreed to take the case, but he told her that he was almost certain her friend Sui Wai was already dead. Sue Keely hired him anyway. She told him to leave no stone unturned. After paying him for four weeks' worth of work, she decided it was hopeless. Sui Wai was gone. She was either dead or back in Hong Kong or in a horrible Chinese prison somewhere. It was not easy for Sue Keely to accept what had happened to the brave woman who had so desperately wanted to be a whistleblower. It was the end of September, and Sue Keely finally accepted that she was never going to see her friend again.

CHAPTER 27

M*atthew and Isabelle Ritter accompanied* Rosemary Davis back to her room. They knew this would be traumatic for her, to revisit the scene where she and her husband had been attacked and where Harrison had been tied up, drugged, and kidnapped. It was now the middle of the night, and thankfully no one else was in the hall. Rosemary almost fainted and stumbled against Isabelle when they entered the room and saw the blood on the floor. Furniture was overturned. Isabelle was feeling her own stomach churn in disgust. She couldn't wait to get away from this room. It reeked of blood.

Rosemary wasn't much help, as she sank into the couch and stared at the chaos in front of her. "You can't stay in this room, Rosemary." Matthew Ritter was tired and angry and frightened. He didn't want to be involved in this mess, but he was. He especially didn't want Isabelle to be involved in it, but she was, too. "Nobody can stay in this room. It's a war zone."

Rosemary Davis nodded her head in agreement. She went into the bathroom and came out with wet towels. She got down on her hands and knees and began to mop up the blood on the tile floor. Matthew wanted Isabelle to stop the woman from trying to clean up what was impossible to clean up. Isabelle shrugged. There was nothing that could be done to dissuade Rosemary from her task.

Isabelle and Matthew found the Davis's luggage and began to pack their clothes. Matthew went to the lobby of the Albergo to find a luggage cart. Isabelle had cleaned out the closet, the dresser drawers, and the bathroom by the time he'd returned. They piled the Davis's belongings onto the cart. Isabelle found the iron on the floor, wiped it clean, and returned it to its place in the closet. Isabelle found a plastic laundry bag, took the bloody towels from Rosemary, and put them in the bag. Matthew and Isabelle each took one of Rosemary Davis's arms and lifted her from the couch. They abandoned the room.

Isabelle guided Rosemary, who was in a daze of disbelief and exhaustion, out of the room and down the hall in the direction of the Ritter's hotel suite. When they reached the Ritter's room, Isabelle convinced Rosemary to get rid of her blood-soaked clothes, take a shower, and wash her hair. Her clothes were now stiff with dried blood, and her beautiful honey-colored hair was hard with crusted black tendrils. Isabelle sent Matthew to the lobby to see if he could rouse anyone at the desk to find a new room for Rosemary.

Matthew came back with a new keycard. He had arranged for Rosemary to have a room that was just two doors down the hall from the Ritter's. Because of the quarantine, there were quite a few empty rooms at the Albergo. He pushed the luggage cart that had the Davis's luggage on it. Isabelle walked Rosemary, now wearing one of the inn's white terrycloth robes, down the hall to the new room and insisted that Rosemary get into bed. Rosemary was willingly following directions but was in another world. She had lost her fight. Maybe after she had slept, she would come to her senses and be reasonable. Maybe she would be willing to call the authorities who could begin to search for her husband. Every minute that the hunt for Harrison Davis was delayed, the less chance there was going to be of finding him—let alone finding him alive.

Both Isabelle and Matthew were also going on automatic. They were exhausted from the late night and from the drama and the stress of taking care of Rosemary Davis. Isabelle called on one more ounce of her considerable strength and took the bloody towels and Rosemary's bloody clothes to the Albergo's guest laundry located on another first-floor hallway. She put everything in the washer and added the soap. She was too tired to wait for the load to finish. She would come back in the morning to put these things in the dryer. She could only hope that the blood would come out of the clothes. She walked down the hallway and returned to her own room.

Matthew opened the door for her when she returned to their suite. "What in the world are we going to do about all of this? We have ourselves in the middle of some big time trouble, and the usual remedies are blocked. She won't let us call the cops or the FBI or anybody. What should we do?" Matthew was hardly ever in a quandary about what to do or how to get out of a jam. He was a problem solver. But he was stumped this time. He pleaded with his eyes for Isabelle to give him some suggestions, or at least one idea.

Isabelle sank down on the bed, looked at her husband, and muttered, "I have absolutely no idea what we ought to do."

Matthew was so tired, overtired really, but he found it impossible to fall asleep. He was trying to figure a way out of the mess they were in. He wanted to save Harrison Davis, but with all the time that had elapsed and was going to elapse before anything could be done to find the man, Matthew was reconciled to the idea that Harrison was a lost cause.

He had no clue, at this point, what he was going to do about Rosemary Davis. She needed help in the worst way, but she wouldn't let anybody help her. Matthew Ritter also needed help. He needed to consult his friends.

Under normal circumstances, he would have talked things over with Richard Carpenter. But the current circumstances were anything but normal. And Richard had not been himself since he'd been shot at the Mexican restaurant. He had been out of sorts and withdrawn, and Matthew didn't think it was all because he'd suffered a physical injury. Matthew knew that three of his good friends had taken off on motorcycles that didn't belong to them and chased after the van that held Harrison Davis inside. They had taken a huge risk but had been successful in rescuing the man they didn't know. What in the world would the Camp Shoemaker crowd think when they were told that Harrison Davis had been kidnapped for a second time?

Even if Rosemary didn't want anyone to know anything, she was going to have to trust and confide in somebody. She was an intelligent woman. That was obvious. But she was understandably also a very traumatized woman. If she was going to have any hope of getting her husband back and if she had any hope of having a life of her own going forward, she was going to have to tell somebody what the heck was going on. Matthew decided he had to call on the other members of the reunion group to help him out of this predicament.

The next morning, after they'd had a few hours of sleep, things looked brighter to Matthew and Isabelle. When Isabelle checked on Rosemary, she was still sleeping. They left her alone. The poor woman needed all the rest she could get.

Because some of the Albergo's guests were leaving early on Sunday morning, the Albergo was offering a Saturday morning brunch. The pre-COVID Sunday brunch had been a buffet. Buffets were no longer popular, or even legal, anywhere, now that the highly contagious virus could be spread with touching or breathing.

The Albergo brunch was held late on Saturday morning, and everyone had pre-ordered their meals before they went to the ballroom. Mimosas and champagne were served, and Sidney finally got her plate of squash blossoms. Elizabeth and J.D. had ordered the Albergo special club sandwich. Isabelle tried to join in the fun. She had ordered the shrimp and oyster po boy on an Italian roll that should have fulfilled all of her Creole dreams. But she was so exhausted from being up most of the night and so distressed over Rosemary Davis's situation, she scarcely touched her food.

The Albergo's special offering today was "Eggs Benedictus" an Italian and Pacific Coast seafood interpretation of the brunch classic. The large toasted crostini were heaped with crisply cooked prosciutto and poached eggs. The usual Hollandaise covered the Italian-style ham and eggs, and a large portion of Dungeness crab meat topped the Hollandaise. Ribbons of fresh basil, a dusting of Parmigiano Reggiano, and tiny capers completed the magnificent creation from the Albergo's kitchen. Most of the group ordered the special.

Almost everyone was enjoying the mimosas and relaxing as they ate their brunch. Matthew hated to bring the happy party to an end, but he needed help. He'd purposely seated himself next to Cameron, and when they'd both eaten all they could, Matthew quietly shared with Cameron what had happened in the middle of the previous night. Cameron was understandably shocked when he heard that Harrison Davis had been kidnapped for a second time. How could that have happened?

When he'd heard the entire story, Cameron was angry—with Rosemary and with his friend Matthew. How could Matthew have failed to call the authorities to look for Harrison? Many hours had passed since the abduction. Whatever trail anyone might have followed was now completely cold.

Cameron had helped to rescue Harrison Davis once, and now the man was gone again. Nobody had any idea what had happened to him this time. There were no motorcycles nearby, and even if there had been, nobody knew in what direction they should go.

Matthew and Cameron decided to call a group meeting. Rosemary and Harrison Davis were not their responsibility. But the entire Camp Shoemaker crowd had witnessed the kidnapping at the Winer winery. They had all rejoiced when Harrison Davis had been returned to his wife with only minor damage. No one understood what was going on with these people, but it was obvious they were in trouble. The group of friends somehow felt an obligation to Rosemary Davis. How had this happened?

Cameron stood up and announced to the table, "Everybody is invited to Sidney's and my suite after brunch. We have a problem to discuss and need your input. We are asking for your help, your imaginations, and your brain cells to try to figure this out. I know that many of you, and I am thinking about Richard Carpenter and Tyler Merriman in particular, would rather go off to your rooms and take naps. But we need you. So as soon as you have finished with your brunch, your presence is required."

The Camp Shoemaker crowd looked around the table at each other. Isabelle couldn't quite meet the eyes of her friends. Matthew was clearly agitated.

"All right. What the heck is going on around here?" Olivia always got right to the point. She did not beat around the bush.

"My husband won't tell me anything about the secret mission he was involved in that resulted in the successful rescue of our fellow Albergo guest, Harrison Davis. J.D. knows how angry it makes me when he won't tell me anything. Richard Carpenter has been shot in the shoulder, and nobody seems to have any idea who shot him or why. Nobody wants to talk about the shooting. Nobody wants to go to a hospital when they need to go. Nobody will even consider calling the sheriff or the police or any kind of law enforcement when they need to be called. Isabelle looks like she hasn't had any sleep in days. She has terrible dark circles around her eyes. She won't look at me. She knows something, but she isn't talking. What is wrong with you people?"

"That's what we are going to discuss at the meeting in our room." Cameron insisted again.

Sidney had no idea why Cameron had called the meeting. "I am as anxious as the rest of you are to find out what is going on."

"Well, I'm not going to the meeting. I'm going to take my nap. What is so important that we have to have a meeting about it?" Tyler was being a contrarian, and not for the first time. "I am not going to a seminar where I am going to have to listen to people talk about voter suppression. I am just not going to do it."

Matthew spoke up. "This isn't about any of that stuff. Harrison Davis has been kidnapped again, and we are trying to figure out what to do about it. We are trying to figure out what to do about Harrison's wife Rosemary who came to our room last night at midnight covered in blood. She's all right, but Harrison is gone. So, is that enough information to get you to postpone your nap?"

"Call the police or the FBI or the sheriff! That is the only sensible thing to do. You should have called them last night."

Gretchen was definitely one of the most sensible people in the group and probably one of the most sensible people on the planet. She wanted to do what any normal person would do under the circumstances. She had long ago lost her patience with Rosemary Davis and her claims that her husband's secret work precluded calling law enforcement. Harrison Davis had been lucky once because three guys who liked to ride motorbikes had taken things into their own hands. Gretchen was entirely correct when she insisted that this time they had to turn things over to the authorities. "She came to your room covered with blood, and you don't want to call the sheriff? Are you completely crazy?" Gretchen stared at Isabelle and Matthew.

Isabelle spoke up to defend herself. "Of course we wanted to call the sheriff." She paused. "But we didn't."

"We probably are all completely crazy, except for Gretchen, of course." Gretchen glared at her husband when he said this. Gretchen didn't know what he and Cameron and J.D. had done to rescue Harrison Davis the first time. Bailey knew he was taking a position that would infuriate his wife, but he was very afraid that, if they brought in anybody official now, the details of their motorcycle rescue would have to come out. Bailey readily admitted to himself that they were no longer coloring inside the lines.

"We could all walk away from this right now, and anybody who wants to is more than welcome to do so. I can't walk away from it, for a number of reasons. So, those of you who are able to give up your naps and participate are invited to come back to our room now. We are just going to talk. Bailey is not going to put on a disguise … yet!" Cameron was trying to add a little humor. He looked around and saw only grim-looking faces staring back at him. He could see that Gretchen was angry and that Isabelle was in great distress.

Elizabeth seemed entirely clueless which was very unusual for her. Olivia would come to the meeting because she was curious and wanted to find out what was going on. Lilleth looked like she wished she'd never hooked up with this Camp Shoemaker crowd. And who could blame her for feeling that way?

"There's a saying or a proverb somewhere about saving somebody's life. It says if you save a life, you are responsible for that life. That's not exactly the way it goes, but it is something like that. So that makes me responsible for this Harrison Davis dude. He seems to be having a serious streak of bad luck lately, but I feel as if I need to do whatever I can to try to save the guy. After the risks we took when we saved him the first time... well, we don't want all of that to go to waste." J.D. was also seriously worried that the details of Harrison's first rescue would come to light.

"Is there a valid reason why Rosemary doesn't want us to notify the authorities? Does she have a rational explanation about why she refuses to involve law enforcement? It seems to me that the kidnapping of a scientist who has been working on the COVID situation would be a high priority for the FBI." Elizabeth was a reasonable person, and this was the reasonable solution. "It's very bizarre, that Harrison's wife won't allow anyone to help find her husband. I'm with Gretchen on this. Unless I hear a good explanation from Rosemary herself, I vote to call in the FBI. Rosemary seems like a very smart person, and she has every reason to be afraid. Her husband has been kidnapped twice. But she is so adamant about not allowing any law enforcement to become involved, and I don't understand that. I think we need to hear from her exactly why she refuses to call in the FBI."

"I propose we say to her that we can't, in good conscience, be responsible for what happens to her husband. We need to tell her that, unless she gives us a compelling reason why we can't call in the authorities, we are going to do the sensible thing." Sidney agreed with Elizabeth. The women in the group seemed to be in favor of common sense, and the men seemed to be in favor of being Clint Eastwood.

"Where is she right now? Let's get her to come and talk to us, or at least talk to a few of us. All of us grilling her at once might be overwhelming for anybody."

"She is very traumatized. After everything she has been through, it isn't any wonder. She is hiding in her room, and I doubt she will come out any time soon."

There was a knock on the door. When Sidney opened it, Rosemary Davis was standing there. She looked as if she hadn't slept in weeks. She looked like she was about to collapse.

"May I come in and join your discussion? Isabelle sent me a text that you needed to hear from me and that I owe you an explanation. She's right. I do owe you all an explanation. Several of you rescued Harrison from his first kidnappers, at great risk to yourselves. You have been so kind to me when I needed help, and I have been so preoccupied with my own troubles, I've not been appropriately grateful. I've not been forthcoming about my situation. I have been almost rude to some of you at times. I apologize for these things. There are critical reasons why I have not wanted to involve anyone else in Harrison's and my drama."

Rosemary seemed to be more confident as she continued to make her case. "More importantly, there are quite a few good reasons why I do not want to involve law enforcement, at any level, in what is going on. I am here now to plead my case and beg you not to call the FBI. Harrison and I discussed what we would do in case something happened to him. He was adamant that he would rather go to his death than get law enforcement involved. He knows there are many leaks inside the FBI. Some are intentional and some are accidental. Harrison's life is over. My life is in your hands. I will tell you all about it." Rosemary Davis was almost overwhelmed by her grief, but she wanted to tell them her story.

CHAPTER 28

"*Something went terribly, terribly wrong in China.*" Rosemary struggled to regain her composure and present herself as the professional woman she had been for most of her life. She had been a teacher, and she was accomplished at making a convincing speech and giving a lecture. "My husband is a geneticist. He has a PhD in genetics and a PhD in virology. He studies the genetics of viruses. You cannot begin to imagine how busy he has been during the past few months. He has been researching the novel coronavirus, as many others in his field have been, in an effort to find a way to combat this terrible enemy and find a vaccine.

"Harrison determined some time ago that SARS-CoV-2 was engineered in a laboratory. There has been much lying and covering up. There have been excuses and obfuscation around this issue. The Chinese do not want to admit that they have been developing something this lethal in a laboratory. They have lied about the origins of the coronavirus from the beginning. To be fair, if one can even hope to be fair about something as horrible as this, Harrison does not believe that the Chinese government ever meant to set this menace loose on the world. It was never meant to escape the laboratory as it did. It was an accident. There is no doubt about it that China is making genetic weapons, but this time, Harrison thinks with COVID-19, it was an accident.

"Harrison wouldn't tell me everything. He will be the first to admit that he doesn't know everything that happened. He doesn't think that even the Chinese know what all really happened in Wuhan. He knows what he knows because he understands genetics. For many reasons, facts are hard to come by, and knowledge is incomplete. He has attempted to explain how and what went awry in Wuhan, and part of what he has concluded is speculation."

Rosemary's audience was silent and waited for her to continue. "The Chinese might want to kill us, but my husband doesn't think they originally intended to kill us and the rest of the world with this virus. He believes there was an intent to kill; but he is certain that the original intent to kill was local, very much more specific and contained, and genetically targeted."

Rosemary continued. "Harrison's job is to study the relationship of genetics to disease. He looks at differences in distributions of geographic DNA and in racial DNA. He looks at why Tay-Sachs disease is typically found in people with a certain type of ancestry. He studies why sickle cell disease is more common in people who have African DNA than it is in the DNA of people of any other race. That's the kind of thing he is interested in. He's a researcher. His ultimate goal is to find a way to protect us, to ensure that these terrible diseases do not inflict themselves on anybody. I'm not a geneticist. I am primarily a chemist. I understand some of what Harrison does, but I don't understand it all."

Rosemary knew she had to trust these people to get them to see things her way, and she did trust them. But she was reluctant to get into the speculative and sticky parts of Harrison's research with anybody. She didn't fully understand what he had discovered, almost by accident, and she did not feel comfortable telling others about it. But these people had gone all out for her and for Harrison. She owed it to them to tell them everything she knew.

"When it became apparent earlier this year, that COVID-19 was going to be a worldwide catastrophic event, Harrison was one of many researchers called on to redirect their efforts and expertise in the direction of trying to understand this anomalous and dangerous pathogen. Harrison was particularly intrigued because certain demographic groups seemed to be affected differently from others. Males as a group became sicker and died more frequently from COVID-19 than did females. People with certain blood types definitely got sicker than people with other blood types. People with Type A blood were not able to fight off the virus as well as people who had Type O blood. This fascinated Harrison. These selective genetic factors were significantly different from anything he'd encountered in his years of disease research."

Rosemary paused and took a deep breath. "Once Harrison gets onto something, he wants to understand it completely. He goes full force to try to get to the bottom of it. He worked day and night to try to figure out why this virus affected various groups so differently.

"He found that these differences in the way people were affected by the virus and whether or not they died, could be traced to differences in their DNA. Of course, we all know that older people and people with co-morbidities such as diabetes, obesity, high blood pressure, and lung disease, are going to get sicker and die more often. That is not unexpected and also is the case for the yearly flu and most other illnesses. Those whose bodies are already fighting diabetes or some other serious chronic condition are not going to be able to fight

COVID, or anything else, as effectively. We know that old peoples' immune systems don't work as well as young immune systems do. This is all common sense, and although very unfortunate, these factors do not really interest a geneticist very much. It is the unexpected differences in people's abilities to fight this disease that captured Harrison's attention."

Rosemary's new friends were mesmerized by the story she was telling. And she had yet not come to the really interesting part, the shocking part, the part that made Harrison Davis a dangerous threat. "I haven't told you anything so far that is at all controversial. All of this has been in the news and in the scientific journals. You know most of it already." They nodded their heads. Yes, they already knew most of it, but they had not heard it from the acolyte of a geneticist.

"Remember that Harrison is looking at this virus from the perspective of what it has mutated into, that is, what we have now. He does not know what it looked like when it was first developed by the Communist researchers in the Wuhan lab or what these military scientists in China had intended it to look like in its final form. Although there is no doubt whatsoever that the virus started out in the lab, it might have become attached to bats and/or pangolins. One very plausible theory is that laboratory animals that were being used for testing accidentally escaped the lab and spread the disease outside the lab. We may never know for sure about that part of the story. But originally this virus started out in the laboratory. Communist China is in the business of making genetic weapons. Harrison is absolutely certain of that."

"The part of this that got Harrison into so much trouble was what he discovered next. As I have said, I do not understand how he put it all together, and some of it is speculation on his part. But his speculation, his discoveries, and the body of evidence he has amassed, became very threatening to some powerful people. His work and the data he's collected became so dangerous that people have kidnapped him and people have tried to kill him to keep him quiet. They want to keep him from going public with his discoveries."

"What could possibly be so explosive that he can't be open about what he's discovered? I would think anyone who can shed light on where this terrible disease came from would be considered a hero. He ought to be nominated for a Nobel Prize, not hiding out and certainly not being kidnapped and having his life threatened." Tyler spoke up. He always wanted to cut to the chase.

"What he thinks he discovered is that Chinese military scientists in Wuhan were attempting to engineer a virus that would attack certain very specific ethnic groups within China. Harrison believes that the virus was never intended to become a pandemic and never intended to infect anyone beyond China's own national borders. It was certainly never intended to escape the laboratory and infect the world. But somehow the lab animals and the bats and the other creatures that the Chinese consider fair game for food got infected. Things got out of control and mutated in odd ways. What was never intended to happen has ended up creating chaos all over the world.

"China has a terrible human rights record. They have a diverse population, and they do not embrace this diversity. Their policies of Sinicization are constantly at work to try to dilute that diversity. They have a particular problem with their Muslim minorities in Xinjiang Province as well as with the Tibetans. They have done everything they can to tame their ethnic minorities on all fronts, to bring them to heel. The troublemakers in Xinjiang especially have continued to cause problems. Again, this is not anything that is news-worthy. Everyone has known for years about the things China has been doing to its ethnic minorities. Their human rights record is abominable.

"What is new, Harrison believes, from looking at how this virus that started out at a laboratory in Wuhan has mutated, is that the Chinese were attempting to develop a disease, a virus, that would attack and kill only people with very specific DNA profiles."

Rosemary finally had said the incriminating words. She had spilled the beans. She had revealed to these people the dangerous game the Chinese had been playing. "So, the Chinese were in fact attempting to find a way to kill off certain ethnic groups within their country. It would not have been acceptable for them to go in and machine gun these people as they worshiped in the mosques in Xinjiang Province. But if a disease 'accidentally' found its way into the Turkic Uyghur population and for some reason killed mostly ethnic Muslims, that would not be the government's doing. It would be a freak of nature, an accident of DNA.

"Harrison had his opinions about the reasons the virus was being developed in the first place, and these reasons are not noble ones. The political motives behind the development of such a deadly disease are grossly malignant and can only be considered under the broader heading of genocide.

"But before this holocaust virus could be fully developed, something went wrong. The creation of the virus was intended to be very specifically targeted. Before that very specific targeting could be achieved, the research went completely off track. Nobody will ever know exactly what happened at that military lab or how the bats and the pangolins and all the rest of it got into the mess. Harrison doesn't think it was intended to get outside the lab until it had been perfected, that is, fine-tuned to attack very specific ethnic minorities in China. When one is dealing with something so heinous and so dangerous, precautions must be extraordinary. The Chinese did not take the precautions they should have taken. It all 'went to poop' as Harrison would say. The virus, in going haywire and sideways, and getting loose and mutating and all of that, retained some of its properties that ensured it would attack people with certain DNA characteristics differentially. Males versus females. People with Type A blood versus Type O blood. There are undoubtedly other genetic differences that we will discover in the future. This is a very weird disease."

Rosemary had the group's attention now. "The final piece of the puzzle for Harrison was the discovery that the body's interferon response in some people was crippled by genetic flaws and by rogue antibodies. This is getting into the weeds for me, the chemist, so forgive me if I am not totally coherent in my explanations. Harrison said that Type I interferon, which is important in fighting off all viruses, is impaired in some people with certain kinds of DNA. These people have an aberration in their genetic code. Of the patients who carried these antibodies that attack interferon, 94% were male. This is striking, and it means that something on the X chromosome protects females. It is all about genetics, Harrison thinks. He doesn't know exactly what they started out to do with their experiments in Wuhan, but he does know that it didn't turn out the way it was intended to turn out."

"You can imagine what an enormous outcry there would be if the world at large knew that the Chinese had tried to develop a virus that would kill only certain ethnic groups, only people with certain kinds of DNA. The Chinese Communist government has always tried to cover up everything anyway. You can imagine how desperate they would be to cover up this information that Harrison has uncovered. They want Harrison dead. They want anybody dead that might be able to even half-way prove what they were trying to do." Rosemary looked as if she was beginning to fall apart.

"My husband is a dead man. He knows too much." She began to sob and then regained her composure. "He is a terrible threat to the Chinese Communists and their already horrible human rights reputation. Other scientists will inevitably discover what Harrison has discovered. Can they kidnap or kill everyone who stumbles on the truth of what they tried to do? Of course they will deny to the end that they ever tried to do it. They will blame it on the bats and the poor pangolins and the wet markets. They will promise not to eat dogs for breakfast any more for a while. What else would you expect them to say? They will say it is fake news, that it is political, and that it is a way to unfairly shame China. They will say it is a racist attack. They will say that those who speak the truth are suspect and have ulterior motives for speaking out and saying bad things about the Chinese. They will say that people from the Chinese medical research community who speak up are traitors and dissidents and have betrayed their country. They will claim that anyone who speaks the truth are capitalist pigs and are trying to bring down Communism. They will smear any and all of those who say anything against the Chinese Communist government. If discrediting those who try to speak the truth doesn't work, they will resort to more severe measures. They will kill them, if they can, before they can speak out. Harrison is in their sights. They have kidnapped him twice. They will kill him." Rosemary's eyes filled with tears again. She had worn herself out giving this long and complicated explanation. "I have no hope. I don't know why they haven't just killed him. I don't know why they want to kidnap him and keep him alive. I suspect that by now they probably have killed him."

She got control of herself for one more small speech. "The one bright spot in all of this was that he felt he might be on to something in terms of prevention by developing a vaccine. His whole career has been devoted to trying to fool DNA, to fool people's bodies into not allowing their DNA to make them sick. Because there has been so much data collected about COVID-19, he was excited about finding a possible way to block it. He was hopeful. When he began to think there might be light at the end of the COVID tunnel, he stayed up all night. He was determined to crack the code, to discover the secret to making a vaccine. When he thought he was definitely on to something, he worked himself into a state of complete exhaustion.

"Harrison shared his discoveries only with his immediate supervisor. He showed his supervisor the facts he had unearthed, his 'proof' that the coronavirus had been targeted for specific DNA characteristics. He told his supervisor of his breakthroughs on the path to developing a vaccine. Harrison, of course, does not know who his supervisor might have told about these discoveries. And there is always the possibility that his supervisor, or someone else, has been 'bought' by the Chinese to keep the truth from coming out.

"Then his laboratory was vandalized and set on fire. He was supposed to be in his lab that night, and there is no question, he would have died if he had been there. But he wasn't. They missed him that time, but he realized someone wanted to destroy his research and destroy him. After his laboratory was attacked, we knew we had to get away. We had to go into hiding. We decided to run, and we have been on the run ever since." Rosemary sighed as she talked about running and hiding. The woman was at her wits end.

"If he was really on to something in terms of a vaccine or a cure or a discovery of that sort, every government in the world would want him. Even the Russians, who say they have a vaccine that works, would want to muzzle him and co-opt his findings. They would not want Harrison's research to interfere with or overshadow their own discoveries. The Russians, if they currently have the only viable vaccine for preventing COVID-19, would be able to make trillions of dollars and hold the human race hostage. They would be able to extort every other nation in the world." Cameron was the businessman and could always spot where the profit motive drove governments, companies, and individuals.

This comment about the Russians meant more than the obvious to Cameron, Bailey, and J.D. who knew that thepeople who had kidnapped Harrison Davis the first time had been Russians. This had puzzled them. Had the Russians really believed the man was on to something? Somebody had given them the orders to take him out of circulation. Who knew at this point whether his Russian kidnappers had wanted to pick his brains to find out what he knew or if they just wanted to silence him and put him in a box in the ground. Those who knew that men with Russian DNA had been responsible for the first kidnapping were now having second thoughts. Hadthe Russian mafia been hired to eliminate Harrison Davis in order to obscure the fact that the Chinese were really behind his kidnapping and disappearance?

Rosemary wanted to tell her audience a little bit about what they had been through. She wanted them to know what Harrison had done to preserve his research and the provisions he had made so that the world would know the truth. "After we left Seattle and were staying in a motel in Oregon, Harrison spent days writing down everything he had in his head about his research. He explained everything he had discovered in very convincing scientific terms. He laid it all out. He made several copies of this extensive report that explained his very dangerous discoveries. He put copies in a safety deposit box in a bank. He sent copies of the report to his brother, to his lawyer, and to several other trusted colleagues and friends. He included a letter with each report. In the letter, he explained to those he had entrusted with the report that his life and my life were in danger because of what he had discovered. He said that we intended to disappear and were working on acquiring new identities. He asked his friends not to open or read his report until he told them that we were safe.

"Harrison knew that once they read his earth-shattering information, they would not be able to keep it secret. He told them that once we were established in a new location with new names, they were free to disclose his report to the world. This is why we have been so adamant about not involving law enforcement. Once the authorities become involved it will only be a matter of days, or even hours, until the press is involved. We have been desperate to keep this all a secret until we were able to establish ourselves in our new lives."

Rosemary's complicated and distressing story was a great deal for the group to take in. The implications for what Harrison Davis had discovered and what Rosemary Davis had revealed were huge. It could cause a revolution in China. It could make China a pariah in the world for decades, if not centuries. If this information were to become public, there would potentially be many mindboggling consequences. It was difficult to imagine how overwhelming the ramifications would be. No wonder the Chinese had kidnapped him a second time. Of course they had to silence him. His voice could not be heard. Every one of the people in the room was imagining the worst for poor Harrison Davis.

Would his body be found behind a dumpster? Would the Chinese take him out to sea and drop him overboard? His death would never be a public event. There would be no body. He would simply disappear from the world. Gloom settled on Rosemary's audience.

Rosemary could see the despair she felt reflected in the faces of those around her. "I have one glimmer of hope, one question that I need to ask someone who is an expert about how cell phones work. I kind of understand, but not really. I know that it is possible to trace where people are through their cell phones. Harrison won't have a smart phone or an email address. He refuses to participate in any of that. But he does carry an old flip phone that only makes and receives phone calls. It does not take photographs. You cannot play videogames on it. It does not do Facetime. I insisted that he have the primitive phone so we could stay in touch when we were traveling. He keeps it charged. I haven't been able to find the old flip phone in our room, so I am thinking he probably has it with him. He must have put it in his briefcase. That was where he usually kept it when it wasn't charging. I can't imagine that whoever took him would allow him to keep it, but if somehow somebody could trace that phone, we might at least know where he has been, or where the phone has been.

"I hope you understand now why we didn't want any exposure to law enforcement or to the press. It was just too dangerous. We were making plans to disappear forever. That hasn't been easy when everybody in the world seems to be after him. But we had some small hope. We just wanted to live our lives. Harrison didn't want to be famous or take any credit for anything. He loved his work. He loved doing research. He lived for that. But when he realized that his work had put us in terrible danger, he was willing to give it all up. He was willing to sacrifice what he loved most in the world and go into hiding with me." She finally broke down and sobbed, knowing her plans to save herself and her husband were never going to become a reality.

CHAPTER 29

T*he group of Camp Shoemaker campers and their* wives and girlfriends were speechless. Rosemary Davis's revelations had been unexpected and overwhelming. Her audience was reeling.

Olivia was the first to speak. "I for one am on your side. I do not want to call the FBI or the sheriff or anybody. I absolutely get why you don't want them involved. I personally am going to do everything I can to save you. I am going to help you hide and relocate and find a new identity and a new life. I suspect that others in this group will be with me in this effort." Olivia had a big heart. She was always helping and supporting those who were down on their luck and in trouble. When she said she was going to pull out all the stops to help Rosemary Davis, she meant what she said.

Elizabeth and Sidney spoke at the same time. They were both in agreement with Olivia and would do whatever they could to help Rosemary Davis. Gretchen reached out and squeezed Rosemary's hand. All was forgiven. Lilleth gave her a thumbs up, and Isabelle smiled and nodded her head. The women had spoken. Law enforcement would not be involved.

"Okay. Okay. No cops and no feds. We are all in to save Rosemary. We have resources, so we can do this." Bailey was relieved that no authorities would be involved. He was totally on board with that decision. "The harder part is what we are going to do about Harrison. If we could just...."

Cameron interrupted Bailey to ask Rosemary for the phone number of the old fashioned flip phone that Harrison hopefully still had either on his person or in his briefcase. The minute she gave him the number, he excused himself and walked into the bedroom. He already had his own cell phone out. Things were beginning to happen.

"I have an idea about why they have kidnapped Harrison rather than just murdering him outright." Richard had been quiet until now, but he wanted to offer Rosemary a glimmer of hope that her husband was still alive. "His Chinese abductors must suspect that he has shared his discoveries with someone else, maybe even with a number of other people. In fact, you said that Harrison wrote down everything he could remember about his research. He made copies of this report and sent these copies to friends, relatives, and colleagues. The Chinese suspect correctly that he has done this. They need to keep him alive to grill him, even torture him, so that he will tell them who else knows what he knows. They will keep questioning him until he cracks and tells them who has copies of his report. Then they will go after those people to silence them. It is all about keeping this information from becoming public. I think you have reason to hope that Harrison's captors are keeping him alive in order to find out who else has the information about what he has discovered."

"If Harrison talks, he puts all those other people at risk, doesn't he? I think he would hold out and maybe never reveal their names." Rosemary had hopes that Harrison would be strong enough to resist torture.

"Nobody can hold out against the truth-telling drugs these people have. He won't even know he has given up the information. We need to find him before he's taken out of the country and before he's been given these drugs." Richard Carpenter knew about using drugs to extract information.

Olivia was head-to-head in a close conversation with Rosemary. Elizabeth was on her phone. Sidney had buttonholed Tyler and was giving him a list of things to do. They had a mission. They were used to getting themselves out of trouble on these reunion trips. They were happy to be rallying around and doing something for someone else who needed their help. Except for Richard's having been shot in the shoulder and the motorcycle caper, none of them had been in real danger on this trip. That was about to change.

"We are going to try to find Harrison." Bailey had made the decision they all realized was the only decision that could be made. He spoke to Rosemary. "You are going to have to continue to trust us to do this. Since we can't call in the big guns, that is the FBI, you are going to have to leave it to us. And we have no guns, large or small, with us on this vacation."

Cameron came back into the living room of the suite. "Rosemary, I have somebody working on finding the closest cell tower to where your husband's phone is currently located. I've dialed the number of the flip phone, and we think it is here in California. My people are working on getting the right cell tower and an exact location. Can you please get your luggage together and be ready to leave the Albergo in an hour? I have notified my pilot who has already begun doing pre-flight checks on the plane. We want you out of here and in a safe place while we work on finding you a new life and perhaps finding your husband. The plane will be taking you to Sidney's and my ranch in New Mexico. No one knows that you know me. You will be completely safe there. There's a ranch foreman and some ranch hands in residence. There is a housekeeper who is also a terrific cook and will take good care of you. The ranch hands will never see you. You can trust the ranch foreman and the housekeeper. I have done this before, and my people know what to do. Can *you* do this? Your husband was willing to give his life to save you. Are you willing to take this opportunity to fly away from here to save yourself?"

Everyone could see that Rosemary hated to leave Paso Robles while her husband's status was still undetermined. She was hesitating.

Sidney spoke up. "I will text you every two hours with updates on what is happening here. Most of us will be staying at the Albergo anyway. Not everyone will participate in the search for Harrison. You will know everything that we know as soon as we know it. I promise. Please keep your phone charged. Pack your bags."

With tears streaming down her face, Rosemary left the Cameron's suite. Isabelle went with her to help her pack and to give her moral support and encouragement. They would get the Davis's luggage and boxes together and be standing by to leave as soon as the plane was ready.

Elizabeth had been on the phone with a real estate agent in Tucson. Now she was speaking with an old friend from the days when she was a government employee. Gretchen was trying to find a photographer who would come to the hotel within the hour to take photographs of Rosemary for a new passport and driver's license.

Rosemary returned to the suite to have her photo taken. Bailey would have liked for her to have had the time to dye her hair a different color for the passport photos, but time was scarce right now. After the photos were taken, Rosemary pulled her thick, beautiful hair back into a ponytail and tucked it up under a baseball cap. Sidney helped her put on one of Cameron's windbreakers that had a hood. The coat was much too large for Rosemary, but since she was already wearing blue jeans, the oversized coat made her look like she could be a man. The disguise was not nearly up to Bailey's standards, but it was the best they could come up with at the last minute.

Rosemary wanted to be sure she did the right thing. "I don't think any of the furniture in the room is damaged, but if anything was broken, I will pay for that. There is probably still a lot of blood in there. I will pay for the clean-up. I know the manager here. She knows my word is good. I've told her I can't answer any of her questions and not to ask. I have told her to let you know how much I owe her for the damages."

Rosemary tried to say goodbye and thank you but was too distraught to speak. A rental car had been arranged and would be in the parking lot at the back entrance to the Albergo within the next five minutes. Tyler pushed the luggage cart, and Isabelle and Olivia walked Rosemary to the car. Bailey was going to drive her to the plane. Tyler was going along to assist with the very quick transfer of luggage and boxes from the rental car to the private jet. Cameron wanted it to take less than two minutes, including putting everything on board. They all heaved a sigh of relief when Bailey drove the rental car out of the Albergo's driveway, and Rosemary was headed for the airport. The airport was just a few miles away. She would be in the air within fifteen minutes. Another collective sigh of relief would be forthcoming when she was safely aboard the plane and on her way to New Mexico.

"One of us should have gone with her. She's all alone and feeling it acutely right now. I should have volunteered to go with her. I just didn't think of it in time." Lilleth was feeling guilty that she hadn't done more to help. It had all happened so fast. It was no wonder everyone felt overwhelmed.

Cameron came out of the bedroom. He was excited. “We think we have found the phone. It’s not that far away from Paso Robles. I will tell you all about it. Should we let Rosemary know or should we wait to tell her until she’s in the air?”

“If she thinks he is nearby, she might refuse to leave. I think we should wait to tell her until we have actually have the phone in hand. Harrison may not be anywhere near that phone.” J.D. was adamant.

“I promised her I would let her know everything as soon as we knew it. I promised her. I keep my promises.” Sidney had a definite point of view.

“How long until that plane is scheduled to take off?” J.D. wanted to know.

“They’re just arriving at the airport now. The plane is ready to leave and will take off the minute she’s on board. Please Sidney. Just this once, agree with me.” Cameron knew better than to try to talk Sidney out of doing something she was determined to do, but today he was begging. “It’s for her own good.”

“I would feel as if I were betraying her if I don’t do what I said I would do.” Sidney picked up her phone and dialed Rosemary’s cell phone number. The call went directly to voice mail. Sidney left her the message that Harrison’s phone had been located, and she asked Rosemary to call her back. Sidney had fulfilled her promise, and maybe Rosemary would not check her phone until she was in the air on her way to the ranch.

“The flip phone is located close to a place called Harmony, California. It’s an unincorporated place on the Pacific Coast, close to the intersection of Highway 1 and State Road 46. State Road 46 is the highway just out of town, the road with all the wineries on it, the main road that we’ve been driving on every day. It’s the road to the coast. Harmony is only thirty miles from here. Of course, we don’t know if Harrison is anywhere near his phone, but it's a place to start. We've been able to track the phone, so at least we know where Harrison has been." Cameron was ready to follow the phone.

Olivia knew all about Harmony. "When I knew we were going to be in this area for a week, I read up about things to do. Harmony is an interesting place. It used to be the home of a large dairy cooperative that closed in 1955. Lots of cows. The town is tiny. The dairy was called the Harmony Valley Creamery or something like that. After the creamery closed, the town became an artist's colony. Then it became known for glassblowing. I guess it is pretty quaint out there in Harmony. It's a throw-back to the old days. I think there are only fifteen or so people who live in the town now. It's not even really a town. I was thinking it might be fun to go out there and see it while we were in Paso Robles. We've not had the time, and I'd forgotten about it."

"Why would they take Harrison there? With only a few people living there, wouldn't you think they'd notice right away that there were three Chinese guys holding a hostage in their town?" J.D. had questions.

"I'm telling you I don't think there is a real town there. I don't know. It seems to be a kind of tourist attraction. We could go there and check it out." Olivia was reading from her phone. "There's a glass blowing place in the old creamery building. They sell stuff like hand-blown glass and pottery. You can actually watch people blowing glass and making pottery. There are other historic buildings to see…a chapel, the old post office, some nice gardens. The town was founded in 1869 near a bunch of dairy farms by Swiss people. There used to be a school. Lots of references about the place being 'quirky' and 'quaint.' It looks pretty interesting."

Olivia continued. "I couldn't figure out how those Chinese people would know about this obscure place, but guess what,

Harmony has been in several movies, documentaries, and TV shows. It was even in an episode of *Perry Mason* back in the day. That episode was called 'The Case of the Absent Artist.' Ha! It was also the setting for a South Korean movie produced by the Seoul Broadcasting Company. Maybe that's how those Chinese people heard about it."

Cameron was ready to begin the hunt. "Bailey has the rental car at the airport. He'll be back soon. I rented a really 'Plain Jane' little economy car so it would not attract attention. We can drive out to Harmony in that to try to find the phone."

CHAPTER 30

Bailey and Tyler returned from the airport. They were delighted to report that Rosemary Davis was on her way to New Mexico. Cameron was anxious to leave for Harmony, but he gave Bailey a minute to catch his breath. Cameron, Bailey, and J.D., the 'motorbike boys,' were going to look for the flip phone. They had no idea what they would find, and the others were on standby to be ready to assist, if the three got into trouble, or if they were lucky enough to find Harrison Davis.

From Rosemary's account, they knew that three men had participated in Harrison's abduction, so they needed at least three warm bodies to even go near Harmony, California. The three promised their wives that they were only going to look for the phone. They promised they would not try to rescue Davis without help, even if they were able to find where he was being held. Bailey would drive the rental car, and Cameron would have his eyes on the GPS app on his phone. He would tell Bailey where to go to find the flip phone. J.D. was in charge of the bungee cords. He thought they might come in handy and had brought along the two large ones that had helped to hold Harrison Davis upright on the motor scooter earlier that week.

Isabelle excused herself to go back to her room to sleep. She had been up most of the night with Rosemary Davis. Matthew Ritter was sound asleep on the Richardson's couch. He also had not had much sleep the night before. Richard Carpenter still had a sling on his arm. He would be more of a liability than an asset in any confrontation. Tyler was still in favor of bringing in the authorities to handle the situation. Tyler was probably exhibiting more good sense than his friends were.

The rental car chased the blinking red dot on Cameron's phone down Highway 46. Less than a mile from Harmony, the dot told them to turn north off the main highway and drive into the woods. There was no road to turn onto, not even a dirt road. They did not have four-wheel drive, so they hesitated to take the rental car off road. The small car was designed to squeeze into parking spaces where full-sized cars were not able to fit—not to drive off into the wilds. But it was all they had right now. Cameron was cursing to himself that he had not rented a bigger, better vehicle, something with four wheel drive at least. But they didn't hesitate. They drove the low-slung sedan over the rough ground, doing the best they could until one of their tires went flat. No one said a word. Every one of the three had known it was going to happen.

The Ritters and the Carpenters had driven their own cars to the reunion. The Steeles had driven an enormous rented motor home to Paso Robles. Three of the couples had flown in on Cameron's plane. No one had rented a car when they'd arrived. They were short on vehicles because they'd depended on the Albergo to provide transportation everywhere. Bailey was angry that COVID, already having messed up everybody's entire life, had also messed up their rescue efforts.

Because they were desperate to find Harrison's flip phone before dark, they didn't have time to change the tire on the economy car. Cameron would call the rental agency and have them pick it up. Time was slipping away. They abandoned the sedan with the flat tire and trudged through the woods, following the track of the red dot blinking on Cameron's phone.

It was rough going, making their way through the tangled terrain. The brush was thick and there were no paths. They kept following the red dot for at least a half mile into the middle of nowhere. Suddenly, they saw a car stopped between two trees. The red dot stopped pulsating. They had found Harrison's phone, or at least Cameron's smart phone indicated they had located the flip phone.

"How the heck were they able to drive this car all the way back here in the woods? That Subaru's not four-wheel drive either, and it's bigger than our little pipsqueak of a car." J.D. owned a trucking business and most cars seemed like pipsqueaks to him.

"They know something we don't know. There is obviously another way, a better way, to get here than the way we came. My phone locator app doesn't take you on the best highway. It takes you the most direct way. There is clearly a better road to drive on to get here, but we didn't come that way."

The vacant car was unlocked. J.D. began trying to get into the trunk of the car. Harrison might be in there. Bailey and Cameron searched under the seats and in between the seats. They looked in the glove compartment. They looked everywhere and finally decided the phone was probably in the trunk. They kept working to get into the trunk of the car because they hoped they might find either the flip phone or find Harrison Davis alive inside. At the same time, they also dreaded breaking into the trunk, afraid of what they might find there. What if they found Harrison's dead body in the trunk of the car?

They were trying not to talk because they realized the bad guys might be nearby. If Harrison wasn't in the trunk of the car, they hoped they would find him not very far from where the car was parked. It was possible to open the trunks of some cars by pushing a button on the dashboard, but this car was not one of those. They were intent on getting into the trunk and almost didn't hear the two men talking to each other and rustling the leaves as they walked through the woods. Just in time, the three friends ran from the car and hid wherever they could find to hide.

The two men were speaking what sounded to Bailey like Chinese. The men were not wearing masks, and they looked Chinese. Of course, Bailey had no idea what they were saying to each other. They had a key and easily opened the trunk of the car. They took out a briefcase. The briefcase matched the description Rosemary had given them. One of the men took the briefcase, and the other one locked the trunk of the car. Harrison Davis had not been inside, dead or alive.

The two men walked back in the direction from which they'd come. J.D. had been an avid outdoorsman when he was younger, and he'd had some training as a tracker. He motioned for his two friends to follow him. Cameron indicated the red dot that was keeping track of Harrison's flip phone had begun to move again. They were following the briefcase and following the phone. They tried to be invisible as they stayed behind the two Chinese men who were walking deeper into the woods.

Just as suddenly as the car in the woods had appeared, a huge corrugated metal warehouse appeared among the trees. It had been built a long time ago, and was now entirely rusted on the outside. The motorbike trio hid where they could see the wide metal doors that appeared to be the only entrance into the building. One of the bad guys fiddled with a lock on the doors. With difficulty, the two men pulled one of the metal doors aside. They entered the warehouse.

Bailey surreptitiously circumvented the building, looking for another way to get inside. All he could find were two long windows that were up high on the walls near the roof. These windows on opposite sides of the building were too high to see into if you were standing on the ground.

Bailey texted the information about the windows to J.D. and Cameron. He also included in his texts his opinion that this building was likely to be the place where Harrison was being held. They texted back that they agreed. They wanted more than anything to get a look inside that building. They were desperate to confirm his location. They texted back and forth to formulate a plan.

Bailey weighed the least of the three. They decided that Cameron and J.D. would try to lift Bailey up high enough onto their shoulders so that he could look into one of the warehouse windows. These three men were all seventy-seven years old. They were vigorous and in good shape. But their bodies were old and their bones were brittle. They were not teenaged cheerleaders trying to execute a pyramid cheer. This would be quite a feat if they could accomplish it. They positioned themselves to try to lift Bailey onto their shoulders. As they knelt down, he climbed up on their shoulders. It was painful. It was clumsy. It was almost impossible. Bailey fell to the ground twice before his friends were able to stand up with Bailey standing on their shoulders and hanging on for dear life. He held on to the side of the building. He grabbed hold of the window ledge and pulled himself up. He began to lose his grasp on the rusty metal. He realized his arms were not as strong as they used to be. But he held on and tried to lift himself up just a little higher to have a better look inside.

Then he saw what he had been hoping to see. Harrison Davis was in the building. Bailey was only able to get a quick glimpse before his hands began to slip again. Harrison was chained to the floor. He was lying down on the concrete, either sleeping or unconscious. Bailey thought he saw Harrison move or roll over a little bit. This meant that he wasn't dead. There was hope.

Bailey tried to pull himself up on the window ledge again to get a second look, but his strength gave out. This was definitely work meant for younger men. Cameron and J.D. scrambled to try to catch Bailey as he fell. They rushed to cushion his fall as he crashed to the ground. In the end, they all ended up in a pile of arms and legs and bodies on the cold September forest floor. They had some bumps and bruises. Bailey thought he had hurt his ankle and maybe his shoulder in the fall. But they had accomplished more than they'd hoped they would. They had located the flip phone, and they had found Harrison Davis. They were pretty sure he was still alive.

It was almost dark. Bailey was limping. His ankle was killing him. With a friend on each side holding him up, the three knew they had to get out of the woods quickly. J.D. texted Tyler that someone was going to have to drive from the Albergo to pick them up. J.D. let Tyler know that driving their rental car had ceased to be an option. The three would be waiting on Highway 46, and J.D. told Tyler exactly where to drive to meet them. He told Tyler to hurry. If it had not been for Cameron's smart phone with its GPS, they would never had been able to find their way back to their worthless rental car with its flat tire. It was going nowhere. Cameron guided them towards the highway on foot. Would Tyler be able to see them in the dark as they waited by the side of the road?

Tyler borrowed the Ritters' Mercedes SUV to drive to Harmony to pick up his three friends. He'd been asleep when Cameron called and had to wake the Ritters to get their car key. Cameron had sent a text to everyone in the group to let them know they'd found where Harrison Davis was being held hostage. It was late, so most of the reunion group were already asleep. They would get the news in the morning.

The three were very tired after walking through the woods, especially since they'd had to almost carry Bailey the entire way to the main road. Even after they'd reached the place where they'd left their rental car, they'd still had to cover a significant distance to reach Highway 46. They knew Tyler would be arriving in the Ritter's SUV, and they knew it took thirty minutes to drive from Paso Robles to Harmony. They huddled together beside the road. It was dark, and the Central California night air was cold. It was almost October.

They finally saw the Ritter's car approaching and flagged Tyler down. Bailey had to be helped into the front seat of the car. His ankle was swollen twice its normal size by now. No one even dared suggest that he go to the hospital ER to have his ankle taken care of. They knew what Bailey's answer to that would be. Tyler wanted to hear everything that had happened, but the three were so worn out, they were asleep long before they arrived at the Albergo. Tyler roused them when they pulled into the Albergo's parking lot.

CHAPTER 31

Harrison Davis sensed that there was someone else in the building with him. He felt it more than he knew it to be real. Had he heard something to put the idea into his head? Maybe it was just wishful thinking. Maybe he just hoped there was someone else here inside this metal prison, another human being to share his loneliness and his despair. He had been chloroformed, and then he had been given some kind of an injection, probably to keep him unconscious. Or maybe the injection had been some kind of truth serum that was intended to make him tell all. He decided he probably hadn't told them everything they wanted to know, or he would no longer be alive.

He had no idea what day it was or where he was. He was no longer blindfolded, and his hands were free. But his leg was manacled and attached to the floor with a chain. His captors had placed a bucket nearby. They had left bottles of water and a bag of food close to him. He grabbed a bottle of the water and briefly wondered if it were drugged. He decided to drink it anyway. The food smelled repellent to him. The thought of touching the plastic bag that contained the food made him gag. He noticed that someone had thrown his briefcase on the ground, but it was too far away for him to reach. If he could get to the briefcase, and if his flip phone was inside, and if it still had a charge, and if there was any cell phone service out here in the wilderness, he might be able to call Rosemary. He didn't know where he was so he couldn't tell her anything about that. It didn't matter anyway. He tried as hard as he could, but he couldn't reach his briefcase.

He was sure he'd heard a noise, an inside noise. He strained to hear it again. Maybe his ears were playing tricks on him. Maybe he had finally gone over the edge. Maybe what he had heard was just a sound from the outside, an animal screeching or crying, birds flapping, a dog barking. Maybe it was just this ancient metal warehouse creaking in the wind. He drifted into unconsciousness again.

When he woke, he definitely heard someone crying. He couldn't tell exactly where the crying was coming from, but he was certain it was coming from inside the building. He shouted at the top of his lungs. "Who's there? Is anybody here with me? Are you crying?" He paused to listen. The crying stopped after he'd shouted out. "Please." His desperation was broadcast in his voice. "I am being held prisoner here in this warehouse. Please give me some kind of sign that you are also here in the warehouse. Please let me know I am not alone."

There was no reply. There was nothing but silence for a long, long time. Then he thought he heard a small voice say something, but he couldn't understand what that small voice was saying. Harrison shouted again. "Speak louder. I can't hear you. I can't understand you. Do you speak English? I am an American scientist. I will not hurt you. I'm here against my will. I'm being held hostage. I mean no harm to anyone. Please talk to me." He wondered if he was hearing a recording of some kind, a human voice that was designed to trick him, to work on his psyche to convince him to give up his secrets. He listened for the small voice again. He wanted so badly to hear that small voice one more time.

At last, he heard it. "I am being held hostage here, too. And I am also a scientist. I have been here for many weeks. I don't know how many exactly. I think I am going to go completely insane. I think I am going to die soon. Please talk to me and tell me where I am. Why won't they just let me die? Why are they keeping me alive?"

Harrison realized he was listening to a woman's voice. She spoke perfect English with an accent of some kind. He decided he had nothing to lose by telling the truth to whoever this person was who said she was also being held captive in the building. "My name is Harrison Davis. I am a geneticist. I've been kidnapped by the Chinese because of what I know. I have been doing research on the coronavirus. I discovered some things the Chinese don't want anyone to know or talk about. I believe they intend to torture me and then kill me. I think we are still inside the United States. I don't have any idea how long I have been here. I've been drugged and have lost track of time."

The woman's voice seemed to be coming from the far end of the long building. Her voice was not strong. It sounded almost like a child's voice. "I am Sui Wai. I escaped from Hong Kong so I could tell the world what the Communist Chinese government created in Wuhan. I had intended to be a whistleblower, but I trusted the wrong person. Now I am here. I have already been tortured. I know they intend to kill me. They have said they are going to take me back to China to make an example of me. They've told me that is why they have kept me alive."

The two small windows high up on the walls of the metal warehouse indicated that it was nighttime. These two windows were the only way to view the world outside their prison. The two scientists talked to each other throughout the night. They found tremendous solace in sharing their stories. Sui Wai had been held for much longer than Harrison had been, and she had sunk into a state of total hopelessness. Finding Harrison Davis had given her a tiny ray of hope.

They admitted and accepted that they both were doomed. They shared their scientific findings. They told each other what they had done to try to get their stories out to the world. They talked about the things they had done to try to save themselves. They decided that their jailors had put them both in the same warehouse for practical reasons. It was easier to secure and take care of two hostages if they were in one location. They speculated a great deal about how they might escape, and in the end they decided escape was impossible. They agreed that it would be better if the kidnappers didn't know they had discovered each other's presence in the warehouse. They would be docile and pretend to be asleep whenever their kidnappers came to question them. Otherwise, they had no plan, no hope for the future.

After the sun had come up, two men arrived with more bags of food. Harrison pretended he was still under the influence of the drugs he'd been given. He lay still as long as he could. One of his captors kicked him hard in the side. "Wake up Mr. Harrison. You'd better eat something. We are moving you out today, and it may be a very long time before you have the chance to eat again." The man had an accent, but his English was good. Harrison continued to play possum. He was afraid to open his eyes to see what the man looked like, but Harrison was almost certain, from the sound of the man's voice, that he was one of the people who had abducted him and driven him to the warehouse.

CHAPTER 32

C*ameron was having a crisis of conscience within* his own mind. On the one hand he thought the most sensible thing to do was to immediately call the authorities and have them try to rescue Harrison from the warehouse. He felt it was impossible and foolhardy for a bunch of elderly amateurs to try to save Harrison on their own. A SWAT team of FBI agents was needed, not a geriatric assembly of do-gooders. He hadn't asked Bailey and J.D. if they had changed their minds about calling in the cops, but he suspected, after they'd seen what they were up against, with Harrison chained to the floor, they would have to agree that they were way out of their league. It was time to call in the professionals.

They would never have to mention the first kidnapping or the first rescue. The important thing was to free Harrison Davis. Capturing the Chinese kidnappers had never been on their agenda. Cameron knew that the people who were in power in Washington would ultimately trade the Chinese agents for some people the United States wanted in return. Or the U.S. would just give the people back to China without any kind of exchange. Once politicians became involved in anything, things went downhill quickly.

They had decisions to make, and they needed to make them tonight. If they were going to call the FBI, they would have to spend a considerable amount of time explaining to the feds what was going on. Would the FBI believe a bunch of old codgers? Cameron had some connections he could call on, and so did the others in the group. But the reality was that the FBI didn't put together a SWAT team on the spur of the moment and storm onto private property in the middle of the night because a group of vacationing friends said a man had been kidnapped. Cameron was genuinely worried that the FBI would dismiss them as a bunch of kooks or file their report about Harrison Davis in the senility file.

Everyone else had gone to bed. When Cameron had called needing a ride, Tyler had been asleep, and now he was heading to his room again. It had been an exhausting day for everyone. Tyler thought they should call the FBI, but no one was listening to him. He was going back to sleep.

Cameron knew he wouldn't be able to go to sleep. He put in a call to a friend of his at the FBI. The call went to voice mail. The man had shut off his cell phone. Of course he had. It was the middle of the night. Sensible people were in bed, asleep. After Cameron had left a message for his FBI contact to call him, he thought back over everything Rosemary Davis had said about the leaks at the FBI. She and Harrison had not wanted law enforcement to become involved because they'd not wanted the press to become involved.

As Cameron began to think through all the things that would have to happen for the FBI to do something to rescue Harrison Davis, he became more and more discouraged that law enforcement would be able to respond quickly. There was no time to waste, no matter who tried to rescue Harrison. By the time Cameron fell asleep, sitting in his chair with his phone in his lap, he had decided they were going to have to do this on their own. He had begun to make a list of things they would need. They would have to be at Home Depot when it opened in the morning. However feeble their amateur attempts might be and even though Harrison was chained to the floor, maybe it would be possible to rescue one man.

Unfortunately Bailey was now sidelined, along with Richard. Two of the intrepid force from Camp Shoemaker were injured and out of the fight. Bailey would be furious to have to sit this one out. When they arrived back at the Albergo, Bailey wouldn't allow J.D. or Cameron to wake up Matthew Ritter to look at his ankle. Bailey promised to put ice on it tonight, but he was so tired, that wouldn't last long. Bailey would be asleep before the ice melted, and the ice would melt long before it did much good for his swollen ankle. Matthew Ritter would see to Bailey's ankle and wrap it in the morning. Cameron and J.D. would go to Home Depot.

It seemed as if he had just dropped off to sleep when Cameron heard someone knocking quietly at the door. He left the safety chain on as he opened the door and looked into the hall. It was J.D. who'd come knocking. It was 5:00 in the morning.

"What in the world are you doing here at this hour of the morning? We need our sleep." Cameron wanted to know.

"I think we need to move fast and try to get Harrison out of that warehouse. I couldn't sleep." J.D. had been awake all night thinking. "After we came back last night, I was all for calling the FBI or the state police or somebody to go in there with guns blasting and rescue our guy. But the more I thought about it, the more I realized they're not going to believe us. And because they are not going to believe us, it will take days for us to explain to them why Harrison Davis is important and convince somebody that he's in danger. Even then, will law enforcement be willing to take action? Maybe. By the time all that BS has transpired, Harrison Davis will be long gone. He will either he dead or on his way to China or someplace else far away from here."

"Yeah, I went through the same thought process and also decided we wouldn't be able to explain it to the authorities in time for them to do anything about it. On TV, the SWAT team goes right in. In real life, they plan these things for days and weeks in advance. The FBI are the ultimate planners. Nobody at the FBI is going to believe us anyway." Cameron didn't have much hope the FBI would move quickly enough.

"I also had an epiphany. I tried to put myself inside the heads of these Chinese guys. That was not easy, let me tell you. I'm not a racist, but they are inscrutable to me." J.D. was a logistics expert. If you were in the trucking business, you had to be. He knew how to move things and get his people where they needed to go. "I was in the U.S. Air Force, but, as you know, I also have a real interest in boats and ships and watercraft of all kinds. That first day when we were out on the coast, in the Cayucos Beach area where we had the picnic, I noticed something odd. I had my super-duper high tech, I-can-see-anything-with-these, binoculars with me. I was looking at everything. When I was looking out over the water, I thought I saw something a long way off the coast that didn't look right to me. I know what most U.S. military ships and submarines look like. I keep up on what NATO ships look like. I even subscribe to a magazine that keeps me informed about these things. Can you believe it? Anyway, I thought I saw a submarine way off the coast that wasn't a U.S. sub and wasn't a NATO sub. It was a peculiar shape. I wondered what in the world it was doing inside U.S. territorial waters. All of a sudden, it was gone. I couldn't find it again. I decided it was most likely some new craft they were testing at Morro Bay. That's very close to here. I also wondered if it could be one of those mini-subs that Mexican drug cartels are using to get their drugs into the United States. Supposedly, that's one of the latest ways to smuggle drugs into the country."

"What does this have to do with our Harrison Davis problem?" Cameron was questioning how this was relevant.

"I think those Chinese thugs who kidnapped Harrison Davis are planning to put him on a submarine and take him to China or someplace else to torture and then kill him. I think that weird, ugly thing I saw in the water earlier this week was some kind of Chinese submarine. I think that's how they are going to move him out of the country. I think it's waiting off the Pacific Coast to transport him."

"It could be, but that's a pretty far out theory, J.D. You aren't even really sure you saw a Chinese submarine, are you?" Cameron was asking.

"How else can they get him out of the country? They can't fly him out or drive him to China. The longer they keep him in that warehouse or anywhere in the U.S., the more likely they are to be caught." J.D. knew more than he wanted to admit.

"I don't think these Chinese guys who have Harrison Davis are very good at what they do. This whole thing has been pretty amateurish. The way they broke into the Davis's room here, the set-up in the rusty warehouse... all of that is really bush league." J.D. had not been impressed with the Chinese bad boys who were running the operation or with the operation's planning.

"The Chinese have lots of upscale spies and secret agents of various kinds here in the U.S. But those guys are academics and into industrial espionage and things like cybercrime.

They're white collar types. They work for United States Congressmen and sit in offices in suits. Some of them are very high end prostitutes and go out on dates with those Congressmen. But it isn't easy to hide Chinese thugs. People in Chinatown don't want anything to do with them. Most Chinese people who live in the United States don't want anything to do with Communist China or their spies. Our American Chinese people are smart and law-abiding and hard-working. They own businesses. They are doctors and lawyers. Their kids get good grades in school and go to good colleges. They are responsible and patriotic citizens of the United States. They are the best of us. Many of them left China to get away from the repressive and criminal Communists in Beijing." J.D. had given this a great deal of thought.

J.D. continued. "I think those Russians who kidnapped Harrison the first time were hired by the Chinese. Russians look more like Americans. They can hide themselves pretty easily here without attracting attention. The Chinese didn't want their fingerprints on the abduction of Harrison Davis, so they hired the Russian Mafia to do it for them. Those two guys in the van probably had no idea who was paying them to kidnap Davis. But that didn't work out, so the Chinese had to go to plan B. They have this submarine, lurking off the Pacific Coast, waiting to transport Harrison Davis. Their first kidnapping plan fell apart when the Russian guys died in the car crash. Now they are scrambling to put together another way to get Harrison out of the country. That's just my opinion."

The only thing J.D. hadn't shared with Cameron was about the phone call he'd made earlier that night to a good friend who worked at the Pentagon. That good friend had reluctantly told J.D. there was in fact a Chinese submarine sitting off the coast of California, close to Morro Bay. He assured J.D. that the U.S. military was very aware that it was there and were keeping a close eye on it. They did not know why it was there, but it had been in the area for more than a week. Of course, the phone call to his friend who worked at the Pentagon had never taken place, and no one had ever told J.D. anything about any Chinese submarine.

"Okay. Let's assume you're right. What does this have to do with us? We can't fight the Chinese navy. What do you suggest we do?" Cameron agreed with J.D. but didn't have a plan.

"Of course we can't fight the Chinese navy. We have to get Harrison before he's taken to the submarine. Once he makes it there, we will have failed. We may already have failed. It may already be too late. Maybe saving Rosemary Davis is all we will be able to do. I am still thinking this through myself." J.D. didn't really have a plan yet either.

The urgency of the situation grew even as J.D. speculated about what he thought would happen. "We have to get Davis out of that warehouse this morning. If I were the Chinese, I would want to move him as quickly as possible. The Chinese submarine can't just pull into Morro Bay or some other marina and pick up Harrison Davis. These incompetents have to have a way to get him from the California coast out to sea and then get him onto the submarine. The best way to do this, if it were my operation, would be to use an inflatable water craft with a very high-powered motor. Something like a Zodiac, something like the U.S. Navy Seals use. It's something they can do at night. They bring the thing up onto the beach anywhere, any beach, put Harrison on board, and sneak back out into the Pacific to deliver him to the submarine. They let the air out of the inflatable and either sink it or stow it on the sub. They are gone, and no one saw a thing. easy-peasy."

"If we are going to save this guy, we have to get him today, don't we?" Cameron concurred with J.D.'s analysis.

"We do. And I am so tired, and we don't have enough people to bring this off." J.D. was discouraged.

"I say we try to do it anyway. If we could just get Tyler off the law-enforcement horse he's riding, he could be a big help. Richard and now Bailey are out due to injuries. Matthew might come with us, but he leans more to calling the cops, too. It might turn out to be just you and me." Cameron had made his decision. "We could enlist the women. They can all drive, and Lilleth is very athletic. I know, I know. We are all old. Our bones break easily, and we can't move as fast as we used to be able to move. But we have brainpower. That puts us way ahead of those Communist idiots."

"Olivia woke up because I couldn't sleep and was pacing the floor. I think she found a better way to get to that warehouse in the woods. We suspected there was a road that the thugs were taking. We were following the red dot on your phone when we took that crap car off-road. Turns out there's a dirt road, but it isn't on any printed map or in the road atlas. Olivia has skills. She found a couple of classified satellite photographs of the area. They are very detailed. I've copied them onto my phone. I will be able to find the dirt road that goes to the warehouse. We need to get moving now. We have to beat these guys to the warehouse, or we will have lost our chance."

Cameron was beginning to form a plan. "I've made a list of things we need. It's not long, but we can't get into the warehouse without metal shears. And we can't cut Davis loose without something to cut the chain that's got him attached to the floor. Remember, Bailey said he was chained to the floor. We need to go to Home Depot."

"We don't have time to go to Home Depot. Even if it opens really early, it won't be early enough for us. There's a shed behind the swimming pool that has a bunch of tools in it. I was scouting around the other day and came across it. It is mostly gardening and landscaping equipment, but I will bet we can "borrow" the things we need from there." J.D. was a scout. He always knew where to find things, no matter what it was you might be looking for.

"We borrowed motorcycles and a motor scooter to rescue Harrison Davis the first time. I guess, if we are sure to return the tools, we can borrow them from the Albergo." Cameron would be sure they returned whatever they borrowed.

It was still dark outside when Cameron and J.D. found their way to the landscaping shed behind the Albergo's pool. J.D. had brought his lock picks with him, so they made quick work of the locks on the door. They found some cutting tools they thought would help them get into the warehouse in the woods and break Harrison Davis free of his chains. Both Cameron and J.D. knew a lot about tools. They locked the door behind them and hoped no one would be looking for the metal shears or the bolt cutters this morning.

CHAPTER 33

The sky was just beginning to show some daylight as they sped along Highway 46. They were going way over the speed limit in the Ritter's Mercedes, but they figured the local cops didn't have their radar traps set up yet. It was Sunday morning after all. The dirt road that would allow them to drive almost all the way to the warehouse in the woods turned off Highway 1. If they'd not had Olivia's Google Maps satellite photos, they would never have found it. They made the turn off, and then they drove and drove. They began to wonder if they'd made a mistake and taken a wrong road. Finally, they saw the warehouse up ahead. They needed to hide their vehicle, but they wanted it to be close by. They didn't know what condition Harrison would be in when they freed him, and they anticipated that they might have to carry him to the car.

Cameron had the bolt cutters, and J.D. had the metal shears. They could have used two sets of metal shears, but there had been only one in the Albergo's shed. They'd decided to cut their way into the warehouse on the end of the building opposite the double doors where the Chinese guards had a lock. It was slow going. Even though the metal was rusted, it was corrugated. The warehouse had been made of sturdy material when it was constructed decades earlier. When J.D.'s arms were tired cutting, Cameron took a turn.

Finally, they had made an opening they thought they could crawl through. They pushed aside the metal flap they'd cut, and J.D. got down on his belly. He made it through the hole and found himself in a bathroom. He didn't see her at first. He was guiding Cameron through the opening and telling him to be careful of the jagged edges they'd made with their rough cutting job. J.D. heard the shower curtain rustle and looked at the ancient bath tub. It was chipped and cracked and filthy. He pushed aside the shower curtain, and there she lay in the bottom of the blackened, dirt-encrusted porcelain, cowering and terrified. The creature whose head rose up out of the bathtub did not look like a human being. Her hair was black and flew in all directions. Her eyes were wide. She was so small and so emaciated, she looked as if she were a survivor from a Nazi concentration camp. She was a specter. She was a living cadaver. J.D. reached out his hand to help her out of the bathtub.

"Who are you?" he demanded.

"Who are you?" Came the reply in accented English.

"We're not going to hurt you." By this time Cameron had made it all the way into the bathroom and was also staring at the woman.

"I am Sui Wai. I am a prisoner here. I was a scientist who worked in Hong Kong. I came to the United States to be a whistleblower. Are you here for Harrison? He is my friend. We are on the same side."

Sui Wai was anxious to establish that she was not one of the kidnappers, that she herself was a victim. One glance at the woman made it quite obvious that she was somebody's victim. Cameron and J.D. were shocked to find Sui Wai in the warehouse bathroom. They were expecting to find Harrison Davis in the warehouse, but they'd had no idea there was anyone else being held hostage in this place.

They were trying to move fast. "Are you locked in the bathroom? I mean do we have to break down the door to get out?"

"I have tried to break out, but I have no strength left. I have been kept here for many weeks."

"Is Harrison still here? We have come to rescue him. We will save you, too."

"The men just arrived while you were cutting a hole to get into the bathroom. They are taking Harrison away now. You must move quickly. They will be coming for me next. They are going to put us on a submarine and take us to China. They will torture us, and then they will kill us. I have already been tortured. You must go back out the way you came, at once. They have guns. They would think nothing of shooting both of you. I am going to crawl out through the opening you have made. You must leave now with me. I know what I am talking about. You cannot be found here. They will be angry enough when they find me gone."

Sui Wai spoke so earnestly, Cameron and J.D. had to believe what she was saying. They could hear people in the warehouse, outside the bathroom, speaking what sounded like Chinese.

They'd had a plan, and now that plan had to be discarded. They had to make a decision about whether they would leave the warehouse. Sui Wai was already gone. They made the split-second decision to follow her. Cameron was down on all fours, crawling out of the building back into the woods. Sui Wai had crawled away from the opening in the wall, but she realized she was not able to stand up. She had grown so weak during her captivity, she no longer had the strength to stand on her own. J.D. crawled out of the warehouse. He picked up Sui Wai and carried her to the Mercedes. Cameron picked up the metal shears and the bolt cutters.

The kidnappers' car was blocking the road. They would have to take the Mercedes through the trees to get back to the road to drive to Highway 1. The Mercedes was well-hidden, but they wanted to be in a position to be able to follow the kidnappers' Subaru when the Chinese men drove Harrison away.

"What are you waiting for? Drive away now. We must leave immediately. Please hurry." Sui Wai was insistent.

"We want to follow the car when it leaves. We are going to do everything we can to save Harrison, too, but we don't know where they're taking him. And we don't know how much time we have.

"Please, leave now. I know everything. I will tell you. You must get out of here. I will tell you where to go and when you have to be there to save Harrison. The men will be angry and confused when they find I am gone. They will spend some time looking for me and discussing what to do next. They will make some phone calls. But I know what their plans are. I heard them discussing it… both last night and this morning just before you two showed up in the bathroom. They speak in Chinese, so Harrison has no idea what they are saying. But I am Chinese, so, of course, I understand their every word."

"Are you sure you know where they're taking him and what the timetable is?"

"Yes, I am sure. Leave now before they come outside to get in their car."

Cameron started the Mercedes, maneuvered his way around the Subaru, and sped away from the warehouse as fast as they could drive on the dirt road. As they headed for Highway 1, Sui Wai told them about the conversations she had overheard in the warehouse. "Their plan was to take both of us to a submarine that is waiting off the coast. The rendezvous with the Zodiac raft is scheduled for 9:00 this morning. They wanted to do it at night, but these men don't know the area very well. They were afraid they would not be able to find the right place on the beach at night, the place for the meeting."

"The meeting is not until 9:00? That's more than an hour from now. Why were they planning to get you out of the warehouse so far ahead of the time of the rendezvous?" J.D. wanted details.

"I don't know the answer to that, but I suspect they are worried they will not be able to find the place to meet the Zodiac on the beach. They want to allow plenty of time. I know where the rendezvous is supposed to be. It is in a very remote location, and you have to drive off the road to get there. The Subaru has front-wheel drive, and they think they can drive it on the sand. I heard them discussing all of these things." Sui Wai was certain of her information.

"The meeting place is 3.1 miles south of Cambria. There is a very rugged stretch of beach there with rocks in the water and rough waves. No one ever swims or walks their dogs there. It is inconvenient to get there, and it is not pleasant to walk along the beach in that spot. There is a tricky current and rogue waves that come up on the beach. They say the Zodiac will be able to manage the difficult approach."

J.D. was in the passenger seat, and he was madly sending texts.

Sui Wai continued. "They have said that there is not a good place to hide their car close to the meeting place, so they will have to park the car and walk with Harrison Davis to the beach. They have GPS to tell them exactly where to wait for the Zodiac. They say there will not be any other people around. There are three of them, three Chinese. Two are going on the Zodiac. One was going to handle Harrison and one was going to handle me. The third man is an agent in place here in California. He works for someone in the California state government, someone very important and powerful. He doesn't usually do this kind of work, that is, kidnapping and guarding people. This Chinese agent works in cybersecurity in some financial division of the government. He lives here with his family in California. He is not going back to China with the others. He will return the rental car after the Zodiac has left the beach to deliver the hostages to the submarine. Of course, now there is only one hostage. They will be infuriated by that. They will have to know, when they see the hole that has been cut in the wall, that I had help in my escape. They will be on even higher alert, if they think I have someone helping me. You have thrown a monkey into their plans. Bless you for saving me. Thanks be to that monkey."

"You mean a monkey wrench?"

"Yes, the wrenchy monkey." Sui Wai had pushed herself to convey all of this information to the two men who had rescued her. She wanted them to know everything she knew so they could rescue Harrison Davis. "They have weapons. Automatic weapons. And they are not afraid to use them. They will kill both of you if they have the chance." Sui Wai was at the point of collapse. She had been on the verge of crumbling for days. At last she'd told Cameron and J.D. everything she knew, and she had used up all of her energy. She was fading fast now.

"Sui Wai, listen to me. Before we try to make that rendezvous at 9:00, I have arranged for someone to meet us to drive you to the hospital. You are in desperate need of medical care. You have been starved and tortured. I am afraid we might lose you yet because of your medical condition." J.D. insisted.

Fear sparked in Sui Wai's eyes. "You cannot take me to the hospital under any circumstances. I would rather die than be taken by the Chinese again. I will throw myself out of this car right now while it is moving if you threaten to take me anywhere near a hospital." Sui Wai was ready to open the back door and jump out onto the road.

"Hold on there now. Don't do anything rash. If that's the way you want it, we promise not to take you to the hospital. But you need medical care." J.D. understood that during the COVID epidemic, no one wanted to go near a hospital for fear of catching the disease, but he was shocked once again that this woman was terrified of being taken to a hospital because she was certain it would lead to her being kidnapped again.

"I will be fine. I have someone in Ojai, California who will come for me and take care of me."

"Ojai is more than two hours from here. By the time you locate this person and they arrange to drive to Cambria, I'm afraid you will have lapsed into unconsciousness. You are almost that far gone now although you may not realize it."

Her voice had grown weaker and weaker. She was giving up the fight. "If you promise you will not take me to the hospital, I will do whatever you say." Sui Wai lay down on the back seat, completely spent.

J.D. told Cameron what was going on with his plan. "I texted Elizabeth. She is driving her car to meet us. Richard still can't drive. If Elizabeth can locate Sidney right away, she's going to bring Sidney with her to help with Sui Wai. Elizabeth has visited Paso Robles several times. She knows her way around the area. She knows her way to the hospital. She was going to drive straight to the emergency room with Sui Wai, but I just let her know the plan is going to have to change. I told her where to meet us. She said she would be there in thirty minutes. That will still give us time to make the rendezvous on the beach. Sui Wai really needs to go to the hospital, but Elizabeth can drive her back to the Albergo.

Matthew and Richard can take care of Sui Wai there. They've taken care of someone in a hotel room before. I think Sui Wai is dehydrated and needs rest and some food. I think our two docs can manage whatever is necessary to save her. They can talk her into going to the hospital."

"I don't want to take her anywhere near that rendezvous, and I was frantic about what in the world we were going to do with her. Why did you contact Elizabeth? Why not Olivia?"

"I didn't want a huge motor home anywhere near where we are. Those waves painted on the side... are you kidding me? It's impossible to try to make that thing inconspicuous. The Carpenter's SUV is big and obvious enough. And I've got another assignment for Oliva and Tyler. Tyler is on board, but I can't reach Olivia. I've left her a message to call me back. She's probably mad at me because I won't tell her anything and because I keep running off with you and having adventures. She feels left out. She will call me back in a few minutes. She always does, even when she's angry with me. And I have something important lined up for Tyler and Olivia to do. She's going to drive him to the coast in the motor home. It won't be as out of place at the marina where they're going.

CHAPTER 34

E*lizabeth arrived in her elderly Ford Expedition* right on schedule. Cameron and J.D. had arranged to meet her on Highway 46 near an old barn they'd driven past every time they'd made a trip to the coast. Elizabeth knew it well, and the men in the Mercedes were already parked there. There was a dirt driveway where both cars could pull off the road and make the exchange. Elizabeth unlocked her car, and J.D. was lifting Sui Wai out of the back seat of the Mercedes. The scientist was even less able to walk now than she had been when they'd left the warehouse. She was fading, and Elizabeth didn't think she was conscious any longer.

Suddenly, out from behind the barn, a woman riding a horse and dressed in a cowboy hat and blue jeans appeared holding a shotgun. She had it pointed at J.D., and she meant business.

"Put her down now. If you think you're going to use my property for your human trafficking schemes, you can think again. I would just as soon blow your nuts off as look at you. You are trespassing on my property. You will lay the woman on the ground and leave now. I have the license plate of your fancy car, and I will be calling Sheriff Hernandez to tell him to come and get you. This woman is in very bad shape, you scum bag. How dare you come to my ranch and think you can get away with this." J.D. lay Sui Wai down on the ground and walked away. The stubble in the field was still wet with morning dew. He hated to leave Sui Wai to the elements, but he didn't want to be shot. He raised his hands in the air and stumbled backwards towards the car where Cameron was sitting in the driver's seat.

When Elizabeth had seen the woman on horseback riding towards the cars, she knew there was something familiar about her. But the woman in the cowboy hat was too far away for Elizabeth to see her face. As the woman galloped closer and began to shout at J.D., Elizabeth realized who the woman was. She was even wearing the concho belt she'd worn in the restaurant. Elizabeth couldn't hear what the woman was screaming at J.D., but she knew that shotgun was definitely loaded. Elizabeth rolled down her window.

"Hey there. I recognize you from La Buona Ricetta. You go there with your family, and you sit at the big round table. I've seen you several times. Don't shoot him. I can explain all of this. It's not what it looks like it is. We are trying to save this woman, not harm her."

The woman did not put down the gun. She rode her black beauty up to the driver's side window of the Expedition. "And who the hell are you?" The horse's nose was almost inside the car, as Elizabeth tried to quickly explain to this cowgirl about what was in fact a very complicated situation.

"I'm staying at the Albergo in Paso Robles with a group of friends. We had dinner the other night at La Buona Ricetta, and you were also there, dining with your family. Please let me explain what's going on here." The woman on the horse never lowered her gun during the explanation Elizabeth gave her about why they were on her property, and why the emaciated young woman who was lying on the ground in the pasture was unable to stand up. Elizabeth understood how the scene must look to this woman, and it was definitely true that they were trespassing on her ranch. J.D. stood wide-eyed next to the Mercedes, afraid to move. Elizabeth was eloquent, gracious, and apologetic. She introduced herself and asked the cowgirl for her help.

Cameron was getting nervous behind the wheel of the Mercedes. He was afraid they were going to be late for the rendezvous with the Zodiac.

"My friends have to leave now. Please don't call the sheriff. I will explain everything. I need your help. This woman needs medical care immediately. Can you get her into the car?" Elizabeth waved J.D. and Cameron on their way. She knew they had some kind of a deadline although she was not clear on the details. It didn't matter. What mattered was that the woman from the restaurant hadn't shot any of them, and it looked like she was going to participate in the effort to save Sui Wai.

The cowboy hat, the wide blue jeans, and the concho belt got down from the horse and stuck her hand in the driver's side window of Elizabeth's SUV. "I'm Henley Breckenridge. This is my ranch. I remember your group from the restaurant. Sorry I scared the shit out of your friend. Let's get this poor thing into your car. You can follow me up to the house. I'm a vet, and I mostly take care of horses and dogs. But I've saved the life of more than one human being. You can trust me to take care of her. I don't know why you didn't take her to the hospital, but I am assuming you have a good reason. I know you are going to tell me all about what that reason is."

Elizabeth shook Henley's hand. "I'm Elizabeth Carpenter. Do you have someone who can help you get her into the car? I'm disabled and use a cane. I'm afraid I can't be any help to you."

"Sure thing. Hang on a minute. I've got help." Henley took her cell phone out of the pocket of her jeans and punched some buttons. "Help will be here in a jiffy."

Elizabeth couldn't remember the last time she'd heard anyone use the word "jiffy." She liked this woman. Sure enough, two young men appeared in minutes and gently lifted Sui Wai into the back seat of the Expedition.

"You can drive to the house. Follow me. Just go slow."

Elizabeth didn't really understand completely who Sui Wai was or where she had come from or how exactly she fit into the scenario of trying to save Harrison Davis. J.D.'s text had been brief and urgent and cryptic. Elizabeth drove her car slowly and followed Henley Breckenridge through some fields and a stand of pine trees. A sprawling white stucco building with a red tile roof was up ahead. Elizabeth was approaching it from the rear, but even the back side of the hacienda was beautiful. She realized the Spanish style house was one of several buildings in this housing compound. All the buildings were white stucco with red roofs.

Henley Breckenridge directed Elizabeth where to bring her car. The two young men reappeared and carefully transferred Sui Wai from the Expedition into the house. Henley told them where to carry her patient. Elizabeth wanted to see the inside of this elegant ranch house, so she struggled to get herself and her cane out of the SUV. Henley led her into an enormous kitchen, through a dining room that held an antique wooden table that would seat at least twenty people, through a large front hall, and into a lounge where a fire was burning in the carved stone fireplace. The warmth was welcome on this cool and foggy late September morning. Henley pointed to a chair, indicating that Elizabeth should sit.

"Let me get things started for this woman you've brought to me. Carmen will bring you some coffee in a minute. Carmen helps in the kitchen. It's only 9:00 in the morning, and already my day has gone completely haywire."

The room had beautiful antique furnishings and colorful rugs over the tile floors. The furniture and the rugs looked as if they had been there forever. Henley Breckenridge didn't look like the interior decorating type, so Elizabeth was betting that this room hadn't changed much in the past half-century. A young woman, Carmen no doubt, arrived carrying a large silver tray which she put down on the low upholstered bench in front of Elizabeth. In addition to the silver coffee service, there were cups and saucers, silver spoons, cloth napkins, and a plate of pastries on the tray. "Please serve yourself, Ma'am." Carmen left Elizabeth to enjoy her coffee in front of the fire. Elizabeth had not expected this elegant hospitality, let alone a silver coffee service. She heard Henley giving directions from another part of the house. The woman's voice boomed.

"Call Maria over here to help you. You need to get this woman cleaned up, but it will take two of you. Be very gentle. She's been beaten and tortured. She has many bruises on her torso and on her limbs. Try not to inflict any more pain on her than she's already endured. She hasn't bathed in weeks. The dirt in her hair and on her skin have been on there a long time. Poor thing. I can't begin to figure out what's wrong with her until I can see her skin under all that dirt." There were more noises. Henley's voice boomed again. "No, don't cut her hair yet. If she has head injuries that need stitches, we may have to cut some of her hair then. When she is all cleaned up, put her in the guest room behind the garage. She will be on the first floor and easy to get to, but she will be able to rest. Anyplace else in this chaotic household is too noisy. She doesn't need to hear us shouting and something going on all the time. She needs to heal. And she needs to eat. Tell Margarita to bring some of her chicken broth, the non-spicy kind. This woman has almost starved to death."

Henley came into the lounge and served herself a cup of coffee. She popped two pastries into her mouth and wiped her hands on her jeans. "You said you would tell me all about it. So start talking. I can see she's been starved and beaten. She has cigarette burns on her back. What the heck is going on here? She looks like a victim of human trafficking, but you have told me she is a scientist who wants to be a whistleblower. Talk to me Elizabeth Carpenter."

Elizabeth could see that Henley Breckenridge was not only smart, she was well-educated, in spite of her rough-and-ready cowgirl persona. Elizabeth proceeded to tell her everything she knew about Harrison and Rosemary Davis. She told Henley about Harrison's scientific discoveries, about how the Davises refused to involve any official law enforcement people in their situation, about Harrison's two kidnappings, and about their antipathy towards going to a hospital ER. She told Henley what little she knew about Sui Wai. She also told Henley what she didn't know. She suggested Henley get Sui Wai's story from the woman herself. Elizabeth had only become aware that Sui Wai even existed this morning through a text from J.D. Steele. Henley was obviously captivated by the complicated story Elizabeth had to tell. Elizabeth speculated that it took a pretty outlandish tale to capture Henley's interest.

"She keeps muttering something about Ojai and White Fox Farm. That must be her home. As she recovers her strength and becomes more coherent, I will be guided by her wishes about what to do with her. It sounds as if you and your friends have way too much going on right now. Leave this sad soul to me. I will be sure she recovers and is healthy again before I send her where she wants to go. If she is talking about Ojai,

California, that's just about a three-hour drive from here. She will recover, and she will be all right. I worry about her heart a little bit. Some people who have been tortured... I have a cardiologist friend who can check her out, under the radar of course. I think I understand why she doesn't want anybody to know where she is."

Elizabeth stood to leave. She thanked Henley and gave her a card with her cell phone number on it. "You might need to get in touch with me. I know that Sui Wai will want to know if we are able to save Harrison Davis. I'll let you know what happens today." Henley wrote her own cell phone number and her email on a piece of paper towel she had in her pocket. She handed it to Elizabeth. Elizabeth left to drive back to the Albergo. She felt Sui Wai was in good hands and would receive good care. Elizabeth was now anxious to hear the news from the coast.

CHAPTER 35

Cameron and J.D. were running behind schedule, but they managed to find a place to hide the Ritters' car. They had a plan, but it was ad hoc and last-minute, sketchy to say the least. Because they had no real weapons, the two didn't think they could take Harrison away from his guards while he was on the beach. They knew the Chinese thugs would have automatic weapons. Cameron knew little about guns; J.D. was an expert. But they'd not had time to buy weapons of any kind, not even a sharp knife. J.D. always carried a pocket knife, but that wasn't going to get them very far with this crowd.

J.D. had been on his phone with Oliva and Tyler, trying to coordinate a boat rental. J.D. loved boats, and he had several. When he'd heard from Sui Wai that the hostage plan was to take her and Harrison Davis from the beach in a Zodiac and rendezvous with a Chinese submarine that was waiting off-shore in the Pacific Ocean, J.D.'s brain had leapt into overdrive. He knew they could not hope to confront three men with automatic weapons and secure Harrison Davis's release on land. But he knew what his boats could do, and he knew that one of his boats had the speed and agility to accomplish what he wanted to accomplish. He knew his super-duper cigarette boat could outrun any inflatable watercraft. But that perfect and amazing boat was thousands of miles away at his lake house in Missouri. His only hope was to find a similar boat to rent, borrow, or steal in the immediate area.

J.D. wasn't able to locate a boat at a local marina that was identical to the model he owned. But he thought he had found a boat that was similar and just as fast. The one he'd found to rent might even be a little bit faster. A boat that had to perform well in the ocean would be somewhat different from one which performed well in a lake. J.D. was juggling all these things in his mind at the same time he was having a conversation on his cell phone with Tyler and texting with Olivia.

One problem was, with these very fast boats, the companies that rented them out wanted to send along "a captain" to pilot the boat. That was the last thing J.D. needed for the Harrison Davis rescue scenario. He did not want "a captain" anywhere near what he had planned for the go-fast boat he intended to rent. J.D. was a former lawyer and a slick talker. He had a way about him that was able to convince people they wanted to go along with what he wanted. With a few hundred dollars added to sweeten the pot, J.D. was able to find a boat owner that was willing to send their rental without a captain. J.D. gave his credit card number over the phone. It was a deal.

J.D. was in the process of texting his instructions to Tyler and Olivia who were already speeding down Highway 46 in the motor home. Lilleth had insisted on accompanying them. She was an outstanding athlete, and she was younger than the others in the reunion group. She also knew how to operate a fast boat, maybe better than Tyler did. She wanted to help. All three were on their way to the Agua Azul Marina to look over the boat rental and take it out on the water. Time was short, and they had to have the boat in just the right place at just the right time for all of this to work as planned.

The only motor vehicle they'd had immediately available to them to drive from Paso Robles to the Pacific Coast was the gigantic motor home J.D. and Olivia had leased to drive to The Circle Bar Q Dude Ranch. It was not inconspicuous, but many people who came to the Agua Azul Marina arrived in motor homes. The huge motor home would not be out of place in the marina's parking lot as they rushed to finalize the paperwork on the very fast speedboat and take possession of their rental.

J.D. had texted them the exact position of the rendezvous on the beach, the spot where Sui Wai had said the Zodiac was to come ashore to pick up Harrison Davis. J.D. told Tyler to keep the speedboat hidden until the last minute, if possible. But it was important that those who were in the go-fast boat be able to see what was happening on the beach. There would only be one chance to intercept the Zodiac. They could not be late. The timing had to be exactly right. Tyler and Lilleth would have to watch as the inflatable watercraft picked up Harrison. They would have to go after him as soon as he was on his way to the submarine.

J.D. loved his fast boat and used it all the time at his lake house. He was beside himself that he would not be driving a similar fast boat during this rescue operation. Nobody could drive his boat and make it perform quite the way he could. But there was no way he would be able to get aboard the rented boat. He had to trust Tyler, Lilleth, and Oliva to do what he told them to do. He didn't want Olivia on the boat. J.D. wanted her to stay with the motor home, so he was delighted when Lilleth said she wanted to accompany Tyler. If their goofy, crazy, half-baked plan worked, it would take two strong people to lift Harrison Davis out of the ocean water into the speedboat. Olivia wanted to participate, but she was not crazy about the very fast racing J.D. liked to do. Olivia was more of a cocktail party on a pontoon boat kind of a person.

J.D. realized it would be a downright miracle if his plan came together. Timing was everything, and he felt acutely that he did not have control over the situation. He could trust others, but he mostly liked to do it all himself. Olivia finally had texted him to stop sending them directions. She told him they had the boat, and Tyler and Lilleth were already on their way to the spot where J.D. had told them to wait. Everybody knew what they were supposed to do and when they were supposed to do it.

If they were able to rescue Harrison, their plan was to immediately return the boat to the marina. If Harrison was able to walk on his own, they would get him inside the motor home as quickly as possible. From the moment he climbed out of the boat and onto the pier, he would be visible and vulnerable. If he was able to walk, he would have to walk a considerable distance to reach the safety of the motor home which was in the marina's parking lot. If he'd been beaten or tortured and wasn't able to walk on his own, Tyler and Lilleth would have to carry him or somehow make sure he got into the motor home with as little exposure as possible.

Cameron's plane was waiting at the Paso Robles Municipal Airport. It was ready to leave at a moment's notice. Olivia was to send word to J.D. and Cameron to let them know if and when Harrison was inside the motor home. Cameron would notify his pilots that their passenger would be arriving in thirty minutes. Olivia would drive the motor home directly to the Paso Robles airport. During the long trip from Missouri to California, she had become accomplished at maneuvering the huge beast on the road and in parking lots.

Once he was inside the motor home, Harrison Davis would put on a disguise—a blonde wig and a red outfit that Bailey had insisted he wear. Bailey had pointed out that driving onto the tarmac at the airport with a huge motor home would not be an inconspicuous arrival or result in an inconspicuous boarding of the plane. Harrison had to be in disguise. If anyone was watching, they would report that a blonde woman in a red dress had exited the enormous motor home and boarded the private jet.

Olivia had covered the license plates of the motor home with mud, but the vehicle was so big, it was not going to fool anybody. The sides of the exterior were painted with large and colorful, red, black, and silver waves that could not be ignored. The plan was far from being perfect, but it was the best they could do at the last minute. Hopefully not that many people knew about Cameron's private jet, and maybe no one would be watching at the airport. By the time the plane had taken off, they hoped Harrison Davis's trail would go cold. They would all meet back at the Albergo late in the afternoon for cocktails and debriefing. Olivia could only hope and pray things would happen as they were supposed to happen. She knew they were all crazy to be doing what they were doing. And she was not going to miss a minute of it.

J.D. and Cameron had hidden the Mercedes. They had to walk quite a ways from where they'd left the car to the beach where they could watch what happened to Harrison Davis. There were not many places to conceal themselves in the brush and rocks near where the Zodiac was supposed to come ashore. They thought they'd found a pretty good spot where they would have sufficient cover. It wasn't much of a hiding place, but they would be able to see what happened at the water's edge.

There were three Chinese brutes holding onto Harrison Davis as they pushed him along toward the rocky beach. He stumbled often and looked terrible. His hands were bound together with plastic ties, and his legs were also secured so that he could only shuffle his feet forward with small steps. The three guards were all carrying automatic weapons. Cameron and J.D. were satisfied that it would have been impossible to rescue Harrison while he was on the land. They'd made the right call. It would have to be done on the water, but the guns could still cause a big problem. The kidnappers and Harrison had arrived at the beach on foot which meant they'd left the Subaru parked someplace.

Because there had not been many good places to hide in the scrubby brush, Cameron and J.D. grew nervous when the Chinese gunmen began to search the immediate area. The two dug down deeper into their hiding places. They knew Harrison's captives were on a timetable, and they'd hoped to be able to stay hidden until the Zodiac arrived to take the men out to sea. But their luck ran out.

One of the men with an AK-47 discovered them cowering in the sparse vegetation. He pointed his weapon at them and shouted to his companions. Soon all three Chinese men were standing around them with guns pointed. Neither Cameron nor J.D. understood a word of Chinese, so they could only imagine what these three were saying to each other. There seemed to be a difference of opinion about what should be done with them. Finally, one man ran in the opposite direction from the water. The two captured friends assumed he was going back to their car for something.

Sure enough, the man returned with plastic ties and secured Cameron and J.D. One of the men with a big gun pushed the two ahead of him over the rough ground to where the Subaru was parked. He forced the two into the back seat and tied their legs together and to each other. He locked the car door. J.D. and Cameron were not going to be able to walk away from this any time soon.

When the bad guys had left, Cameron managed to slip his phone out of his pocket, turn it off, and push it under the front seat. Seeing what Cameron had done, J.D. also turned off his phone and put it under the seat. The men with guns had been careless. They had not thought to take Cameron's and J.D.'s cell phones away from them.

Back on the beach, the kidnappers were checking their watches. The Zodiac was late. The three didn't think anyone would be using this stretch of beach this morning, but the longer they hung around, the more risks they were taking. Finally they saw the black rubber raft speeding towards them. They had coordinated it all through GPS, so everyone knew exactly where to be. It only took a few seconds to force Harrison Davis into the Zodiac and for two guards to climb in behind him. These two were going to the Chinese submarine with Harrison. The Zodiac immediately took off into the Pacific, heading for the rendezvous with the sub.

When the Zodiac had left the beach and gone about two hundred yards, a sleek red cigarette boat appeared, heading directly towards them. Two men on board the Zodiac still had their machine guns, but they'd been caught off-guard. The men had thought they were out of danger and on their way home. They had put their guns down in the bottom of the raft and were not expecting trouble.

The cigarette boat accelerated. The Zodiac accelerated. The high performance powerboat was going to win this one. It put on a burst of speed and struck the Zodiac from an angle heading sideways. The go-fast boat could have completely overrun the slower inflatable craft, but they didn't want to kill the man they were attempting to rescue. The big powerboat was made of much sturdier stuff, and it shredded the rubber side of the Zodiac. The speedboat slowed and accelerated and rammed the Zodiac again and again until it was left sinking into the Pacific. The faster boat did not seem to have sustained any damage from the repeated and intentional collisions with the Zodiac. The two Chinese guards in the Zodiac were thrown into the water. Harrison Davis had also been thrown into the water. The driver of the Zodiac was trying to keep the remnants of his watercraft intact and afloat, but it was looking more and more like a hopeless task. He, and what remained of the inflatable, were going down in the Pacific.

Tyler pulled the speedboat close to Harrison who was sinking. His arms and legs were bound. Tied up like Harrison was, even the best swimmer in the world would not have been able to save himself. Lilleth jumped into the cold Pacific Ocean. She dove down under the water to find Harrison and pulled him to the surface. She had him in a cross-chest carry and swam with him as fast as she could towards Tyler's waiting arms.

The speedboat had stopped and was idling in the water. Tyler pulled Harrison into the boat, while Lilleth pushed from below. Once Harrison was safely onboard, Lilleth climbed in. She was still holding onto the gunwales, ready to fall into the cigarette boat when Tyler pushed the watercraft forward at its top speed. Lilleth shouted that she'd almost ended up back in the water. But she hadn't. She scrambled to get herself the rest of the way into the boat as it raced toward the Agua Azul Marina.

Whatever was going to happen to the Zodiac and the men who'd been in it was none of their concern. Tyler had his pocket knife with him, and as they sped down the coast, Lilleth sawed away at Harrison's bonds. She finally freed his legs and began working on his hands. Tyler and Lilleth were back at the marina in less than five minutes, and they quickly pulled the rented boat into its slip. Harrison was weak and soaking wet. He was not able to walk steadily. Lilleth decided it was more important to get him quickly to the motor home than it was to finish getting his handcuffs off.

They lifted Harrison out of the speedboat and pretty much carried him down the pier. They received some odd looks, as it might have appeared to some boat owners who watched them hustle the handcuffed man along, that they were taking him someplace against his will. They hoped they could make it to the motor home before anyone decided to call the cops.

When they arrived with Harrison at the motor home, they'd expected Olivia to be overjoyed that they had been able to accomplish their almost impossible mission. But she was frantic with worry. She'd not been able to reach either J.D. or Cameron. They had both turned off their phones and weren't answering. Olivia was supposed to let them know immediately if Harrison had been successfully rescued so that Cameron could notify his flight crew. Harrison had been rescued, but Olivia was not able to reach anyone to let them know the good news. J.D. had promised to give her a blow by blow about what was happening with the Zodiac, but she'd heard nothing at all from her husband or from Cameron. What could have gone wrong? Where were they?

She knew it was important to leave the marina right away, so as soon as her passengers stumbled aboard, she pulled out of the marina parking lot. She had been supposed to head directly for the Paso Robles Municipal Airport, but that plan had depended on Cameron alerting his pilots. Now she had no idea where she should go.

She decided to drive to Harmony and pretend she was a tourist visiting the town and hoping to find the glassblowing exhibition. She was almost in Harmony anyway. She was anxious to get the motor home off the highway. She thought the motor home would be less conspicuous if it was parked near a tourist attraction. Other motor homes were bound to be parked there. She was frantic about J.D. He'd been taken hostage in Maine, two years earlier, and Olivia had made him promise he would never let that happen to him again. Now he was gone, again, and Olivia had no idea what had happened to him.

Olivia was torn. Did she drive Harrison to the airport in Paso Robles anyway, or did she try to find J.D.? Cameron's pilots were on standby, waiting to hear from him if there would be a flight leaving within the hour. Cameron couldn't know that Harrison had been successfully rescued, so he could not notify the pilots to be ready with the plane. Olivia's decision was made. She was going to try to find J.D.

Olivia explained to Tyler and Lilleth about not being able to contact J.D. or Cameron. Lilleth removed Harrison's handcuffs, tried to get him to drink some water, and helped him into his disguise. He'd objected briefly but was too weak to stand up to Lilleth's persuasive explanation about why he had to wear a woman's blond wig and all the rest of it. Lilleth insisted Harrison lie down on the couch in the motor home's living area. They'd brought along some protein bars, but Harrison Davis was in no condition to eat anything. They rode along in the motor home, feeling depressed and wondering what to do next. Olivia was able to find a parking lot where other motor homes were parked.

CHAPTER 36

W*hen Cameron had been tracking Harrison* Davis's flip phone in an effort to find out where he'd been taken, Tyler had been very curious about how it was possible to locate the cell phone. Cameron had used special software to find Harrison's flip phone. Tyler had watched carefully everything that Cameron did. He asked Cameron if he would share the proprietary software with him. Cameron had hesitated because only law enforcement and cell phone companies were supposed to have these particular apps that tracked cell phones. Cameron had finally relented and shared the software with Tyler. He knew Tyler was not a terrorist and would probably never have much of a reason to use the specialized programs. Cameron knew that Tyler mislaid his phone quite often and suspected that he wanted the apps to be able to find his own phone when it was missing. Tyler hadn't had an occasion to use the tracking software yet, but now he was going to give it a try.

Tyler already had J.D.'s and Cameron's phone numbers programmed into his phone. He fumbled around with his phone for a while. Within fifteen minutes of attempting to activate the software Cameron had given him, Tyler shouted that he'd found them. At least he'd found both of their phones.

"They're here, in Harmony. Both of their phones are here in Harmony anyway. I've found them. They aren't very far from where we are now."

"Let's go. Let's find the phones and find them." Olivia was not going to put off riding to the rescue and finding J.D. "Tell me where to go."

"Shouldn't we tell somebody what we're doing?" Tyler was asking.

"Who in the world would we tell and what in the world would we say? No! We are going to find those phones, and I am going to find my husband ... right now."

Tyler was looking at his phone, watching the red dots pulsate. It looked like they were within a half mile of the phones. "Okay, I'll tell you where to go."

Tyler gave directions while Olivia drove. She turned off Highway 1 onto a very narrow dirt road. "I don't know if this monster is going to be able to make it through on this narrow road."

"Well, we don't have another vehicle anywhere in sight right now, so this one is going to have to do. The motor home doesn't belong to you, does it?"

"No it's rented, but ...."

"No buts allowed. Keep on driving, even if you wreck the paint job and even if you have to drive over some bushes and trees. This thing is a tank. It can make it. This could be a matter of life and death."

Olivia drove the motor home over the bushes and through the trees. She could hear the tree branches scraping against its sides. She kept on driving through the woods until she arrived close to the rear of the rusted metal warehouse. There was a

Subaru parked on the dirt road, and that car seemed to be where the missing cell phones were located.

There was no place to hide the motor home. The only place to park it was exactly where it was stopped. Olivia didn't think she would ever be able to turn it around to drive it out of the woods. "This looks like the place J.D. described, the place where Harrison was held captive. That place was in Harmony. This has to be the same place. Do you think they're inside?"

"I would bet on it." Tyler was out of the motor home and tracking the two cell phones. Lilleth was just behind him. The Subaru was locked. Lilleth's two older brothers had taught her many things. Some were useful and some were not. Some were legal and some were not. She had the Subaru's doors open in thirty seconds. Tyler recovered both phones from underneath the front seats of the car. He gave the phones to Olivia. She put them in her purse.

Tyler and Lilleth walked around the warehouse looking for a way to get inside. They didn't see the place where J.D. and Cameron had cut their way through the corrugated metal. The only entrance they found were the double doors in the front. They were locked. Lilleth knew how to break into a car, but breaking into these doors was beyond her. They went back to the motor home to give Olivia the bad news that they didn't think they would be able to get into the warehouse. Olivia hesitated for only a second or two. She asked Tyler and Lilleth, who were standing outside the driver's side window of the motor home, "How many people were in the Zodiac when it left the beach?"

"Besides Harrison, there was the guy who was driving it plus the two guards." No one had any idea what Olivia was thinking at this point. Olivia adored J.D. Nothing was going to stand in her way of getting him back.

"That means there's probably only one or two of the kidnappers here in this building. Get out of my way." Olivia settled into the driver's seat of the motor home and refastened her seatbelt. Harrison was still lying on the couch of the motor home, but that didn't seem to matter to Olivia. She started the engine and backed up the huge vehicle as far as she could. She drove around the Subaru and accelerated. She put her foot all the way down on the gas pedal and roared forward into the side of the warehouse. She quickly backed up the motor home. She rammed it forward again. She backed up and surged forward. All of this happened in just a few minutes. Tyler and Lilleth watched from the sidelines aghast.

The people inside, whoever they were, could not possibly imagine what was attacking the warehouse. After seven tremendous crunches into the rusty metal building, Olivia had loosened the side of one of the corrugated metal wall panels. She grabbed a tire iron she'd retrieved from the motor home's toolbox. She climbed out of the motor home and pushed her way through the narrow wall opening she'd made. She went into the warehouse swinging. Tyler and Lilleth looked on in shock and horror. What was she doing? Whoever was waiting inside would have guns.

Olivia saw J.D. and Cameron lying on the concrete. They were chained to the floor and were not moving. Even with all of the noise of the motor home crashing into the side of the building, they were still asleep … or dead. Olivia felt sick to her stomach. She saw a Chinese man cowering in the corner. He was staring at the front end of the motor home which was now several feet inside the warehouse. The engine looked like it was completely kaput, and steam and smoke were rising out of the front of the wrecked vehicle.

The man in the corner looked frightened, and he didn't have a gun in his hands. Olivia went after him with the tire iron.

She was relentless. She pummeled him until blood was pouring out of his head. She kept after him until he was unconscious. She had lost control. Or had she? She was beside herself with anger. If this man had killed J.D., she would finish him off and beat him until he was not only dead but had no unbroken bones left in his body. Tyler was able to put his arms around Olivia and hold her arms at her sides. Tyler held her still while Lilleth pried the tire iron out of her hands. They didn't know if the man she'd been attacking was dead or alive.

Lilleth took over from Tyler to restrain Olivia. Lilleth was strong and was able to hold on to Olivia until she had calmed down. Tyler knelt beside his two good friends and found they were still breathing. He found a pulse on both. They must have been drugged.

"We have to take the Subaru. That's the only way we're going to be able to get out of here. We have to find the keys. I will search the guy in the corner. Put Olivia in the car and lock her in there." Lilleth hated to lock Olivia inside the Subaru but decided it was the only way. They had to leave the motor home where it was. It could not possibly be moved. Lilleth guessed that J.D. and Olivia had paid a fortune for insurance on the motor home. Because motor homes are difficult to maneuver on the road and in parking lots, most people who are renting one sign up for the additional insurance that's offered. Maybe Olivia and J.D. would say they'd had an accident, or maybe they would report it missing and presumed stolen. No one would believe them if they actually told the truth about what had happened to the motor home. Who in the world would ever do a crazy thing like deliberately driving a motor home into the side of a building?

Tyler found the keys to the Subaru in the pocket of the unconscious kidnapper. Lilleth and Tyler climbed into the motor home to rescue Harrison Davis. His face was white as a sheet after the wild ride Olivia had just taken him on. Tyler and Lilleth escorted Harrison Davis to the Subaru and put him in the front passenger seat. He was not in good shape and needed medical care, but they were doing everything they could to save everybody. Olivia seemed oblivious to the fact that they'd brought Harrison to the car. They locked Harrison and Olivia in the Subaru.

Lilleth retrieved Olivia's purse, Harrison Davis's clothes, and the keys to the motor home's ignition. The Steeles had pretty much cleared all of their belongings out of the motor home because they knew they would be leaving it in the Albergo's parking lot for a week. There were few personal items left for Lilleth to carry to the Subaru.

With considerable effort and with the help of Olivia's tire iron, they were able to break the chains that held J.D. and Cameron attached to the floor. Tyler and Lilleth half-carried and half-dragged groggy Cameron and groggy J.D. to the Subaru. It was a tight squeeze, but they put both unconscious men into the back with Olivia and locked the car again. Olivia was sobbing as she held J.D.'s head in her lap. The last thing that remained for them to do was to carry the bloody body of the Chinese agent to the Subaru and put him in the trunk of the car.

Once that was done, Lilleth squeezed herself into the passenger seat of the Subaru beside Harrison Davis. It was a bucket seat, and Harrison was not a small person. It was crowded and tremendously uncomfortable with two of them sitting in a seat designed for one. Three of the people in the car were unconscious or almost unconscious. One of the people in the front seat was a man dressed as a woman, wearing a wig and a red dress. One person in the back was crying hysterically and was covered with blood. They were worse than a clown car.

Tyler drove the Subaru almost to Highway 1. He pulled off the dirt road and parked the car in the trees. It could not be seen from the highway. Lilleth called Sidney who thankfully picked up right away. Sidney also was panicked because she'd not been able to reach Cameron or J.D. Lilleth explained quickly that they had both been found. Of course, Sidney had not known they were ever really missing. Lilleth assured her that Cameron was fine and so was J.D. At least they would be fine when the drugs had worn off. Sidney wanted details. Lilleth told her Cameron looked as if he'd been beaten up, but he was not seriously hurt and was not going to die. Lilleth told Sidney that Harrison Davis had been rescued, and they needed to get him to the Paso Robles Airport.

"We have a car problem, Sidney. The motor home is not an option any more. I will tell you all about that later. You will have to drive the Carpenter's Ford Expedition to meet us. Get the key from them and get on the road ASAP. We don't know where the Ritter's Mercedes is. The only car we have available to us, the Subaru, belongs to the Chinese thugs. It isn't our car, but we are all in it now. We have stolen it, so we can't drive it on the highway. You'll have to drive to Harmony to meet us."

Besides the fact that the Subaru was a stolen car, the motley crew of people crammed inside would immediately be suspicious to anybody who glanced in the window. If they were stopped for some reason, there would be no good explanation about why they had a half-dead man in the trunk. The motor home would probably never again go anywhere—if it could even be towed away from its current final resting place. They had no idea where the Ritter's Mercedes was hidden, and they needed another vehicle in a hurry. The Carpenter's 2004 Ford SUV was their only option. Lilleth told Sidney where to come to meet them. The sooner the better.

Sidney called back almost before Lilleth had a chance to hang up. "The Ritters have OnStar, or one of those services that knows where your car is at all times, in case you are in an accident or lost or something. We need to locate that car, and it doesn't sound as if either Cameron or J.D. will be able to tell you, any time soon, where they've parked it. I'm sure the Mercedes is someplace near where you guys are, and counting heads, we really need two cars. I will get Isabelle working on locating the Mercedes. Where are you going now?"

"We don't know where we're going. For now, we are staying put, exactly where we are. We can't go anywhere. I mean, we're waiting here to meet up with you, and then we have no idea what we are going to do. There are six of us packed into a car intended to hold four. Oh, excuse me, there are actually seven of us in the Subaru if you count the man in the trunk." Lilleth was making a snide joke, but no one was laughing. "Can you call your pilot and tell him we have the package? As soon as you can meet us, somebody has to drive Harrison to the airport. We can get him there in the Expedition or in the Mercedes, if we can find it, but he needs to get there. I don't think anybody wants to wait around for him to be abducted a third time."

"I'm leaving now in the Expedition. I'm bringing Gretchen with me. It was all I could do to get her to leave Bailey. If she's not there to keep him locked in the room, she's sure he's going to call a taxi and follow us and try to get in on the action. He can't stand to be left out. Isabelle is talking to her car-tracking service and will text Gretchen with its location. Gretchen and I are going to find the Mercedes before we meet you. We need two cars to take all of these people back to Paso Robles. Stay where you are, wherever you are… off the road. I don't blame you for not wanting to drive the Subaru on the highway. That would be madness. Where will you leave it?"

"We plan to leave it exactly where it is now. We're going to wipe it down so none of our fingerprints can be found in or on the car." Lilleth had her clever brothers to thank for one more thing. "When you and Gretchen arrive to pick us up, we intend to abandon the Subaru as quickly as we can get everyone into the other cars."

Thirty minutes later, Gretchen and Sidney found the Ritters' Mercedes hidden in the foliage and scrubby trees near the beach. Gretchen had the extra key, and the two cars quickly made their way to the dirt road just off Highway 1, the rendezvous point with the Subaru.

Tyler had decided what needed to be done and began giving orders. "I think Sidney and Gretchen should drive Harrison in the Expedition to the Paso Robles Municipal Airport. The old car won't attract as much attention there as the fancy new Mercedes would. Gretchen and Sidney can get Harrison onto the plane. He isn't able to walk on his own. The pilots can help with Harrison. Sidney knows the pilots, and they know her. She can take charge of getting Harrison and the jet on the way to New Mexico." Tyler looked around and everyone seemed to agree with that part of the plan.

He continued. "Lilleth and I will drive the Mercedes with everybody else in the back. When we get to the Albergo, we will need help to get them out of the car and into their rooms. Lilleth will text the Ritters and the Carpenters to let them know we are bringing our two drugged friends back to the hotel. Hopefully we can sneak them in that back door near where the washers and dryers are located. These two probably need minor medical treatment and a chance to sleep off whatever drugs they've been given. Richard and Matthew can figure it out and do whatever needs to be done for Cameron and J.D.

"I'd prefer to have a medical person fly with Harrison Davis, but we can't take the chance of getting an unknown doctor involved in our mess. From what I understand, the plane will land on a private runway at the Richardson's ranch in New Mexico, less than a half-mile away from the house. It's just a little more than a two-hour flight from Paso Robles to the ranch. I'm not a medical person, but I think Harrison will be okay on the plane without medical care for that long. He's tougher than he looks. He's a little beat up, but I think he's mostly in shock." Those who were paying attention to what Tyler was proposing nodded in agreement. Everyone was worn out. Everyone wanted this all to end.

"Sidney, can you contact people at your ranch and let them know Harrison needs medical care when he arrives?"

"Already done. Rosemary knows he's alive and has been rescued. She is helping make the arrangements for Harrison's arrival. A car will meet the plane as soon as it lands. We've arranged for a doctor we can trust to be in the car with Rosemary. Harrison will be in good hands. You can imagine how overjoyed she is to know he's okay."

"Let's get this done people." The Ford Expedition, with Harrison Davis on board, pulled out onto Highway 1 headed for the Paso Robles Airport. The Mercedes followed, headed to the Albergo. The Subaru stayed behind, abandoned in the dirt with a criminal locked in the trunk. Tyler promised himself that, when he had a free minute, he would try to find a pay phone and make an anonymous phone call to the FBI telling them about the man they could find in the Subaru.

After they'd put Harrison on the plane at the Paso Robles Municipal Airport, Sidney and Gretchen returned to the Albergo with the good news that Harrison Davis was on his way to New Mexico. He'd even rallied enough to give them a faint smile and say thank you as he was carried onto the plane.

Cameron was waking up from his drugged state. Sidney was sitting beside his bed ready to explain everything that had happened since he'd been taken off the beach and chained to the floor in the warehouse. Richard Carpenter and Matthew Ritter had cleaned up Cameron's injuries and decided his bumps and bruises were nothing serious.

J.D. was recovering in one of the queen-size beds in his suite. Olivia was sound sleep in the other queen-size bed. Matthew Ritter was resting on the couch in the suite's living room. He would be keeping an eye on both the Steeles.

When J.D. had come out of his drug-induced sleep, Gretchen told him about what Olivia had done to rescue him and Cameron from the warehouse. She was concerned that Olivia's behavior had been out of control. Gretchen and Olivia were close friends, and Gretchen had been shocked when she'd heard the story about what Olivia had done.

J.D. told Gretchen he didn't think Olivia had been out of control at all. "She saved my life. She was willing to do whatever it took to make sure I lived. I have only admiration for what she did. The only weapons she had were the motor home and the tire iron. If she hadn't smashed into the side of the warehouse, what would have happened to us? If she had not immobilized the Chinese agent, he would have grabbed his machine gun and killed Cameron and me, and probably her, too. Extraordinary situations sometimes call for extraordinary solutions. She loves me and wants me to be around for a long time. I feel the same about her. I would have stopped at nothing to save her life."

Gretchen told Bailey everything that had happened and everything that he'd missed. He wasn't doing well with his crutches and had decided to throw them into the hotel's dumpster. He would then consider other ways of getting around. He was furious that he'd missed the action. He swore that would never happen again.

Elizabeth had spoken on the phone with Henley Breckenridge a couple of times that afternoon. Henley had hooked Sui Wai up to an IV. Sui Wai was awake and had been able to drink some chicken broth. Henley had stayed beside her patient most of the day. Sui Wai had told Henley about her friend Sue Keely who lived in Ojai. Henley was going to wait a couple of days before she made contact with Sue Keely. She knew that Sue Keely would head for the ranch in Paso Robles as soon as she heard Sui Wai was there. Henley felt Sui Wai needed more time to get back on her feet before she engaged with her previous life. Elizabeth told Henley that Harrison Davis had been rescued and was on his way to a new life. She made sure that Henley knew it was important to convey the information that Harrison was safe to Sui Wai. She also told Henley that she'd sent word to Harrison that Sui Wai had been rescued and was going to be all right. The woman who had been tortured needed more time for rest and restoration before she took on her whistleblower persona again. Sui Wai had begun to tell her story to the eccentric cowgirl with a big heart.

The reunion group had been scheduled to leave on Monday morning, but Isabelle had arranged with the Albergo's management for them to extend their stay for two more days. Isabelle and Matthew were going to join the Carpenters in their room for dinner and order room service and at least one bottle of wine. Tyler and Lilleth had collapsed and were sleeping, too tired to eat. The group would, at some point, try to have a debriefing about what all had occurred in the past twenty-four hours. It was still "Quandanche Quarantena" for a few. All the other guests except the Bruces had left the Albergo.

CHAPTER 37

O*n Monday morning, Tyler and J.D. were doing* nothing except lying on the chaise lounges beside the Albergo's pool. J.D. had made a quick recovery, and after a good night's sleep, he was almost back to normal. With all the other excitement, they'd nearly forgotten about the Ridenours or the Bruces or whoever they really were. Owen Bruce appeared beside the pool, pulled up a lawn chair, and sat down with Tyler and J.D. He did have on his mask and was almost socially distanced.

"I wanted to thank you for putting me in touch with that private investigator of yours. Jack. I sent him a text that night, and he called me right away. My mentioning your name got his attention. He said Tyler Merriman's name opens many doors. I told him everything that's happened, and he was interested in my story, as you thought he would be. He said he would get on it, and two days later, he had results. I'm impressed, and I told him so. He said his business has changed a lot over the past several decades, and it's now almost ninety percent computer searches. He said he rarely does an in-person stakeout and only once in a while gets on a plane to track somebody down.

Most of his investigating can be accomplished through the internet. I am telling you all of this because it was through his computer searches that he found out some interesting and pertinent information regarding my case. I'm almost positive he's been able to identify the person who is the one most likely to be trying to kill me and my wife."

"That's pretty quick work, I agree. But how does he know, or how do you know, that you've been able to figure out who is after you? How could he possibly track all of that down using a computer?" Tyler knew his PI was good, but he was surprised that he'd been able to produce results so fast.

"It amazed me, too. I was astonished at how much he had figured out. I'm pretty computer-savvy myself, but he's in a class by himself. He's a real genius at detecting over the internet. I didn't ask if he'd broken into any databases he wasn't allowed to access, or if he had done anything illegal. How he does his internet research is his business. But he did find out some amazing stuff. Let me tell you." Owen was also clearly impressed with the results of the investigation so far.

"I'm delighted he was able to help you, but did he help you enough that you are going to be able to keep yourselves safe? That's really the bottom line, what you really need to have happen." Tyler was hoping for a real-world solution, not just information.

"The bottom line is that my sister's ex-husband, Rodney Childress, fathered a son he never knew he had. The ex-husband is long gone, but the son is still very much alive somewhere. I think he is the person who is after me. From looking at this person's hundreds, maybe even thousands, of computer searches, Jack thinks this previously unknown progeny has some kind of distorted notion that he's entitled to my fortune. Let me explain. I'm fascinated with how Jack found this guy, and found him so fast.

"I'm sure you know all about these DNA services that have sprung up in the past few years... Twenty Three and Me and Ancestry.com. There are others. People send in their DNA swabs for various reasons—to find out about their ethnic heritage, to find out where their ancestors came from, to find long-lost relatives, and so forth. Sometimes people find out things they wish they hadn't found out.

"Apparently, the first thing a high-tech PI does is to run the names of people close to you through all kinds of databases, hundreds of them. I gave him six or seven names, including my sons' names, my sister Angela, two co-workers, and of course my wife and myself. The first thing Jack turns up is my sister's ex-husband, Rodney. They were divorced almost thirty years ago, and he's been dead for at least twenty-five years. He died in 1995. So, I didn't even put him on my list of people to look at.

"But, sure enough, he was the one who rang the bell. At least for Jack, and also for me. Apparently, Rodney Childress, my sister's deceased ex, has a son that nobody ever knew anything about. My sister sure as heck didn't know anything about her husband having another child, and I am almost positive Rodney didn't know anything about him either. When Angela's boy was killed in 1983, she and Rodney were completely destroyed. They tried to keep their marriage together, but it didn't work. Rodney always drank too much, or at least I thought he did. Their son's death pushed him over the edge, and he became a full-time alcoholic. Angela and Rodney divorced, and a few years later, Rodney died of something related to his liver. Liver failure or something like that.

"This new son, who has just popped up, is now in his early thirties. So I am guessing that Rodney sired him shortly after he and Angela divorced, but maybe before. The boy's mother raised him as a single parent and never told him anything about his father. Apparently, earlier this year, the son, whose name is Keith Doyle, bought one of those DNA kits. We don't know, at this point, why the boy decided to have his DNA tested. Maybe he wanted to find out who his biological father was. Who knows?

"The computer screening that Jack's company does looks at who has done searches for their relatives using DNA. Jack wants to find out if anyone has searched for or found out anything about people close to you. Rodney Childress's name came up. This kid, Keith Doyle, had submitted a DNA sample, and Rodney's brother, Alan Childress, showed up in the database as being some kind of a familial match to Keith Doyle. Rodney himself had never submitted a DNA sample for anything, so he wasn't in the database. But Rodney's brother, Alan, had his DNA tested a few years ago, so Alan was in one of the ancestry DNA databases. Anyway, Rodney's son was able to track down Rodney through the brother, Alan, who is Keith Doyle's uncle. Are you following all of this? It's complicated."

Tyler and J.D. nodded. They were following, and they were fascinated.

Owen Bruce continued. "So now Keith Doyle knows his biological father's name is Rodney Childress. Keith does a bunch of computer searches to try to find out about Rodney—where he lives, how much he's worth, and everything about him. Doyle finds out that Rodney is dead, but he also finds out that Rodney was once married to Angela Bruce. So he Googles her and finds out she is related to me. There's way too much information about me and my businesses and my money out there, so I imagine dollar signs start to roll around in the kid's eyes. He's no blood relation or any kind of relation at all to me or to my sister, but he must have some cockamamie idea that he's entitled to some of my money. He did thousands of computer searches on me, my businesses, my houses, my finances—everything about me.

"Here's the thing. And this is the clincher, at least for me. Jack also found out that Keith Doyle got a job working for the company that does the landscaping at my farm in Indiana. Keith was able to find out what landscaping company I use, and he got a job with them. He worked for my landscaper for three months. I'm sure he was spying on me, or at least he was watching me whenever I was there and he was working in the yard. I checked some dates and know that he was working at the farm at least one time when my wife and I were out of the country. We were on a trip to Norway. That must have been when he stole my grandfather's revolver. I figure he broke into the house and into the gun room. He must be a pretty good burglar because he picked the locks and didn't leave any traces. I've got an alarm system, but during the day, when people are at the house, the alarm is turned off. It wasn't until I asked our houseman to check on the gun that anybody knew there'd been a robbery. The gun was in a special case... kind of on display. That's probably why Keith decided to take that one. I keep it in a glass case on a table beside my chair. My point is, it had a prominent position in the room, *and* you could see what it looked like because it was in a glass case. I kept it there because I loved to look at it. It was important to my grandfather, and it was important to me. It's a beautiful thing, even though it can't shoot worth a darn. Of course, Keith would not have had any way of knowing about the gun's lack of accuracy. The gun looks really good, kind of old-fashioned, and like it's worth a lot of money. I'd love to get it back. More than that, I'd love to have Keith Doyle locked up."

"It sounds like you have solved at least part of the mystery. You probably know 'who done it.' Do you know where the guy is now? He has to be in Paso Robles. Or at least he was here.

You know the gun was in Paso Robles a few nights ago." Tyler was into the mystery now and wanted to help track down the man who had stolen the beautiful but faulty gun and used it to shoot one of his old Camp Shoemaker buddies.

"Jack's people are working on that. He's also working on finding out if it's Keith Doyle who has been trying to access my medical records. Somebody has been trying to get into them. Jack has a way of finding out who that is and if they were successful. Medical information is supposed to be carefully guarded, but it really isn't. Doctors' offices usually don't use encrypted computers. In the old days, your medical file was kept in a filing cabinet, a metal thing that stood on the floor. Remember the break-in at Daniel Ellsberg's psychiatrist's office? The Pentagon Papers? Somebody broke into that doctor's office and got into his filing cabinets. Now, it is so much easier. Everything is stored electronically. You don't have to go out in the rain or even leave your parents' basement to find out all about a person's medical history and medical problems." Owen Bruce found it very disturbing that medical records could be so easily hacked.

"That's depressing." Tyler was not as concerned about the medical records, but he could see that any kind of information would be useful to the person who was after Owen Bruce. "This Keith Doyle person has obviously figured out that you're in Paso Robles. Why has he not been here, to the Albergo?"

"He may have been here. We don't know. Jack is on it. He's getting photos of Doyle. I have surveillance cameras at my houses and at my office. The cameras must have captured Doyle's face if he was poking around the farm in Indiana. If Doyle has a driver's license, he will have a photo on file in some state. There are lots of ways Jack can get a picture of Keith Doyle. I'll need a photo for when I turn this over to law enforcement. Jack says he will have a photo to send us today.

Alexandra and I need to know what he looks like so we can be on the lookout for this nut job." Jack, the PI, had worked a miracle for Owen Bruce.

"And," Owen Bruce continued, "Alexandra and I have been pretty careful about where we've gone and what we've done since we arrived at the Albergo. You haven't noticed them, but I have a security detail staying here. They have rooms on either side of ours. My wife hates having them around all the time, and I don't like it either. This vacation was supposed to be a fun trip for us, especially for her, to get away from it all. That's one reason I tried to pretend those gunshots were firecrackers. I gave the guys a night off when we went to Tio Theo, and that was a big mistake. Of course, Keith Doyle struck that night. He must have been watching me and waiting for an opportunity. And of course, he was waiting for us to come out of the restaurant. Jack is very good. And you were exactly correct about him; he's right on top of this case. I hope he can find Doyle. If Jack can locate Doyle and get the goods on him, I will go to the authorities with what we have."

"That's a relief. When you refused to go to the hospital and wouldn't call the police, I didn't understand what you were thinking. Now I get it. If anyone can find out what you need to know to make a case, Jack's the one to do it." Tyler had another thought. "You're a high profile person and a very wealthy person. Are you absolutely sure this does not have anything to do with any of your companies? You must have competitors, unscrupulous business rivals, and all of that. Everybody who's in business has competition. What about international crooks who want to steal your secrets?"

"When all of this started, I naturally assumed something having to do with my businesses was behind the threats. But, my companies are different from most big companies. Shares in my companies do not trade on Wall Street. There are no public shares out there. Nobody can make a bundle off of insider trading or anything like that. I have no intentions of ever going public. But there are plenty of people who would like to steal my inventions. I'd assumed it was someone trying to steal something from me. It was finding the rounds from my grandfather's gun that convinced me this was personal, not a business rival or thugs from Russia or China after my formulas." Owen was now quite certain Keith Doyle was the man who was after him.

"You've convinced me. It has to be this Doyle guy." Tyler agreed.

"It has to be, although, at first, I was sure it was somebody threatening me to give up my scientific secrets. But I didn't really understand why they were going about it the way they were, like killing my wife's cat. Jeeze! Who does something like that?" Owen Bruce shook his head and sighed a big sigh. "Because of the timing, I did think it was related to my business. I will tell you this in confidence, but it really isn't much of a secret anymore. It will be announced publicly in a day or so. One of my companies is going to introduce two very significant scientific breakthroughs. I had hoped to be able to announce these revolutionary products myself, but that is looking less and less likely. My wife and I have decided we will continue to hide out here at the Albergo, under our assumed names, until Keith Doyle is in custody. Even after he's found, we will want to avoid having to talk to the press. Alexandra has really been on edge and doesn't want any publicity about any of this.

"Let me explain about these breakthroughs. Quite by accident, while we were developing another product entirely, my researchers came across some interesting characteristics about a chemical that is used in making plastics. We've been working with it and have altered it in two very distinctive ways. We've discovered that when we add certain substances to the plastic that's used to make PVC pipe, we can make plastic pipe that's as hard as steel. Plastic pipe is much less expensive to make than steel or copper pipe, and now we have found a way for that plastic pipe to last forever, or almost that long. One of the problems with PVC has been that it deteriorates over time. Pack rats chew up your irrigation system. Acidic water eats away at your plumbing and your gutters. With the addition of my company's chemical concoction to PVC pipe, that won't happen anymore. Plastic pipe will be able to last longer than copper pipe. You can imagine what implications this has for the price of copper and the environment and on and on. This is a game-changing innovation. The other thing we discovered, really at the same time, is a way to make plastic bottles, plastic straws and cups, and all of these things biodegradable. No more acres of plastic floating on the ocean. No more dolphins strangled because they tried to swallow a plastic bag."

Tyler was impressed. "That is exciting news. I'm impressed and can see how a lot of people all over the world would like to get their hands on those formulas."

"We tried to keep it secret until we had all our contracts lined up and signed. Finalizing the legal business took many, many months. We didn't want news to get out about the products, but of course, there were leaks. That's pretty much inevitable. There are implications in the commodities markets ... copper futures and copper mining for example. But it's all wrapped up now. I'd promised Alexandra that when everything was finished, I would bring her here for a long vacation. She loves this place. Then the COVID pandemic struck. Anyway, here we are. I trust Jack to be able to find Keith Doyle. I intend to have law enforcement throw the book at him—for attempted murder, burglary, stalking, killing our cat, and everything else the authorities can come up with. I've got some friends at the FBI, and now that I know who's behind all of this, I'm going to get them involved, too. I'm counting on the FBI to find this guy." Owen Bruce was convinced he'd identified the person who was after him. Now that miscreant just had to be found.

CHAPTER 38

S*idney, Gretchen, and Isabelle walked to downtown* Paso Robles. They'd wanted to visit SLO Confections, the special bakery and candy store that everyone had talked so much about. They rationalized that if they walked to the bakery, they could eat whatever they bought there and not worry about the calories. It had been a rough couple of days. They needed chocolate. They were masked and got in the socially-distanced line outside to wait their turn to be allowed into the store.

When they made it inside, they inspected all the glass display cases that held the beautiful sweets SLO Confections produced. Some of the display cases were refrigerated and held chocolate eclairs and custard tarts with fruit on top. It was going to be difficult to decide how to choose from among the many extravagant and mouth-watering choices.

They nodded when they saw Mrs. Ridenour inside the bakery. Or maybe she was Mrs. Bruce. Whoever she was, she was wearing wonderful clothes, as always. Today she had on perfectly tailored navy blue silk pants and a matching silk windbreaker lined in what looked like a navy and yellow

Hermes silk scarf. Her masks always matched her outfits. The three walkers from the Albergo looked rustic in their sweatsuits and sneakers.

Isabelle wanted to buy some brownies. She and Matthew loved chocolate, and there were several varieties of brownies in the glass cases. She questioned the salesperson. "Tell me about the different kinds of brownies you have. There are so many. How does anyone ever make up their mind about which ones to buy?"

The saleslady laughed. "Mostly they just buy one of each."

Isabelle pointed to three trays. "What's the difference? These all look very similar."

"These two don't have any nuts. Lots of people are allergic to nuts. These, as you can see, have chocolate icing. These don't. The ones on this tray all have nuts inside the brownies. These are made with walnuts and have a walnut on top. These are made with pecans and have a pecan on top. These are made with almonds and have chocolate almond icing on the top. And there are toasted almond slivers on top ... to let you know what you are eating. That one's my favorite. The chocolate almond icing is the best. We sell more of these than we do any of the other kinds. Once you've tasted the almond one, you'll never go back."

"You take your brownies seriously here. I've never seen such an assortment." Isabelle was still trying to decide. "What about those over there in the other case? Are those brownies, too, with the powdered sugar on top?"

"Oh, yes, those are brownies, too. We keep them separated from the others, though. They are made with hazelnut flour and ground up hazelnuts. They have a few very big fans, so we always have them on hand. But a lot of people are allergic to hazelnuts, so we always explain the ingredients to anyone who asks about them. They have powdered sugar on the top which sets them apart, and we keep them in a separate case."

Alexandra Bruce had been listening in on the conversation Isabelle was having with the salesperson. She had questions. "Are the hazelnut brownies the only ones that have powdered sugar on top?"

"Yes, ma'am. We only put powdered sugar on those."

"Do you supply your baked goods to the restaurants in town?" Alexandra asked.

"Yes, we are proud of the fact that so many of the restaurants in Paso Robles buy their desserts from us. We custom make exclusive things for some of them."

"Do you furnish Tio Theo with desserts?"

"Yes. They send Keith in every day to pick up an order."

"Keith?"

"Yes, he's the new guy who picks up for Tio Theo."

"New? Since when?"

"He's been in every day now for almost two weeks."

Alexandra Bruce took a chance. She pulled her cell phone out of her purse and found the new photograph that had just arrived in an email. She held the phone up so the salesgirl could see the face on the screen. "Is this Keith? Is this the person who picks up the order for Tio Theo?"

Isabelle had made her decisions about which brownies to buy, but she was fascinated by the conversation that was going on between Alexandra Bruce and the SLO Confections salesperson. Gretchen and Sidney had made their purchases and were also intrigued by the intensity of Alexandra Bruce's questioning.

"His hair's longer and darker than in that picture. But, yes, that's Keith, the new guy from Tio Theo."

"Are you sure?"

"Yes, I'm sure. I've got a good memory for faces. He was in here this morning, just before you came in."

"Do you remember if you ever sold him any of the brownies with the powdered sugar on top?"

"We don't sell those to restaurants, and we don't usually sell the ones with the walnuts or the pecans to restaurants either. So, no, we would not have sold any of those to him."

One of the other salespeople interrupted her. "Wait a minute. I don't know what this is all about, but one day last week, one of Keith's first days in here, he bought a box of those hazelnut brownies. I told him we didn't sell them to restaurants, but he insisted they were for his own personal use, not for Tio Theo. I put them in a separate box from the order for the restaurant. But he did buy them. Just that one time."

"Thank you. That is all I need to know." Alexandra Bruce took her box of sweets and walked out of the bakery. She was already on her phone. She could not rid her mind of the image of the plate of desserts that she and her husband had been served at Tio Theo last week. Owen didn't like powdered sugar. He said it got on his clothes and in his mustache and made him sneeze. But he loved chocolate, and he loved brownies in particular. The dessert tray had arrived at the table with several kinds of desserts, including two brownies topped with powdered sugar. Owen had eaten both brownies. No wonder he had fainted. No wonder he'd had a terrible allergic reaction. He was deathly allergic to hazelnuts. It was a blessing he had vomited, or he would probably now be dead.

"Owen." Alexandra Bruce was insistent over the phone. "Call the FBI. Now! I know where Keith Doyle is working. He is still in town, and I think he's working at Tio Theo. He tried to kill you when we ate there the other night. He tried to poison you. Please, trust me on this. Call the FBI. Get this murderer off the streets."

Everyone was feeling well enough to have cocktails and talk things over. There was a lot to say. They were mostly being thankful, very thankful for many things. They had a late reservation at La Buona Ricetta. Their limo had picked them up and driven them to the restaurant. Between Elizabeth, who always had a hard time getting in and out of the limo, and Bailey, who hadn't yet thrown his crutches in the dumpster, it took longer than usual for the crowd of twelve to make it to La Buona Ricetta.

Just as they were walking in, Henley Breckenridge and her entourage were leaving. Henley was delighted to see Elizabeth, and after waving hello, Henley stepped back into the restaurant and called the maître d' over to speak to him.

"See that guy in the black leather coat?" She pointed to J.D. "I'm buying him two drinks and a bottle of wine tonight. Charge it to me. I owe him." She winked at J.D. who stood in the doorway staring at Henley. She pointed to Elizabeth. "Put her whole meal on my tab. I'm buying her dinner tonight. She's my friend." Henley blew kisses through her mask to the group and made her way to the sidewalk, concho belt clanking.

As they were paying the bill at La Buona Ricetta after another outstanding meal, Olivia told them all just to stay in their seats. She had news, big news.

No one could imagine what big news she could possibly have. They hoped against hope it didn't have anything to do with the coronavirus or the Chinese or any of that. They were so worn out by all of it. They needed a break from any and all kinds of big news.

"You are going to want to hear this. I promise." Olivia loved having a scoop, and she did indeed have one this time. "I've stayed in touch with Elle, our concierge from the Penmoor, from last year. We email each other from time to time. She has just emailed me to let me know that the same man, the one they think pushed Richard down last year and caused him to push Elizabeth's wheelchair into the lake, has done it again. He pushed another woman in a wheelchair into the lake, and she drowned. The guy was wearing the same black outfit with the hoodie that he wore when he pushed Richard. This time the creep pushed the woman's wheelchair into the lake himself and then ran away. Somebody saw what he'd done and ran after him and tackled him. Somebody else called 911, and the guy was arrested. Now he's been charged with murder, because the woman died. She was belted into her wheelchair, and she couldn't swim. She managed to get the belt undone and get out of the wheelchair, but she couldn't make it out of the water. She drowned before anyone could get to her. She was older than Elizabeth and not in as good shape. She was definitely not as good a swimmer."

Richard Carpenter's ears had perked up, and he wanted all the details. "Who was this guy? Why in the world would he want to attack women in wheelchairs? He must be mentally ill."

Olivia was still reading Elle's email. "Apparently this guy comes to the Penmoor every year for a vacation. He stays a week and climbs Pikes Peak. That rhymes. It's like a thing with him. His name is Zebulon Sheets. Because his name is Zebulon, he thinks he has a special connection to Pike's Peak. Oh, Richard, you are going to love this one. Hang on to your wigs, folks. This bad guy is a doctor. The guy who pushes the wheelchairs into the lake is a doctor. Can you believe it?"

"He must be a very troubled human being or a very evil one." Elizabeth had been the man's victim the year before.

"Apparently this guy is famous for hating old people. He thinks everybody should kill themselves when they reach age seventy-five."

"Everybody over seventy-five is going to be dead anyway, if they don't hurry up and get a vaccination for this COVID-19 crap." J.D. found the news about the deranged killer very disturbing.

"He sounds like Dr. Kevorkian." Bailey was trying to get his mind around the fact that anyone would do what this man had done, let alone that a doctor would do something like this.

"He's much worse than Kevorkian. Kevorkian helped people die who wanted to die. This guy takes it upon himself to help people die, whether they want to or not. Big difference." Lilleth wanted to clarify that Zebulon Sheets, M.D. was not a humanitarian.

"What kind of a doctor is he? I hope he's not a gerontologist." Matthew liked to take an occasional poke at his own medical profession.

"I don't know what his specialty is, but apparently he's written an article about why life after seventy-five is in the toilet. He says people over seventy-five are pathetic and non-productive and a drain on society. According to Zebulon Sheets M.D., people over seventy-five are not contributing anything to the world and need to leave it." Olivia could scarcely believe what she was reading.

"I guess this is his own personal solution to the Social Security deficit problem and how to get the Medicare budget under control." Tyler liked to look at the financial side of things.

"Tell me they are going to throw the book at this madman and keep him in jail until he is seventy-five." Gretchen wasn't yet close to being seventy-five, but she wanted justice to be served.

Isabelle was non-judgmental and philosophical, but these acts of cruelty and the mindset of this physician really upset her. "I am stunned. I thought this was a random act when it happened. I didn't think anyone had specifically targeted

Elizabeth or Richard. But it is very disheartening to hear about a person who is so twisted and so mean. It sounds like this man was living on the dark side, even before he decided to push disabled people into the lake. What a miserable and perverted soul he must be. No wonder, with his dreadful outlook on life, that he wants it to end early. Do they know if he's done this before he pushed Richard? Or is this something that might have afflicted him due to early-onset dementia, or because of some kind of traumatic brain injury? It sounds like this guy may have been suffering from dementia all of his life."

"It sounds as if he's definitely been suffering from being a kook burger all of his life." Cameron was cutting Dr. Death no slack.

"The good news is that now we know who pushed Richard. We know we were not targeted personally. I was targeted because I was old, disabled, and in a wheelchair ... everything this guy hates. He doesn't know me. He judged me because of my age and physical disabilities. He is very gerascophobic." Elizabeth was relieved to know who had caused her to end up in the freezing lake at the Penmoor. She was thankful he had been caught and hoped he would not spread his hatred of the old and infirm anywhere else in the world from now on. Maybe they would assign him to the geriatric section of the prison as an extra punishment for his misdeeds. Maybe the judge would sentence him to collecting bedpans in an old folks' home.

"I would like to offer a toast to my dear friends, including and especially those who are over seventy-five. I want to give you all credit for the good things you do every day and for the extraordinary things you can do when you need to. You worked together to save Harrison Davis's life. It wasn't an easy feat to accomplish. But it was a triumph of brain power over firepower. I do not apologize for being over seventy-five and still being alive. I am proud to have lived this long. I hope to continue to contribute to society. I pray for a vaccine against this plague. Soon." Richard had tears in his eyes when he looked at Elizabeth, the wife he'd almost lost to the cruelty of a lunatic the year before.

Everyone raised their glasses to drink to Richard Carpenter's toast. Others offered their own heartfelt and humorous toasts. This group of people, many of whom were over seventy-five, were not fading into the woodwork or going down without a fight. Their lives were rich and full in so many ways.

EPILOGUE

The house next to Elizabeth's and Richard's winter home in Arizona had just come on the market. The people who owned it had spent little time there. They had a place in Florida and preferred to spend their winters in the sunshine state. The house on the golf course wasn't brand new, but it had been very lightly used. It was well-built. Elizabeth thought it would be perfect for her new friends Annabeth and Peter Davidson. They were currently living in New Mexico and loved the weather there. It was so much nicer than the weather in Seattle where they had lived for many years.

Peter's brother had sold their house in Seattle for them, so they were ready to find a new place to live. Peter was a retired research scientist, and Annabeth was a retired chemistry teacher. Elizabeth put them in touch with a good real estate agent. They looked at the house online and made a trip to Arizona to see it in person. When they came to look at the house next door, they stayed with Elizabeth and Richard. They loved the place and signed a contract on the spot. Their cash offer was accepted. They had plans to update the appliances and paint all the rooms. They were making some changes to the flooring. The furniture from their house in Seattle was in storage, and Annabeth couldn't wait to see her things again. Elizabeth was thrilled that these two lovely people were going to be her next door neighbors. She was looking forward to getting to know them better and having fun times in the future with Annabeth and Peter.

Less than a year after the deadly pandemic cast its evil self into the homes and lives of every family on earth, several vaccines against COVID-19 became available. Thanks to the hard work and brilliance of many researchers who had labored night and day, day after day, to make this happen, the Camp Shoemaker crowd could hope to live to fight another fight and to meet for another reunion. As difficult and complicated as it turned out to be for them to get their shots, they did it. By hook or by crook, every one of them got fully vaccinated. Children and grandchildren and friends cheered. But too many others were grieving. There had been too many deaths, too many losses. Those who had survived were thankful and looked forward. Tomorrow is another day, and this group of friends will live to see it.

WHEN DID I GROW OLD?

When did I grow old?
        It is now so still around me.
        When did all the noise turn to quiet?
        The cacophony of busyness that engulfed me
                for so many years, has subsided.

When did I grow old?
        Did it happen slowly as the years passed by?
        Did it happen as I filled my time with immediacy …
                moving from one crisis to the next?
        Did it happen all of a sudden when I found I had to use
                a cane to get up and down the steps?

When did I grow old?
        Did I fill those years that passed with goodness and giving
                and love?
        Did I spend too many days in anger and hoping for retaliation
                for things in life that didn't go my way?
        Did I spend too many hours organizing and cleaning and
                worrying about my material possessions?
        How much time did I spend shopping? Sorting out
                my closet?

When did I grow old?
        Was it when I learned that I was deaf in one ear
                and there was no help for that?
        Was it when I realized there were so few days ahead
                and so many already gone?
        Was it when I accepted that I would die?

When did I grow old?
    Was it a gradual process as the hairs on my head
        one by one turned white?
    Or did it happen overnight? And what night was that?
    Was it when I became a grandmother?

When did I grow old?
    Did I spend this precious time I have been given
    To make a difference?
    To make the world a better place?

When did I grow old?
    Is it today when I know that however this life was spent,
        it cannot be respent?
    It was what it was ...
    Full of imperfections and mistakes and trying hard
        and often struggling and falling short
    And full of joy and good luck.

When did I grow old?
I just don't know.
Or, maybe I'm not old yet.

MTT 5-7-2014

ACKNOWLEDGMENTS

Heartfelt thanks to my readers and editors. I couldn't have done this without you. Thank you to Open Heart Designs and Jamie Tipton who implemented my cover ideas and who does everything else to turn my manuscript into a book. Thank you to the photographer who always makes me look good. Thank you to all the friends and fans who have encouraged me to continue writing.

AUTHOR'S NOTE

*I wrote the chapter about voter fraud and voter sup-*pression in the summer of 2020, many months before the November 2020 election. Some readers have suggested that I delete this chapter because of what has occurred in the real world. They say this subject is too controversial. I have decided to keep the chapter in the book. It is a controversial topic. I've refused to cut the chapter because of controversy and have declined to be intimidated by the frenzy of the moment or the loud voices on either side.

ABOUT THE AUTHOR

A former actress and singer, **Henrietta Alten West** *has lived all over the United States and has traveled all over the world. She writes poetry, songs (words and music), screenplays, historical fiction, spy thrillers, books for young people, and mysteries. She always wanted to be Nancy Drew but ended up being Carolyn Keene.*

More Books By
Henrietta Alten West

I Have a Photograph

Book #1 in the
The Reunion Chronicles Mysteries

Available online
everywhere books are sold.

Released 2019, 277 pages
Hardcover ISBN: 9781953082947
Paperback ISBN: 9781953082930
ebook ISBN: 9781953082923

Preserve Your Memories

Book #2 in the
The Reunion Chronicles Mysteries

Available online
everywhere books are sold.

Released 2020, 362 pages
Hardcover ISBN: 9781953082008
Paperback ISBN: 9781953082015
ebook ISBN: 9781953082022

CPSIA information can be obtained
at www.ICGtesting.com
Printed in the USA
BVHW010729140721
611802BV00015B/16/J

9 781953 082060